CORPSES AND COGNAC

Deadly Drinks #2

Dorian Graves

Dorian Graves Fiction
Eugene, OR

Dorian Graved Fiction
3950 Goodpasture Loop, M 341
Eugene, OR 97401
www.doriangraves.com

Publisher's Note: This is a work of fiction. Names, characters, places, and incidents are a product of the author's imagination. Locales and public names are sometimes used for atmospheric purposes. Any resemblance to actual people, living or dead, or to businesses, companies, events, institutions, or locales is completely coincidental.

Book Layout © 2017 BookDesignTemplates.com
Cover designed by M. Brackett – https://mbrackett.art/

Corpses and Cognac/Dorian Graves -- 1st ed.
ISBN 978-1-7348960-2-2

To Chris
Here's to many more laughs and adventures
With the best brother and Buckoman I could ask for

1 - JARROD

I hadn't planned to be run over by a minotaur's motorcycle.

If I'd been standing in the middle of the road, being ambushed by a motorcycle would make some sense.

But this happened deep in the woods, perhaps a mile off a dirt road only frequented by logging trucks, in the last dregs of summer when falling leaves are fragile and flammable in equal measure. I had beasts in these woods on my hit list, but not the minotaur. I reeked of blood from my own wounds, and also of cheap whiskey, because I'd upended half a bottle over my head to deter my intended mark—which certainly hadn't been a minotaur—from attacking me.

One might ask what kind of idiot has instincts that scream "grab the motorcycle and throw it into a goddamn tree" instead of getting out of the way. The answer is me, Jarrod Gallows.

"What," the minotaur croaked in the second he and his bike were airborne, "the ever-loving shi—" The crash of his impact shook the forest.

The hidebehind I'd just fought, my actual intended target, twitched at my feet, scraping foot-long claws against the forest floor. The silver manacles I'd clasped around its wrists were the only reason it didn't use the surprise minotaur attack as an opportunity to flee, or to escape out of sight and stab me in the back, as its name suggested. I should've ignored the ambush and lugged the hidebehind to the car. But I'm a paranormal investigator by trade because I'm always too damn curious for my own good.

I grabbed one of my pistols and kept it aimed on the minotaur as I approached. I waited to speak until the bull-headed man sat up and stared at me, terror in his eyes and splinters of bark sticking into his skull.

"You've got two seconds to explain."

The minotaur patted the ground at his side for a weapon. He found only crumpled metal. "Forgive me, Lord Nalem. I was, well you see..." he cleared his throat. "I mistook that hidebehind for, well, for *you* until it was too late. Appearances can be deceiving, right?" His laugh was closer to a pitiful bray.

I wanted to pretend I'd heard him wrong, but I wasn't drunk enough. "Right. Which is why you'll be more surprised if you actually find him." My family bore plenty of curses, but I wasn't the one forced to be a vessel for the ancient, eldritch asshole known as Nalem.

"Yeah, I guess I...wait. You're not him?" The minotaur bolted to hooves—and took in our surroundings with rapid, wild eyes. "But you're a hulderkind! I was told to look for a hulderkind, one with a, what did she call it, a malicious aura..." The minotaur looked to me. Down to the hidebehind, a bristling ball of fur that seemed to be crafted from shadows with glowing coals of hate for eyes and long, gangly limbs that ended in even longer claws. Me again. "Well, shoot. I...must've muddled your auras together, huh?"

I nodded. In all honesty, I had no idea. Other supernatural beings, like the super-strong and hollow-bodied huldras on my mother's side of the family, were taught to sense each other through some sixth sense from a young age. I'd never had the knack. Otherwise, the minotaur wouldn't have been able to ambush me.

The minotaur buried his face in his hands with a mournful moo. "The rest of the herd will never let me live this down. But if you're not Nalem..."

I considered leaving him there. Nothing good ever came of dealing with Nalem, and I should've spared him from the torture that had plagued my family for years.

Plus, the hidebehind kept hissing, and I feared it might try to break away soon.

I offered the minotaur a hand instead. "If you're that desperate to see him, follow me." The minotaur took the offering, so I pulled him to his feet even though he was almost twice my size. "Jarrod Gallows. Paranormal investigator. Grab what's left of your bike and follow me."

While minotaurs may look human from a distance, they've still got a bovine head and hooves, plus a layer of hide over all that muscle. This one was light brown and dressed in motorcycle leathers liberally covered in patches and spikes. Only thing throwing the picture off was his puppy-like demeanor. His giant arms, which I almost swore were as long as I was tall, scooped up the motorcycle parts like they were little more than a fallen bag of groceries. "My name's Bolton," he said, "and I really appreciate this. I've got a special message for Nalem, see. An old friend needs his help."

I scoffed at that. "Better hope he's feeling sociable."

I dragged the hidebehind after me as I led Bolton toward where we'd parked the car. My job was to capture the local pair of hidebehinds before they could mate and spawn. Problem was, hidebehinds were fast and prone to backstabbing, so much that almost no one ever saw their faces and lived. It was rare for them to drop their guard even around their own kind. I had a hard time looking at the one I'd caught; it was like staring at a gaping hole in the universe, albeit one that kept trying to claw me even with the manacles searing its wrists.

I asked Bolton as we walked, "Tell me, what do you know about Nalem?"

Bolton hummed as he thought, almost loud enough to drown out the sound of his hooves crunching leaves. "He has power over bones, that's the big thing. Living and dead. I was told to never shake hands with him, heh. He's ancient, too. Made a lot of enemies. But he's loyal deep down, to his friends and his dreams."

That last part struck an anger in me I worked hard to keep buried. "I helped him kill his own ex-wife. After he'd helped her capture me and my partner and almost sell us, of course."

"They must not've been friends," Bolton answered with a shrug. "I guess all I really know is, my entire town's in trouble if we can't get his help. And if that happens, things'll be bad enough that even the humans will notice."

I swore under my breath. Human minds can't comprehend the supernatural—their minds twist and warp to explain away anything monstrous or magical that they see. There were rare exceptions. My father was one, my boyfriend had been another. But if a situation were bad enough that multiple humans would notice, would be forced to comprehend something their minds shouldn't be exposed to...

No, I couldn't think about that now. There was the car up ahead, a Mercury Grand Marquis that had once been red, but spray-painted black with the words "CRUSHER 00" painted in white along its sides. I'd gotten it from a destruction derby for the low price of exorcising a ghost. It was a tank of a car, but to my disappointment, it was currently vacant. The others hadn't made it back yet.

"This is...your ride?" Bolton asked.

"Sure is." I popped open the trunk and tossed the hidebehind in. I'd spent most of my last job's check lining it with silver for containing creatures like this hidebehind. Maybe I could get more jobs rescuing supernatural beings this way, instead of extermination gigs. "Feel free to leave your motorcycle parts here. Don't think anyone else will come by to steal 'em."

Bolton did so, then for some reason knelt next to the Merc and bowed his head as if in prayer. He said when he stood, "It's certainly...well loved. May it continue to guard you well."

I offered my thanks, confused as I was, and we returned to the woods. When my brother—or Nalem—is out and fighting, he's easy to find. All one has to do is follow where the bones should be but aren't. Layers of decaying skin and muscle lying flat on the ground, torn so the skeletons could be freed. Holes where long-buried remains have been unearthed through sheer force of will. I felt a dull ache in my jaw as he reached out with his powers from afar and tried to pull, only to remember that he hadn't killed me yet. The last days of summer were warm enough that the corpses stank as they rotted, nestled by decaying leaves and flies gorging themselves before the Autumn chill arrived.

I heard a crack up ahead. Couldn't tell if branch or bone. Undergrowth rustled behind us. Bolton stumbled to a stop. "I think there's another one of those things behind us," he whispered. He balled his meaty hands into fists the size of my head.

I also shifted into a fighting stance. No guns; didn't want to risk killing my targets. "Are you actually sensing it this time, or is this just wishful thinking?"

Bolton sniffed the air. "This time, I'd bet my—"

Whatever it was, he would've won that bet; a lanky-limbed, bristled form darted out of the trees behind us and pounced onto the minotaur's back, digging its claws deep into his hide. Bolton bellowed in pain. He swung a wide hook, but the hidebehind blurred as it dragged its claws through his flesh, and all he hit was solid earth.

Before I could react, two more figures burst out of the foliage. The first was tall and skinny enough that his bones jutted through his near-white skin, stumbling toward us like a newborn foal taking its first wobbling steps. The other was a bear—not all of it, just the skeleton and a couple stubborn scraps of rotting flesh that wouldn't fall off its bones. It also, for some reason, had six legs and a set of horns.

"Hey! Perfect timing! I've almost got this hidebehind, but it just occurred to me, how am I supposed to handcuff the darn thing? Am I supposed to cuff it to me, or can I like...cuff it to this elkbear I made?" The only person who would even think to ask that was Retz Gallows, my lanky little brother with a fascination for magical, skeletal taxidermy. In fact, he was so proud of his creation that it took another scream from the minotaur for him to actually notice the fight. "Oh, shit. Who's our new friend there?"

"Don't ask questions during a fight." I snatched the silver manacles out of my brother's grasp and ran over to the scuffle. "Watch and cover me."

There hadn't been much reliable research on hidebehinds, but I'd learned about the two things they abhorred most: silver and alcohol. I'd had plans to drink the remaining half of my cheap whiskey, but I instead uncorked the bottle and ran toward Bolton and his assailant. The hidebehind hissed at me and my booze, bristling like an expanding black hole. Its teeth were almost as long as its claws. I splashed the whisky over it, and it screamed.

As planned, the stench distracted it enough that it forgot to dodge as Bolton smashed his elbow into the hidebehind on his back. The creature fell off like a dislodged tick. Before it could regain its bearings, a swarm of bones surrounded it, pushing it into the ground. Behind me, Retz cheered about teamwork as the horned bear skull floated over his head.

I approached the skeletal trap. The hidebehind tried to claw me through the gaps in the bones. I dumped the rest of my bottle over its fur, and as it tore at itself to get the smell out, I grabbed hold of its wrists and clasped the manacles on. The hidebehind hissed and screeched and writhed. Its cry was like a child throwing a tantrum.

"Sorry. Don't feel like bleeding any more today." I shoved the empty bottle back into my coat. Since I had to wait for the hidebehind to calm down before I could carry it, I pulled out a small tin of salve and offered it to

Bolton. "Here. It's got some yarrow and other herbs to help those wounds."

The tin was tiny in the minotaur's hands. One finger was enough to scrape out most of the salve. "Thanks. Whoever named those things was pretty spot-on, huh?" He reached to apply the salve to his wounds, and his finger came back red. "Ah, how bad does it look...?"

"Like a butcher hacked at your back," Retz said as he sauntered over. "Makes me glad I don't bleed. Or have skin on my back to tear up, now that I think about it."

As expected, Bolton cast a confused look, until I assume his supernatural sense kicked in. "Another hulderkind? That means..."

"Means you're pretty lucky to find two of us in one day, huh?" Retz's easygoing smile was all too human, but his body was even stranger than mine. He didn't have enhanced strength or a tail like I did, but he also didn't have muscles, blood, or any other internal organs. Just his skeleton—something not even other huldra had— and a hole in his back he had to hide from humans. Retz never mourned his lack of humanity, even if even the most advanced supernatural experts we'd met had no idea how he could physically exist. He was far more content to gloat about his ability to avoid bandages and bathrooms.

Bolton shook his head. "I guess. I was actually going to say, that means you're the one who's Nalem, aren't you?"

If not for the hidebehind, our neck of the woods would've been shrouded in silence.

"Nalem's not available at the moment," Retz said after a time. "Please leave a message after the beep." He waved one hand; the bones surrounding the hidebehind floated behind him, hovering over his body like haunted armor. "Beeeeeep."

Bolton shuddered and looked away, busying himself with applying the salve. "Uhmm, okay? Uh, Lord Nalem, I have been sent to find you for help. Not just because our entire town of Arcata is in trouble, including some of your staunchest allies, but...I was told you know Sea Mother? Giant leviathan buried under our town? Her skull went missing, and now we've got an upset leviathan ghost on our hands. So, uh, you can call me back at five four—"

"Stop, you absolute buffoon." The voice was my brother, but the words weren't. Neither was the arrogant scowl, somehow looking down at Bolton with a barely repressed wrath even when the minotaur easily dwarfed him in size. "You dare tell me that a skull of a holy beast, buried underground and built into the foundations of the town itself...went missing."

Bolton paused, seeming to consider his words, before nodding. "Yup, that's what happened. No one knows where it went. The room built into it collapsed, and then the ghost appeared, and she's been throwing a fit. We've kept her confined as best as we can, but we can't exactly stop her from going up to the surface to look for her head. And the humans are starting to notice what she's doing, even if they can't understand what they're seeing."

I'd seen Nalem's anger plenty of times, and had been on the receiving end more often than not. Times like this when his teeth sharpened into fangs, his finger bones turned into talons that split his skin, and all the nearby corpses around sharpened like knives? That was a rare enough wrath that it set even me on edge, my body threatening to panic under the memories of what Nalem had inflicted on me as a child the few times I'd pissed him off so royally. The hidebehind hissed as its cage dug into its body.

"Of all the damnable incompetence! Must I babysit this entire planet, lest they tear themselves apart without my watchful gaze? Where is Ginny, did she...pah, it does not matter." Nalem spun on his heels, arms crossed. The bones holding the hidebehind wrapped into a ball, then bones came together under it and formed legs, making a walking cage reminiscent of Baba Yaga's legendary hut. "We must make haste to Arcata. On our way there, you will tell me everything, and I shall determine how much suffering to inflict upon your clan."

"So, you'll help?" Bolton brightened, apparently not hearing Nalem's threat. "We appreciate you, my lord! So much has happened, I don't even know where to begin—"

"Then keep your mouth shut until I request your report, lest I fuse your teeth together to assist you in such efforts." Nalem turned to me. For a second, I thought he'd make the same threat to me, one he'd carried out in the past. But I wasn't a child or powerless anymore. Nalem kept his haughty glare and said, "As you are bound to protect me, you will of course join me on this mission."

"We've got to complete this job with the hidebehinds first," I told him. I tapped the scarf on the side of my neck. It hid a curse that demanded I complete any supernatural task asked of me, or else turn into a rosebush. Gods knew I couldn't protect anyone as a flower. "Then we'll head over to Arcata. Ghosts are serious business, especially if they weren't human to begin with."

Nalem's sneer turned into a cruel smirk. He often claimed to be a god, and lording over others was one of his favorite pastimes. "Glad you're choosing to be sensible, for once. Let us be on our way." The menace fled from his face as control reverted back from Retz. He shook the sharpness from his bones, though his fingertips were pierced and would take some time to heal. Not long, as we'd inherited the swift healing of our huldra side of the family, but he'd still have to cover his hands around humans for the rest of the day to be safe.

"Hope you're happy," Retz said to Bolton, smiling but full of sarcasm. "Well, you heard him. Let's get going before either Nalem or these hidebehinds throws another hissy fit."

The trek back wasn't difficult, especially with the hidebehind secured in the walking cage. I kept my eyes and ears alert for any signs of Farris, my boyfriend and the final member of our squad. Cell service was low, but I sent him a text that we'd found both hidebehinds, just in case he'd gone deep into the woods.

"So. You been Nalem's vessel long?" Bolton asked near the end of our trek.

"Almost all my life. Nineteen years now, or thereabouts? Turns out, the terrible twos are a lot more

terrifying when you've got an ancient evil in your skull."
His eyes glazed over, a sign that his end of the
conversation had shifted into his thoughts. His birthday
was in a couple days. He hadn't even turned one before
Nalem had entered his life.

"And you're...one of his followers?" Bolton was
looking at me this time. Genuine curiosity in his eyes.

I balled my fist so tight, the chain of the handcuffs
crushed together. "I'm just here to help out my brother.
Nalem and I...don't agree most of the time."

"Nice of you to be supportive, at least. There's
nothing more important than family, right? That's why
I'm here, you see, on behalf of my herd. You see, one of
our own was..."

Without warning, Bolton's ears twitched. He looked
off into the distance, staring past the trees and fallen
leaves toward the direction of the car. "Oh no. Not here.
But wait..." He glanced back at us. "Turns out, thanks for
breaking my ride. I think something followed us here,
but no worries—there's some iron in the bike pieces to
defend us with. Stay here while I sort things out, okay?"

He charged away, head down and horns pointed
straight ahead, hooves leaving deep prints in the dirt
and leaves.

"The hell was up with that?" I asked.

Retz tilted his head. "He said he needed iron from his bike, right?"

"Sure did. Don't think modern vehicles have much of it that's not in an alloy, but..."

"Have you heard from Farris yet?"

I didn't get the change of subject, but I checked my phone. Farris O'Reilly, my boyfriend and assistant paranormal investigator, had texted back a selfie of him at the car. The phone caught his mortal visage, sun glinting off his flowing brown hair and a charming smile that made my heart skip a beat whenever I saw it. A nice photo, but it didn't catch the undead pallor that now clung to his skin, or the shadows that billowed from his limbs and missing eye.

That's when it hit me. I still thought of my partner as human, not the undead Faerie he'd become. And that meant he was no longer safe from the ire of monsters forbidden from attacking humans, but free to target an otherworldly being like a Faerie if they sensed one nearby.

I ran.

"Do you sense him fighting anything yet?" I shouted back to Retz.

Retz called back, "He's still charging. No, wait, hit a tree, I think. Also, he's still got some broken ribs and a fracture in one arm. Think I should bother fixing that later?"

"Let's find out if he really is targeting Farris first, and why." There shouldn't have been anything else around, as the hidebehinds had apparently scared away all other sentient beings in the area, human and supernatural alike. Yet one didn't need iron for something mundane like a bear. But why fight a Faerie just because he sensed it? Sure, most didn't stay in our world for long—why Farris could was one of the many mysteries surrounding him—but it had sounded like Bolton had dealt with his kind before.

No sense in asking myself. Time to stop a fight first, ask questions later.

Before we even reached the car, we heard the combatants. Bellows met manic, frenzied laughter. The snap and following crash of a large branch echoed through the forest. The hidebehind in the cage licked its lips with a jeering coo, excited for the prospect of blood. I considered drawing one of my guns, but settled for a less lethal option by pulling out the empty whiskey bottle instead.

Once we broke through the forest to the clearing where we'd parked, Bolton had Farris in a headlock. Not an easy task, as Farris had limbs made of shadow and tipped with steel-and-glass claws. Also, a habit of going berserk in a battle, which seemed to have happened as he'd sunk his fangs into Bolton's arm. The minotaur howled and reared back a fist. Light glinted off the tiny metal rings that'd he'd grabbed from his bike. When they struck Farris in the side, his skin sizzled. Was that the iron—but how?

With worry spiking my temper, I ran over and slammed the bottle against the minotaur's back, the force of my blow shattering the glass and embedding shards in the wounds from the hidebehind. As anticipated, he released his hostage and reared around to fight me.

"Bolton, stand down. This man's our ally."

"B-but he's corrupted! Aberrant! Can't you sense it? They're the reason I had to come find you!"

Before I could ask what he meant, Bolton was struck from above. Farris had climbed on top of the car and jumped off to attack with what looked like a wrestling move he'd seen on TV, landing a kick with metal-shard claws. Bolton collapsed from the force of the blow. Not realizing I was there, Farris reared back his claws and prepared another blow.

I caught his arm when he swung. "Farris, this is a misunderstanding. Get ahold of yourself."

Farris snarled. I stared deep in his remaining eye, now feral gold instead of warm brown, searching for the humanity I knew still lurked within.

"Careful!" Bolton bayed. "He's going to take you away, and if you ever come back—"

"This isn't one of your aberrant," I growled, "he's my dumbass boyfriend. And he's going to calm the fuck down, aren't you Farris?"

Farris swatted at me in his berserk state, leaving scratches across my cheek that dripped blood. To drive the point home of what he'd just done, I knocked our foreheads together. Some of my blood got on his skin. He blinked. Er, winked, what with having only one eye.

"Babe, what the *fuck*." Farris wiped the blood off his face before realizing where it had come from. "Oh shit, was that me? Hell, I'm sorry, don't know what got into me—"

"This idiot did." I grabbed Bolton by the nape of his neck and pulled him up with my hulderkind strength so the two of them faced each other. "Bolton, for your sake, I hope your explanation for why you need Nalem's help also explains why you attacked the love of my life unprovoked."

"Your..." the minotaur narrowed his gaze at Farris. "So, this isn't an aberrant that's kidnapping humans and turning them into monsters?"

Excuse me, what?

"Something tells me this is going to be a long car ride," Retz said as he nonchalantly walked up behind us, opening the trunk to deposit the other hidebehind. "Nalem's getting antsy about this leviathan skull, so let's save the apologies and earth-shattering reveals for the road, okay? And anyone who sits in the back seat, try not to bleed on my stuff this time."

And to think, I'd started the day expecting a relatively simple case. We hadn't even reached the main road before I had my notebook out and a swarm of questions buzzing for answers.

If I dared help Nalem with a case, I sure as hell needed more information. And maybe even more importantly, a drink.

2 - RETZ

As a rule, Nalem loathed people. To him, people were either enemies or tools, or both if they had half a shred of competency. Hell, the only reason he tolerated me was because we shared the same body. He could put on a show of playing nice if the mood suited him, but at the end of the day? Nalem was a self-made god in his own mind, and gods didn't have friends.

At least, that's what I'd thought. This outrage strong enough to shake my own bones made me reconsider.

"If you don't want us to crash, stop using my body as a punching bag," I thought at him. I had a hard enough time driving Jarrod's stupid Marquis, which handled about as well as a three-wheeled shopping cart full of bricks; I didn't need Nalem tearing up my body on top of that.

He grumbled, but retracted the spikes piercing my skin. Nalem didn't have a physical form of his own, but he left sensations across my bones as if he had a body to move around inside of me. He mimicked pacing around my skull as I drove, tearing through theories on how a leviathan skull disappeared without anyone noticing. I could've tried peering into his thoughts to figure out what was going on, but I had to keep my focus on the twisting mountain road to Arcata, a small town on the coast of northern California. Dappled sunlight filtered through the redwood branches along the highway, as signs warned about the chance of tsunamis along the coastline.

From the back of the car, Jarrod grilled Bolton for any detail he could snatch about our newest case. In my rearview mirror, I watched his brow furrow in concentration as he jotted down notes in his unintelligible scrawl. I couldn't quite see Farris even though he was leaning against Jarrod; his body seemed to sag into the shadows of the car. The rest of the back seat was obscured by my duffel bag full of hair-dressing supplies, a couple stray bottles emptied of their alcoholic contents, and the usual half-contained explosion of Jarrod's laundry. At least I'd convinced him to change into something that wasn't drenched in whiskey and blood.

In the passenger seat, Bolton's voice rumbled in response to one of Jarrod's questions. "What are the aberrant? Well, it's hard to explain. They aren't human, not anymore at least, but their auras don't feel anything like I've ever felt before. 'Cept your partner, which...sorry again about trying to kick your ass there, Ferry."

"It's Farris," he grumbled in the back seat. He looked ready to say something else snarky, but Jarrod shot him a warning look. "And it's...fine. Not like I died again or anything."

I winced at that, seeing as Farris's monstrous state was my fault. Well, technically it was Nalem's, but only because I hadn't been conscious enough to stop him.

Awkward silence threatened to make itself at home. Bolton cleared his throat and continued, "I don't know what happened to turn folks into aberrant. See, the first one, Monica Bowers? She came back looking the same, so none of the humans investigating the disappearances realized she'd ever gone. We can tell, though. She can see us now." Bolton had somehow managed to prop his hooves up on the dashboard, the only way he could comfortably stretch out even in our giant boat of a car. "Talks to us sometimes too. Says it's for her paintings. But most of the time when she talks to someone in private, human or not, they go missing in the next few days."

Jarrod scratched notes into that old notebook of his, pencil scraping across pages smeared with graphite. "Any signs of struggle?"

"That's the thing, there ain't. No signs of a repeat visit either. More like they got up and left, but they never disappear when under watch. Always wait until you think they're safe, and then..." Bolton's eyes drifted from the redwoods around us to his hooves. "One of the people who disappeared was Bertha. Daughter of our clan's herd-caller. We watched her for a week, and the second we stopped, off she went. Haven't seen her since. But there've been others. Humans we'd seen around town, we catch their faces in the woods, but they ain't right anymore. The one I saw first-hand had white feathery wings and was all stretched out like some kinda bird."

"Have they attacked anyone?"

"Only folks who get too close to wherever they're camping. But we've also seen them watching Monica when we're doing the same. Waiting to talk to her, we think." Bolton reached into a pocket in his motorcycle leathers and pulled out some of those tiny metal rings. "We make sure to keep iron on hand just in case they try anything. I gave up most of mine to the forge recently, though. Clan's trying to make something more effective than kitchenware and spare parts."

Jarrod's brow scrunched tight enough that his eyebrows almost collided. "Iron, huh? But he said..." His mutterings retreated back into his head as he snagged a bottle from somewhere in his giant coat and took a drink. He offered the bottle to Farris, whose hand hovered over the bottle's neck before pushing it away.

"Right," Jarrod muttered before setting the bottle back. Not like the dead could get drunk, after all. "So...how'd you figure out they were weak to iron?"

"Ginny's the one who figured it out. I mean, I don't know *why* she had her cast-iron skillet with her out in the woods, figured it's a boggan thing...but she said the one she hit with it sizzled like a salted slug."

"Sounds like my trusted boggan," Nalem muttered in my head. He flashed me memories of this figure; short with nut-brown skin, bright green hair, and a mouth that'd make sailors cross themselves. Memories included her laughing as she peeled potatoes on a ship, swearing at a broken shovel while digging deep into the earth, putting up planks of wood between what looked like the longest ribs I'd ever seen. *"I've worked with her across many lifetimes. I left her to watch the establishment we built together, Levi's Tomb."*

"Which is...built in the bones of some leviathan?"

"Not just any. Her name is Sea Mother." Nalem reached for control of my mouth, and I let him. "Did Ginny impart any information to you about the disappearance of the skull? Any connection with these other disappearances?"

Bolton shook his head. "I mean, we all think it's got to be the aberrant, but we don't have proof of them taking anything 'cept supplies from campers. And we sure don't know how they took a whole skull the size of an apartment. They must've done it while Ginny was out shopping or somethin', seeing as she works at the bar and sleeps in the back room."

I caught memories of those rooms. Ginny bargaining with traders for supplies. Men and monsters alike rolling into town first on stagecoaches, then in early automobiles. Glasses raised to Nalem in toast. Those same patrons giving way to a figure covered in eyes, each one appraising those bones. A voice deep in those memories saying, "Not quite traditional, but what is a tavern but a temple to the community itself?"

"You don't want the Harvester to know the skull's missing," I said to Nalem. Why else would his memory drift towards his father, boogeyman of the supernatural world? *"So, this city and this leviathan, Sea Mother...they're important to both of you?"*

Nalem didn't grace me with an answer. Apparently, that last memory wasn't one he'd meant to share. Still, if failing to find the skull would draw the Harvester's ire, I wanted to get things sorted out soon as we could. Not only did I have Nalem in my head, but my brother had made a pact with the Harvester—and while I didn't want to suffer along with Nalem for any of his transgressions, I wanted to avoid consequences for my brother even more.

"Then stop asking questions and keep your eyes on the road." Nalem looked through my eyes at the winding path, at the surf hitting the sand and the sun growing closer to the horizon. I was struck with a pang of nostalgia that wasn't mine.

"You must've lived here awhile."

"I've lived here for many lifetimes. Such is true regarding most of the planet, all things considered." Yet as we left the highway and descended on the town, I saw as much of the past as I did the present. Many buildings were decorated with colorful murals, and Nalem remembered those places as they'd been constructed, and stretches of forest that preceded them. We passed a sign for Humboldt University; a feud between academics and loggers recorded on old newspapers sprung to mind. An ocean breeze pulled along the smell of jasmine. I

imagined damp sand between my toes. I'd never been to a real beach before.

I let the unvoiced memories wash over me. It wasn't often that I caught a glimpse of who Nalem used to be, what he'd once cared for in any of his lives before being planted in my body.

"Here, turn over here." Bolton directed us toward town square, where storefronts surrounded a small park and its statues. Bohemians and transients kept to the park, some playing music or resting with their dogs, as shoppers wandered the sidewalks with small boutique bags dangling off their wrists like jewelry. We parked near a building that resembled a supersized general store from a couple centuries ago, with its square pillars and white paint with slate gray trim. I wondered why we were stopping. Then I let my senses drift around the building—and under it.

"How'd you get a leviathan corpse under there?" I asked, aloud so Jarrod and Farris knew what I'd sensed. They glanced around as if expecting to see the ghost materialize right then and there.

"I put it there, of course. Incorporated it into the storehouse's structure when it was first built, creating a basement floor only other supernaturals could find." He paused as I got out of the Marquis. *"I admit, I failed to consider that a general store would be such a hotspot for*

*humans. I did not think many would stay here once the gold
rush had ended."*

We followed Bolton into what he told us was the
Jacoby Building, which turned out to be a collection of
stores, restaurants, and art studios all under one roof.
In the middle of the first floor was a small wooden
stage, probably for traveling performers back in the day.
It shimmered as we approached, I assume because it
was enchanted to react to our supernatural nature, and
revealed a trap door in the floor of the stage. A crooked
plaque materialized next to the door, reading "Levi's
Tomb" with a logo of a bottle of ale emblazoned with a
reptilian skull-and-crossbones. Nalem had me tap my
foot against the door, which revealed a spiral staircase
made of wooden planks and old bones, blue and green
fog billowing out of it. None of the humans nearby
seemed to notice; as Nalem had claimed, it was hidden
to their eyes.

"Of all the buildings I expected Nalem to hide a
leviathan, a bar was not one of them," Jarrod admitted
as he peered around me.

"Not that we're complaining or anything," Farris
added, looking over my other shoulder. "Except it seems
pretty quiet for a bar, don't it?"

"We've gotten pretty quiet now that there's less of us." Bolton shoved past me and descended the stairs into the tavern, each step creaking in his wake. I lost sight of him when the mist encircled him.

Gripping the railing for dear life, I followed him into the blue-green fog. The inside of the tavern was more solid, from the glowing glass orbs held in place by fishing nets to all the strange creatures on their driftwood-built barstools. Instead of brick and stone, the tavern's supports were bones larger than I'd ever seen, connected by slats of aged wood instead of skin and sinew. One end of the room was plastered in caution tape, right where the neck should've connected to a head. Everyone in the bar spoke in hushed tones around their tables, voices obscured as an old Screamin' Jay Hawkins record yowled from the jukebox.

The entirety of Levi's Tomb shuddered once I reached the base of the stairs. For a second, the room was filled with soft, spectral silver light as a ghost larger than the entire room flickered into sight. I couldn't see it all in that brief second, but considering it looked somewhere between a giant serpent and one of those prehistoric sea creatures, I guessed this was our leviathan. Nalem raised our hand to touch a patch of scales, but they were already gone.

"I'm glad at least Sea Mother's happy to see your negligent ass, my lord!" The bartender pulled herself up onto the countertop in order to be seen over her patrons. Seeing her in person, she was short enough to make Jarrod look giant, and her moss-green hair was styled into a frizzy bouffant. She stomped to the edge of the bar and pointed at the nearest stool. "Sixty-five years! In case you forgot how to count, that's how long you've been gone, you ingrate!"

I expected Nalem to shout back. Instead, he eased his way into control of my body, and he smiled. "My dear Ginny, is that any way to treat your benefactor? Your patron, lord, and in case I dare need to remind you, the savior of all that is good in your life?"

Ginny stomped on the bar, glasses shaking from the force. "Sure, but I'd appreciate a reminder more than once every few decades. As I'm sure twinklehooves over there told you, shit's hit the fan while you were away. Now sit your ass down, 'cause we sure as hell ain't going over it without a drink." Her gaze flickered behind me to Jarrod and Farris. "Who're these bozos?"

My brother rushed to get his introduction out before Nalem could beat him to it. "Jarrod Gallows, paranormal investigator, brother to Nalem's vessel, Retz. Farris O'Reilly here is my partner. Due to...extenuating circumstances, we're working with Retz and Nalem for the time being."

Ginny narrowed her eyes. "What's the hardest thing you can drink?"

For once, Jarrod smirked and answered with a note of humor, "I once drank a troll under a table with a couple rounds of Tree Smackers."

Ginny's laugh was more of a bark, but she gestured for some of the other patrons to pull up more stools anyway. "Good! I like you. Take a seat, I'll see if I can whip up something just as hard. My lord, I've already got your favorite in the works. Unless that's changed in the past few decades?"

Nalem shook his head as he took his seat. "I do hope you've grabbed the good cognac this time."

"As if I ever don't!" She leveled a glare at the other patrons, who were all gawking at us. "Didn't your mothers ever teach you lot it ain't polite to stare? This here's Lord Nalem! Scourge of the living and dead alike—and the damn idiot who's going to fix our bar and put our favorite leviathan back to rest! Show some respect or fuck off and puke in your boots somewhere else."

I couldn't name all the kinds of beings around us, such as dog-faced women and men sculpted from water, but all of them turned away when Ginny ordered them to. None dared to leave the bar, not alone.

Bolton raised his hand behind us. "Uh, Ginny? Does that include me too?"

"No dumbass, you can't wear boots to puke into in the first place." Ginny snatched a beer and tossed it to the minotaur. "However, I do need to have a talk with Nalem in specific, and without you blathering in the middle of it. Some of your herd's coming in later; why don't you grab a chair and a cold one for 'em?"

"Yeah, I can do that. Uhmm." He leaned over us and sheepishly added, "Nice to meet you all. And, ah, praise be to Nalem?"

"Praise be," agreed Nalem. He put his hand out as if expecting a celebratory drink, only for Ginny to hand us a cold glass of water instead. He grumbled and drank it anyway.

"Is it any problem that I'm underage? I mean, I turn twenty in a few days." It occurred to me that I'd never drunk alcohol before either. It had been offered to me once or twice, but I hadn't wanted to find out what Nalem could get away with if my inhibitions were shot.

Nalem took a long sip of his water. *"I doubt your lack of biology will be affected by one beverage. And if you somehow kept drinking and became an alcoholic one day like all the other men in your family...well, I doubt you'll grow old enough to let that be what runs you into the ground."*

I couldn't tell if he meant that or wanted me to squirm. I looked over at Jarrod, who was reminiscing with Farris about the drinking contest he'd mentioned. There was a hint of a smile on his face, like he wasn't sure if he should drop his guard and enjoy the moment.

"If it's any consolation, I doubt your brother will live that long either. And look, Farris already bit the dust, so he can't get inebriated at all." It wasn't a consolation, and he knew it.

The drink Ginny set before me was small and golden-orange, with a mandarin peel delicately curled around the rim. "One Sidecar for ya', my lord. As for you chucklefucks, Shut the Hell Up."

Jarrod looked embarrassed for two seconds, assuming that he'd somehow been talking too loud, only to find a glass of suspicious reddish liquid. Farris had one as well, which he sniffed with crestfallen amusement. I bet that even if he couldn't get drunk, he'd race Jarrod to finish it anyway.

Ginny summoned another bartender to take over the bar, this one a crow-like bird woman with what looked like a katana strapped to her back. The boggan mixed her own drink and sat down in the free seat next to me. "To old ghosts," she toasted. We echoed her and clinked our glasses before sampling our drinks. Mine tasted like someone had set an orange on fire and lobbed it straight down my throat, but somehow not in an awful way. Nalem settled down and enjoyed it.

"There. Now we can talk." Even when she lowered her voice, it still carried as if everyone else had gone mute. "First off, sorry if Bolton there caused you any trouble. I know he ain't bright, but he's the only guy I could spare and trust to survive getting you lugs over here."

"He did his best to help," Jarrod said; I couldn't tell if he meant it, or if it was a ploy to appear professional. "He mentioned you weren't only troubled by this leviathan ghost, but some…strange beings he called aberrant? Somewhat similar in aura to Farris here?" His notebook was out and ready to go, even if I was worried about his drink spilling onto it.

Ginny made a face into her drink. "Yeah, not that we know much about them. Most of 'em steer clear of us, so we only catch a look in passing. Humans with unnatural bits stapled on, skittish as hell. We know at least one who looks like a regular mortal, though. Some folks like Bolton think the aberrant are stealing people away or corrupting 'em somehow, but that doesn't seem quite right to me. They're too skittish, for one. Been no traces of scuffles anywhere around town when folks disappear, for another."

"There are ways to get around that," Jarrod muttered as he wrote. He fished a tranquilizer dart out of his coat and waved it us. "Hypnotism. Toxins. Hell, even one of these could fit the bill."

Nalem and I peered over at the dart. "Did you steal that from a certain late lamia?"

"Is it really stealing if she's dead?" Farris asked as he nabbed the dart. He flipped and tumbled it along his fingers the way some folks did with coins or pencils, watching as it caught the lights in the bar, somehow not stabbing himself in the process.

Ginny said, "You've got a point there. Could be they're playing me for a fool or something. But you know who never did? Lady Delight, if we're speaking of lamia. Glad to hear you've finally gotten her into a grave, milord."

"Because she tried to eat you once." I could tell Nalem was teasing, but he sounded too distracted for it to stick. Fighting Lady Delight, a snake-woman who ran a supernatural menagerie—and was also one of Nalem's ex-wives from another life—was our first case with Jarrod and Farris. We'd ended up being hired to kill her, after a bit of double-crossing first, and I still wondered if Nalem felt at all bad about it. But when I tried to prod his scattered thoughts, I didn't even catch a glimpse of her floating around his memories.

Instead, I saw two scenes in the back of my mind. One was a glint of silver scales under the waves, a full moon overhead with more stars than I'd ever seen, blood dribbling down skin with the taste of raw fish clinging to tongues. The other came with the warmth of a hot sun beating against shoulders, cleaning dirt out of cuts, wood into nails into bone buried deep in the earth. In both memories, Sea Mother watched, her head tilted like a curious bird. She was a giant of a being, head large as a whale and body at least twice as long, with a serpentine body and long wispy frills along her spine and the sides of her face. There was only life in her eyes under the moonlight.

"How long since this befell her?" Nalem asked, cutting off wherever the conversation had wandered in our distracted absence.

Ginny blinked, drink raised halfway to her lips. "Huh? Oh, you mean Sea Mother. Hell, four months or so ago? Didn't exactly mark it on my calendar, y'know."

I caught calculations intertwining with the past. How long seemed too long to a leviathan, living or dead? Was four months a long time between feedings or seeing the sunlight? How long had Sea Mother lived, even before meeting Nalem, before meeting...

Nalem hissed through his teeth. "You should have summoned me sooner."

Ginny scooped an ice cube out of her glass and flicked it at me. "In case you've forgotten, Mr. Savior of All That Is Shit, you never left a forwarding address. Didn't know if you had a vessel that could break away for the trip, or even when you'd last died." She seemed to consider another ice cube assault but drank more of her cocktail instead. "Soon as word passed through the grapevine about your scuffle with Lady Delight last month, I set Bolton on your trail."

The air shimmered again around us. As if she understood that we were talking about her, Sea Mother's ghost crowded the room, scales curled in along themselves in order to fit. The other patrons didn't even jump when she materialized, apparently used to this spectral outbreak. Meanwhile, Farris dropped the tranquilizer dart he'd been fiddling with and fell out of his chair. Jarrod snatched the dart before it could crash and shoved it into his pocket. Farris wasn't so lucky, landing with a surprisingly sturdy thud for someone mostly made of smoke.

"Let us hope we have time enough, then," Nalem murmured. Sea Mother angled her head over us; it was fainter than the rest of her body on account of her missing skull, so I had to squint to make it out. Nalem raised his hands and cupped them around the end of her long chin. She settled into his grasp even as she sunk through our skin and bones, closing her eyes with a contented trill. Frills on the side of her head vibrated with a high-pitched buzzing. I was reminded of a cat somehow—an oversized, scale-covered cat who could eat sperm whales as her kitty treats.

"Should've known your pets were as weird as your hobbies," Farris grumbled from the floor.

"She's not a pet." Instead of stroking her scales, Nalem ran his powers along her bones—again, the same way one would pet a cat, head to tail. "Leviathans represent the duality of life and death, the cost it takes to exist and the impact even our small lives have on the world. She is sacred, not a mere beast to dole mindless affections upon."

Once more came Farris's observations from the floor. "I'm sure little old ladies say the same things about their cats."

Nalem shot a look at Ginny. She hopped back onto the bar, stomped over to Farris's seat, and kicked his entire glass of Shut the Hell Up to where he was lying on the floor. Jarrod grabbed his own glass and downed it before Ginny could kick it onto his poor boyfriend, then slid off his stool with a hand towel procured from his coat to dry Farris off with.

I found it funny, but Nalem didn't spare them a second glance. He spoke to Sea Mother in a language I didn't recognize, though I heard him fumbling through meanings and sounds in my head. Whatever he was saying, he hadn't spoken it in a long time. Contented, she faded back into the air, scales winking out of existence like stars before sunrise.

"She's been around since before humans first stood on the earth," Nalem explained to me, though he accidentally started in the older language before shifting his thoughts back to English. *"Her bones will long outlast us, as they should. We cannot let her become a poltergeist—it would shame everything she stands for."*

I wanted to ask why. I wanted to demand a good reason to help him when he'd done his best to hurt everyone I'd ever cared for. But much as I wanted to be cold, I couldn't bring myself to say no. Was it the rare note of genuine concern I felt from Nalem, and my curiosity over why Sea Mother was one of the few exceptions to his hatred? Did I only agree so the town didn't face the wrath of a poltergeist even older than the bastard stuck in my head? Or did I just have a sick sense of adventure?

I sipped the last of my drink and agreed to do what I could for the leviathan. For now.

We stayed at Levi's Tomb awhile longer, reluctantly unwinding after a chaotic day. Jarrod pulled Farris up off the floor and tried to continue his investigation, but the booze dragged his focus away toward swapping stories with Ginny about misadventures across the country. Bar patrons wandered over to me throughout the night to pay their homage to Nalem. A few greeted me as well, surprised that a couple of hulderkind had made it out of the woods and into their bar. Some of the patrons pressed tokens into my palm, old coins or tiny carved statuettes of bone. Offerings for Nalem, no doubt, but part of me thought of them as early birthday presents anyway. Screamin' Jay Hawkins crooned and cackled over the jukebox late into the night.

While Levi's Tomb did have rooms along the rest of the leviathan's body, they were deemed unsafe to stay in while Sea Mother's ghost was at risk for turning poltergeist. The hour after last call found us wandering the streets of Arcata in search of a cheap hotel. The air was crisp, fog rolling in from the ocean shrouding the streetlights in a muffled glow. Farris drove the Marquis around until we found a place not far from the university campus. Our last job gave us enough money to afford two rooms, one for me and the neighboring one for Jarrod and Farris. I was so tired that I wandered into mine and collapsed onto the bed without even turning on the lights.

Except, with my bad luck, Nalem fell asleep before I did. And he snored.

As I debated between scrolling my phone or tossing and turning for the next hour, I overheard voices from the next room over. The walls weren't thick, after all. I prayed my brother and his boyfriend hadn't decided on drunken sexcapades. Then I heard my name. I pressed my ear against the wall.

"Hard to tell. Either way, it's best we don't tell him."

"We going to try to find the skull first?"

"Of course. And figure out what's up with these so-called aberrant while we're at it. But the second that leviathan hurts anyone..." I heard rustling. Must've been Jarrod pulling yet another alchemical concoction out of his coat. "We've got this."

"Dirty diet cola?"

"It's a near-complete bottled exorcism. Just needs some grave dirt. After that ghost at the racetrack a few weeks back, figured it'd be smart to prepare another for such a situation." A pause. "Hey, true holy water's expensive. Diet cola has the same cleansing properties for a fraction of the price."

"Just don't use it as a mixer."

"Ha. Already made that mistake once."

They drifted off, but my eyes were stuck more open after that. Great; now they had a plan against Nalem, and I had to pretend I hadn't overheard.

I loved when my own thoughts could label me a traitor.

3 - JARROD

rue to its name, Shut the Hell Up granted me a hangover so strong, I wanted to growl its name at anyone who even looked at me. It came with the kind of headache that resisted everything from hair of the dog to shower sex. I'd already tried both. As I sat at a table in the motel lobby, traces of breakfast and a cup of black coffee in front of me, my eyes were ready to jackhammer out of their sockets and shatter my glasses on the way out.

"That good, huh?" Farris asked. He at least had the sense to keep his voice low; he'd had plenty of hangovers just as bad when he was alive. We'd been investigative partners and drinking buddies for a couple years we started dating, after all, and he'd been one of the rare humans who could almost drink me under the table.

"Best drink I've had in ages," I croaked. I fished my notebook out of my pocket so I could feign productivity. Unfortunately, shitfaced-me had left notes so torn and smudged, I couldn't even sort them out when sober.

Instead of eating, Farris had taken a variety of
foodstuffs from the hotel's small continental breakfast
and stacked them into strange alters of dry toast and
packaged cereals. His hands trembled as he worked.
They often did, since his death, but these tremors were
more pronounced than normal. To think that such a tiny
ring of metal had hurt him so much. It hadn't even been
specially crafted, like all the fairytales said. No cold iron
from the heart of a meteor or whatever. Just a
stereotypical motorcycle piece.

Guess we'd have to avoid cast-iron skillets for the
foreseeable future.

"So. About this case. Is it..." Farris tapped the side of
his neck and kept his eye on my scarf.

I shook my head. "No one's ordered me to do any of
this. I'm free to investigate and decide what to do as I
see fit." Farris hadn't been the first Faerie I'd
encountered. That first Fae, my own father, had granted
me a curse after his death: complete any supernatural
task of me, or else turn into a rosebush, of all the useless
possibilities. This pact rooted itself deep inside me,
growing in intricate patterns along my limbs and
around my neck. The scarf I always wore appeared knit
to mortals but was actually a set of interwoven leaves

that hid the runes around my neck. No one else saw how it tried to choke me if I strayed from a case.

My father had told me the stories about iron hurting Fae were lies. He'd claimed they were another baseless rumor humans had thrown at the myths they couldn't comprehend to exert a false sense of control. Why would he lie to me about something that could hurt him? Before I could dwell on it, brain fog drowned the thoughts. I didn't have time for obsessive worries right now.

Farris stacked a couple packets of jam. "Good. I mean, I'm all for helping people out, saving the day and all that, but...sometimes it's nice to have the option to walk away, y'know?"

I eyed him over my coffee. "You're expecting complications."

"Duh. We're working with Nalem's groupies to save his oversized dead goldfish?" Farris leaned back in his chair and fiddled with his eyepatch. He tried to blow rings in the smoke that drifted from the empty socket. I was too hungover to remind him we were in public. "If Nalem wanted you dead—real dead, not one of our thirty-one flavors of undead—all he had to do was ask Ginny to poison your booze. Heck, I'm surprised you didn't fear that too."

I mentally cursed myself. I'd been so worn and parched that I hadn't even thought of it. The hangover was bad enough that I might not have noticed if I'd been poisoned.

Farris tugged a piece of toast and a packet of jam out of his jumbled tower and offered them to me. I accepted and snagged a napkin from his art project as well. Somehow, that's what upset its precarious balance. A flash of frustration stronger than I'd expected passed over his face, claws clicking together to resist doing something worse. He settled for cleaning up the mess.

I lowered my voice since a couple other hotel guests were staring at us. "Are you alright?"

"Yeah. All s'good here."

"I recall you adamantly promising to be open with me, to encourage me to do the same."

Farris looked up from his cluster of breakfast detritus. He allowed me one vulnerable glance, frustration and helplessness warring for control. Then his attention slipped away at something up and behind me, and his winning smile plastered itself back into place. "Well, look who finally rolled out of bed. Did your mattress have a weird crater in it too? Like a dead body was left there for a week?"

I turned to see Retz wandering over. Somehow, he
was already dressed in his usual prim and proper attire,
all vest and slacks and rolled-up shirtsleeves, and even
had his hair dried and styled. Mine was still sopping wet
from the shower.

"No, but there were cigarette burns all over the
blankets. And a stain I'm hoping is Kool-Aid? I think it's
a little bright for blood..." Retz grinned as he passed us,
deciding to brave the civilians at the breakfast bar
instead of Farris's cone of confections. "Next time, I'm
picking the hotel, okay?"

"Long as you pay for it," I said.

We made small talk as we ate. Retz was thankful
Nalem was still asleep, sparing him from demands of
baked goods drowned in syrup. He also hadn't realized
his headache that "just started" was a hangover. Farris
laughed at that, but without his usual humor. I resolved
to get an actual answer out of him later. For the time
being, I worked on deciphering my notes to make a plan
for the day.

Retz already had his decided. "I mean, I'm here
because Nalem and I can sense that skull, right? So
that's what I've gotta' do, search the areas nearby and all
that. Might check out near the campgrounds too, see if I
can get any more info on those aberrant. And I'll need
the car to cover more ground. You coming along?"

On one hand, I wanted to make sure Retz stayed safe, and Nalem kept out of trouble. On the other, I kept reminding myself that Retz wasn't a kid anymore—he was turning twenty in a couple of days, right on the Autumnal Equinox this year. And like how Autumn brought death and decay, I'd seen the destruction Retz could cause when pressed. He could handle himself. I had to remain practical, not protective.

I said, "I'm investigating that painter the others mentioned, Monica. Even if her case isn't connected to the skull's disappearance, it's worth checking out."

"Because she's a human who can see the supernatural after she started acting different, right?" Retz pointed his fork at Farris. "Think it might be connected to what happened to you?"

Farris paused in the reconstruction of his tower. "I mean, shit, might be. It's worth a look, at least." He had no memory of his past before we'd run into each other, and his ability to see the supernatural as a mortal was rare enough. Who was to say how long he'd had such a skill, or what he'd been like before? Retz had a point; this could be the break in Farris's own personal mystery that we needed.

I knew that hoping never accomplished anything. But we all have our vices, don't we?

From my notes, I deciphered an address for Monica Bowers' studio in downtown Arcata. Retz dropped us off on his way to survey the area in his search for the skull. The morning cloud cover from the ocean had yet to burn off, but the streets were bright with murals. Dyed homespun clothing hung in store windows. I wandered the sidewalks in search of the studio. Farris found a free newspaper that looked like it had been printed in some indie garage. He read about half of it before deciding to use it as origami fodder, though he kept tearing the paper by accident with his claws.

Our objective ended up being a small second-story flat upstairs from a gaudy crystal shop. The place reeked of cheap sage, and oil paints too once we made it upstairs. I resisted the urge to cover my nose with my scarf as I knocked on the door, and instead focused on Farris's particular mix of musk and brimstone. Wasn't the sort of smell you'd wear as a cologne, but at least it was familiar.

It took a few knocks before the bustling inside the studio stopped. A slow and airy voice said, "I'm not expecting visitors. You are...?"

"Buck and Dharma. We're the art reporters. We've got an interview?" I'd learned from experience that it was easy to fake an email conversation long since lost or accidentally deleted in a clogged inbox. I had one of a number of fake business cards at the ready, and an art review website pulled up on my phone. Farris had a cheap camera we kept for gathering evidence, though I had to elbow him to put the newspaper away instead of wearing it as a hat.

The door, held in place by a chain, opened a crack. Murky brown eyes looked us up and down. "Shit, I'm sorry. Didn't get that onto my calendar. I'd forget my head if it wasn't glued on."

As Monica fiddled with the chain, I saw behind her a sparse room splattered in paint. Canvases in varying stages of completion covered easels and most of the walls. I recognized most of the subjects from Levi's Tomb: there was Bolton working on a motorcycle, Ginny scowling at cheap vodka brands in the middle of a liquor store, her tengu bartending assistant feeding crows outside a supermarket. Slices of life with a touch of whimsical mythology, that's what I'm sure the critics said. That's the only thing they had in common; from the styles to the color palettes, every painting seemed to come from a different person.

"There. So, remind me again what...wait, chairs. Hold on." Monica wove through her maze of easels, gathering paint-splattered stools for us. She was shorter than me, her skin smooth and made up like a porcelain doll, matched by polished pink nails and flawless blonde curls. This perfect appearance was offset by her jeans and a smock where not an inch of the original fabric showed under all the paint, and one smear of green marred her cheek. She spoke as if awakening from an unsettling dream, a pleasant smile glued to her face.

Farris leaned in and whispered, "I bet someone hasn't left this room in a while."

Monica dragged over a chair and some stools. We sorted through our introductions, "reminded" her of our website and the interview we'd scheduled as Farris snapped a few photos. She took it in stride, as if forgetting such meetings was commonplace. She kept a small sketchbook in her lap, but I couldn't see what she drew as we talked.

I tossed her a few preliminary interview questions before asking, "What inspires you to create these paintings?"

She spoke carefully, pausing to plan her words as she spoke. "To show people what I see. No one believes me when I tell them what's really there. So I show them. But they still don't *want* to look. Not even the subjects."

"You've shown your paintings to the individuals you've painted?" I asked, with an affected note of surprise. "I can't believe they don't like it. Most people would be flattered. It's not as if your work is satirical or anything."

"Sometimes, bare truth is more offensive than satire." She began turning over her sketchbook but caught herself. For a split second, her soft, unshakable smile grew wide and knowing as if she were in on a cruel joke we hadn't heard the punchline to, barely fitting her face. I blinked in case my eyes were playing tricks on me. When I looked again, there was that genial grin peeking out from behind her sketchbook.

Farris elbowed me in the ribs and tilted the camera screen at me. He'd caught the strange face she'd made— it wasn't hers. Even the bone structure was different. At least photographic evidence meant the paint fumes weren't to blame.

"That's a fair point. What's so appealing to you about the truth?"

"Because everyone lies. About who they are, what they want...and that's how everything gets complicated. People don't want to be themselves and can't let others do the same. That's why you're here, after all."

I stopped writing mid-sentence. Farris jerked his face away from the camera screen.

"I mean...we're here for an interview, miss. That's it."

"See, here you are, proving my point. Let's be honest here, Mr. Gallows." Had I let my name slip? Monica leaned back in her chair. Her mouth didn't fit her face anymore. "You're here to gawk at a curiosity because you're hoping she holds answers. Well, she doesn't, but lucky for you, I'm always happy to help."

I straightened and resisted the urge to immediately put a hand to a pistol hilt. "Seems you have me at a disadvantage, considering that's not the name I used when I came in. Who am I talking to?"

"Are you sure you want to add any more mysteries to your plate right now?" Monica, or whoever was speaking through her, smiled with perfect white teeth. "Call me the Ringmaster, as that's the title I've come to wear. And I do believe we can help each other."

"Depends on the price. What're you doing to this woman?" I briefly glanced at Farris; he held the camera still as he could, though it trembled in his hands. He didn't look scared.

"Of course he's not scared," the Ringmaster said out of the blue. "He's in a lot of pain, you know, being out here. Same reason why I speak through Monica dear. Lucky for me, we've been friends a long time, so she's kind enough to let me borrow her body here and there to go where I no longer can."

Farris held the camera tighter in a vain attempt to stop it from shaking. "You're a Faerie too, then."

"Am I? Perhaps. I'm sure I'd look grand with insect wings—though you don't have any either, so perhaps that's all fiction too. Pity, always liked Tinkerbell." The Ringmaster leaned over the top of the sketchbook. "See, information's all the payment I need. I only came into this semi-charmed life, or afterlife, whatever it is, in the past couple of years. You have knowledge I lack. I answer your questions, you answer mine, everyone wins."

Farris muttered "Except if you can read minds, you can just grab whatever answers you want right outta' our heads, and that don't seem fair. How can we trust you?"

The Ringmaster didn't answer right away. His gaze was trained on me, eyes now a soft yellow-green instead of brown, and Monica's hands furiously scribbled across the page.

"You can trust me," the Ringmaster said, "because of what else I can offer you. A way out."

I raised an eyebrow and kept my pencil trained on my notebook. "Out of what? I'm not trapped anywhere right now."

"Going to make me spell it out, hmm?" The Ringmaster's smile widened. The pencil pointed at my scarf. "You've got a curse riddling your body and no idea how to get rid of it. This body wasn't even made to match your head. You can keep telling yourself you don't hate it all you want, but if you don't love it either, what's the point? And even if none of that were true…"

For a brief moment, the Ringmaster's grin lapsed. The face looking at me had the gall to look…sad. Pitying. I swear I even saw the smallest beads of tears form, black as ink instead of clear.

"Do you really think, between Nalem and carrying out your father's work, that you won't live longer than a few more years? That's not a lot of time to spend with your loved ones like dear Farris here."

"I don't…" I didn't dwell on those thoughts often. Only when I was particularly practical and sober. But those who hunt monsters either die or become one themselves; just look at my father. Look at Farris— except no, I made a concentrated effort not to look at him, didn't want to see what he thought about my own mind being laid bare before me. The adage about those who fight monsters rings true in my line of work, especially with Nalem involved.

"What if I told you that I can help you leave all that behind?" I hadn't seen the Ringmaster move, but a pair of hands with manicured pink nails now rested over mine. "If all you long for is information, that's fair. I can tell you where the leviathan skull rests. But if you wish for more than that?" With a flourish, two golden tickets appeared in the Ringmaster's hands, softly setting them into mine. "All you need is one night at the carnival to change your life."

I didn't take the tickets. Kept staring the Ringmaster straight in the eyes. "And everyone else who's gone missing? Do you know about them?"

"I know that none of them were kidnapped," The Ringmaster said softly. That smile was so tight, beads of blood—black again, not red—grew along the gums. "Everyone comes to my carnival willingly."

Tickets were pressed into my hands. The face shifted back to Monica, all soft jawline and deep brown eyes. She rubbed her cheeks briefly, but the smile stuck to her face.

"Does that happen often?" I asked her.

"I think I'm done with questions for today," she answered. Her eyebrows crinkled in contrast with the rest of her face. "Please."

I nodded and fished one of my few actual business cards out of my pocket, offering it to her. "In case you have any follow-up comments. Thank you for your time."

We left quickly. Kept quiet until we were blocks away. I'd thrown the tickets into a pocket without looking at them, but I swear they weighed heavier than anything else in my coat.

No surprise, Farris broke the silence first. "So...that Ringmaster was just spouting shit to get under our skin. Right?"

"Right," I agreed. Glad we were on the same page of avoiding the subject. It had been...some time since I'd had such loathing thoughts. Mostly since I'd started traveling with Farris. He made me a better and more well-adjusted man, albeit one with tits and a huldra cow tail. He gave me a reason to keep going. But just because I'd been doing better, didn't mean the shadows of those thoughts didn't still lurk at the edges of my brain. Part of why I drank was to keep them away so I could do my damn job.

Farris grabbed my hand tight and refused to let go the rest of the way back to the hotel. I squeezed back.

"We both know it's a trap, right?"

"Of course. But it's also our only lead." I checked my phone. Nothing from my brother yet. "Let's see what Retz is able to find. But if nothing else, this Ringmaster warrants investigation. Especially whatever it's doing to Monica."

Farris chewed his lip with glass-shard teeth. Keeping himself from asking questions about me so I didn't do the same to him, I guessed. We didn't dive into heart-to-hearts too quick. Had to find a safe place to let our guards down first. So he asked instead, "Any idea what this Ringmaster might be? I've never heard of a monster that reads minds and sculpts life-sized barbies in its spare time."

I had absolutely no idea, but I knew someone in the business of hunting monsters who might. "I'm giving Alexander a call."

My father had died four years ago. His number in my phone had long since gone silent, but I didn't need it anymore. Once we returned to the hotel room, I sat down on the bed and closed my eyes. Took a moment to focus my jumbled worries into something coherent. *"Sir, it's me. I'm on a few unofficial cases, and I need some advice. Nalem's involved."* I knew it was enough when I fell.

Instead of hitting the bed, I landed on a patch of moss. I opened my eyes to a meadow walled in by thorns, vines reaching so high the white roses at the top took the places of stars in the sky. This was a vision, my body unconscious on the hotel bed, but I clutched moss and felt it tear in my grasp. The air was cool and floral. My scarf unfurled from around my neck.

A figure lurched out of the thorns and loomed over me. One long claw, gnarled and twisted like a tree root, reached out and prodded my forehead.

"Been better, been worse." Same went for Alexander. What remained of his skin was pulled taut over his face, roses the color of cataracts where his eyes should've been. Interlaced vines and roots made up the rest of his body, as it had since the moment he'd died in Arcadia years ago. Until that point, we'd quested together for a way to save our family from Nalem and helped as many folks with supernaturally inclined troubles as we could along the way.

Other than Farris, he was the only person I dared trust. For the most part.

Alexander spoke few actual words these days, seeing as they were responsible for the curse planted in my and Retz's bodies. We had a bastardization of sign language that served us well enough. He tapped the air where his glasses once rested, then drew one claw down to an open palm to signify a book. "You need my advice?"

"I do, on a couple fronts. One is a leviathan ghost, soon to be a poltergeist. It's interrupting the town it's buried under because its skull has gone missing. Retz and I are following a couple leads, but..."

"Which town is it under, and how?" Alexander asked.

"Arcata, California. Its corpse has been incorporated into the structure of an underground supernatural bar. Levi's Tomb?" I paused. Alexander nodded; he'd heard of the place before. He knew a fair amount of such haunts. "Turns out, Nalem built the place in a previous life. And this leviathan is apparently important not just to him, but the Harvester. They call it Sea Mother."

"You're worried about the repercussions of exorcising it."

"Seeing as I'm stuck near Nalem as his bodyguard, and I need the Harvester's help to eventually bring Farris back to life, I don't want to piss them off. But I also can't let a poltergeist that big and ancient run rampant through the town. I've got most of a holy water vial ready to go, and its grave dirt shouldn't be hard to find if it's buried in town."

Alexander drummed his claws along the bark of his arms. "If it becomes a threat to humans, the Harvester will have to understand its removal and set his own feelings aside. He's sworn to protect humanity above all else. As for Nalem..."

My father's gaze swept the edges of the clearing. Unseen figures scurried away through the underbrush. I wondered how many bore cursed roots like me. Once the glade had descended into quiet, Alexander whispered with his actual voice, "I have a plan to deal with him soon."

"You finally found something? And it won't trigger my curse or kill Retz in the process?" He nodded and I nearly reeled back. My chest felt far too tight for my heart, but in a good way. We'd spent so long searching. People I loved had died for it. If our work really was almost at an end...hell, maybe the Ringmaster was right, and I should start making plans for a longer life. Not that I had any idea what that'd look like.

"Well sir, what is it? How can I help?"

Alexander tapped out three dots in the air to form an ellipsis. Wait. It'd be revealed in time. My thoughts raced and I wanted nothing more than to know right then, but I knew Alexander's logic. Cautious and resolved as I could be, we couldn't risk Nalem catching wind of any plans too early.

"In the meantime," Alexander signed, "continue your search for the skull. Be cautious. Keep your brother out of trouble." He turned away, and the world began to dim. "There are matters I must attend to."

"But sir, I had more questions." I struggled to stay in the vision, even as the roses overhead blinked out like stars at encroaching daylight. "There's a body-swapping being called the Ringmaster, and I don't know what—"

"A young Fae, around for even less time than I and far less experienced. But powerful. I have eyes on him, so remain vigilant, but worry not if your paths cross. I will be able to protect you."

The fading stopped, and Alexander turned back to me, his body creaking like some ancient tree preparing to fall. "You and your brother still believe that, yes? That all I do, I do with your best interests at heart?"

"Of course we do," I said, even though Retz had voiced his doubts a couple times since a misspoken order had almost complicated the case with Lady Delight. What had brought this on? I suppose even Alexander had doubts on occasion. "And soon, we'll finally be able to go home again."

Soon as I said that, I expected to be chided for naivety. Even without Nalem, how could we ever return to normal? I'd spent so long as a mercenary of all things mythical, I had no idea how to do anything else. Plus, I still had to help Farris figure out his own pact-bound task and bring him back to life. Alexander couldn't go home either, being dead and unable to leave Arcadia.

And Retz...how would he cope without Nalem in his head, even if it saved his life?

Alexander said nothing on that front. The edges of my vision blurred. I think I heard him say "We still have much to do, before we can rest." Then the clearing was gone, and the only thing overhead was the cheap staccato of the hotel ceiling.

4 - RETZ

"**I** once heard redwoods are some of the oldest forms of life on the planet. How do they stack up to you?"

Nalem took a brief break from our bone-sensing powers to follow my gaze directly up; we couldn't see the treetops or the sun.

"I am older than individual trees. I may have even walked these woods when they were mere saplings. But as a species? They have been here since I first walked along these shores, and likely before even that."

I didn't find many places reverent, at least not in the traditional awe-inspiring way folks who didn't have a self-proclaimed god in their skulls used the word. But this ancient place, overgrown with shadows and life, the earth beneath my feet teeming with so many bones even I would take ages to count them all...it was almost enough to make me lose myself in the scenery and forget why I was there.

But right on cue, I spotted an empty glass beer bottle poking out of a log like it was nature's cupholder, and not too far away a snack wrapper pretended to be a mutant fern leaf in the undergrowth. And in the distance, humans. At least, they felt like humans. Mostly. Something about their bones felt too soft and smooth from a distance, like they were made of the same plastic as the discarded wrappers. These had to be the aberrant. And while I didn't sense a leviathan skull with them, I hoped they could lead me in the right direction.

I'd driven as close as possible to where I'd sensed them, out near an abandoned campsite. Paved roads gave way to gravel and then dirt, so I had to walk most of the way. Only my bone senses and the slight increase in debris confirmed that I headed the right way.

I almost didn't notice the first guard watching me. I felt bones like birds, lightweight and hollow, but then I got close and realized the skeleton was all stretched out to human proportions. Thing is, I couldn't get a good look at the guard; no matter how close I looked at the branches where I felt their bones, I only saw needles and bark. I wanted to keep looking, but Nalem ordered me to keep walking. If the other supernaturals were in the dark about the aberrant, there was a good chance they were also clueless about us. Meaning, they didn't know about Nalem and I...and we didn't get that element of surprise often. So, I had to keep moving forward without revealing that I knew where our invisible watcher was hiding.

After I walked away, the watcher flew toward the camp, arcing their flight so they didn't cross my path. I caught a whiff of strong paint, reminding me of the art classroom in school. But the bones I felt were far stiffer than a bird's. More like a toy model. I wondered how it was possible such a thing could fly, even if they were light as a bird. Then again, maybe it was hypocritical of me to question, considering my own seemingly impossible anatomy.

The camp itself wasn't the idyllic collection of tents and cookware showcased in magazines and travel blogs. A ramshackle collection of shelters loomed before me, seeming taller with the redwoods at their backs. There were a couple raggedy tents, lean-to's made with tarps strung from low branches, even a rickety RV falling apart around its own frame. Backpacks full of supplies rested near sitting logs. The campfire had been recently doused, smoke trailing from the embers. A couple dogs growled, except one that wandered up to me and sniffed my hands in hopes of a snack. But in terms of people, it didn't look like anyone was home.

Looked being the key word, of course. I felt plenty of skeletons around me, curled up inside their makeshift

settlements, or even hiding against the trees in
otherwise open view. But I couldn't see them, and these
plasticine bones kept still as abandoned action figures
left on a kid's shelf after being outgrown.

"Don't reveal you can sense them," Nalem ordered.
*"Search the camp for clues. If they're unwilling to interfere, so
much the better. If they do, we'll be ready for them. Plastic or
no, bones will still snap all the same under my command."*

That would endear us to this secretive little group.
Though if they could hide in plain sight, no wonder folks
blamed them for things going missing; it made for a
pretty clean getaway, and according to other
supernaturals, tracking down their auras could only go
so far. I wondered how the aberrant got away with it,
when another strong whiff of paint hit my nostrils.
Surely that couldn't be it. No amount of paint could
completely camouflage a person, much less an entire
camp of people, right?

Per Nalem's instructions, I rifled through the meager
possessions scattered around the camp. Not much,
other than hoarded non-perishable foods and toiletries,
and a couple scattered wallets with cash I didn't dare
take. What I did find were photos. Tons of photos,
mostly of the same few people through all stages of life.
Some had families. Others were always pictured alone.
At one point I followed a trail of scattered envelopes,

which led to a gift bag full of cards from birthdays and holidays past, resting just outside of a lean-to made of soft blankets covered in cartoon characters.

"*Paraphernalia of the kidnapped, perhaps?*" Nalem mused as he turned over a card. "*Behavior emblematic of many stalkers, to be sure.*"

"*Wouldn't you think folks would notice if their photos and stuff had gone missing?*" I asked. Then again, not like I had a huge collection of them. Mom used to take tons of photos of us as kids, but as we got older and moved around, the pictures were relocated to photo albums that Dad always claimed "got lost" in the moves. I think, even before he left, Dad had tried to distance himself from us—from me, at least—in preparation for the day he'd face Nalem. Not like we ever had much other family around to send us cards, but I figured other folks placed a lot of importance on them to make such a big industry out of it.

"*Seeing some of the subjects, acquiring these would require a more...personal connection to the target and their possessions. Again, not unheard of with stalkers, but there has been no mention of anyone's homes being disturbed. Nor would I find it sensible for there to be a whole group of kidnapping stalkers with no further known attachments to those who've disappeared.*" Nalem twisted the card we were holding again, held it up so the scant light struck the glitter heaped on the card. Sadly, no clues lurked in the art on a kid's tenth birthday card." *At least, no one at the tavern could draw any parallels between the missing. Not even Monica was a common thread with all of them.*"

I turned to chuck the card back onto the collection in the blanket lean-to when something caught the corner of my eye. Another shelter had logs grouped together into a square shed, with a futon on one end and a long metal dog bowl containing the remains of a wilted salad. I felt a figure huddled on the other side of the wall from where I stood; if I wasn't mistaken, this one wasn't even humanoid, but a cow. What caught my attention was a license plate with a Harley Davidson frame hung up on one wall of the shed. Even I recognized that as a motorcycle brand.

Didn't Bolton say one of the minotaurs had gone missing? I wracked my memory for the name, then nonchalantly walked around the shed, pretending not to notice anything. All the bodies kept stock still, even when I approached the bovine skeleton. It felt plasticine up until the neck; everything above that felt like natural bones. When I looked straight at it, all I saw was the forest undergrowth and the back side of the makeshift shed.

I lowered my voice and said, "Bertha? Is that you?"

A pair of deep bovine eyes blinked, seeming to appear right out of the forest floor. But before I could say anything else, a rope wrapped around my neck and pulled me backwards. I didn't sense any bones directly behind me.

"Everyone, scatter!" called a commanding voice right under my ear, seconds before I hit the ground. When I looked up, a woman loomed over me in a sundress and jean jacket, both covered liberally in paints the same hues as the forest. A combat boot stamped on my chest, pinning me down. I couldn't see any bare skin, just the sort of canvas artists painted on. Instead of a face, a red X was painted over the front of her head. "How did you know her name?" she asked, though it was really more of an order the way she spoke.

As she'd told them, the camouflaged beings bolted in every direction, though Bertha lingered longer than the others. Their movements were stiff, action figures only able to move at one or two joints as they ran. Feeling their stilted bodies made my own limbs feel stuck in place, claustrophobic in my own body.

I put up my hands to show they were empty. "Ran into part of her herd. Told me she was missing."

"And how," the faceless figure hissed as she leaned in, "did you know where she was?"

"I...have a discerning eye when it comes to paintings?" I tried a charming smile. She didn't budge, not even the rise and fall of a breathing chest. Not that I could tell, because I didn't sense any bones from this woman. Not unheard of. My mom and other huldras were the same way...but they did have faces. Where was this woman's voice even coming from?

I continued, "Let's just say I'm not entirely human. Doesn't seem like you are either. You're the so-called aberrant, I take it?"

"Not by choice."

"That's the boat a lot of us are in, truth be told." I tried to look as un-threatening as possible. Instead, the thick soles of her boot ground against my sternum. "I'm Retz Gallows. Paranormal investigator, as a matter of fact, and I'd heard this town has a ton of missing cases. Humans, supernatural beings, a giant leviathan skull buried under the town...don't suppose you could give me any leads?"

The faceless woman toyed with the end of the rope she held. I wondered if she noticed how my flesh didn't bruise.

"And how do I know you're not one of *his* henchmen? You look like his handiwork. Let me guess, didn't like your size, so he ripped out your organs 'til you were bone thin?"

"No, I was born this way. But we don't need to go into my bizarre anatomy—"

"We do." She leaned in and pulled a knife out of her boot. "If you want my trust, you've got to prove that you don't fucking ooze."

"Nalem? Any advice?"

"This is our only lead so far, and you heal fast. If she attempts to do any serious harm, I will intervene." With our own body, of course; couldn't warp her bones if she didn't have any.

I nodded and tried to hold still. "Go ahead. It's gonna' get weird in there, but no ooze, scout's honor."

She paused; either she wasn't actually used to hurting others, or she highly doubted that I was ever a scout. But she grabbed one of my arms and sliced across my forearm. As promised, I didn't ooze anything. I also didn't bleed. What did come out was a vine, looking like a cross between a rose stem and a gnarly blackberry bush, sharp and prickly and reaching for a brief moment of light. The cut was light enough that my skin immediately began to knit itself shut, and the vine slithered back inside. If the faceless woman looked in the wound right before it shut, she would've seen the vine wrap itself back along my bones, all floating together in empty space.

"As you can see, I've got my own fair share of curses,"
I said. Well, the curse was Nalem's, really. Dad planted it
in me so he couldn't murder, not that it stopped him
from ordering me to do it. "So, can we talk?"

Pressure lifted from my chest. The knife returned to
its boot. "We can. Why are you investigating the
disappearances? You're not like the other detectives and
stalkers we've avoided lately."

I sat up now that I was free to do so. "My brother and
I were told about folks going missing and you folks
showing up instead. I'm sure my brother's more
interested in the hows and whys than I am, and he'll
want to pick your brain later if you're willing. But me,
I've got more pressing matters. There's a ghost that's
going to turn the town into a wrecking yard if I don't
return its skull. So, you got a leviathan head hiding
around somewhere? It probably looks kinda' like a whale
head, at least in terms of size."

The faceless woman regarded me a long moment
before answering. "I've seen it. But it's somewhere you
sure as hell don't want to go."

"I don't get the luxury of only going where I'd like,
especially not when an entire town's in danger." Or
more importantly for my sake, not when Nalem's got a
stake in what's going on. If I failed to help him reunite
Sea Mother's parts, I'm sure my head would be next on

the chopping block. "I know you're new to seeing how much magical shit goes on around you, but trust me, poltergeists aren't a fun time for anyone."

From the way she stood, trying to hold her ground with arms crossed, I could tell this was a lot to take in. If she was right about becoming whatever she was against her will, it must be even worse. Most humans had it easy, their brains twisting to erase any trace of the supernatural so they didn't have to comprehend how it broke the laws of everything they ever knew. But being thrust into such a world, having that safety net ripped away, must've been a lot. Especially when no one knew what these new beings were and got themselves too scared to help. These aberrant certainly didn't seem dangerous. Then again, I'm sure I didn't at a glance either.

I offered a hand to her. "Maybe I can help you and your friends. Give you some tips on how the world really works. Talk the others around here into cutting you some slack. Long as you're not the ones kidnapping folks like everyone thinks, of course."

"No one's been kidnapped," she muttered. "All of us walked into this willingly, if blindly." She rubbed her hands on her dress, wiping off paint, before taking my hand and shaking it. "You can call me Artemisia. You're the first person who hasn't tried to chase us down."

"As I said, I don't really care much about where you came from, long as you aren't causing trouble for me or the rest of the town. Got bigger worries, like that skull." Still no bones, even when directly holding her hand. "I'm sure we both have a ton of questions for each other. Tell me where that skull is so I can save the town, and I'll help you and the others out however I can as thanks. Fair?"

Artemisia nodded. "And if you come back changed like we've been, I'll help you as I've done for the others."

"You're not worried about me making it back at all?"

Artemisia's hand lingered as she let mine go. "The person who did this to us doesn't think he's cruel. If he works on you, it's because you wanted it, and then he lets you go as soon as his "help" is done. So no, he won't keep you in his world. Then again, by all reports I've heard, he thinks the skull was either a gift or a bribe. I'm sure he can make all sorts of twisted shit with it...so the question is, do you want it back more than he wants to keep it?"

"*A gift?! Who dares think they have any authority over Sea Mother? None who would be so foolish to break her corpse knowing the specter that'd arise from it, surely!*" Nalem's thoughts raced, but I had to hold us steady. Artemisia and her aberrant didn't know what we were. Whether we could really trust them or not, it'd be in my best interest to keep Nalem and the full extent of my powers secret for now. Getting to reveal those on my own terms was rare, and I didn't plan to waste it.

"Who's this person that has the skull, and where can I find him?"

"He goes by the Ringmaster." Artemisia lifted one finger bubbling with paint. "Get me something to write on, and I'll draw up a map to the so-called Happiest Place Out of This World."

Jarrod held a pair of gilded tickets up to the light. One had my name, and the other had his. "One Time Entry to the Carnival of Bliss!" they declared. I had a map painted on a canvas bag scrounged from the aberrant camp; we hadn't found anything smaller that could hold Artemisia's paint. We had the bag, a box of half-eaten pizza, and Jarrod's notebook spread out on the bed in his and Farris's hotel room; their bed didn't have a divot in the middle like mine did.

"This has got to be a trap," Jarrod said, and not for the first time. "If Nalem and the other supernaturals are the only ones who knew about the leviathan skull and what kind of destruction its poltergeist could bring about, someone really wants to lure him into that carnival. Question is, why?"

"Dunno. Sounds like this Ringmaster guy reworks people's body with literal plastic surgery. Why you'd want to do that to someone who doesn't even have a body of his own doesn't make any sense to me. Especially since if Nalem really wanted to, he could adjust my bones into whatever features he wants, and it's not that hard to put on a wig and a pair of contacts. All he really couldn't cover on his own are my skin and like, my nose and ears."

Jarrod rested his head on his knees as he looked over the map again. He'd mentioned the offer the Ringmaster made through Monica. Said he wasn't considering it, but bravado couldn't cover up him subconsciously sitting in ways to hide his body, or how he kept fiddling with his clothes and hair.

"Look, you don't have to go," I said. Whatever the Ringmaster had told Jarrod, it clearly left him on edge like we were back to before Jarrod had come out and gone away with Dad. "I can go get the skull myself and be back before you know it."

Jarrod held up his hand, which for once wasn't covered in his battered fingerless gloves. While the curse from Dad spread down his arms and ended at his wrists in looping patterns, the mark on the back of his hand seemed inked in black that shimmered silver in the right light. It resembled a stylized tree with eyes in the roods and leaves like sun rays.

"Harvester said I have to protect Nalem from Arcadia, and that's where the map leads. And even if that wasn't the case...you're my little brother. Who else around here has your back?"

Oh, Arcadia. Land of the Faeries. Mostly because folks became Fae if they died in Arcadia, like Farris and Dad, and this Ringmaster too by the sound of it. The place also didn't agree with Nalem, tripped up his senses and was full of undead beings he couldn't use his powers on. I'd already run into one circus in Arcadia and then had to get my ass rescued out of a hall of mirrors. Heading back into such a place wasn't my idea of a fun time, but again, we didn't have much choice. If that's where the skull was, that's where we had to go.

Then again, Jarrod had a point. We'd already lost each other for ten years; we sure as hell wouldn't let that happen again. If he said he had my back, I believed it. I'd just have to look out for him too if this Ringmaster was already getting so deep under his skin.

"So, what's the plan?" Farris asked from the corner of the room. He hadn't joined us on the bed, not having a stomach for either plans or pizza, so he'd commandeered a desk chair and slowly spun in it while watching us. "We know where the skull is, but it's with some body-warping freak who can also kinda' read minds. How do we get around that without, y'know, giving away what we're doing to a fuckin' psychic psycho?"

Nalem nudged for control of my mouth, both for pizza and to speak. He grabbed a slice with pineapple on it, probably just to spite me. "I have some experience with mind-readers and have developed techniques for counteracting their skills. However, it only works with myself and my vessel, where one can linger on the edge of subconsciousness while the other remains aware of their actions. It is...tricky to explain and trickier to pull off. Lucky for us, Retz here is one of the most pliable vessels I've worked with. A perk of raising one from infancy, I suppose."

"This sounds an awful lot like you making a plan and not letting any of us in on it," Farris grumbled.

"Exactly. If you knew of the plan, you could give it away. We know not what limitation this Ringmaster's mindreading may have, nor do I have time to instruct either of you on the art of shielding your puny little minds." Nalem sighed around his slice of pizza, as if our companions were the real disappointment here. "My suggestion is that we scout from a distance. See what reconnaissance can reveal from outside the carnival; even in his own domain, I doubt his powers extend far past the fairgrounds. If he doesn't know how to keep Sea Mother properly bound, I may even be able to retrieve it easily. Otherwise, we can return to the mortal realm and I can chart our true plan of attack."

Jarrod and Farris exchanged long looks with a hundred questions passing silently between them. I waited for them to speak as Nalem gave me control of my body back. I absently pulled at a cigarette burn on the comforter, trying to ignore the taste of pineapple on my tongue.

"Reconnaissance wouldn't hurt," Jarrod finally said, "as long as it remains just that. Though I'd prefer speaking with those aberrant you found first."

I said, "They were skittish, and it totally makes sense why. We've got to prove we're being honest about why we're here. So we get the skull, save the town, and then we can move onto settling this misunderstanding between the aberrant and all the local supes. Everyone wins."

"That's awfully magnanimous of you and Nalem," Farris mused. He looked ready to say more but held his tongue in order to stare at me. As if I should pick up his thoughts like this Ringmaster apparently could.

"Nalem's not always screwing folks over with his schemes. He honestly cares for this place. It's...the closest thing he's had to a home, at least as far as I've ever felt. So why wouldn't he want it to stay peaceful?"

Jarrod put up his hands. "I understand you two have good reason to be suspicious of each other, but now's not the time." Jarrod shot both of us looks to keep our mouths shut. "I understand that Nalem...cares about this leviathan more than he normally does. We can acknowledge how important that is. But knowing Nalem's propensity for scheming, and considering recent events, I think Farris is being cautious. Which is also smart, wouldn't you say?"

My first instinct was to argue otherwise. I bit my tongue and nodded instead. Really, it was fair, wasn't it? Nalem had screwed both of them over plenty, and now we were on his home turf. It made sense to question that. Even if he behaved and didn't betray them now...there was always later.

"Or are they so blinded by their own paranoia, they cannot believe a good deed when they see it?" I felt light taps in my shoulder blades, as if someone patted my shoulders. *"Honestly, you should be used to this by now, little one. Even your own family will always doubt your intentions. If you offer*

kindness in order to receive the praise of others, you'll find it withheld no matter how hard you work."

"*No thanks to you.*" I couldn't tell what irked me more; the suspicion, or how warranted it was.

I said, "Right now, we all have the same goal. Stop Sea Mother from becoming a poltergeist, which means getting that skull back before she turns. Let's focus on that, and we can interrogate the aberrant and Nalem and everyone else in town once we know it's not gonna' get torn apart. Sound like a plan?"

Jarrod agreed. Farris did too after a reluctant moment. We turned our attention to the painted map, comparing it to maps on the internet and figuring out our reconnaissance plans. Jarrod did most of that. Farris and I did our best to ignore each other. And I tried to figure out how to make them believe that Nalem and I honestly wanted to help, and more importantly, if there was even a point to doing so.

5 - JARROD

"**L**ooks like this is as close as we can get by car."
Retz slammed the Marquis door shut and
ambled onto the grass of the park. The sun
dipped low enough for our shadows to stretch toward
the forest and its trails. Not too far away, children
chased each other around a wooden play structure,
enjoying their brief respite from school schedules and
homework. I remembered being that age, protecting
Retz from bullies. I'd had to, or else Nalem might've
enacted a vengeance far fiercer than a bloodied nose.

Retz must've guessed I was reminiscing as I got out
of the car. "C'mon bro. I don't care how many beers
you've had; you still aren't allowed on the monkey bars
anymore."

"At least I never fell off of 'em." I brushed Retz aside.
"Farris, do you sense anything?"

Farris leaned against his door, eye trained on the
woods ahead. Turns out, portals into Arcadia lurked all
over if one knew where to look, and a "perk" of Farris

becoming a Fae was an innate sense for these
otherworldly bolt holes.

"Definitely a portal nearby," Farris muttered. His
voice was dazed, but his pupil shifted into feral slits, a
predator catching a whiff of prey. He left the car and
made his way toward the woods without even shutting
the door. I did so and hurried after him. I already feared
I'd have to remind him we were on a reconnaissance
mission instead of a chance for a Fae to let loose.

We weren't interested in the open area of the park,
but deeper along the trails. The scent of jasmine
mingled with crisp redwoods as we left the reminders of
childhood behind. An unpainted road wove between the
towering trees, but we soon veered onto a walkway
covered in little more than dirt and sticks. Ferns
threatened to consume our path and sawed-through
trunks of fallen trees had been left to rot in the untrod
spaces between the hiking trails through the woods.

Forests are never quiet the way folks claim. This close
to civilization, the grumbles of car engines came to us
filtered through the trees. These were public trails in
summer, so we passed other humans finishing a hike
before dinner. Voices carried in those woods, as did
every stepped-on twig or gravel path crunched
underfoot. The only ones who kept truly silent were the

figures carved into trees, faces and animals leering from their bark trappings.

Yet there was a certain stillness once we reached the portal to Arcadia. It didn't stand out; there were many fallen trees in these woods, and the portal was half a redwood log propped up against a large stump, forming a triangle. Yet I felt its power thrum through the Fae-curse planted in my skin, and the air in the wooden arch faintly shimmered. No birds sang near this place. No animals scurried. Even the rest of the trees gave their fallen kin a wide berth. Nature knew what didn't belong.

But humans had no clue. How many had fallen through this portal—or if the Ringmaster was to be believed, had walked through willingly?

"Remember," I said, "reconnaissance only. Don't go into the carnival. We'll leave at the first sign of trouble."

"Unless we can get the skull out immediately, in which case, fuck shit up and run screaming. I know the drill." Retz winked at me, and I hoped he was kidding. "Wanna' enter together on three?"

He'd barely started to count when Farris strode ahead, not seeming to hear us. I grabbed his hand to make sure he didn't get too far. Stepping through the portal came with spinning vertigo as the world swerved and collapsed into itself. Green leaves and redwoods around us shifted to midnight blue, and the treetop branches drifted off into nebulas full of alien constellations instead of leaves. The path we stood on was as dark as the sky above, but the trees further along that trail were slathered with golden fliers, no inch of bark exposed. The smell of ocean and cedar was twisted by the reek of over-buttered popcorn. A distant calliope dragged out its notes in the distance.

Retz stumbled out of the portal right behind us, but as soon as he heard the music, he nearly turned around. "Gods be damned, how many spooky circuses does Arcadia have?"

"Let's hope it's enough for this to be mere coincidence," I said. I still had some trouble looking at mirrors, remembering the taunts of my reflections in the last fairground's funhouse. I squeezed Farris's hand; his expression was still dazed. I wondered if the sight reminded him of our last time in Arcadia. When he'd died. We hadn't been back since.

Farris blinked a couple times before squeezing my hand back. "I'm okay. Though if there's another merry-go-round at this one..."

"Then we'll tear it apart if it attacks, but please, for once in your lives, try to be stealthy."

I failed to account for Farris being undead. His life was already forfeit, and apparently so was his ability to sneak. He crept around like in the B-list movies he'd watched in hotel rooms, all exaggerated movements and stage whispers. I would've chided him for it, but it was refreshing to see him acting like a theatrical goof again. Then there was Retz, who navigated just fine with bones around, to the neglect of his other senses. With no bones to orient him, he kept getting distracted and almost walked into a number of tree trunks.

"When we get to the carnival," I hissed, "I'm sticking you both in trees as lookouts. Except then you'd probably fall out and break your necks."

"That's what you get for taking us anywhere," Farris said with a teasing wink. He reached the first flier-covered tree and tried to pull one away. Even with his claws, it remained stuck to the bark, held in place with thick black ooze. It sunk under his claws and stained the glass black. "You guys might wanna' look at this," Farris growled, "but don't get too close." We hurried over to look.

"Welcome to the Carnival of Bliss, where YOU are the Star of the Show!" read the flier, with a logo shaped like a big top tent scrawled across the top. The illustration was of a human so ordinary I couldn't focus on their features, walking through a hallway of circus posters. Familiar figures—the ringleader, the strongman, animal tamers and supposed freaks of nature—leaned out of their paintings as if the guest was the main attraction. As soon as I saw the art, I knew who'd painted it: Monica's signature mundane touched by whimsy was tough to miss.

The gilded coloration of the flier reminded me of the tickets. I pulled one out, and sure enough, the paper was the same shimmering gold as the flier with a matching font and big top logo. Except the bottom read "One Night Only," and in the middle, a name. My name, in the right light. If I turned it wrong, I saw the name I'd been born with, as if that had been written first before someone tried to rub it out.

The flier in front of us shifted when I pulled out the ticket. For a brief moment, the human on the poster wasn't a stranger, but eerily familiar. Shaggy dark hair, murky eyes behind thick glasses perched on a long needle of a nose...it still took me a moment to recognize it as my own face with the giant grin plastered on. I shoved the ticket back into my pocket fast enough I scraped my fingers against the zipper.

"No offense," Retz said, "but if you ever smile like that at me, I might have to break your teeth."

"Don't make me pull out your ticket." I turned away from the flier before I gave into the temptation to tear it apart. I didn't look that horrifying when I smiled, did I?

I wasn't the selfie-taking sort, or what most folks would call a cheerful person. But I was just a serious person. A grump. Going through a lot of shit. Nothing wrong with that, right?

Farris wrapped an arm around my shoulder, a heat-seeking missile for self-doubt. "I think your smile's real sweet when you bother to show it. Whoever drew that is no skilled hand at caricature, okay?"

Not for lack of trying, it turned out. The farther we went along the path, the more fliers had actual carnival guests featured, all of them with grins sharp and wide as a crescent moon. Some were human. Not all. We stopped when we found a flier featuring a minotaur teenager, judging by her fashion. Thanks to Retz's report, we knew what became of her once the smiles had faded. That, more than seeing myself on the fliers, made my guts churn and my hands ball up into fists. Whether or not she came willingly didn't matter if this minotaur was still a kid.

As Retz pointed out soon after, we had more to worry about. The carnival had a fence higher than any of us were tall, wooden boards plastered with fliers and illustrations for various carnival acts. The tent tops I could see seemed composed of radioactive, glowing paint instead of fabric, colors dripping into each other. Surrounding the fence and spilling from the gates were clouds of candyfloss, white intermingled with blues and pinks, flecked with squirming black bugs. The abandoned carnival with the house of mirrors had also been flooded with the same confections.

"I'm starting to think this might not be a coincidence, and Fate's got a funny plan here," Farris said, keeping his voice low now the carnival was in sight. "Except the one we crashed didn't have a leviathan head hiding in it, right? And that was a couple months after this skull went missing."

"It didn't, but this one does." Retz's gaze went distant but snapped back as he scrunched his eyes shut and shook away whatever feedback he'd gotten. "And something live is strapped to it. Don't know what, but it means I can't float it out."

A loud honk alerted us that even if he could've, he'd be quickly discovered. We scurried off the path and behind the trees as a flashlight swept over the area outside the fence. Patrolling the perimeters were...I hesitated to call them clowns, even though they had the proper garish paint and attire. Their squat bodies were topped by bulbous, oversized skulls like blown-up balloons, so unstable that each step put them at risk for tumbling over.

"Fuck," Retz muttered as he ducked behind me.

I whispered back, "Sense something?" I forced both hands onto pistol hilts instead of the ticket.

"I understand why some folks are terrified of clowns. I fucking get it now." Of all the times to discover that my brother was coulrophobic...

"How the hell can you be scared of clowns? You make scarier shit with bones all the time. You have one of the biggest terrors of the supernatural world living in your head. Explain to me how clowns are more terrifying than that."

"Other than not having bones for me to fuck up?" Retz peered over my shoulder and pointed at one as it passed by the carnival entrance. "Look at their heads. Wobblier than a baby. Gross. And all that makeup...can you imagine the grease? The pimples? You see how frazzled their hair is too, right?"

Farris rolled his eye. "Bet their heads would pop if stabbed. Like a fuckin' water balloon."

Retz grimaced. "You're probably right, but why'd you have to go putting that mental image in my head?" He sighed before pointing at the carnival and the tallest tent. "Skull's around that end. There's a body strapped to it, but...it doesn't have a head. At least not one I can feel, though it's got to be alive somehow if it's blocking my control of the skull."

"Is it human?" I asked.

Retz closed his eyes. "It's...bipedal. Similar for the most part, really broad and...oh. That's not good."

"Does anything about this seem fine and dandy to you?" Farris growled, looking about ready to charge through the front gate for a chance to shred the clowns. I had a firm grip on his hand to keep him from making any rash decisions.

"The body has a tail like yours Jarrod," Retz said quietly. "And hooves."

I took a deep breath to keep myself calm. Instead, I nearly choked on the reek of candyfloss, buttered popcorn, and the iron tang of blood.

"Let's get to that reconnaissance. If we stick to the trees, we should be able to avoid the clown patrols." Raising hell now wouldn't get us any answers. Wouldn't reunite that body with its rightful head either, if what Retz implied was true. We had to figure out what this Ringmaster was doing, and how, before we could make our move. Facts before fights, that's what Alexander taught me.

As with the forest on the mortal side of the gate, most of the trees here were wide and difficult to climb, even without being plastered in fliers. Farris managed to claw his way up, though his fingers came away slick with ooze when they pierced the gilded paper.

Retz and I kept an eye out for smaller trees, and failing that, something with a low branch. We found one with branches that hung over the carnival fence, a prime spot for reconnaissance.

I told Retz, "Should be easy to climb if one of us lifts the other. Climber gets the boost to reach the top, then tosses a rope over for the other to follow."

"Like we did back on the playground as kids, huh? Except, where're we going to get a rope?"

I reached into one of the back pockets of my coat and pulled out a bundle.

"Next thing I know, you'll have an entire car in that coat of yours."

"I did carry an RC car for a mission once. Does that count?"

Retz groaned and knelt next to the tree. "What'll count is you climbing up there. I'm sure I'd drop the rope or something if I went first."

"I appreciate your honesty." I was lucky Retz inherited Alexander's height, but even once he stood up, I could barely reach the branch while perching on his shoulders. "Retz, can you manage a couple more inches?"

"Depends. Why are mortals full of meat, and how do you make it lighter?"

"You know, there's a whole industry of folks trying to figure that out, so they'll look as emaciated as you." I tried standing on tiptoe, but that nearly caused us to fall over like the bulbous clowns. "Would you rather I jumped?"

"And have you pulverize my shoulders? No thanks, Rocket Man." Retz whistled a few notes, followed by a wretched creaking noise as we ascended. I made the mistake of looking down. Retz had extended his leg bones, the skin visible at his ankles taut and about to tear. I grabbed the branch and hoisted myself up. Retz fixed his legs and collapsed to the ground.

This branch didn't seem quite sturdy enough for both of us, even light as Retz was. I climbed a bit higher, occasionally glancing down to make sure the clowns hadn't noticed us. They ambled along the fence, occasionally honking at a stray bug in the candyfloss or a flier that somehow broke free and glided down to the ground. None of them looked up except when one's head lurched back, forcing the clown to stare skyward with an unflinching smile as it struggled to maintain balance. Makeup pooled down their faces like sweat.

I made it to a branch that drooped over the fence, tied the rope, and tossed it down to Retz. Then I made the mistake of looking down into the depths of the

carnival itself. In the maze of painted tents, I saw
someone I recognized.

"Shit. *Shit.*" I started pulling Retz up before I even
made sure he'd grabbed hold. He flew up on account of
how light his skin-and-bones body was and clung to the
branch before glaring at me.

"Warning next time?" He snapped. Instead of
answering, I grabbed his head and tilted it toward the
figure I saw. "Oh. Wait. What the hell is she doing here?"

I couldn't remember the lamia's name. But I couldn't
forget the red-and-black scales combined with a punk
haircut and too much eyeliner. She still had her leather
jacket and refused to put on a shirt, which showcased
the spiraling green tattoos across her chest and arms. I
didn't have to roll up my own sleeves to know how well
they matched.

When we'd fought Lady Delight to keep ourselves
from being sold in a supernatural marketplace, she'd
had a number of other lamia working for her, including
this one, her right-hand woman. When she'd had been
injured in Arcadia, I'd gone out of my way to patch her
up. Last time I'd seen her, she asked me why. I never got
to answer before she and the rest of the menagerie had
been swallowed up by vines and tunnels created by
Alexander. I didn't know what he'd done with them.

Never got a straight answer out of him, other than that they were "somewhere safe".

"Is she still...all together?" I asked Retz in a low voice. She didn't look scared, at least, though maybe she hid it under hisses and glares.

"Doesn't feel plastic to me," Retz answered, "but that curse is pretty deep in her bones. Same as yours."

"Figured it was." But why was she here? I knew Alexander had cursed a few others, so while seeing it on someone else upset me, I wasn't as surprised as when I'd last been to Alexander's realm in-person. If she was cursed, however, it was incredibly unlikely she'd run away. Interrupting an escape would be as simple as ordering her to stay. And if she'd somehow snuck out without Alexander noticing, he'd find her easily enough. He'd always been a skilled tracker, even before he could visit folks in visions like he did me.

If someone bearing his curse was here, it was under his orders. Sure, he'd told me that he had eyes on the carnival...but I'd met that lamia, and stealth wasn't her strong point, and I doubted she could hide from a telepath either.

Not that I expected Alexander to tell me everything. But he usually kept me abreast of any investigations he was working on in Arcadia, especially if it involved a past case. He'd seen the carnival this one seemed to mimic; he'd rescued us from it. So why keep it secret that he'd found a similar carnival, or that he had a stolen being handling his dirty work?

Huldras are beings of instinct, however much I try to ignore that fact. Seeing the lamia lost among the carnival tents was the straw on top of everything else I'd already discovered in the past twenty-four hours. I ignored my own warnings and climbed as far as I could along the branch. I didn't answer Retz when he loudly whispered my name, or look back to see if Farris had joined him. I gauged how far I was from the fence. With the strength I inherited from my mother, I jumped and grabbed the top, then looked down to make sure there weren't any bulbous clowns underneath. I found a covered carnival wagon that looked significantly sturdier than the bleeding-paint tents and leapt onto that, then made my way to the ground. I stayed quiet as I could, but the lamia still noticed me.

I expected her to be angry. To shout something about my family ruining her life. Instead, she sighed and pointed at the curse on her neck. "Here to play hero again? Either you're digging these roots outta' both of us, or you're dead meat."

6 - RETZ

"**S**o what are we s'pposed to do?" Farris asked, both of us peering over the fence from our branch. Neither of us knew how to follow up Jarrod's blatant disregard for his own rules.

"*Hypocrite,*" Nalem murmured in my head. "*I doubt the fool even figured a way back out first. How fortunate that you do not follow the same huldra tendencies.*"

Far as I could see, Jarrod and the lamia were just talking. I racked my brain for her name; Zalin, wasn't it? Our first meeting hadn't gone great, as she'd turned into a two-headed snake and tried to kick my ass before I could meet her boss. She'd never seemed nice, but I doubted that was a factor for Jarrod. We all saw the cursed marks they shared, and when Jarrod wanted answers, everything else fell by the wayside.

"I think I can get him back out afterwards," I said carefully, even as I plotted it out. "Wait, I didn't bring the viola case, almost all my extra bones are in the padding. But I do have mine and a couple spares in my pocket, and I think if I float enough down there, I can make a ladder for him to climb..."

Farris gave me a disturbed look before quietly lifting up the rope.

"That'd work too," I said.

"Maybe one day you'll realize you don't have to solve every problem by tearing yourself apart with your freaky-ass powers." He coiled the rest of the rope while keeping an eye on Jarrod. "Alright, you any good at plans and shit?"

"I mean, Nalem has some—"

"Forgive me for not trusting the guy who ordered my heart ripped out." Farris looped the end of the rope into a lasso; I hoped this wasn't another trick he'd picked up from TV. "All I know is, I'm no chess master. That's Jarrod's job. And seeing as he's having a brief case of curiosity killing the cat, I'm hoping you got some idea of getting us out of this mess that doesn't involve making a scene."

I nodded and looked down. Of course, Jarrod and the lamia had wandered off in the two seconds I'd looked away. However, the thick field of cotton candy captured their footprints—well, the soles of Jarrod's thick boots and the trail left by Zalin's serpentine lower half. I could feel their bones close by; they were headed in the direction of the skull. There were other living bones in the carnival, but none of them were moving, and they didn't feel whole.

Where was that Ringmaster? Hard to tell. Faeries didn't have bones, at least in a way I could sense them, so all I had was "something's static-y over there and makes me want to vomit." Closest contender for that was Farris, seeing as he was perched right next to me.

Deep breath. No, bad idea, this place reeked, and Farris fuming with brimstone didn't help. I clapped a hand over my nose and tried to think. Problem was, the Ringmaster could read thoughts, though we didn't know how much or how long he could do so. Heck, maybe he read my thoughts as I thought them up in that tree. How could anyone plan around that?

"I'm experienced with telepaths," Nalem said. *"There is a technique for handling them with two minds, but even I cannot teach you in a matter of minutes. I will also need to determine how deep the Ringmaster can read, so I will have to, as mortals say nowadays, go dark. It will be as if I am absent. I'll be unable to help you–but if I do need to interfere, I may catch him off guard."*

Great. No Jarrod and no Nalem; I really was going in blind. What would they do in my shoes?

I finally answered Farris, "Alright, goal one is to stay stealthy, but we might not be able to hide from a mind reader. So...one of us should focus on tracking Jarrod and getting him out. The other should be ready to peel off and cause a distraction, then circle back out."

Farris smirked, baring his glass shard teeth. "Distractions are my forte. You can track Jarrod, so I'll trust you getting him back in one piece." He pointed a finger at me, almost stabbing me with his claws. "And I do mean one piece. If so much as a single hair is missing from his head, I'll..." he trailed off upon realizing that any threats on my person would likely piss off Jarrod. The things we did to keep my brother vaguely happy and sane. "I'll get the pettiest revenge I can, that's what."

I wouldn't call what we had a plan, but at least we weren't charging in mindlessly. Farris lassoed the rope around the tip of the closest tent. I crawled over first, being the lighter of the two of us, and only almost fell once. I clung to the end for dear life while Farris crossed in a matter of seconds. He smirked at me, the show-off, before signaling me to look down. One of those bobble-headed clowns marched between the fence and our tent. We held our breath, hoping those bulbous eyes didn't look up at our rope.

Farris pantomimed what I'm pretty sure translated to "watch me do something stupid". He poised to pounce. Claws dug into the painted canvas before he dove down. The clown stumbled out of Farris's path without even realizing he was there, moving in herky jerky motions. I expected him to crash into the ground and come up covered in cotton candy.

Instead, the shadows cast by the tent shimmered, and he disappeared from sight.

I almost called his name before remembering that I was supposed to be stealthy. I tried to ask Nalem what happened. Silence. Shit. I peered over the surface of the tent, but the shadows had returned to normal. And the clown's head jerked back up. Its bulbous eyes went wide as it emitted a scathing honk from its nose, a sound suspiciously similar to strangling a goose. I tried to jump from the tent to land on the clown and take it out action-movie hero style, which I'm sure had been Farris's plan, but missed by several feet. Landed right on my face and looked up to find shiny red shoes charging toward my head.

I rolled out of the way and launched a handful of emergency vermin bones I kept in my pocket into the clown's nose. They tore through and out the back of its head like darts through a water balloon. The clown's face deflated as it oozed black sludge, and it stumbled around blind until it wandered into a smaller tent, collapsing the painted canvas in upon itself. Sweet air turned chemical with the smell of paint. I got to my feet and gagged.

I still didn't see Farris anywhere, and I couldn't sense him either. I'd lost my brother and his stupid boyfriend in a couple minutes. So much for stealthy reconnaissance. And to remind me how much we'd fucked up, more scathing honks echoed in the distance. I cast a last glance at the shadows, but no spooky golden eye looked back at me, and no claws reached to scrape my ankles. I ran off in the direction I sensed Jarrod, and hoped wherever Farris had fallen, he'd catch up later.

If I was already on the ground and heading toward the skull, I might be able to free it by removing what I assumed was Bertha's body, make a clean escape, and fix Sea Mother before anyone could raise a fuss. Did I expect things to be that easy? Maybe; I pick the worst times to be an optimist. I also didn't have Nalem to shoot me down. Honestly, the complete and utter silence in my head had me more on edge than anything those clowns could manage.

The carnival itself was a maze, and all I had was a direction in which to run. I passed colorful stalls and painted tents straight out of the cartoons Jarrod and I had watched as kids. A wall of stuffed animals lined along a target range silently pleaded for release with sad glass eyes. A popcorn machine boiled over with butter

and nearly-burnt kernels, unmanned and untasted.
I paused around a cage holding a lion with a roar like a
crying child, but despite how human its voice sounded,
every inch of it was numb to my senses. It pawed at the
bars as I left.

I'd ask how fucked up someone had to be to think
this place was actually fun, but I should be the last
person to question it, considering my particular
hobbies.

After popping the head of another clown before it
could honk the alarm, I heard low murmurs. My powers
told me Jarrod and Zalin were nearby. There was a wall
of tents in my way...but could it really be that hard to go
through paint? I tore an opening in one with my
vermin-bone knife and strode in. The paint covered up
the slash quickly and pooled down my shoulders like a
waterfall of molasses. This tent seemed empty inside,
not even a trace of cotton candy; it just existed to
support the illusion of a bustling carnival. And it got me
close enough to hear voices over the din of the calliope.

"It's not spying if the Ringmaster knows you're here.
He understands that, right?" I couldn't see Jarrod, but I
felt how tightly his fists were balled, the way his teeth
grit when he wasn't talking.

Zalin snapped, "I don't know how to get it through your thick head, hulderkind, but that's the entire point. I'm a goddamn test. Your old man wants to see this Ringmaster at work, and he's pegged me as an acceptable casualty if he fucks it up."

"But the Ringmaster said folks only come to him willingly."

"Real stinker, ain't it? I'm under orders so I can't leave of my own free will. Only way to escape the curse is to let the Ringmaster plop me into a new, curse-free plastic body. Creeper's ringing all his hands waiting for me to say yes—have you seen him yet, by the way? All those hands?"

"I haven't—"

"Of course not. You don't know what's going on, just waltz right in and think you can save the day 'cause you're human when it suits you." Her hands wrapped around something close to Jarrod's chest, likely the lapels of his oversized coat that had once been Dad's. "I hate when half-humans like you do that. Makes the rest of us look bad." Hold on, what did she mean by...?

A hand clapped over my mouth. I sensed no bones, and the skin was loose over musculature like a plastic glove. Another hand grabbed the collar of my shirt, and two others grabbed my wrists and pinned them behind my back. They pulled me backwards, out of the tent, and held me upside-down in the air.

I looked at my captor. Imagine a man. Imagine a centipede. Then mash them together. He was blond and almost handsome from the torso up, with a curled mustache and a jaunty top hat that screamed charming gentleman villain. Then add extra arms along his sides and give him a black and red suit tailored to fit. Keep stretching the torso back until he's built like a centaur and stands at least seven feet high, but instead of horse legs or even people legs, just keep adding arms. Ooze caked under the fingernails of his many hands that tore up fistfuls of cotton candy as he walked.

"Retz Gallows, I presume? Didn't expect to meet you quite this soon. What a pleasant surprise! You should've come in through the front with your ticket, gotten the whole royal welcome. But I understand your caution. Seems like you've had some scary run-ins with carnivals in the past, hmm?" One of those hands reached up and patted my head. I tried to ignore those too-long fingers, the way his entire anatomy didn't make sense and made me want to hurl.

From the other side of the tents, Jarrod called my name. Maybe he heard the Ringmaster, or maybe Zalin had sensed me. I shouted back, "Jarrod! Be careful, the Ringmaster's right here—"

"Careful?" The Ringmaster asked, seemingly offended. "Whyever would you need to be careful? This isn't a horror story, my friend. This circus is a place of fun and healing. Not like the last one you attended!" He winked and added, "I personally made sure of that."

"Didn't anyone ever tell you it's rude to snoop in other people's heads without their permission?" I tried to kick the hands holding me, but his grip wouldn't budge. "Now put me down this instant or—"

"Or what?" The Ringmaster asked, faking innocence. "You can't control my bones. Using your own would hurt you more than it would me. And I'm only moving you somewhere out of the way until the clowns calm down. Coming in over the fence without presenting your ticket gave them quite a fright, you see."

"Likewise." I stared up at this Faerie's face, as it was the last part of him human and anatomically correct. I expected some form of malice, but honestly, he looked more awkward and earnest, like a host for one of those educational kid shows. Heck, that'd explain the clown theme and all. If I didn't look down at the arms, I had a hard time matching him with the shadowy figure Artemisia had warned me about, shoving people into plastic doll bodies left to hide in the woods.

His smile faltered when I thought about the aberrant in the campgrounds. "I gave them what they wanted. I can't control what they do with their lives afterwards." He placed a hand on my finger and answered the thought I was still in the middle of thinking. "That includes Bertha. She was such a sweetheart during her visit, you know. And if someone like her wants to cast aside responsibilities and the burden of family, who am I to say no and let her suffer? This is no place for pain, my friend."

I could've argued morality and ethics, but being a vessel for Nalem makes any argument I make ring hollow. I chose to switch tactics and buy time for Jarrod to reach me so we could bullshit some sort of escape plan. "If your goal is to avoid pain, then I'm going to need that leviathan skull back. The ghost it belongs to is getting pissed at being in pieces, and it's going to wreak havoc in the mortal world if left that way. Unless you don't care about anything outside your carnival...?"

"On the contrary, I'd return the skull right now if I could. Thing is, I've promised to hold onto it until a certain someone has been saved." A pair of hands lightly rapped their knuckles on the side of my head. "Wherever is Nalem, by the way? I've been dying to meet him."

The last thing I wanted was for two powerful idiots, who thought power gave them the right to warp other people's bodies on a whim, to meet. Nalem would either get in over his head trying to establish his own supposed godhood, or he'd find a way to make a deal with the bastard in front of me. Good thing he was...wait.

"Deep in your unconscious, hiding his presence to later scout out my weaknesses?" The Ringmaster gave an impressed nod. "Didn't realize you could do that. Then again, it seems there's much I still don't know. As I told your brother, perhaps we can make a deal. I save your lives, you give me the lowdown on all these supernatural wonders I missed out on before I discovered this land. But much as I'd love to chat with him once you're done stalling, we simply don't have time for that on tonight's billing."

Turns out, a swarm of hands could scurry as well as a pair of legs, even if they came up with fistfuls of dirt and wisps of sugar. The big top loomed ever closer, its edges leaking a monsoon's worth of paint. My imagination ran wild with what could be inside. Some carny-themed operating room? Mannequins that'd copy my face the second they saw me? More clowns?! I squirmed and tried to think of some excuse to escape.

The Ringmaster chuckled, but not the delighted at my suffering sort that Nalem often did. This was exasperation, pure and simple. "I don't think you understand my goal. I'm trying to keep my promise and save both of you from a grisly end. Now, I cannot make you use your ticket, but have you ever considered what your life could be like without Nalem?"

"You know what you're saying is impossible, right?"

"Are you saying you've always believed your family's goal was a fool's errand?" The Ringmaster reached up to his face and pinched his own cheeks, then pulled out his nose so his face was a mockery of mine. "Let's see...ah, you've had to convince yourself this is your lot forever, so you'd have no option but to get used to it and cope instead of wasting away in want of a hero. And so, you trap yourself in your own tower. This burden can only be yours and yours alone—so you'll never be disappointed when no one saves you."

Ah. He didn't just hit the nail on the head, he struck it right through the wood and broke it.

"But here's the thing: you *can* be saved. That is why I'm here. To help. To return to you the joy so wrongfully taken from you. So, let me ask again: what do *you*, Retz Edward Gallows, want out of a body?"

My brain wanted to dwell on what the Ringmaster had plucked out of my head. Because as much as I wanted to deny it, he had a point. I'd never let myself think about what might happen after Nalem, if Dad and Jarrod were somehow successful in their quest. I expected to die with him. And even if he could be removed without being destroyed, why would I let someone else suffer him while I walked free? At least I knew how to handle him. To...mostly contain him.

Except, not when it counted. He'd hurt my family over and over again. Farris was an undead abomination because of him. And for what? To feed his own delusions of power?

"I...don't know what I'd want," I admitted. I'd been in this body for so long, I couldn't imagine myself looking like anything else. Hell, folks said all the time they wished they looked like me, rail-thin and bright-eyed. And what's more, I looked like my family. Jarrod and I both inherited Dad's long woodpecker nose, Mom's dark and fluffy hair, even the same cheekbones if one ignored how gaunt I was. Changing any of that would be a kick in the teeth to them and all their attempts to save me instead of murdering my ass to get Nalem out of their lives.

The Ringmaster softly patted my head, like I was a child. "You don't have to decide right away. It's a lot to think about. One night to change the rest of your life! But we'll get to that. First, I need to talk to Nalem. Can you convince him to return from your subconscious, or...whatever exactly it is he's doing?" He paused, those long fingers dangling right over my head. "Is this common, people sharing one body? Or how your body works in general? You don't even have a heart, do you...what is that in its place? I can barely tell it's there." The Ringmaster prodded my chest with a giddy grin, like a child figuring out how a new toy works. "To think, this could've been going on all around me in life, and I never knew. There's so much I couldn't see before!"

"And for good reason," I said as I sent a mental ping to Nalem. I'd let him decide the best course of action, but at least the Ringmaster could see I'd tried. "Most folks don't handle their first glimpse of the supernatural well, if they remember it at all. Can you imagine, if one day out of the blue, you realized someone had a cow head? Or a hole in their back like me?" And what about the aberrant, I thought super hard at him. They didn't get the option to hide in plain sight, because of how they were made. They couldn't show their faces around humans anymore. They truly had to flee to the outskirts of society where no one could find them, and he was the reason why.

A twitch rocked the Ringmaster's grin and shook all the way along his fingers. "If it happened so suddenly with no cause, maybe. It definitely shocked me after fell into this world. But if I'd always seen them, from birth onward? I'm sure I'd find them all as common as you do. Why aren't we allowed to see?"

Turns out, I could tell when the Ringmaster started closely reading my thoughts, because he read them so much more forcefully than Nalem did. Telepathy between Nalem and I barely even registers with me anymore since it's the way we've always communicated. It's subtle as air passing through your mouth to breathe and talk. But with deep dives, all those memories flicker to the front of your mind and away again, like flipping through a book in search of that one specific page. Nalem always did this so carefully that I sometimes didn't notice why I suddenly remembered certain topics, but when the Ringmaster barged through my head, my entire life flashed before my eyes in a rush of sound and color.

"You think yourself worthy enough to summon me?" Nalem's voice rang deep and strong through my head, reverberating around the false impressions of fingers. *"You know not what you invoke, Faerie. When it comes to our world, you are but an infant reaching for the face of God."*

"You've got me mistaken," The Ringmaster said, clinging to his smile to hide how fast he retreated back to the surface thoughts of my mind. "I'm not the one who summoned you here. After all, the skull's a gift and nothing more. My goal is to save your life, my friend."

That piqued Nalem's interest, though he didn't drop his guard. Not many professed wanting to protect him so openly. Fewer kept the promise behind closed doors. *What does one such as yourself think I need protection from? You have died but once. I have risen again more times than all your ancestors combined.*

"But that won't happen if you die here, now will it?" The Ringmaster set me down, then sank onto his knees—er, elbows—so he didn't tower over me so much. He'd already caught on to how Nalem expected to be treated. "The skull was left to guide you here, but someone else found that beacon first. Someone who wants your head more than anything else. But if your killer doesn't know you've evacuated this body, you can make a clean escape...and be in a form of your choosing, to boot. No more being shoved into people's heads who don't resemble your true self."

One hand scooped up a handful of cotton candy, mushing it together and pulling it taut until it somehow resembled a clipboard. Ink leaked from one finger, and the Ringmaster began to draw while looking just past my shoulder, as if he could see Nalem. "And this body is about as far from your true self as you can get, now isn't it?"

Nalem always had a witty, arrogant comeback. Except to that.

"At least creating a body for you shouldn't be difficult," The Ringmaster said, emboldened by the lack of answer. "But in order to make this work, I'll have to move both of you out. It might be a last-minute move, but I can't fake the death of a body like yours. The actual flesh and bones have to fall. But my friends, the bodies I make are durable. They'll last you as long as you need."

"Okay, but why?" I asked. "You've peeked into our minds, and I'm sure Nalem's reputation has warned you why this is a stupid idea."

The Ringmaster shot me a look, as if questioning why I might argue against a plan that'd save my life. He kept smiling, but pity clung to his eyes.

"I've only died once, but I wouldn't wish it on anyone. And if I could get a second chance, shouldn't everyone? Wouldn't we all be better, if only our bodies and minds were truly in sync?" Then he reached down and grabbed my hands, looked straight into my eyes this time. "Nalem's been on this track for a long time, going nowhere. Sometimes, we need a change of perspective to fix things like that. Or we need a chance to live life on our own terms, without anyone else's rules tying us down."

Did he really think that'd be enough to fix Nalem? This was a guy building an army and plotting to take over for Death itself, not a minor villain with a bad hair day. Yet there was this weird giddiness that kept pulling at my thoughts, that maybe this could work. I knew better than to trust a Faerie, even more than I shouldn't trust Nalem. But what if this was the way out?

"Nalem? Is this Fae doing something to my head? I should be turning tail and running, but..."

Nalem sighed, low and deep in my thoughts. *"He's not influencing our thoughts. You're feeling hope for once in your pitiful life. We'll have to squash that."* Yet he didn't make any efforts to run either. He ran through scenarios, weighed options. Sea Mother featured in his thoughts. So did a woman with sandy skin and cold gray eyes; his sister, who I'd only ever seen in memory and mocking funhouse mirrors.

"So? What do you think?" The Ringmaster stood again, one hand offered to me as others gestured to the big top. "Are you ready to finally live life on your own terms?"

I wasn't sure what answer would come out when I opened my mouth.

Turns out, it was a yelp of surprise as something burst from the shadows and bowled me over. Except instead of hitting the ground, I fell past the cotton candy and into darkness, the bright colors of the carnival swiftly disappearing into a pinpoint of light. Even though I was moving, I didn't feel air rushing against my skin. It was eerily similar to the numbness of when I went under and let Nalem take full control. The only sensation I had was a cold arm around my middle and the acrid tang of brimstone.

"Thank Fate I found you!" Farris cheered, the only sound in this void. "Er, you didn't catch up to Jarrod, I take it?"

I tried to answer, but no sound came out. I settled for shaking my head. I asked Nalem where we were. For once, he was as clueless as me.

"Let's see if I can get a read on him like I did you. Only reason I found you first was 'cause if I returned to Jarrod without knowing your ass was safe, he'd have my head. Not literally, of course..." Farris reached his hand out. A prick of light opened up in the darkness, growing as we rushed toward it. "Alright, we're going to shoot right out of the shadows. Try not to hit your head!"

High-pitched calliope notes heralded our return to the carnival, all the colors and smells bombarding my senses. Even without Nalem directly in control of our body, we nearly hurled from the sensation since Arcadia fucked with his perceptions at the best of times. We were back at the point where Farris had first disappeared.

"Jarrod's not here," Farris growled, claws out and ready to tear the surrounding tents apart. His eye darted to me. "Where is he?"

"Gimme two seconds now I'm on solid ground again." I sent out my skeletal senses in search of my brother. "Mind explaining what just happened?"

Farris shrugged. "Guess I can teleport between shadows? I must not've fallen into any since becoming a Faerie. Or maybe it only works in Arcadia? Guess we'll find out when we try to bat outta' hell."

"A power like that could be useful indeed," Nalem mused as he followed the tendrils of our senses. Sea Mother's skull was still blocked off by the remnants of Bertha's original body, somehow alive without her head attached. Jarrod and Zalin were partway between us and the big top, stalled. Jarrod must've convinced Zalin to help track me down by my aura, since he'd never figured out how to do it on his own. *The question is, will the Ringmaster come after us first as the higher priority target, or Jarrod because he's closer? Either way, we should make haste. I*

have a few theories about who would dare work alongside the Ringmaster, and none of them leave us room for error."

I grabbed Farris's sleeve. "Jarrod's this way, and we've got to hurry. Ready?"

"Sure thing. But if this leads to another one of Nalem's tricks..."

I broke into a run and pulled him along. "We can bicker later, but right now, all of us want the same thing. We want Jarrod safe and to get out of this twisted place."

Then I'd have to make a harder decision: who to really trust with saving my own life.

7 - JARROD

"**H**ow long has your boyfriend been able to teleport?" Zalin hissed.

"Since today," I said. Not because I doubted Farris would keep secrets from me, though he was a terrible liar. But he was enough of a mischief maker that, had he known how to teleport any earlier, he would incorporate it into every possible scheme, stunt, and con job.

Zalin and I had reluctantly teamed up in order to locate Retz. I needed her ability to sense the auras of other supernaturals, and she needed me to help her escape the carnival. Plus, she told me, she wasn't just sent here to spy on the Ringmaster. She was told to watch out for my brother and me too.

Either way, she'd led me through the carnival. I'd cleared out the clowns in our way without raising the alarm thanks to a silencer on my pistol. We'd almost reached Retz, but by the time we'd climbed on one of the game booths in order to plan our rescue, Farris had beat us to the punch and disappeared into the shadows.

Below us, the Ringmaster laughed–in surprise or in response to our own poor timing, I don't know–and the stuffed prizes in our booth laughed along with him.

"Will surprises never cease," The Ringmaster said. I considered slinking away, but of course he chose that moment to look up at us. "Like you two getting along after previously being enemies! Though really, you two are so similar deep down. Half-humans torn between worlds, clinging to one half of their identity for meaning even if the source is, if I may be biased a moment, quite toxic...and instead of letting yourselves heal, you stay sharp and push folks away. But it's hard, isn't it?"

The Ringmaster reached a hand toward us, as if offering to help us down onto solid ground. "Aren't you tired of being alone?"

"I wasn't alone until these assholes uprooted my entire life." Zalin bared her serpentine fangs, though she seemed poised to push away from the booth and flee. "Unless you can somehow bring my lady back...and I mean really bring her back, not a blow-up Barbie version of her, then you've got nothing to offer me."

"And I'm sure we'll repeat this argument tomorrow night, and the night after that ad nausea." The

Ringmaster winked before turning his attention to me. "What more can I offer you, my friend? You've found where the skull is, and what it is I've done for the aberrant. Whether or not you believe what you've uncovered isn't something I can help with. Perhaps it's time for me to learn a thing or two as we'd discussed, if you don't terribly mind..."

It wasn't quite a headache that assaulted me. More of a numbness spreading through my brain as a flurry of thoughts passed through my mind. Past jobs, creatures encountered, stories from Alexander...when the Ringmaster had said he wanted knowledge of the supernatural world, he didn't mean a brief overview. He wanted everything I'd learned, over twenty years of knowledge squeezed out over the course of a couple minutes. My limbs gave out and I found myself splayed atop the booth's roof, unable to even focus on the idea of getting back up.

I also didn't notice Zalin's absence until something wrapped around my ankle and yanked me off the roof. The candyfloss didn't do much to cushion my fall, and as I was dragged across the ground, strands of the stuff found their way up my nose and into my mouth when I tried to speak. I sputtered, gasping for air.

"Consider this payback for the time you healed me," Zalin snapped. "Will you be able to walk if I let you go?" I attempted an answer, but between my thoughts fighting to regain order and a mouthful of candyfloss, I didn't manage anything intelligible.

Zalin had a few choice words about that, followed by "Our cover's blown anyway. Alright, I'm going to shift into snake form so we can travel faster. Try not to freak out or I might hold you too tight to keep you still. Then again, I s'ppose you've got your brother if I do break anything by...accident."

I appreciated the warning, as finding myself in the coils of a lamia's true form triggered my huldra instincts to punch my way out of trouble. Last time this happened, my leg had been fractured and I broke a lamia's skull in response. I managed to remain calm this time. Zalin held me up high with her tail so she didn't risk smacking me against the painted tents, which gave me an overhead view of the carnival. I had a hard time committing the nonsensical maze to memory, but I did note a few key areas, such as the game booths we'd fled, a county fair sort of area covered in ribbons, and a conspicuously blank area near the back covered in caution tape and construction cones.

Also, the Ringmaster wasn't chasing us. For a moment he simply watched, allowing his smile to slip into disappointment. Was he upset about letting us get away while he'd read my memories, or by something he'd found in my head? He shook it off and galloped toward the back of the carnival, but stuck to one side along the fence, avoiding our path. It took me a moment to realize why; the Ringmaster headed for the skull to make sure it remained here. Even if we escaped, we'd have to come back to grab it. And by reading our minds, he knew there was no way Nalem could leave it alone.

Unless I got to the ghost first and staged my exorcism before it could become a poltergeist. Could I get away with it?

"The Ringmaster's avoiding our path," I shouted to Zalin. "We should be clear to head out of here."

"Then let's hope this works," Zalin said with one head, though I still had no idea how the snake heads managed human speech. The other one shouted moments later, "You stupid motherfuckers, stop running! I'm here to help you–look, I've got your hulderkind here." She whipped me around to dangle over Retz and Farris, who had bone daggers and claws out respectively.

"She's telling the truth," I called out to them. And then to Zalin, "Okay, you can let me down now." Which she did by dropping me from twelve feet in the air.

Farris caught me, and we tumbled to the ground. Zalin slipped into her more humanoid form next to us.

"Glad to hear you aren't planning to kill us," Retz said with a nervous chuckle. "Unlike someone else, according to the Ringmaster."

Zalin snapped back "And I'm sure you could figure out who that is, if you and Nalem both put your single brain cells together for a second."

I pulled Farris up with me as I got to my feet and stood between my brother and the lamia. "We'll have time to figure that out later. For sake of information and survival, we're putting our differences aside and working together for the time being. Let's get out of here and regroup. Zalin's coming with us if that doesn't activate her curse."

I didn't blame Retz and Farris for their confusion. After all, I'd panicked and broken my own rules for reconnaissance, inadvertently putting them in the Ringmaster's way. Now I was demanding to rescue a woman who'd captured us not two months ago. But both of them were smart enough not to ask questions while we were still in dangerous territory. Retz turned to Farris and asked, "That shadow-warping thing...think you can get us back to the mortal realm with that?"

"Good question," Farris said. And then, as we heard the approaching honks of clowns, "guess we'll find out.

Everyone, grab hold." He already held my hand, and I grabbed hold of Retz with both my free hand and my leaf-scarf. Zalin reluctantly took Farris's other hand. He bit his lip as he tried not to dig his claws into her skin.

"Alright, on three. One, two..."

Farris stepped into a shadow and sank, pulling us along. Vertigo took over as we should've hit the ground and kept moving, the world above spiraling away. We hovered there for a moment, just under the shadows, as Farris tried to pull Zalin along. The tips of her fingers burst with thorns, the green of her curse creeping along the rest of her arm. She jerked her hand away and pulled herself back to the surface with her tail, clutching the cursed limb to her chest until it settled back into flesh. Even when she'd been dying or kidnapped, she hadn't looked so terrified.

I tried to shout that we'd be back for her, but no sound came out. Then I realized that there was no air.

Farris noticed. Swore, somehow still able to speak in this liminal place. Angled himself toward a pinpoint of light and shot toward it. I tried to keep my body's instinctual panicking to a minimum as the familiar wooden blanks and blue-green mist of Levi's Tomb rushed into view.

We broke through the shadows in the floor. Instinct gulped air into my lungs. Patrons yelped at our sudden arrival, some reaching for weapons or preparing natural defenses before Ginny shouted at them to stop. Retz hit his head on the underside of a table, and we both hit the floor.

"Holy shit, my lord, are you okay? And you, Fae, do you need help?"

I almost answered for them before looking back to Farris. Only his torso had made it through the shadows, his skin ashen and claws digging into the wooden floor as he tried not to scream.

I got to my knees and wrapped my arms around his torso to pull him up. The shadows seemed to suction him in. Even with my strength, a couple other patrons had to grab his arms. I tried to mutter something comforting to keep him calm, but I think all I managed was a stream of "okay, you're going to be okay, come on, you'll be okay." It took us about a minute to heave him out of the darkness, shadows closing up once his feet were through. He stayed draped over me until I staggered to my feet and got him into a booth.

"Been a long time since I've seen Fae magic like that," Ginny said as she stomped over, waving the other patrons to look away and return to their business. "What got you running out in such a hurry?"

Retz answered for us, "We found the guy who's been kidnapping folks and making the aberrant. Also ended up with way more questions than we know what to do with and couldn't get the skull yet 'cause *someone* left half a minotaur strapped to it." Retz glanced at Farris and me. "Can you get us drinks? Maybe something to eat too. Something as far away from carnival food as you can manage."

Ginny nodded and hurried back to the bar. The other patrons failed to hide their staring, but I ignored them as I kept Farris upright. He leaned against my shoulder to stop from falling over, one hand gripping my thigh under the table in a vain attempt to keep it from shaking. He didn't need to breathe, but his body went through the motions of nearly hyperventilating as smoke billowed from his limbs and empty eye socket.

"That didn't happen the last time you did that," Retz said as he slipped into the booth seat opposite us.

"Didn't hurt as bad," Farris growled. It'd been a while since I'd heard him so pained; he hadn't sounded that bad even after dying. "Coming back here feels...full of needles. Or bees. Needle bees."

Comfort wasn't my strong suit, especially against the pain of existing in a dimension actively trying to destroy you. I offered what I could. We settled into awkward silence as we waited for our drinks, a Janis Joplin song drifting around us from the jukebox. Farris recovered enough to mostly sit up on his own, smoke clouds diminishing to thin wisps.

Retz spoke first, his arms crossed and fingers digging into his sleeves with nothing else to do. "Well, we all know how we fucked up sticking to the plan, so let's just...skip over that and talk about what we found out. Anyone want to go first?"

Farris shrugged. "All I figured out was the shadow teleportin' stuff. Afraid I missed all the rest of the action. Sorry."

"You're the last person who needs to apologize," I said. "You saved our asses after I put everyone in danger. We owe you."

Farris managed a weak smile. "Thought we weren't talking 'bout the fuckups. Alright detective bros, what'd you all find?"

Even though Retz had brought up the topic, he seemed reluctant to go next. I sighed and said, "As you know, I found Zalin. When we'd invaded Lady Delight's castle, I'd seen her fall into one of the holes made by Alexander's vines. Seeing her at the carnival with a curse like mine confirmed my suspicion that Alexander had taken those he'd captured for his own use." Much as I hadn't wanted to believe it, or anything else the lamia

had claimed. "Zalin claimed she'd been left in the
carnival for two reasons. One was to test the
Ringmaster's abilities, because the only way for her to
escape the carnival seems to be escaping her own cursed
body. The second reason was to alert Alexander when
we arrived at the carnival."

I paused, not wanting to admit what this all meant.
"It seems Alexander is working with the Ringmaster.
I'll...need to question him about it."

"Like he won't lie out his ass to keep you on his side?"
Retz shook his head. "...I'm sorry, shouldn't have said
that. I mean, you know Dad and I don't quite see eye to,
well, roses or whatever he's growing...but look, what I
learned is that the Ringmaster's working with two
people. One gave him the skull to lure Nalem there, so
the Ringmaster could put Nalem in a new body and give
him a second chance. The other heard about this plan
and wants to break in and kill Nalem, and maybe me too
while they're at it. If Dad's working with the
Ringmaster, I'll give you three guesses which plan's his."

"But he told me..."

This time, Farris cut in. "He wouldn't have to worry
about your curse or how to spare Retz while stopping
Nalem if you think about it. All your old man would
need is for the Ringmaster to chuck both of you in new

bodies, and then he's got nothing to worry about when murdering Nalem."

"He wouldn't force us to make that decision."

"Would he need to?" Retz asked softly. "I'm sure the Ringmaster gave you a pitch like he did me. From both his and Dad's point of view, it'd solve all our problems. No Nalem for me, and for you..."

He didn't have to spell out the rest. Everyone who knew me could list the myriad of ways my body and brain didn't match up. Logically, it made sense. And the Ringmaster seemed earnest in his goal of helping others, even if his methods were misguided. And yet when I thought about the idea...

How could I leave my body behind, after all it had survived? Could I really just cast aside all my scars, the years of testosterone treatments, every inch of skin Farris had kissed? Something about the idea made me inexplicably upset. I couldn't stand when my head and heart were so at odds.

Before we could fall too deep into our own thoughts, Ginny reappeared with our drinks. She hadn't fussed with fun names and bright colors for these. Retz got another sidecar, which he took without question, while Farris and I got a straight whisky on the rocks. The boggan also slid a plate of pretzel bits and beer cheese on the table before looking between the three of us with worried eyes. "No leviathan head, I see. Are you all...?"

"We're fine Ginny," Retz said. He tilted his head, signaling that he was listening to Nalem before speaking further. "Nalem and I want to speak with you a bit later, concerning some...suspicious information we heard at the carnival. We also need to talk to the minotaurs about what we found. Think any of them will show up at the bar tonight?"

Ginny shook her head, green curls escaping her constructed hairdo. "They already came and left. Quicker than usual, I might add. Seems they're up to something big, though I couldn't get anything out of 'em. If you've got something to say to them, I'd suggest you get to it first thing in the morning, before they've got a chance to head out."

"What time even is it?" Retz fished his phone out of his pocket, eyes widening as he checked. He flashed it at me; "Geez, we were in there way longer than I thought."

"Time flows strangely in Arcadia," Ginny said with a shrug. "I'll cook up you bozos a real meal, and then you should get some shut-eye. If you're starting off with minotaurs first thing, you'll need all the energy you can get."

Even with the evidence before me, I didn't want it to
be true. But even if I tried to tell myself that Alexander
would never hurt innocents in his quest to save
Retz...I'd seen the followers he'd cursed. And before
that, the cases we took up, the beings we hurt both
human and not, for answers. I retraced my memories,
already raw from the Ringmaster plundering my
thoughts, and found that every event looked far darker
in hindsight.

It couldn't be true, right? I would've noticed
something wrong with Alexander if he'd really stoop
this low. I...should've.

I belatedly realized the others were talking, but I
didn't register what they were saying. My face felt
warmer than if I'd been drinking for hours, and my eyes
threatened to well up. I dug my nails into my palms
until it hurt. Tried to convince myself that I was
overreacting because the carnival had left me worn and
mentally off-kilter. I was in no condition to think
rationally right now.

Food, sleep, and time would put everything in better
perspective. Then I could figure out what pieces of this
puzzle I was missing. What Alexander was really up to,
something that might explain all I'd seen.

I nudged Farris and asked, "You okay to stay here a little longer before we head to the hotel?" He nodded and buried his head into my shoulder.

"After we talk to the minotaurs about what happened with Bertha and all that," Retz said, "we should speak to the aberrant too, if they'll let us. Sounds like I might be able to convince the Ringmaster to put them back in their old bodies. Or something like them. I sensed a number of them in the carnival, though all of them were fuzzy with his powers. He doesn't seem to throw them away, at least, and he's got to have some way of keeping them alive."

"Think they could find Arcadia again?"

"Artemisia's the one who gave me the map. I think they could make it on their own." Retz popped a pretzel into his mouth, chewing thoughtfully before speaking. "Though we'll still have to grab the skull and make it back before Dad shows up."

Or, I thought to myself, we could bypass the carnival completely if I exorcised the leviathan ghost. Then we'd have no reason to go back. After all, even if I'd promised to come back for Zalin, she'd captured and hurt us. Anyone else would forgive me for not helping my former enemy. It'd be so easy to walk away, leave

Nalem's damn devotees to fend for themselves, stop
poking my nose into Alexander's plans.

How tempting, to be a coward for once. I munched
on a pretzel and considered it. But I knew, in the back of
my mind, I wouldn't be able to leave this alone no
matter how much I wanted to pretend. The Ringmaster
wouldn't leave us alone after giving us those tickets.
This town and its monsters wouldn't let us forget if we
forsook it for our own comfort. I wasn't the sort to leave
a mystery unsolved, and even if Zalin had been my
enemy, what kind of monster would I be if I left them
trapped and tormented after offering to help? Especially
a half-human like me, someone who'd trod the wrong
path in search of acceptance.

But more than that...if Alexander really was working
with the Ringmaster, if this really was his final plan to
rescue me and Retz...I couldn't live myself if I let him go
through with it, seeing how many lives he'd ruined on
the way. Had it been anyone else, I wouldn't have
hesitated before figuring out how to stop them.

There was the real source of my fear. I didn't know if
I could stand up to Alexander. Did I have it in me? And if
all the evidence correctly condemned him, would I be
able to deliver justice? Much as I tried not to think about
my huldra half, my mother always said that the purpose
of our hulderkind strength was to judge the way only a

force of nature could do. But I'd always been too human to agree. Too much like my father. And if I confronted him over what he'd done, I'd also be confronting myself over what I'd allowed to happen.

Or maybe I was overthinking everything, and I hadn't even finished my drink yet.

I think all of our minds were heavy with what we'd learned at the carnival, so we slipped into companionable silence as we ate, drank and recovered. Retz seemed especially hard hit by whatever he'd discussed with the Ringmaster, and I wasn't surprised when he drifted away to let Nalem take over the rest of dinner. At least Nalem read the room enough to avoid taunting us.

Sea Mother appeared once Nalem took over. Even with a different body than the one he'd been born in, she recognized his vocal patterns. She sniffed Nalem. After finding stray black stains, a massive tongue flicked out to lick them off, followed by a deep growl when she passed right through without removing the ooze.

Nalem mimed stroking from her snout to the frills along her neck. He spoke to her in a language I'd never heard before, words rough and halting yet lyrical.

"Ya' still act like it," Farris muttered, words muffled because his face was pressed against my arm.

Nalem jerked toward him. "Excuse me?" I felt a tug in my bones, as if Nalem were trying to will me to walk away so he could glare at Farris unimpeded.

Farris didn't bother to look at him, or even open his eye. "Y'said you weren't a kid anymore. But you're still a childish bastard. Just lettin' her know."

Turning his back on his ethereal companion, Nalem grabbed my other shoulder. He tried to force me to stand up and walk away, and I felt the sharp pull of bones suddenly in motion when muscles weren't ready. Farris tightened his hold on me and sat back up. His empty socket puffed smoke like a factory about to be slammed for pollution laws.

"Tell me who taught you," Nalem demanded. He pushed past me so he was face-to-face with Farris. "How does an insolent mortal such as yourself know what tongue I speak?"

"Like it's hard? I mean, it was. Your pronunciation was awful." To my surprise, Farris pulled away and added, "No idea how I know that. I just do. Maybe if you hadn't killed me, I'd tell you once I remembered."

"Lies. You cannot forget your entire identity but recall a language thousands of years dead that no one in your home dimension should be able to speak." Nalem's arms twitched. I imagined Retz was holding him back from throttling Farris. "Say something, then. And do remember to enunciate."

I prepared to push the two away, but Farris was faster. He winked, said a word both harsh and soft, and pulled me away. The world went dark around us again, but only for a second. My face hit metal springs as we were spat out of shadows, and then my back hit the floor. Seems we'd ended up under a bed.

"Man, this mattress sags," Farris said next to me. He sighed and splayed his limbs across the floor. "Should be our hotel room. Can you check?"

I inched my way out from under the too-low mattress. Same cigarette burns on the mattress, and on one chair sat my backpack of clothes and extra supplies. "Yeah, this is ours. You weren't sure?"

"We've been in a lot of hotel rooms." I waited for Farris to crawl out but heard a frustrated groan instead. "In case you're wondering what I said? I'm not sure, but I'm pretty sure it's the equivalent of 'fuck you'."

"I figured that." I crouched next to the bed and peered under it. Farris seemed to sink back into the shadows, his face barely discernible in the darkness. I reached out and grabbed his hand. "Hey. You okay?"

Farris's grip on my hand was light, not even digging his claws into my skin. "No."

"Want to come out here and talk about it?" No answer. "Do you...need help?"

A long pause. "Yeah."

I lifted the side of the bed with one hand and pulled Farris to his feet with the other. He collapsed against me. I set the bed back down, and us on it. His skin had turned ashen, freckles like pockmarks of soot. My hand on his back was the only thing keeping him up.

"Is it the warping that's bothering you? Or a side-effect from the iron?" A worse thought struck me. "The Ringmaster—did he do something to you? Or those springs on the mattress, were they made of iron?"

"None of those." Farris ran a hand through his hair, scraping metal and glass against his scalp. "Okay, I know we said we'd be honest with each other, but. Something I haven't told you. Well, I did, but I didn't keep telling you. It hurts, being in this world."

I'd noticed. I wasn't an idiot. The dead weren't supposed to exist in our world, and Faeries were no exception. Farris could survive when others of his kind couldn't, but he'd paid the price for it. He'd told me it felt like the world was trying to kill him some days, when he'd first changed. But he hadn't mentioned it for some time. Even though I saw the way his hands trembled and how he tired out after a fight, I'd thought he'd been getting better.

I grabbed Farris's hand as smoke started to rise from his scalp. "It's been a rough couple of days. Between the iron and Arcadia…"

"See, here's the thing. Arcadia *helped*. Soon as I ended up there, all the pain just…went away. Nothing hurt." He laughed, a hollow sound that scraped his throat. "Heck, I could juggle without getting a preview of what arthritis prob'ly feels like."

"…So teleporting us from the carnival to Levi's Tomb…the pain all came back at once." His answer was a mute nod. My guts coiled in on themselves and burned—but I couldn't tell who I was angry at. Him for not telling me, or me for needing to be saved and hurting him in the process.

"Why didn't you say something?"

"Because…I dunno, figured you'd either treat me with kiddy gloves on account of me bein' so fragile, or you'd tell me to suck it the fuck up. Pain is weakness leaving the body sorta' shit." Farris buried his face in my neck, head resting on my shoulder, long curls of hair and smoke tangling with my scarf.

I wanted to say it wasn't true. That I wouldn't treat him any differently, that nothing would change between us. That nothing had changed already.

"We'll to fix this. I know it hurts, but it's not forever."

"You don't know. And you don't make promises. Thanks for playing anyway."

Shit. Comfort wasn't my strong suit. That had always been one of the reasons Farris and I got along so well; we hadn't talked about our past or pain, so we hadn't had to worry about patching up each other's hearts. I'd never planned for anything to last beyond that.

"I'm sorry. Trying to help." I wasn't even sure if I was supposed to hold him, or if my touch hurt him more. The anger stewing in my chest smoldered into frustration, and I had nowhere to direct it. "Is there anything I can do? Now, or ...in general?"

Farris hummed against my neck, faint and flickering like a dying heartbeat. "This is gonna' sound cheesy, but having you around makes me feel a bit better. So...mind not running off for a few more hours?"

I eased Farris back down onto the bed, even if it was covered in stains and cigarette burns. The night sky was tinged orange, as if there was some grand party on the horizon.

"For you? If I could, I'd never run again, just to stay by you."

Even as I said it, I knew life would never let me be so lucky.

8 - RETZ

I spent most of the night overthinking how our conversation with the minotaurs would go. I didn't know how they'd react to their chieftain's daughter being stuck in a plastic cow and her real body tied to a leviathan skull, but I doubted it'd be an easy talk. I imagined just about every awkward direction the talk could go, from sobbing to enraged chucking of furniture. And honestly, I'd prefer the chucking. I wasn't great at calming folks down in general, much less beefy minotaurs twice my size.

The one outcome I didn't prepare for? Them not even being home.

"What do you mean, they already left?" I asked Bolton, the one minotaur who'd had to stay behind. "It's not even nine in the morning! I thought we'd be interrupting your breakfast or something."

Bolton shook his head as he tightened another bolt on his motorcycle carcass. "The only thing my clan hungers for is revenge."

The minotaur's garage took up its own warehouse, half-built motorcycles and immaculate old cars scattered throughout. Shrines made up of engines and chassis pieces lined the walls, each one topped with a highway diorama containing a miniature vehicle model. Except for the one nearest Bolton, which seemed to have been smashed with a hammer, a clay figure with a green scarf set haphazardly in the middle. A reminder of who'd busted his ride, I guessed.

"How about you start at the beginning," Jarrod said, tugging his scarf up over his mouth to hide a yawn. I don't think any of us slept much the night before, but Jarrod insisted we wake up bright and early in our vain attempt to reach the minotaurs before they departed on their unknown quest. "Did they learn something about Bertha?"

"Not exactly, but they're going to get answers. See, we got some fancy cameras recently, and finally caught the aberrant moving camps. The clan has tracked down their new location and is riding there now to question them." Bolton grinned and added, "plus, we completed our secret weapon. See, remember how I told you all that the aberrant are weak to iron? We gathered up all the spare parts we had around here and made a sword."

"Least that's more dignified than hitting them with a cast-iron skillet," Farris muttered. He seemed better than he'd been at the bar but was still a pale comparison of himself in Arcadia. "So what, they're planning to break into the aberrant's lair and wave a sword around 'til they get answers?"

Bolton answered with a confused "Yeah?" as if there weren't any other options to consider.

Jarrod looked ready to go on a rant about how getting answers through force buried truth under lies to make attackers happy. Instead, he took a deep breath through his nose and asked, "And you're here because…?"

"Because I've got to atone for my ride first." Bolton gestured to the box of motorcycle parts beside him, and an engine block surrounded by rings and screws propped up on a giant workbench. "I broke it due to my own foolishness, so now I gotta' fix it."

Jarrod asked warily, "Is this…common practice? Forgive me for asking, but I've never heard of minotaurs having a strong connection to vehicles." I shot him a warning look, because we didn't have time for his curiosity to sidetrack us again. He glared back and nodded toward the shrines. I think he meant he was trying to get useful information for if we had to fight the minotaurs. Or maybe he wanted me to notice the shrine second-to-last from one end, pink chrome

surrounded by fresh flowers and recently-snuffed
candles.

Bolton nodded, turning back to his engine and
picking up his tools. He spoke in a booming voice to be
heard over his work. "The Ride has always been
important to minotaurs. It's how our ancestors gained
their freedom and left Greece, y'know? The humans
wrote the story wrong, you see; not even all of Athens
could kill us in our own maze. We followed Ariadne's
thread once the humans thought they'd won, and
Poseidon took that thread and lead us to the ships that
became the first rides." The longer he spoke, the louder
and more reverent his voice grew. "Ships took us across
the waves. When Poseidon couldn't follow our clan to
the new world, we asked its gods where freedom could
be found. The Road answered us, and we learned to ride
with wagons. We've evolved as they did, and here we
are, with the motorbike." He raised the still-detached
handlebars in offering to a god we couldn't see.

The three of us looked to each other. Jarrod shrugged
and then bowed his head in brief reverence. We
scrambled to follow suit.

*"Nalem? Er, are the minotaurs right about the whole
Poseidon thing?"*

*"I wasn't in Greece at the time, but I wouldn't be surprised.
He clings tight to his creations, the bastard."* Nalem sank

back into his own memories, likely remembering reasons to curse out various other gods.

The silence broke as Bolton picked up his tools. Jarrod took this opportunity to ask, "I assume the others are out on their rides, then?"

"Yeah. I mean, we got a few Harleys, some Indians and a couple a' Hondas...gotta' keep the herd diversified, right?" I assume that's what the models in the shrines were of, but I didn't know enough about motorcycles to be sure. "Why, you guys joining in? Wanna' see the sword at work?"

"We actually have news for the rest of your clan," I said. "We...I found Bertha. And I found out what happened to her, and what might be able to fix it."

Bolton said, "They'll find it soon enough too, from the aberrant—"

"Bertha got turned into an aberrant, and her body's stuck in Arcadia with a Faerie." I maybe could've blurted that with a bit more tact, but seeing how Bolton dropped the handlebars onto his own hoof and didn't budge, at least I got the point across. "If the rest of your clan attacks the aberrant, then not only will that scare them off so I can't get the info I need from them, but you'll all lose your chance at getting Bertha back. She'll keep running from you, just like how she ran to Arcadia when someone offered her a solution to her problems."

"Her problems? She left...willingly?" Bolton softly mooed as he picked up the fallen handlebars and clutched them to his chest. "That can't be right. Bertha was the next in line to be chieftain. She was happy here. She..." Bolton trailed off, turning his gaze toward the pink shrine and its fading vigil. His face slowly fell. We could all see the pieces falling into place behind his eyes.

Jarrod crept closer. "I can't say I know how she must've felt, but...the person who lured her away, he spoke to us too. It's a tempting offer to make, even to someone whose life seems alright. There's...it's hard to tell, what's going on under the surface for someone else." He waited for Bolton to respond, but the minotaur said nothing, wiping a hairy arm across his face to hide any tears that might be forming. "The person who turned Bertha and the others into aberrant might be able to reverse it. We're working on convincing him to do so. But if you want to help Bertha return to her own body, you need to know why she felt the need to leave it. And to do that, you need words. Not swords."

"Oh, sweet Bertha..." Bolton set down the handlebars on the bench. "Phones don't work that deep in the woods. And even if my ride wasn't in shambles...I have to stay here. In case...well, in case Bertha comes back."

So much for our luck. I was about to ask Nalem if he had any bright ideas, but then I saw something at the far end of the garage. Unused vehicles. Mainly, an ATV that could easily fit two or three people. Even if we couldn't sense auras, I had my powers, and a fairly strong memory of where I'd last encountered the aberrant.

"Don't suppose you know where the key for that red ATV over there is...?"

Bolton blinked away tears in surprise. "Huh? That old thing? Yeah, I could find the keys for it. It's been a side project, no one's really claimed it, so...I suppose you could drive it." Brows furrowed. "Sure you could handle it? Not to doubt the power of Lord Nalem and his vessel, but..." Standing there in my vest and matching slacks, combined with the rest of my fashionable but not-entirely-functional clothes, I didn't exactly look like the sort who drove an ATV regularly.

"I can drive it," Jarrod cut in; I tried to remember if I'd seen him drinking already. "If Retz guides me, we can either catch up to your clan and explain what's going on, or reach the aberrant and warn them." Then he turned to Farris, fingers nervously fidgeting deep in his pockets. "I'll need you to stay here."

"I feel fine," Farris growled. I couldn't sense his bones like with Jarrod, but while he looked better than yesterday...

Jarrod shook his head. "It's not that. Combat triggers you going berserk. That's the last thing we need if we're trying to de-escalate a fight."

Farris groaned, but didn't have an argument. This did nothing to ease the tension between the two. It was obvious enough even I noticed this. "Then I'll stay on standby in case you two need to get warped out, for whatever reason. Retz, hand me a bone. Something small I can fit in my pocket."

I considered giving him one of my throwaway pieces, like a squirrel skull, but I remembered some of Nalem's rants about how our powers worked and had a better idea. So I summoned my viola case from the car, floating it through open windows and the doorway to the garage, and opened up the lining where I'd hidden an assortment of bones. I grabbed two small bones and floated them over to Farris.

"These are from Jarrod's ripped-off toe. I'll try to use my powers on them to signal you if we need help, but if I remember Nalem's explanation on sympathetic connections, that should help you find Jarrod if there's an emergency. And try not to juggle them either, alright? I had a hell of a time trying to find them in Lady Delight's castle in the first place."

Bolton gaped at me, and the others looked vaguely grossed out. Bolton said, "You...why do you have one of your brother's toes?"

"Lamia ripped it off. Saw no good reason why it should sit in a ruined castle forever, so I grabbed it back when we kicked Lady Delight's ass. Got my toe back too, but it turns out it was gone long enough that the skin won't grow back over it, and some people think having a skeletal toe is gross." Goes to show what they thought of me being practical for once.

In the back of my mind, Nalem cackled. *"Look at their dumbfounded faces...! Ah, good job taking my lessons to heart, little one. I am quite interested to see how this experiment works with our Fae's newfound powers."*

Farris grabbed the bones and shoved them into his pocket. "You two stay safe. And let me know the second things go south, got it?"

"Of course." Jarrod quickly pecked Farris on the lips, probably as some sort of peace offering over whatever their issue was. Bolton got us keys for the ATV, and helmets they apparently kept on hand for rare humanoid visitors like us. He also gave me a bulky leather jacket that threatened to swallow me whole, claiming that road rash was no joke. I complained it was hot, but Jarrod rolled his eyes and buttoned up his own bulky leather heat-trap of a coat.

The ATV rumbled to life. I threw out my senses, catching a glimpse of minotaur at the fringes of my range. I directed Jarrod where to go. We rolled out of the garage.

Then we were off, speeding past trees and crevasses fast enough that any cop would've nailed us for a ticket if they'd been able to brave the woods. I'd thought Jarrod was the safest driver out of us, but apparently that rule didn't apply to ATVs. I clung to him for dear life. His hair whipped against my face. I swear I heard a whoop of laughter out of my normally grumpy-as-hell brother.

We drove like that for a while, speeding through the forest as I clung on for dear life. Nalem summoned bones from our surroundings to construct weapons for our fight. After not too long I shouted to be heard over the engine, "Herd of minotaurs bit northeast of us. They aren't bumping around much; might be on a trail. Haven't found any aberrant."

"Then we might have time to talk some sense into the herd." Jarrod sped up as he made a sharp curve around a tree. Judging from his tone, he doubted their willingness to talk as much as I did.

"Nalem, got something to stop our motorcycle minotaur death squad?"

"Would you rather I have more time to trade barbs with you, or that I actually get this finished?" Nalem floated something into view; it looked like a spine wrapped into a loose ring. *"It's a simple device. We land this over a minotaur's neck, tighten it, stab the vertebrae into their neck, and wait to see if they bleed out or asphyxiate first."*

"...Aren't you banned from murdering anyone?"

"Hence why I'm not building a slaughterhouse. But no matter; you can direct and tighten the theoretical noose yourself. Nowhere in the curse does it say that I cannot make the weapons." Nalem dove back into his creations. I imagined maniacal laughter, and while he didn't echo my imagination, he didn't refute it either.

Sick and twisted bastard. What did it say about me that I thought the collars were ingenious?

Turns out, minotaurs have loud engines and louder voices. Their songs were call-and-response like pirate shanties, a deep and powerful alto ringing through the woods and followed by the off-key echoes of the other minotaurs and drumming on motorcycle chassis. The tune was a familiar punk-pop anthem; I recognized it as one of the bands Mom played in her salon, a point of connection for her and her clients.

Jarrod shouted to be heard above the minotaur's war cry. "I'm going to cut them off. Hold on tight!"

I was about to shout back that there was nowhere to make a shortcut; the minotaur's trail curved ahead to avoid this small valley of fallen logs and...no, wait, that was the point.

"Goddamnit Jarrod....!" I wrapped my arms around him like a straitjacket. I swear our ATV almost achieved liftoff before plummeting into the ferns and bouncing back into the air. Oh gods. This would be how I die: not by betrayal, but thanks to my brother dating a daredevil long enough to imitate him.

Crunch. Ouch. The ATV hit something but managed to land on its wheels and keep going. Up above us and to the left, I heard a mix of awed cheers and sympathetic verbal winces. The minotaurs were watching us crash through a gorge.

I shouted at Jarrod, "How drunk are you?!"

"Almost enough for this not to hurt."

The engine revved and we went practically vertical. Animal terror kept my eyes glued shut. The wheels whirred as sticks and shit got stuck in them, but on it ran. We hopped out of the pit Jarrod charged us into and plopped back onto the road. With the sputtering whine of a dying man, the ATV rolled to a stop. I didn't dare open my eyes until Jarrod pried his way out of my death-grip and stumbled to his feet.

"That," bellowed the deep alto we'd heard singing, "was the single stupidest stunt I've ever seen. And I have the dubious honor of having Bolton in my herd."

The leader of the minotaurs was...for one thing, tall even for a minotaur. I had to crane my neck to look at her, and there's about six feet of me if I don't cheat. She had a mottled black-and-white hide and a braided mohawk running from her head down to her tail. Her motorcycle was the size of an actual cow, chrome shiny enough for me to catch my reflection and realize how many leaves were stuck in my hair. Oh, and did I mention the giant iron sword strapped to her back?

"Foolish stunt or no, it achieved its goal. I had no other way of catching up with your rides, amped up as they are." Jarrod offered his hand up to the head minotaur. "Jarrod Gallows. Paranormal investigator. Currently researching certain disappearances and beings connected to them."

The head minotaur snorted. "Isolde. Herd Caller to the Redwoods Clan." Her hand overlapped Jarrod's, but her eyebrow quirked in surprise at the strength of his grip. "Ah. Bolton mentioned Nalem's vessel was hulderkind. You are his brother, then?" As Jarrod nodded, she directed her cold gaze down her snout at me. "You are Nalem, and not Nalem at all."

"Retz Gallows," I said, with half a bow because it pissed off Nalem.

"I see. And you are here to stop me from fighting the aberrant? Or are you just here for the sword, cousins?" Her voice was void of emotion, a stark contrast to her passionate singing. I had a feeling it was on purpose.

Jarrod cleared his throat. "Over the course of our investigation, we've discovered—"

"I was not asking you." Isolde didn't release Jarrod's hand either. She was braced to throw him aside if she didn't like my answer—and unlike most beings I'd met, I didn't doubt she could do it.

I put up my hands, pretending like I wasn't a threat with bone collars hiding out of sight. "We found out that the aberrant are all folks transformed by a Fae. One with...good intentions, but horrible execution. We're trying to convince him to turn everyone back if they want, but in order to do that, we have to talk to them. Which can't happen if you scare them all off." I looked Isolde dead in the eyes. "That includes your daughter."

Isolde's fingers twitched. "You claim this Fae is the one who kidnapped her, then?"

Alright hours of worrying and practicing in front of the mirror, don't fail me now. "This is going to be hard

to hear, but this Fae doesn't steal folks away. People
come to him willingly for a new body if they think it'll
solve their problems. I'm sure the reason Bertha hasn't
come home yet is because she's scared of explaining to
you why she took up such an offer. I know I'd be."

As I'd feared, Isolde passed through shock and
disbelief to settle on wrath. "You expect me to believe
this? From a human known for his betrayals? You
confuse me for a sheep."

I felt her bones move. I raced toward her. Nalem
dropped the collars, and I squeezed tight. Some of them
made their targets and the herd clawed at their necks.
But we were too slow for Isolde, who dodged my trap as
she chucked Jarrod to the minotaurs behind her. I ran
toward the one who'd caught Jarrod and tried to grab
her, but she backed out of the way and prepared to spike
my brother like a goddamn football.

Isolde tore her collar off, crunching the bones with
her bare hand. "Aberrant, Fae, mortal flesh...this sword
will cleave through it all the same." She pulled the iron
blade out of its sheath. "You want my belief? Pry this
from my cold, dead hands."

I managed to grab hold of the minotaur holding
Jarrod, breaking the assailant's hand to free my brother.
"You heard her, Jarrod! Get to prying!"

Jarrod rolled as he hit the ground and rose with his shotgun in hand. He fired at the legs of a minotaur preparing to charge—the shot tore through the minotaur's hide but didn't get much farther into the skin. "Should've known that diplomacy wouldn't work."

"Maybe we should've just run the ATV into their bikes." As the minotaur I'd injured bellowed over her hand, I took the opportunity to weaken the bones in her ribs, and then kicked them in. Let the rest of the herd think I was as strong as my brother.

"And risk an explosion? Retz, fire season is still in effect." Jarrod kept shooting until one minotaur tried to charge him from behind. He dropped the shotgun long enough to catch hold of the minotaur's horns and throw him, letting inertia pull the charging brute into the ground. Jarrod snatched up the shotgun and shot his downed attacker. "The best way to stop a forest fire is to not start one in the first place."

"Thanks a fucking ton, Smokey." I heard a crunch behind me. Isolde had been about to strike, only for Nalem to take the remaining bones and create a shield to protect us. It shattered as soon as the sword hit.

"Hey, if Faeries are weak to iron, wouldn't that get rid of our curses?" Maybe we could turn this fight to our advantage, somehow.

"It would. However, they're rooted so deep in our bodies, that...well, you might live. Your brother would probably find most of his muscles ripped out, including those in his throat. Wonder how that would look?"

Er, right. So much for that plan. I let Nalem return to watching the battlefield while I dealt with the threats in front of me. Isolde reared back for another swing. She wasn't graceful in a traditional sense, but the sword was so light to her that her movements flowed like a force of nature, a flood strong enough to snap trees into toothpicks. I would've been struck in momentary awe, had she not been aiming for my head. I ducked, summoned shards of my shield into my hand as a dagger and tried to stab her leg.

I was flung into the air seconds later. She was smart not to let Nalem get close, but damn, how many times was I gonna' be thrown this week? I had just enough time to brace my bones before hitting a tree. They still fractured where I struck. At least no one heard my sissy screaming over the sound of Jarrod's shotguns.

Between Jarrod's combat prowess and Nalem's asphyxiating collars, most of the minotaurs had already dropped. But Isolde crushed any collars we tried to form around her neck, and she shrugged off shotgun blasts even as blood streaked the white patches in her hide.

She was slow enough Jarrod could dodge her swings, but eventually, one of them would run out of stamina— and Jarrod had been through plenty of other fights in the past couple of days.

Shit. What could I do? I patched up my bones and tried to manage a thought beyond "ouch." Could I cause a distraction? Give Nalem more leeway with my body? Try to call on Farris for backup? Those would all help in the long run, but the giant minotaur was trying to run my brother through with an iron sword right now.

Jarrod parried with his shotgun. It went flying into the ferns. Isolde reared back for a finishing blow.

I had an idea.

I ran up to Jarrod and braced myself behind him, half-crouched with my hands on his back. I could sense Isolde's bones moving before Jarrod saw anything. I strengthened his bones in case my reflexes were off. When Isolde swung the blade, instead of letting Jarrod dodge sideways as he might've on instinct, I forced him to duck under the blade. Isolde's sword kept swinging without something to hit and she couldn't correct in time to slice downward, giving Jarrod an opening. I released control and let him do the rest on instinct; he delivered an uppercut to the minotaur's stomach, then grabbed the briefly winded minotaur and used all his strength to flip her over both of us and onto her back. The sword flew out of her hand as she hit the ground.

I let go of Jarrod and grabbed Isolde, keeping her skeleton pinned. Jarrod recovered his shotgun and aimed it at Isolde's face.

"I don't want to pull this trigger," he said. "But if we let you go, I have to be sure you won't try that again."

I added, "And to think, we could've all had a nice little chat without me dropping your herd like flies. All you had to do was not chuck my brother. Wouldn't that have been easier?"

Isolde fucking bellowed at me instead of speaking. The noise almost startled me enough to let her go, but Nalem kept my grip.

"What the hell are you doing?"

I looked over my shoulder at the path beyond us. There stood a cow, mottled black and white. All I could sense was her head; the rest of her body was made of plastic.

The cow cleared her throat. "You two humans better step away from her right now, before I gore the hell out of your guts."

"...Bertha? I'd say nice to see you again, but..." I gestured toward her and said to the others, "I hate saying I told you so, but here she is. Believe me now?"

Isolde glared at me. I gave her enough movement in her head to look over and see what we were. "Bertha?! You're...a mere cow?" She whipped her head back to face me. "Explain. Now."

Another familiar face wandered onto the trail. Artemisia wore a weary expression of blues and greens on her face, almost completely masking red warpaint. She patted the cow—er, the minotaur. Ex-minotaur? "I told you she wouldn't take it well."

9 - JARROD

How many camps had sprouted up and withered away over time in these woods? I had to wonder as Artemisia and Bertha led us into the aberrant camp, with its lichen-covered handmade signs and a barbecue built from a rusted metal barrel with years' worth of ashes in the pit. The tents were new, but there weren't many, mostly lean-tos of scavenged wood and cheap tarp. Since the aberrant were no longer human-passing, I'm sure most of these goods hadn't been bought in regular human supermarkets.

"As you were, everyone," Artemisia called out to the camp. I swore I hadn't met her before, but every time she spoke, I heard Monica's voice. I didn't have time to ask what the connection might be. "These visitors are safe and here with our permission. They know what's going on."

Retz and I followed her, with the minotaurs close behind. They'd taken a bit to calm down once the unconscious ones had woken, but Isolde demanded a truce until she'd learned the truth of Bertha and the aberrant. I'd asked Retz to keep an eye on everyone's bones for any sudden movements, just in case. I didn't know how long minotaurs held their grudges, but if they were close enough to huldras to call us cousin, their ire might last as long as ours too.

The aberrant who emerged resembled toys more than humans. Some had perfect bodies in sculpted plastic, and I found myself reminded of Dr. Frankenstein's creation; every feature idealized on its own but deemed unnatural once placed together. Some of these folks had forsaken humanity entirely, if they hadn't been supernatural in the first place like Bertha. There were mermaids and angels, limbs stretched into tails and wings but other features untouched. Others resembled dragons, wolfmen with stiff fiber fur, and at least one was a spherical orb with no discernible features at all.

"I did not realize so many had gone missing," Isolde said as her eyes scanned the crowd. She stayed close to Bertha, one hand on her daughter's furred head; she twitched if she touched the cheap fiber on her back instead.

"When the Ringmaster started, he spoke to those on the fringes of society," Artemisia explained, gesturing for us to sit on the logs around the barbecue pit. "The vagabonds drifting in and out of town. The elderly no longer receiving visitors. College students who'd lost sight of their goals. All people who the Ringmaster thought could use a friend and a fresh outlook on life, I guess. Not all of them agreed to go with him. But enough did."

"Sounds like you're familiar with his methods," I said.

"Let's say the Ringmaster needed a lot of practice to get the hang of his powers and leave it at that." I stared at where her mouth should've been and the stains that formed a reluctant smile.

One of the minotaurs asked, "So it's true? No one was ever kidnapped?"

"Nobody here was," Bertha said. It was disconcerting, hearing a jaded teenager's voice come out of a doe-eyed heifer. "Heck, most of us walked to the carnival ourselves. Showed we really meant it. That's why I veered off during a ride. So you didn't...so no one followed me."

I'm sure Isolde's head spun with questions. Why her daughter had left. Why a cow, of all things. What she could've done to keep her daughter safe. Would my mother ask the same things, if I came back to her in a new body? She hadn't the last time I'd seen her after a decade apart, but even with age and testosterone shots,

I still had her eyes and hair, Alexander's nose and jaw, and the little girl in all of Mom's photo albums could still be found if anyone stared at me long enough. If I cast aside all familiarity and claimed it made me happy...what then?

"Tell me what happened," Isolde said, "once you arrived at the carnival."

Bertha scraped a hoof along the dirt. "The Ringmaster was there–not Monica, but the Ringmaster himself–and he greeted me like an old friend. I was...a little scared by all the arms at first. But he was really nice, you know? He let me play all the games and ride whatever I wanted, like we were besties with VIP passes. And when I talked about what had been bothering me, he just...listened."

None of the minotaurs watched Bertha as she spoke, eyes drawn everywhere else in shame. The other aberrant lurked close by, heads hung low, as they carried on tasks like meal prep and laundry. I'm sure the tale Bertha told rang familiar for all of them.

I had to ask, "Did he tell you about what he planned to do? I mean..." I wasn't sure how to tactfully ask if she'd willingly chosen to become a cow.

"He did. And at the time, it all sounded like a good plan. Cows don't bother anyone. Just live a nice life in a field somewhere. I mean, I didn't want to be a cow

forever, but for a little bit? I could see the appeal of that."
She sighed, pressing her head against her mother's side.
"He took me to the green room before the finale at the
big top. We'd done a lot, so I was tired and fell asleep.
When I woke up, I was like this. We went into the main
ring of the big top, and the Ringmaster guided me
through a couple acts with him. And everyone was
cheering for us, for me. They were so happy. Even if all
of them were fake." She smiled, despite herself.

"But it didn't last," I said.

Bertha shook her head. "I only thought it'd be for a
couple days, you know? Spend some time away from the
herd, re-center myself in a body without so much
baggage, then go home. But when all was said and done,
the Ringmaster led me to the gate and said goodbye. I
asked about my old body and...and he seemed so
confused. Why would I want to go back to the body
where I was so unhappy, he asked? I tried to explain, but
he insisted I'd be happier this way. Without all the cares
of society. And then...the gates shut."

Silence fell across the camp. Isolde wrapped an arm
around her daughter.

"Her story isn't unique," Artemisia finally said. She'd
been painting on her arm during the story, though I
couldn't get a clear look at what it was from where I sat.

"Most everyone here shared that same show with the Ringmaster on different nights. And none of us have been able to break into the carnival again to make him change us back. If he even still has our bodies anymore."

"He does," Retz said. "They're even still alive, somehow. He must've known, deep down, that some folks would want to go back." Retz seemed troubled, but I couldn't tell if it was the story that bothered him, or his own memories of the carnival. Or maybe it was the usual culprit, Nalem taunting him for his own sick amusement. "That's why we wanted to come here to talk to you, Artemisia. I know, still haven't gotten that skull back...but I did talk to the Ringmaster. And I think I can get your bodies back, which will also let me get that skull. But I'll need everyone's help to pull it off. And since the Ringmaster can read minds...I can't tell you the plan."

Much as it initially made me suspicious to hear my brother plotting without me, it made sense in context of the Ringmaster. Retz and Nalem apparently had a trick to skirt around the Ringmaster reading minds and discovering schemes; I didn't. What might they have up their sleeves? Especially since Nalem was rarely so altruistic...

Isolde apparently rode the same train of thought. "Others of my herd offer their honor to Nalem, but I do not. What proof do you have that he will not betray us?"

Annoyance flickered over Retz's face, though I couldn't tell who it belonged to. "You know who built Levi's Tomb, right? And who came running as soon as he heard the skull had gone missing? Sea Mother is more important to Nalem than...most people, let's be honest. He'll cooperate as long as we can guarantee its safe return. And right now, we can't get that skull unless we remove the body tied to it. That body is Bertha's."

Retz waved two fingers in the air. Bones flew to him, the skeleton of a small vermin and a larger skull. Retz warped the bones until the vermin bones looked almost human, strapped onto the skull crucifix-style. "Bertha, you already said you don't want to be a cow anymore. And Isolde, you don't want this to be your daughter's legacy, now do you?"

Isolde's gaze turned to me this time. "Tell me honestly, cousin: does your kin speak true?"

I nodded. Zalin had told me about it when I'd asked to see. Explained how Bertha's flesh and bones were topped with a bobbling clown head to keep it alive, laughing at any who came near. She insisted I'd punch the face if I saw it, as she'd almost done much the same.

Didn't see any reason for her to lie about something like that.

"And you honestly think you can convince Aiden to change us back?" Artemisia asked. We stared a moment before the paint from her fingers bled blush-pink. "I mean, the Ringmaster." So, she knew him before he became a Fae. I'd have to interview her later. Maybe she could explain why she sounded so much like Monica when both of them were in distinct bodies. Nothing I'd learned about Monica suggested that she had a twin.

Retz smiled, charming but with a hit of deviousness underneath. I hoped it was him in control, but a small part of me also feared that. If he was the one with the plan to trick the Fae, then maybe he really was as manipulative as his possessor. "My talk with him was really enlightening. Pretty sure I've got some bargaining chips he can't refuse."

I wanted to ask what he meant and who we were even speaking with, but either question might jeopardize this plan, much less convincing the aberrant and minotaurs to work with us. Even if I'd been stupid enough to ask in public, my mouth grew dry, as if yesterday's hangover had returned for another round. I blinked. The edges of my vision grew dark.

Alexander? Why was he calling now, with no warning? My conversations with Zalin and all their implications reared their ugly heads. Maybe I'd have a chance to dispel them, find out what was really going on. I tried to shove my doubts aside and thought, *"Sir, I'm in the middle of some delicate negotiations. Can you...call back later?"*

"I may not get a chance to do so." The dark swarmed in faster. Someone spoke, but the words were muffled.

I tried to say "taking a call, don't mind me" before passing out, but I'm sure I didn't manage anything that intelligible.

I'd never been summoned into Alexander's realm so quickly, and I hit the ground hard enough that I swore I felt it, even though this was only a dream. I wondered if something had gone wrong because everything was so bright. Then I looked up. The roses had disappeared, revealing a roiling brown sky full of floating stone. I hadn't seen that sky since the day Alexander died. I thought the brambles were gone too, but no, they surged away in the distance like a wave. Figures, human and otherwise but all covered in bright green runes, followed behind the walls of thorns. The entire realm uprooted itself...but where was it headed?

Alexander tapped me on the shoulder with one claw, but when he spoke, it was with words instead of signs. "Apologies for calling so suddenly. I wanted to tell you that we're on our way. Give you time to prepare, and plan if need be."

I bit my tongue before I could ask the stupid question: where? I'd already been told. I just hadn't wanted to believe. "It's true, then. You really are working with the Ringmaster."

"Why wouldn't I? As long as he can be made to see reason, his powers solve all of our problems." Alexander gestured at the crowd following the thorns. I hadn't realized how many people he'd stolen to his realm over the years. They'd always been hidden from the glade Alexander and I met in. "I can release them from my curses. Those too dangerous, like the lamia, can be placed in safer bodies. And Retz can finally be normal, while Nalem perishes once and for all."

"This doesn't solve anything!" I rarely raised my voice to Alexander, but I couldn't help it this time. "Have you seen what happens to people after the Ringmaster is done with them? He doesn't turn them into what he wants, but what he thinks is best! They're all plastic and stiff and...miserable."

"He is a young Fae. Doubt he's even been around for more than a couple years. He'll grow into his powers, as I have mine, especially if he has a suitable tutor."

"Is that why you're talking now? You're absolutely certain you won't curse me again?"

Alexander knelt, his claws scraping together as they rested on my shoulder. "Does it matter? You'll move into a new body of your own anyway. Otherwise, no matter how we killed Nalem, your curse would still activate." One knuckle pressed against my chin, tilting my head up to look at Alexander's face, skin barely clinging to the roots underneath. "Don't give me that look. You must have already realized how much a new body would help you too? No more curses. No more huldra impulses or feminine hysterics holding you back. You'll be as you've always known you're supposed to be."

For the first time in my life, I wanted to deck my father in the face.

"Whether or not it's logical, you don't make those decisions for me."

He shook his head with a rumbling sound. Was that...a laugh? "What kind of argument is that? If you'd said as a child that you didn't want to go to the doctor, I would've taken you anyway. That's what parents do. Sensible ones, at least." He stood again, towering over me. I'm surprised he didn't make a dig about how I'd finally be taller in a new body as well. "You're not a child anymore, so don't act like it. See what's best for you and accept it. Otherwise, I will drag you kicking and screaming if I must. It will only prove my point."

I should've been practical. Feigned being sorry, asked how long before he arrived, made a plan once I was out of the vision. Instead, I kept pushing. "Why are you making decisions for all the other people you cursed, then? You aren't their father. I saw what kind of curse you planted on Zalin. Why her? Because she's half-human like me? Did you want to prove that you could force someone into choosing humanity?"

"Yes. Don't make me do the same for you."

"Do I need to remind you that your wife isn't human either?"

"She looked mortal enough that when I was younger, I thought we could surpass that. But when it came to your brother and the monster inside of him, we saw how she handled the situation." Alexander turned away from me, slowly slithering out of the clearing. He didn't even bother to form legs. At least it almost made sense why he no longer had eyes. "I should've brought your brother along instead of you. Perhaps he would've taken to discipline as well as you did. But there's no use reflecting on the past. We've got a mission to complete."

In the past, I would've believed in my father even after hearing that whole spiel. Put all my faith in the idea that what we did was right, that every step brought us closer to stopping Nalem and maybe securing a bit of peace for everyone else. If Alexander had found the

Ringmaster and formulated this plan before I'd met
Farris, would I have agreed to a plastic body?

Probably. Hell, definitely. I'd refused to acknowledge
that Alexander had been changing. Ignored the
increasing shadows in his realm even once I'd met one
face-to-face. Forgave him for my curse even when he
continued to inflict his words on others. I'm sure even if
he'd asked me a couple months ago, I would've accepted
his plan with open arms. If he'd asked before Retz had
returned to our lives and an order from Alexander
nearly killed us both. Before his refusal to rescue Farris
along with me inadvertently led to my love's murder.
Before seeing Zalin and the aberrant and realizing they
weren't the only ones whose fates had been fucked over
by a Fae claiming to have the answers.

All that anger bubbled up into a cluster of words
warring for the right to tear out of my mouth. Rebuttals.
Denials. Curses of my own. They melded into a scream
I'm sure Alexander wrote off as another reason why he
was right. I screamed so long and loud that I felt it'd rip
my throat apart. I didn't notice the darkness closing in
until I stopped to breathe, and I smelled cedar and
jasmine instead of rotting roses.

I opened my eyes and sat up, catching my breath.
Someone had laid me down on a blanket after I'd passed

out, even had a lumpy pillow under my head. A minotaur shouted, "he's awake!" before offering me a bottle of water. I took it and drank, willing the anger to seep away with the cold. My tail lashed out behind me, and for once I didn't bother to still it.

"Are you...okay, cousin?" The minotaur asked. He looked ready to scoot away; he must've heard stories about a huldra's temper.

"I've got a lot to reflect on," I told him. "I...just had an argument with someone I placed too much trust in."

The minotaur nodded in sympathy. "That happens, man. But as they say, your clan is who you choose, not who births you and throws you in a labyrinth. And there's no shame in breaking out and building something new from the rubble, right?" The minotaur flashed me a thumbs-up as he stood and joined the other minotaurs as Retz, Isolde, and Artemisia strode over. He forgot to take his water back.

Retz jogged over to reach me first. "Glad to see you up! That came on pretty sudden. Dad call?"

"Yeah." My tail whipped against the pillow. "Tell Nalem he was right. Alexander's let his power and plans get to his head, and thinks we'll follow him because it's the logical thing to do." I bit my tongue from cursing him out further, as Isolde and Artemisia joined us. "Sorry about interrupting negotiations, but we've got a complication in our plan. Our father, another Fae who I've discovered is working with the Ringmaster, is on his way with a group of cursed followers and his entire realm. He wants to put Retz and me in new bodies while he kills Nalem, and I've got a feeling we're not the only ones he'll have the Ringmaster encase in plastic."

Artemisia swore. "I'd heard the Ringmaster was getting more paranoid. Another Faerie intruding on his carnival and telling him how to use his powers would be a valid reason."

"Any idea when he'll show up?" Retz asked. I shook my head, unable to admit I hadn't been composed enough to find out. "Well...I guess if we're going to get the skull and everyone's bodies, we'll have to do it soon."

Isolde glared down her nose at us, arms crossed. "Forgive me if I find this timing...suspicious."

I put up my hands in a show of innocence. "Words only go so far, but I can honestly tell you I didn't plan to pass out in the middle of our meeting. I try not to be so rude." I tried to stay stoic, but I didn't have the capacity to facilitate negotiations between the minotaurs, aberrant, and my brother at the same time. I needed a drink, or to scream until I got all this out of my system.

Retz seemed to get the hint and offered an arm to help me to my feet. I took it even though I didn't need the assistance. Retz said, "If you'll excuse us, we've got to talk a sec about this suddenly pending family reunion." He pulled me out of the camp clearing. I felt the faint trace of his powers along my bones, as if ready to make sure I kept moving in case I somehow decided otherwise. We didn't stop until Retz said, "Okay, they should be out of earshot now. So...what the fuck?"

"You heard me. Alexander's working with the Ringmaster, like Zalin said. I asked him, and he...didn't even try to deny it. Said it was the best way to solve all our problems. To make us..." I'd spent so long clinging to my human side, but the word stuck in my mouth.

"I'm impressed he came out and said it. Must be real confident in this plan of his." Retz looked about ready to go on about how he and Nalem were right, but I must've looked miserable enough for him to sober. "I'm really sorry, Jarrod. I know you looked up to Dad, and..."

"And now I get to question everything, like I should've done earlier." The man who'd raised me wouldn't have agreed to this, right? Or had I ignored his flaws for so long because he'd accepted me, taught me all I knew, was...my father? I bit the insides of my cheeks, resisting the urge to scream or cry. There wasn't time for that. We had people to save, Fae to fight...

Shocking me out of all these potential reactions, Retz wrapped his gangly arms around me and pulled me in for a hug. We'd always shied away from physical contact growing up, what with Nalem and all, so the act surprised me even as I saw it happening. It was slow and awkward, and Retz didn't know what to do with his hands, and his attempt to pat my shoulder felt like a fly swatter. But I appreciated it. I held him in turn and tried to center myself.

"I just don't know what to do, once we're done with this town," I admitted. "Even if I wasn't directly working for him, I worked under the rules he'd taught me. I accepted the cases that came from my curse even when I hated them. But what if Alexander's been this way for longer than I realized? How am I supposed to contend with that? What do I do?"

All my questions had been rhetorical, but Retz hummed in thought anyway. With only plants and bones instead of organs inside him, the sound reverberated through his body with a strange buzzing. "Can't say I know, other than to keep moving forward. I mean, it's easy to dwell on all the shit you might've caused. I've had to face that with Nalem, whether or not he was in control. But...if all you do is dwell, it's easy to get stuck, and then you can't actually fix anything."

Retz was quiet a moment before saying in a softer, secretive voice, "That's actually why I became a hairdresser. Aside from the fact that Mom did it too, I mean. I figured it was a job where I could provide a bit of happiness to folks, fixing their hair and listening to them talk. I know it's a little thing, never enough to make up for Nalem, but better than sitting at home and thinking about how much I've fucked up in the past."

"That's...really sweet, actually. Think I'd be shit at cutting hair, though." I'd meant it as a joke. But in all honesty, what sort of good could I do? All I knew were the tricks of my trade, and that boiled down to research and fighting. Hell, I hadn't even finished high school, though I vaguely remembered passing the GRE at some point. I couldn't just sit down and get a normal job helping folks. It felt simultaneously too easy to count, and too difficult to consider.

"Uhmm...do you need to cry or anything?"

"That can wait." Even I wasn't stupid enough to claim I didn't need to, but I had to hold it together. I could at least wait until I was back in my hotel room. "Do you? I mean, I know you had your doubts about Alex...about him, already, but the impact of having it confirmed..."

Retz groaned. "Crying feels weird. I don't think my body does it right. I get tears in my eyes, but then my nose starts running too? Like, my entire face starts leaking? It's super gross."

I couldn't tell how seriously he meant that. It was such a Retz thing to say, I had to laugh, even if it bordered on hysterics. Even if Alexander had betrayed all he'd once stood for, at least I'd gotten my brother back. We had Mom back home, and I had Farris. I wouldn't be alone. I might even be okay in time.

"Am I...interrupting something?"

We let go of each other and turned to see Farris, leaning against a shaded tree. Amused as he sounded, there was a hurried edge to his voice.

I told him, "I can explain later. What's up? I don't suppose you got bored." Not when warping caused him such pain in our world.

"I almost did, but a certain leviathan beat me to it. Surprised you haven't felt the quakes." Farris motioned for us to join him in the shadows. "Tell me you guys got some idea on how to calm down the ghost of a giant sea snake?"

He knew I did. I'd told him about the bottled exorcism in my pocket, lacking only grave dirt. And if I banished the poltergeist, we wouldn't have to go into the carnival again, at the price of leaving everyone else to fend for themselves. Knowing I'd likely face Alexander there, the thought was tempting.

But then there was Nalem to contend with. "We can talk to her, try to calm her down," Retz said. A grim determination that had to be Nalem's lurked behind his eyes. "Let's get going, before anyone gets hurt." His eyes flickered to me. Did he somehow know...?

We grabbed Farris's hands and fell into the shadows. I remembered to take a deep breath before falling through this time. Farris pulled us out behind an alleyway dumpster, our arrival heralded by crashing bricks and a roar that almost drowned out the screaming humans.

"Out of the frying pan and into the fire," Farris said. His face was smeared with dirt and someone else's blood. "So, what's the game plan?"

In lieu of answering, Retz stumbled to his feet and ran past us. "I've got this! Stay back and don't get hurt!" The last thing I saw were bones he summoned mashing together into a shield.

"Think he's warning us against the leviathan, or Nalem?" Farris asked.

"Haven't I told you not to ask stupid questions?" I pulled a bottle out of my pocket. Holy water, bay leaves, and other trace elements necessary for an exorcism. All I needed was the grave dirt. How fortunate that this leviathan was buried under the town. "Of course they'll both want to kill us. Get ready to dig."

10 - RETZ

The humans thought it was an earthquake. I'd never felt one myself, but I remembered the safety drills from school. Instead of running from the raging poltergeist they couldn't see, people braced themselves under benches and in doorways, waiting for the shaking to subside. They had no idea an ectoplasmic leviathan swam through streets like rivers, surfacing with enough force to ripple the earth as she toppled cars and chased humans foolish enough to flee. The monsters tried to sneak away without being noticed, but they didn't have much luck either.

I asked Nalem, *"Why is she attacking people? I thought she was domesticated or something."* I ran as fast as I could back to Levi's Tomb; I had to find a way to stop Sea Mother before Jarrod exorcised her. I didn't want Nalem and the Harvester to go after my brother's head.

"Leviathans don't domesticate. The only reason she tolerated our family is because...long story short? She adopted my father and views us all as her kin."

My brain blanked at that. *"How'd your father get adopted by a giant sea snake if killing supernatural creatures is his job?"*

"Becoming the bane of the supernatural world came afterwards. Personally, I maintain the belief he was forced into the role so he'd stop befriending non-human creatures." Nalem's brow furrowed as we vaulted into the market square, narrowly dodging an obelisk statue Sea Mother decided to knock over with her tail. *"Either way, the Harvester will not wish to exorcise Sea Mother if we fail in saving her...but that may not be his choice to make."*

Sea Mother reared over us and roared. Nalem took my voice and called to her with words I didn't recognize, the sound of calm seas and crashing waves turned into a language. She paused at the sounds—but then made a sharp turn toward a foolish bugbear who'd decided to run. Ginny shouted for him to come back, but the leviathan already had her eyes on him. Jarrod and Farris tackled him to the ground seconds before the Sea Mother passed through him.

Here's the thing about poltergeists: They can't actually touch living creatures. Going through them still feels weird as hell. And inanimate objects that don't have a lifeforce are all fair game for a poltergeist to possess. Sea Mother's plan probably hadn't been to eat the bugbear, but to crash into the building behind him and bury him in rubble...and then maybe play with the corpse once he died. Or maybe she wasn't thinking at all. Poltergeists aren't known for their logic: they're ghosts who've gotten so sick of everything all they've got left is rage.

"These fools should've sought me out sooner," Nalem swore as I stopped in the doorway of the Jacoby Building. *"No matter. Hurry, while your brother and his pet idiot are distracted by their heroics. I'm sure they're already scrambling for exorcism supplies—not that anyone in your family has the connections for proper holy water, I'm sure."*

Of course we didn't—and if someone had, that would had been Dad, though he didn't seem keen on helping with this poltergeist. Then again, Jarrod seemed convinced his soda-filled concoction would do the trick when I overheard him talking to Farris, so I had to hurry in case he was right. Maybe all the coke needed to become holy water was for someone to believe hard enough in it. Wasn't that what made gods holy?

We bolted to the bandstand hiding the entrance for Levi's Tomb. The stairs were covered in shards of colorful glass and strands of snapped rope. Inside, I would've sworn a wrecking ball had gone through the bar—turns out a leviathan tail is just as powerful. Furniture was crushed into sawdust, planks pulled away

from the ribs in the walls, the kitchen in the back caved
in to release the fin bones decorating it. Sea Mother
wasn't just hunting; she was trying to free herself.

"She's in an agitated state, so don't affect her bones unless
there are no other options. Missing her skull is what woke her
up in the first place."

"Tell that to her ghost. Maybe she'll stop pretending to eat
people if she remembers she's missing a mouth."

"That's precisely why she's attacking; she's trying to regain
a sense of control over her lost parts. What better dominance is
there than in blood?"

The ceiling groaned. I ran to duck under the bar, but
realized the floor was a trap of shattered bottles and
enough alcohol to burn off every last hair in my nose.
"Well, you and I don't have any blood, so how the hell are we
going to stop her?"

"Without her skull in our possession? I cannot say. I may be
able to persuade her to be patient now I am here, but..."

"But?" As I asked, parts of the ceiling caved in,
exposing pipes from the building above. Dirt and bricks
fell toward my face. I dove under the pool table, which
chose that exact moment to topple over, colliding with
me. I popped open my viola case to release my bone
collection inside, which instinctively gathered into a
shield to ward off the worst of the debris.

"...I do not speak Lemurian as well as my father and his people," Nalem groaned in frustration. Nalem took control for a moment and, with some effort, grabbed the pool table's legs and lifted it back up over us. *"I was taught a mixture of my parent's languages, but never became proficient in either before my initial death. I was then thrust into the culture of that first vessel, and by that point, Lemuria and Atlantis were more fable than fact."* He actually sounded ashamed when he admitted, *"With almost no one else to talk to, I lost my Lemurian. Sea Mother would understand nothing that came from my lips."*

"I'm sure she'd get the gist of it. In your voice or something. Feeling's universal, right?" I sort of understood how he felt; Mom's relatives were all from Germany and pockets of other Nordic places, and I could barely count to ten in any of those languages. Okay, vast difference in scope and all, but I got the shame for not knowing your own family's tongue.

Our surroundings flickered, and instead of the bar, I saw scales closing in. Sea Mother's ghost was so huge that even curled up, she filled the entire bar as she materialized. The air grew cold and stifling in her presence. But the rest of the skeleton remained in place, rubble replacing the blood and muscle that usually surrounded broken bones.

I knew what the skull looked like, where the parts were supposed to fit in, and I had a lot of bones. That gave me an idea. *"Nalem, what if we rebuild her head?"*

Nalem shouted as if I'd smacked him. *"Madness! She'll know it's a mere imitation from lesser beings. And a lot of lesser beings at that; there are few creatures her size in existence anymore, much less in these waters…"* True. Her head was about as large as a whale's, and her body was far longer. It'd take every bone we had and every scrap of roadkill within our reach, at the very least.

The ground trembled again. Sea Mother made this weird keening noise, fins along her body vibrating at a frequency fast enough to buzz. I didn't want to know what the hell that meant. I stumbled out from under the pool table and put my hands up, letting my skeletal collection drop to the floor. She understood I wasn't armed and had no meat on my bones, right?

"Would you rather she knock down the rest of the city while we kill ourselves trying to steal her real bones back? Or worse, give Jarrod a chance to exorcise her forever?"

Nalem still thought my idea was stupid. Light burst in from overhead; the door to Levi's Tomb opened up. Jarrod appeared and bolted down the broken stairs. Nalem summoned the viola out of its case and started to play, the instrument having enough bone inlay for him to control it in midair. The sudden noise caught Sea Mother's attention. *"Stall him. I'll get to work."*

Easier said than done. Jarrod needed just one ingredient for his potion, was twice as strong as me...and most importantly, I didn't want to hurt him. I climbed over the rubble and ignored the icy static that filled my body when I passed through Sea Mother's ectoplasmic form. Nalem built a skull from the bones as fast as he could, but building it with any degree of accuracy took more time than we likely had.

"Retz! Are you alright?" Jarrod examined me, concerned but not willing to come closer. One hand was in his pocket; I could sense he was clutching something, and I bet it was the bottled exorcism.

"Oh, you know, just trying to stop a poltergeist from destroying the city. You?"

"Same. Farris is helping Ginny evacuate the square. You're the last person we need to get out."

"I'll leave when we've got the ghost calmed down."

Over my shoulder, I thought Sea Mother was winding down as her head swayed along with the viola's tune. Except then she tried to charge through it, disrupting the notes and causing Nalem's nascent fake skull to crumble apart, shards of animal bone scattering everywhere. He cursed. She crashed into a wall and must've hit a support beam, because I swore the entire Jacoby Building creaked overhead.

"Poltergeists don't calm down, Retz. They're either led to the next life or destroyed." He had the gall to look sorry as he said, "With a ghost of this size, we don't have time to give her a peaceful end. Please step aside."

"Or what? You'll destroy the spirit of a being who was cheated out of a happy afterlife? Plus, you'll bring the wrath of Nalem down on your head, and probably the Harvester too?" I walked closer. He didn't flinch. "You got two options. Head back upstairs, or we'll see if I can finally beat you in wrestling. How's that?"

As expected, Jarrod didn't turn tail. Also as expected, he could still kick my ass in close quarters. I tried to catch him off-guard by headbutting him in the gut. Turns out, Jarrod does in fact have rock-hard muscles under that coat, and I only succeeded in giving myself a headache. That is, until I weakened his ankles for a split second, causing him to topple over...and onto me. He tried to push himself back up. I grabbed his wrists and held them away with my way longer arms. I thought that'd be the end of it, since I could tell he didn't want to hurt his baby brother either.

Except then, it felt like my legs were being pounded by a hail of stones. No, it was Jarrod whipping my knees with his tail. It didn't look like much, but we had cousins who'd driven people deaf with a few well-timed tail shots to the ears. And to think, the two of us had shared a sibling hug less than an hour ago...

"Retz, be sensible. We don't have time for this." Jarrod drove his elbow into my rib cage, hard enough to fracture. He was losing his nerve. Behind us, Nalem hadn't even reformed a jawbone.

"I'm trying to save Sea Mother's life and yours. Thought you'd be grateful." I let go of one arm, but I took his glasses instead, holding them as far away as possible. The only way I'd ever won our wrestling bouts as kids was when I cheated.

"Not when there are innocent lives on the line, you selfish ass. Why do you only have a conscience when it revolves around you?"

"I mean, you just answered that yourself. I'm a selfish ass."

Jarrod sighed, the way an older sibling does when they *really* don't want to hurt their sweet younger sibling but *have to* teach them a lesson, and socked me in the nose. It went sideways with a loud, painful crunch. Good thing I didn't have a brain or anything else that could be damaged by a busted naval cavity, but Jarrod flinched at his actions. His temper could've killed anyone else.

I swore, tearing up a little because that was a hurt I couldn't fix. I also might've accidentally thrown his glasses into the middle of the room, where they joined the maelstrom of debris created by Sea Mother as she thrashed about the room.

"Shit. I'm sorry. You okay?" Jarrod whispered, trying not to catch the ghost leviathan's attention. He squinted with his one decent eye to see what she was doing.

"I will be once you stop being an idiot," I whispered back. "Also, thanks for the early birthday present, asshole. I'll let you sign the splint."

Jarrod groaned. "Since you only seem to learn from things that actually hurt you, maybe this lesson will stick. Don't put the needs of one before the many, and don't pick a fight with me."

"All good points, but none of those are helping us save this leviathan."

"You mean the one who looks like she'd eat us right now if she could?"

Ah. So she did. Her frills vibrated again like hummingbird wings, and she had the poise of a snake about to lunge. I tried to get Nalem's attention, but he was too busy summoning more bones to recreate her skull.

Sea Mother dove toward us. Jarrod threw me off him and rolled back onto his knees, scooping up a fistful of dirt and shoving it into the vial. Sea Mother veered away from me and toward him, opening her jaw to reveal rows of pointed, spectral teeth. He prepared to throw his concoction into her maw.

Sea Mother didn't dive through him, but instead slipped *into* him. Jarrod dropped the vial to clutch his head as it was filled with the thoughts and memories of a millennia-old leviathan ghost.

I ran to Jarrod's side and grabbed his hands before he could claw at himself. I unclenched his teeth with my powers to prevent him biting his tongue. He'd done that before to keep from screaming. Didn't want him to actually bite it off and choke on his own blood, or some other disgusting fate. I guessed he was either trying to comprehend the new information running through his head or trying hard as hell to shove it all back out. The few times ghosts had tried to escape into me, Nalem made quick work of such intruders. But those had been human ghosts; even Nalem was, if we're being technical. A giant sea serpent was about as far from that as one could get.

"Jarrod? It's Retz. I don't know if you can hear me, but I need you to try." I held his hands tighter, though he was shivering. "Don't fight the leviathan in your head. Trust me, you'll just hurt yourself. I need you to focus on your body instead. Keep control of it."

He managed to take a few deep breaths through his nose before clutching my hands back. "Retz, I...loud. It's loud."

"Hey, I know how hard it can be to get a thought in edgewise, trust me." I eased him onto his knees, so I didn't have to worry about him falling over, and knelt next to him. "But you can do it. Having a strong and stubborn head's in our nature, after all. Can you open your eyes?"

His eyelids fluttered, but then he shook his head. He muttered in apology, "No. I think...they rolled back into my head."

I winced in sympathy. "That's gonna' ache later. Fine, focus on your other senses. Like sound and touch, that's what I need from you right now. Ground yourself."

While Jarrod tried to gain some sense of his self, I shifted the pain of my busted nose to Nalem in order to get his attention. *"Hey, your adopted grandma just possessed my brother. Mind getting her out?"*

"...I'm sorry, but what the fuck did you just say?" Nalem snapped out of his musical reverie, his viola stopping with a sharp cut-off to his song. A half-formed leviathan skull fell to the ground, which cracked off bits of un-assimilated bones. Nalem turned his attention to my

brother's twitching, occasionally keening form. *"Oh. That's...less than ideal."*

"Tell me about it." Jarrod's expression seemed calmer, so I tried talking to him again. "Sorting yourself out?"

"I'm not as used to being possessed as you are," he grumbled. It was a full sentence without pauses, at least. He took another deep breath, tasting the air as he did. Or more likely, Sea Mother did. I'm sure it had been ages since she'd had any air in her lungs.

"Quite a thing, ain't it? Look, Nalem and I are going to try to get her back out, okay?" *"Nalem, tell me you have a plan. You can talk to her, right?"*

"I...can attempt. She won't mock my pronunciation, at least." Nalem eased himself into my face, whispering a few lost words under his breath before starting. From what I could gather, he said something like, "Sea Mother? It's me, Nalem. Steal-a-body child of child. Hello?"

Jarrod tilted his head, teeth slightly bared. His nails cut into my hands. "I'm getting...a lot of images in my head. Memories, I think. Lots of different people. All you?"

"I've visited her in many guises," Nalem answered in English. "Does she seem calmer at all?" When Jarrod nodded, Nalem switched back into Lemurian. "Sea

Mother, I...am your body fix. Uhmm. I am fixing body. For short high-tides. Am hunting for lost head. Understand?" Every time he tripped over his own tongue, I felt his embarrassment as a memory of burning skin along my face, one of those weird sensations I missed out on by not having any blood.

I had to force Jarrod not to grit his teeth when he wasn't speaking, though he tried his damnedest to. "She's not happy. Ugh. Feels like I dunked my head in a sensory deprivation tank overnight. It's...how she's feeling without her skull?"

Nalem shuddered at the description. I got the impression he'd felt the same thing many times before. "That is understandable. Retz wants me to remind you that tearing apart your own mouth will not restore feeling to it, so stop before you chew up your own cheeks."

"I...didn't realize I was doing it. Bit preoccupied right now."

Nalem summoned what he had so far of the fake skull. "Short high-tides head. While I hunt lost head. I fix."

Jarrod made a frustrated noise, then tried to open his eyes. As expected, they had rolled back into his head, showing off irritated veins. He blinked as Sea Mother rolled them forward to look through his eyes. He bared his teeth again. "She doesn't like it. Or how my face works, for that matter."

"Sea Mother, I catch head, but long hunt. Rest time."

Jarrod growled in response. Then his mouth started moving without him, and with a startled expression, he tore his hands from mine and tried to cover his face. Sea Mother had taken conscious control of his mouth.

"Is she...trying to talk on her own?"

"Leviathans are intelligent and capable of understanding language, but their vocal chords don't support human tongue. It...could be possible she remembers enough to try speaking." I felt a swell of pride bloom in our chest. So, old sea snakes could learn new tricks.

"Catch," Sea Mother slowly said, in Lemurian, shoving my brother's voice into its deepest possible range. Once she saw in Nalem's face that she'd been understood, she repeated, "Catch head now."

"Need to hunt, Sea Mother. Rest time for you."

"I hunt."

"...You no hunt, Sea Mother." Nalem gestured to Jarrod's body. "Man has no fangs."

Sea Mother gnashed Jarrod's teeth together. "Man has tools. Man has tail. I hunt." The more she got used to having a voice, the better her pronunciation of

Lemurian was—it almost sounded better than Nalem's, not that I'd tell him that.

Nalem parsed through his thoughts, cherry-picking words to try to voice the actual reason why she couldn't come along. "You dead. Man lives. If you hunt in man's body, both dead. Understand?"

"Excuse me, what?" I interrupted in our thoughts.

"Didn't you know? Ghosts drain the life-energy of whatever body they inhabit, since they have none of their own. It's like burning a candle at both ends." Sensing my unease, Nalem added, *"That's the difference between me and a ghost. My life energy, my spark, is endless and bound within my soul. It fuels any body I choose to inhabit—such as yours."* Ever since I'd learned the story, Nalem had been all too happy to remind me I'd been murdered as a toddler, and it was only his presence keeping me alive.

Sea Mother considered Nalem's claim. She also discovered humming and seemed quite fascinated with the noise. In her distraction, Jarrod took back control of his face, one hand rubbing his cheek.

"Retz, is this what you live with all the time?" He spoke slowly as he recovered his mouth.

Nalem let me answer that one. "For the past nineteen years, yeah. At least Nalem and I have the same kind of limbs."

"That...explains a lot. I might owe you a few apologies—after you get this poltergeist out. And give me my glasses back." His eyebrows knit in concentration, or just focusing on keeping control of his body. "You are going to get her out, right?"

"The arrogance!" Nalem snapped in my thoughts, using his brief reprieve to work on the fake skull. *"As if I'd let him be blessed by Sea Mother's power. Besides, her presence would just kill him faster, and I don't want her to face a second death. It takes time to get used to dying."*

Seeing how Nalem turned out, I didn't want any of us to get used to that.

"We're working on it. See the skull? Does Sea Mother understand what we're doing with it?"

Jarrod peered past me, half-rising to his feet before collapsing back onto his knees. Sea Mother took over with a snarl, switching back into Lemurian. "That is my head? My half-a-moon's-travel head?" Her phrasing was far more poetic than Nalem's had been. The fact irked him a little.

"Yes. While I hunt for lost head. Is...good?"

Sea Mother gnashed her teeth together, then realized they weren't her sharp carnivorous fangs. "Is not good. Look weak and fragile. But for resting...is not bad. Good teeth." She prodded at Jarrod's teeth with his tongue, confused more by his molars than anything. "I now understand your trouble eating fish when you were whelp. Stupid human teeth."

"I...yes. Stupid teeth no good fish." The last of the bones Nalem had summoned floated down the stairs to the renewed tune of his viola. Most of them were from the trunk of the Marquis, which Farris must've parked nearby, but a few came from locally sourced roadkill. They drifted to the last empty patches on the fake skull and melded into place. Knobs and fractures alike smoothed over under Nalem's touch. The coloration of the creation varied from dried-white to mottled brown, but otherwise, it was hard to tell that this hadn't always been a solid leviathan skull by the time he was done.

There was a thunk behind me. I turned to see that Sea Mother had tried to swim to the skull and tripped over Jarrod's legs. Jarrod groaned.

Nalem held back a laugh. "Sea Mother? You swim out of man, into body again. No hunt to learn..." He paused before swearing in my head. *"I forgot the word for legs."*

"Mashing together random words that you do remember seems to be working out alright."

"It only goes so far. This isn't exactly German, I'll have you know."

We were interrupted by another ear-wrenching howl. Sea Mother's ghost burst from my brother's body in a flurry of phantasmal scales. She circled the room, looking pleased to have escaped the laws of physics again, before settling her ectoplasmic body along her old bones. She eased her head into the temporary skull with aching slowness, like someone stepping into cold water but afraid to take the plunge. But she made it in and didn't thrash back out, so I figured this was a good sign.

I ran to Jarrod's side and pulled up. "You okay now?" I brushed splinters off his face and made sure his eyes hadn't rolled back again. I checked for blood spilling from a bite I might've missed during his possession.

Jarrod patted his arms, making sure they were his once more. Then he squinted at the leviathan skeleton now at peace in the middle of the bar. "I will be once I get my glasses back."

"Right. Shit." I tripped over myself to get them from where I'd tossed them. The frames weren't even bent. I handed them back to Jarrod, then noticed a smudge on his nose, so I quickly spit-cleaned it before he could dirty his glasses up more.

"You've spent too many years with Mom." Jarrod slid his glasses back into place, blinking a couple times as his vision returned to normal. "I have a killer headache. That normal?"

"I've found that anyone willing to possess another person ends up being a headache." I earned at swift kick to the back of my skull from Nalem, which proved my point. "You'll give me a chance to help her, right? Not going to stage an exorcism or anything?"

Jarrod's tail swished in agitation. "She did possess me. Almost took my body for a joyride." He looked past me, as if he could see Nalem over my shoulder. "I saw you, in her memories. You and your whole family. She seemed to care for all of you a lot. I admit, I doubt her attacks as a poltergeist were out of malice. Not that it matters if she acts up again."

My brother reached over to the fallen exorcism vial and scooped it up. There wasn't much left in it, some having spilled in the fight, but there was some holy water, traces of bay leaves and other herbs...and a small clump of grave dirt cemented at the bottom.

"I do understand how your curse works," Nalem muttered to Jarrod in my head. *"I could just order you not to fight her. I can order you to do anything. Ever consider that?"*

"If she acts up again, Nalem's going to order you to stay out of it," I said instead of relaying Nalem's threat. "Meaning, we should get her skull back soon as we can. Before Dad gets in the way."

Jarrod and I helped each other up, him still wobbly from the possession and my legs sore from our impromptu wrestling match. If we could barely stand a slap-fight with each other, I had doubts about our ability to handle the Ringmaster if things went south, much less Dad himself.

"Can I ask Nalem a question?" Jarrod said as we made our way toward the stairs, doing our best to avoid the shattered glass.

I gave Nalem control of my mouth. "I suppose. Though I reserve the right to laugh at foolish queries."

"In your first body. Your body. Were you...like me, so to speak?" Jarrod gestured at his torso. "When you mentioned your name, the first thing the leviathan— Sea Mother, I mean—thought of was a young girl. Looked a bit like the Harvester."

Like Loresha, Nalem's sister who I'd only seen in memories. Maybe Nalem's birth body looked like hers. Twins, perhaps?

"Self-identity is a tricky subject when one flits between other bodies on a regular basis," Nalem explained, in his head navigating through memories and tact to figure out how much to say. "My own expression is largely dependent on what my vessels best respond to; I am more masculine in this lifetime because that is what made Retz listen most often. You and I are not the same, in how we reconcile our bodies and minds." He paused as we clambered over a couple of broken steps in the stairs. "Sea Mother's memory is accurate, however. I was born in a woman's body, much like you. Unlike you, I would not mind returning to it."

"But you can't, because that body died a few thousand years ago. You know how your body's supposed to be, but can't go back to it? That's..." Jarrod bit his lip and mulled over the information. "Don't take this as pity, but...I'm sorry you have to deal with that."

"That's where he's wrong," Nalem whispered. I think it wasn't directed at me, but to himself. *"I will return to my true form, without placebos such as those the Ringmaster offers. The day is ever close at hand, and when it finally arrives? This whole world will fear me."*

But out loud, and with a note of vulnerability that I couldn't exactly place as faked, he said "This once, I accept your condolences. But never bring it up again, understood?"

I had so many questions. Then we reached the top of the stairs, and I did a doubletake after catching a glimpse of black curls. As if his original vessel was waiting for us. Then reality hit.

"Glad to see we won't have to kill either of you today," the Harvester said, winking five different eyes scattered across his skin.

11 - JARROD

The Harvester is not human. He doesn't try to hide that truth like I do. He may be compelled to destroy any monster that dare kill a human—or Nalem—but in guarding mankind, he lost his place among them. He didn't bother hiding the memory-laden eyes cropping up on his leathery tanned skin like warts. Seeing him smiling down at us from the main floor of the Jacoby Building, I realized for the first time his teeth were filed into serrated points, same as Nalem's sometimes were, crafted with care to resemble the leviathan's maw.

I'd felt those teeth along my own jaw, phantom sensations lacerating my tongue. I didn't understand why someone would want to mimic that.

"Nice of you to rush in and help," Retz muttered with a sarcasm no one else would dare wield against the Harvester. He'd picked up on Nalem's disregard for the boogeyman all other supernaturals feared—the person who'd put Nalem in Retz's head in the first place.

The Harvester shrugged. "We wanted to determine your dedication, among other things. Nalem, we are proud you have not forgotten your roots." He sauntered over and raised a hand covered in a scaled glove, out of place alongside his khakis and eye-searing Hawaiian shirt. A lingering memory that wasn't mine showed a younger Harvester with only two eyes, sewing scales together on a beach with his feet in the surf. He had been born and raised a human. Something else made him change.

"However," the Harvester continued, "your accent is atrocious. Seems we need to go over vocabulary again, hmm?" He almost tapped Retz on the nose before realizing it was broken and rapping his knuckles along Retz's forehead instead.

Retz winced and rubbed his forehead. "Nalem says he's out of practice, no thanks to you. Also, a few harsher things I probably shouldn't mention, but I'm sure you can guess."

"Habits emerge after a few hundred years or so, yes." The Harvester peered past us down the stairs to Levi's Tomb. The faint outline of Sea Mother's ethereal scales decorated the debris-laden room. "That said, we should not be surprised by this outcome. Nalem has always been protective of those he loves. Less so of his knowledge, it seems."

"Are you just here to check on Sea Mother?" I interrupted before Nalem could voice an insult. "Or was there something else you wanted to talk with us about? Farris's memories, maybe?"

"Hmm? Ah, right. That." His affable façade gave way; whatever he'd found in Farris's memories, he didn't seem pleased by it. A golden eye blinked on the Harvester's knuckle before melding back into his skin. It appeared in his mouth a moment later, where he rolled it along the back of his teeth like a candy gobstopper. "We suppose it would be best to discuss that matter—as well as Sea Mother's actual skull. She won't be placated by a fake for long."

She'd barely accepted it in the first place. Her indignation had rattled through my body, not enough space for an ancient being so vast and wrathful. Her head had been recreated with the bones of prey too low for her to even think about, and she was expected to take it in peace?

She'd only left because I'd fought back against her. I felt for her, but I didn't want to feel her forever. It also helped that Nalem's pleading, barely more legible than a child, had evoked a tender-hearted pity I hadn't expected in the leviathan.

Retz told the Harvester, "We'd love to get her head back, but we've got a few problems. A Faerie called the Ringmaster claims that someone gifted him the skull, and he won't give it back unless he gets to punt Nalem and I into plastic bodies of his own design. We might have a way around that, except now our Dad's showed up, trying to assassinate Nalem and maybe misuse this other Fae's powers. Not liable to end well, y'think?"

The Harvester blew his curly mop of hair out of his eyes with an irritated huff. "It warrants a talk, for starters. And difficult talks are best eased with food—though we're sorry to see the tavern you worked so hard on destroyed, little one."

"So are we. But it can be fixed." Retz tilted his head, concerned as he listened to Nalem's advice. "There's a restaurant a few blocks away where we can talk. It's dark, loud, not the sort of place for eavesdroppers. Or so Nalem claims. Hopefully, it'll be calmed down and open again by the time we arrive."

"We should make sure everyone's alright first," I said. My voice wanted to waver at the end, to placate the Harvester with a question instead of a demand. Even without a sense for monsters, the man unnerved me the longer I watched him—and he watched me back with a thousand blinking eyes scattered across his skin.

"Ginny and the rest of Levi's Tomb have already stepped in, along with Farris," the Harvester said as he waved us toward the exit. "Ambulances have been called, first aid administered, so forth and so on." He winked, one eye only this time. "They didn't want humans to remain untended while we were around, you see. Our reputation precedes us."

The square was still a mess when we made it outside, with uprooted plants, fallen bits of loose brick and wood, and damaged cars. The humans had already glossed over the supernatural elements and declared this to be a short but violent earthquake. Some snapped photos of the debris with their phones. Despite the damage in Levi's Tomb, the rest of the Jacoby Building seemed intact, with nothing worse than a fallen sign and a few toppled displays in the store windows. I hazarded a guess that the otherworldly nature keeping the supernatural bar hidden from humans also took the brunt of the damage. A few patrons of Levi's Tomb were sitting with the more injured humans, those with weaker glamours sticking to the shadows to obscure their features while waiting for the ambulance to arrive.

Ginny talked loudly with Farris, tracing lines in the air as she spoke; I suspected she was explaining her plans to rebuild. Whatever the topic, they ran over soon as they saw us.

Farris wrapped me in a tight hug. "We heard you screaming," he muttered into my shoulder. "I should've gone in there, but there was this gal whose foot got caught in the rubble and—"

"I'm fine. Things took an unexpected turn, but the poltergeist calmed to a regular ghost again." As regular as an undead leviathan could be, at least. Other than her visual memories, her thought process had been a jumbled maze searing into the back of my mind, painful and incomprehensible as an open wound.

"Did she kick your ass, my lord?" Ginny asked. She stood on her tiptoes to examine Retz's broken nose before deciding to elbow his side instead. She then remembered the Harvester between us and paled accordingly. "I mean. Uhmm. Hey there, oh lord Harvester, I humble myself before thee and all that jazz?"

The Harvester's laidback demeanor drifted back into place. "You and your humble jazz are accepted, Luigina. We continue to appreciate your dedication to our child's well-being."

"Someone has to, considering how often the asshole gets himself killed," Ginny grumbled, seemingly more annoyed by the mention of her full name than anything else. "So, what's the plan? Time to steal skulls and fight some Fae?"

"It is. But first, we have matters to discuss. And...what time is it? Breakfast?"

"Lunch," Retz corrected, "please lunch. If Nalem even thinks about maple syrup right now, I'll hurl."

After confirming with Ginny that Nalem's restaurant of choice was open, and that our help wasn't needed further, we were on our way. The earthquake's reach didn't extend too far past the square. The homespun clothes and hippie posters hadn't budged from the shop windows. Ginny, Nalem, and the Harvester took the lead, absently talking about how the town had changed in the past few centuries. I stayed in the back with Farris. We kept our own pace, since I wasn't sure how much pain Farris was in and I needed to ground myself before what I expected would be another enigmatic twist in this whole debacle. Our fingers interlaced. I tried not to get lost in my own thoughts.

"We should take a break from jobs like this for a while," Farris said. "They keep evolving way past our paygrade."

I nodded. "Think trouble won't find us even if we hide from it?"

"I try to be an optimist. Sure it'll pay off someday. Maybe today if that bastard gives me my eye back."

I glanced up at the wrong time and realized we were passing Monica's studio. Her blinds were drawn, and somehow splattered with paint even on the window-facing side. Why did it still feel like she was somehow watching me?

The restaurant wasn't far from there. The interior was dark, its walls painted in deep reds and purples, with a chalkboard menu over the bar; this was far more dive bar than a plain restaurant. Not that I'd complain. We were seated in a booth near the back with a painting of dogs playing poker hanging above us. Having just been possessed, I ordered the stiffest drink the bartender could muster. Ginny asked for a Ramos Gin Fizz with a haughty look in her eye, the Harvester requested an entire pot of green tea, and the others stuck to their iced water. We waited until the server was gone to explain what had happened in Levi's Tomb.

"Being possessed by something so ancient tends to drive fuckers mad," Ginny said with a note of awe once we were done. "Good job keeping your noggin together."

"To her credit, Sea Mother knows how fragile mortals can be." The Harvester dropped an eyeball into his teacup before drinking. "Yet if she's bothered enough to possess others, her skull should be recovered as soon as possible."

"Ain't it your job to ferry folks to the next life?" Farris asked. He was busy constructing his newest piece of silverware architecture. "Why don't you just move your leviathan mom onto...whatever the leviathan afterlife is?"

The Harvester sighed into his tea. "Our jurisdiction is human souls only. We are not equipped to ferry supernatural souls, nor to comprehend their memories. We have a hard enough time working with ex-humans." All of his eyes flickered to Farris.

"Hey, you're the one who volunteered. Got any idea who I am yet?"

I'm not sure if Nalem noticed, but a few of the Harvester's eyes squinted at everyone's least favorite necromancer. As if gauging how much was safe to share—for his sake, or ours?

"Some," the Harvester finally admitted, "but what we have found so far is...hazy. And it is the nature of this haziness that brings us pause. Especially combined with that pact from our beloved wife on your shoulder." He paused for another sip of tea. Farris's restless claws pierced into the seat beside me. Much as I had a pact on the back of my hand, an agreement with the Harvester to keep Nalem alive in exchange for one resurrection of my choice, Farris had a tattoo that was apparently a similar pact from his own world. But we had no idea what he was supposed to do—and while it kept him from fading away in the mortal world like most Fae, it also meant I couldn't use the Harvester's resurrection on him until this mysterious task was completed.

"White Prince, most of your soul has been devoured. Not the careful, targeted erosion of someone who stole your memories on purpose. Your memories and identity, everything about whoever you used to be, have been haphazardly ripped apart. The remaining fragments have attempted to patch themselves together, but most of the gaps are filled with the stuff of dreams and daytime television dramas."

"Devoured?" Nalem echoed, suspicious.

The Harvester nodded with a wry, knowing smirk. "All gobbled up. Likely after the pact was made, which was either a foolish or tactful move on someone's part."

Farris slumped in his seat, arms crossed before he tore up the diner seat any further. "There usually ain't a way to un-gobble things, so I assume that means my memory's sunk. Not even you can get it back, can you?"

"Not on our own. But if whoever took the pieces hasn't actually...digested them, so to speak, there may be hope for repair. A broken soul is no easier to repair than a broken bone, but it can be done."

Nalem nodded along, slowly. "Explains how he knows a smattering of Lemurian."

"Does it now?" Farris growled. "Glad you two know what's going on. Care to enlighten the rest of us? Mostly the guy whose past you're talking about?"

The Harvester smirked. "But of course. It seems you've met our entire family, little one. That is not a feat many can claim or survive. Though we suppose you haven't necessarily lived to tell the tale."

"So I didn't bring Farris into this mess," I said. After all the other shit I'd found out today, that revelation was a small relief. "He's been tied up with your family since before he got here. All I did was introduce him to Nalem."

"That is true. Even without your influence, the two would have collided eventually." The Harvester shrugged. "What a funny thing, when Fate and happenstance do meet."

I was smart enough to leave it at that. To let the Harvester have his cryptic comments and see what I could discern from them later. Considering the looks he'd given his son, the Harvester might find Farris and me later with something he'd kept from his son's schemes. However, Farris had far more gall than me, and kept up the questions, trying to goad the Harvester into giving up some nugget of truth.

Ginny leaned in, whispering at me and avoiding the Harvester's tight-lipped, sharp-toothed smile. "Your boyfriend's got guts. Good thing he can't die again, huh?"

I thought back to how much pain he'd been in the other night. "Yeah. Sure is."

Ginny took a swig of her fizz. "This wasn't whipped half as much as it should've been, just as I figured. S'why my bar is better."

"Sorry it got destroyed, by the way. Any way we can help fix it up?"

Ginny shook her head, the foam from her drink clinging to her upper lip. "Hell, it ain't your fault. That's what happens when you build on old bones; you risk pissing off those who can't let go of the past, whether they mean it or not. Present company included." She took another drink, seemingly giddy in how much she hated it. "Besides, I'm a boggan still, ain't I? Fixing shit's my job and will be long as I stay this way. Be it a building or a drink, I'll make it work 'til the day I boggart out."

"I'm impressed no one's managed to trigger that yet," I admitted. I wasn't sure if it was a curse or something more intrinsic, but the literal act of being thanked triggered a boggart's transformation between busybody and destructive juggernaut.

"I mean, I turn back eventually. It's just annoying to turn into a giant raging beast all the time because some bastards can't watch their tongues. Even Nalem tripped over his manners at first." She elbowed Nalem in the side. "Remember that time in the ship? Me peeling potatoes and you with your head stuck between your knees? You almost thanked me when I held your hair back so you didn't puke into it."

Nalem faked indignation. "How was I to know my vessel at the time was prone to seasickness? The Harvester couldn't have picked a worse mortal at the time if he tried."

"You doubt our ingenuity, little one." The Harvester flicked an eyeball into Retz's glass. "Now we've settled the matter of our Prince's eye for now—"

"—We haven't," Farris interrupted, pointing to his smoking, empty socket.

The Harvester tapped the golden eye on the back of his hand. "We'd taunt you to come and get it, but knowing you're enough of a fool to take that seriously, we shall refrain. Now, as we were saying....this vessel mentioned that Sea Mother's Skull is in the possession of one Ringmaster, correct?"

I nodded in confirmation. "Have you heard anything about him before?"

"Other than your elder sister—and now the White Prince here, we suppose—we try not to deal with Faeries. Our purview is this world and the souls within it, so if a soul has the misfortune to slip between worlds before it snuffs out, there is nothing we can do for it."

I bit back a sigh. "He's able to create things out of this...plasticine ooze, including bodies. He's made a carnival where he offers to help folks fix their lives by shoving them into the bodies he makes, with no option to change back. He's extended this offer to all of us...and is particularly keen on giving Nalem his own body. He won't return the skull until this transfer is completed."

The Harvester cocked his head to one side. "In order to move people between bodies, he must possess the ability to touch and move souls. Which is...worrisome, to say the least. We've yet to meet anyone other than ourselves and our wife who can do such a thing." Most of his eyes turned to Nalem, trying to gauge his reaction, but he kept his face impassive. The Harvester continued, "Have any of you...made plans, regarding this offer?"

"We hadn't, but we've got another complication. My father is on his way to force Retz and I into more human bodies, which also means isolating Nalem to murder him. And he admitted as such to my face. With pride."

The others didn't respond immediately. I thought it was out of disbelief or shock. Then I noticed a wide-eyed waitress had returned and silently set our food on the table. When she caught my eye, she motioned zipping her lips and tossing a key before scurrying away.

Ginny chuckled as she prepped the condiments on her meal. "Congrats kid. That human's going to think about this exchange 'til her dying days."

I sank in my seat, trying not to think about that on top of everything else. It was such a little thing compared to bodysnatching, possession, and realizing my hero had turned into a villain in front of my eyes while I'd refused to see. Farris wrapped an arm around me.

The Harvester said, "In all seriousness, this is distressing news. And we do not only mean that as a concerned parent. Even if your father was able to successfully kill Nalem while sparing the two of you...well, we'll spare you the details for the time being, but it would have far deadlier repercussions than any of you could realize. And not even we could prevent it, with all our power."

"Your incompetence is why we're like this in the first place," Nalem spat. Both father and son glared at each other, holding back words but not the hurt in their eyes. Things hadn't been like this in the memories I'd seen of Sea Mother's. What had changed over the past thousands of years? The two immortals didn't say, but turned away and focused on their meals. The rest of us followed suit, eating as we spoke, even though my stomach threatened to throw everything up.

"Much as I hate to say it," Farris said as he stole one of my fries, "might be smartest for us to leave before shit hits the fan. I'm sure someone else can get that skull back out. Like those minotaurs. They can hitch it to a trailer hookup or something, right?"

Ginny answered, "They're strong, but too short-sighted. They'll run in to get revenge for Bertha and get their asses killed, even if they've got that puny pig-sticker they call a sword." I tried to remember if we'd mentioned finding Bertha at the carnival, but my head wouldn't stop spinning with everything else on my mind. I told myself that Nalem probably filled her in on the way over, or after we'd left the bar last night. She elbowed Nalem in the side. "Come on milord, we can make it a quick job. In and out, no problem."

The Harvester narrowed his eyes. "Luigina? Do you really dare discuss dragging my child into life-threatening danger in front of our own face? Has your sense of self-preservation lapsed so much in these past centuries...?" He let that hang in the air for one moment before smirking with those sharpened teeth. "We jest with you. You of all people know the importance of keeping Nalem safe."

Nalem growled, "And the lot of you think you have far more say over my decisions than you actually do. Regardless, I refuse to flee from this situation, but am aware of its dangers. The Ringmaster, we can deal with. Retz is crafting a surprisingly effective plan, though none of you shall dare inform him I admitted this. Alexander, on the other hand...his ability to inflict curses merely by speaking is most infuriating. And I fear even if we avoid him for the time being, we cannot do so forever."

We fell into silent munching. Alexander was well aware of his powers and how to use them. Hell, I'm sure he could give me an impossible order and turn me into a rosebush where I stood if he wanted. How could someone fight against a power like that? Forced to see my father as a foe instead of an ally, I realized how terrifying his power really was.

The Harvester stared deep into Farris's golden eye on the back of his hand before uttering what sounded like the Lemurian swear Farris had uttered the night before. "There is one option at your disposal. Though we hope our wife will not have our head for mentioning it..." He glanced up at my partner and said, "Does the name Fatebreaker sound familiar to you at all?"

"It's not mine to wield," Farris answered immediately. Confusion blossomed on his face. "Not that I have any idea what it is."

"Then you had best remember swiftly. The memories of it are not in this half of your soul, but as you are the White Prince, the knowledge of your family's secret weapon must be locked somewhere in the shadowstuff you call a brain." The Harvester traced some sort of shape or sigil in the air. Farris watched, confused but intent.

Nalem said, "I've read about Fatebreaker in Loresha's book a few times. It's one of the legendary relics of Moonworld, along with its other half, Fatemaker. Assigned to sister kingdoms. Correct?"

The Harvester nodded and spoke between sandwich bites. "Exactly, and as the name implies, it breaks fates. And what is a curse but a negative destiny? You may not be the firstborn or the next to rule in your family, but the ability to summon and wield this weapon remains in your bloodline. And as this world is not governed by Fate, it is not equipped to deal with curses as yours is. This may well be your only way out. And as further incentive for your memories to cooperate, we make this offer."

Farris's eye blinked in the back of the Harvester's hand. He said, "If you can remember what Fatebreaker is, and summon it successfully in order to protect Nalem, we'll return to you your other eye, and all its memories within."

"You've got yourself a deal," Farris said without hesitation. "Now...any hints about what kinda' relic this Fatebreaker is? Some sorta sword maybe?"

The Harvester shrugged with a wry smile. "As we said, we did not spy it in the memories we viewed. So, you'll have to tell us. What sort of relic is so important that your entire family's purpose is to protect it?"

Farris didn't have an answer to that. His face scrunched up in concentration as he stared deep into his unstable tower of snatched silverware, the way the dogs in the painting overhead stared at their cards, as if they held some sort of clue. No great realization struck him at that diner table. But if he had access to some legend that could counter Alexander's powers, and maybe Fate itself, whatever that meant...who, really, was the White Prince? And what would happen if Farris remembered being him?

Ginny spoke up, "While he's trying to summon some superweapon, we should make a plan. And...figure out who gets to know the plan, I guess, if this Ringmaster can read minds. Shall we head out?"

Nalem looked at Farris and I before speaking. "Indeed, but...I believe a few hours to recuperate will not doom us. It has been an eventful day already." I caught a hint of concern in his eyes that had to be Retz bleeding through. I silently appreciated my brother's support. I needed a few hours to shut off my brain, or else not even alcohol would be enough to hold it all together.

"We'll leave the lot of you be for now," The Harvester said as he stood. "We appreciate you joining us for this...enlightening lunch. And in our absence, do keep Nalem safe."

"Are you going to pay for your share?" was all Nalem asked.

"Worry not; we left it in the cup." The Harvester winked each eye in turn, and by the time I lost count, he'd vanished.

Farris plucked a serrated tooth out of the cup. "And this is...?"

Nalem swore and plucked it out of Farris's hand. "I've told him time and again that teeth are no longer currency, but does he listen?"

"Not to anyone in this dimension," I said. I searched through my coat for my wallet—sadly, one of the lightest things in my possession. "Who's covering for him? For the record, I'm covering for Farris."

Ginny raised an eyebrow. "...He didn't order anything. The fries were your side."

Farris said, "I'm already enough of a high-maintenance boyfriend without being an expensive date too." He finally pulled away from his leaning tower of balanced plates and cups, silverware poking out with condiment-decorated napkins draped across the tines, and the Harvester's teacup placed with delicate care on the top. "Behold, a monument to cheap diners. I'd like to see the Ringmaster's carnival top this."

"I'm sure he'll try," Ginny grumbled. She looked to Nalem. He smirked and made no move to grab Retz's wallet. She gave him a full-forced glare as she grabbed her checkbook. "The shit I do for your family."

12 - RETZ

Once we left the restaurant, parting ways with The Harvester and Ginny for the time being, I dropped Jarrod and Farris at the hotel before driving off to give them some space. Considering...everything that had gone on just that morning, I was amazed Jarrod didn't have a breakdown at the restaurant. His body had been taut like a string about to snap, and he'd barely even spoken with all the mysteries of Nalem and the Harvester. I'd convinced Nalem to give them some time to rest. He'd agreed, citing that we too needed some time. Time to figure out who to trust with our lives.

Nalem insisted on driving, and we wove through unmarked roads and cattle fields to a fairly secluded beach. There were a couple other cars parked nearby, but I barely saw anyone. Nalem walked along the beach toward some unknown location while I gawked at the sights. I'd never been to the ocean before. Didn't realize how many plants grew along the sand, or how loud the waves were. Dried-out kelp and sun-bleached crustacean bits marked where the tide would soon return.

"*You really grew up around here?*"

"*Not on these exact shores as a child, but it is similar enough that I've found myself drawn to this coast across lifetimes.*" We'd brought the viola with us; Nalem claimed we were here so I could practice without bothering anyone, but I felt like he needed to ground himself somewhere familiar before our next attempt to rescue Sea Mother.

We scrambled onto a rocky outcropping and sat down to practice. After tuning strings and practicing scales with only a couple grumbles from Nalem, I worked on a pop song I'd decided to teach myself. It was a simple and catchy melody, but somehow, I kept slipping into the carnival's calliope tune. I ended my practice session early, frustrated and fingers blistered.

"*I was never a fan of circuses myself,*" Nalem claimed as he took control. Even his practice scales sounded far more melodious than anything I'd managed.

"*I'm surprised. I thought forcing others to perform for your entertainment was kinda' your thing.*"

"*Excuse you, but my schemes are far more intricate than mere carnival tricks. Besides, have you seen the poor excuses for taxidermy they lined their freakshow tents with?*" He flashed a few egregious examples through my head, fake mermaids and demons constructed so poorly I had to laugh. I tried not to think about how similar the Ringmaster's plastic bodies were, or what kind of joke he'd make out of my body if I gave him the chance.

What would I want to be if I had a body all my own?

"Do you really want to return to your true body?" I asked Nalem before he fell too deep into music and memories. *"What was it like? Jarrod said..."*

I felt Nalem weigh the merits of answering. *"I did look much like the Harvester and my twin when I was born. My body was frailer than Loresha's, but otherwise, it was hard to tell us apart."* Unspoken scenes of the past drifted through unbidden. A woman with dark skin, I assume the Harvester's wife known as the Weaver, brushing the hair of two small girls. The Harvester, without extra eyes or weariness haunting his features, holding small hands in the surf as the children learned to swim. The taste of raw fish, accompanied by Sea Mother's pleased trill.

"Do you...want to take the Ringmaster up on his offer?" It'd make sense. He hadn't had a body to himself for who knew how long, and if the Ringmaster cooperated, he'd finally look like he used to. Plus, he'd escape this curse Dad planted in us without having to rely on Farris's spotty memory.

"*Nostalgia and self-image both work in strange ways, little one.*" Nalem began a song in earnest, notes drawn-out in minor key. "*I have my reasons for requiring that specific body, and they shall remain mine until my goal is completed. Just as Sea Mother found the false head we made for her distasteful, a simulacrum such as the Ringmaster offers will not satiate me.*" He took a moment to focus on the music, recalling a tune he hadn't heard played in a few hundred years. "*Besides, your body is useful, with its lack of organs. I doubt the Ringmaster would leave me anything so well suited for my needs.*"

Maybe it was wishful thinking on my part, but I might've heard deeper in Nalem's thoughts, "*You have never been truly alone, little one. Be thankful for that.*"

I guess, like me in a way, Nalem had spent most of his life sharing a body with someone else. The prospect of being alone in our own respective heads...I couldn't wrap my mind around it. How did people stay sane, with only their own thoughts and no one to answer?

"*How amusing. Everyone else would think you couldn't wait to leave me behind. Yet here you are, missing a presence you haven't even lost.*"

"*Pretty sure it's Stockholm Syndrome or something at this rate.*" Don't think I'd forgotten that for every kindness Nalem offered me, I got slapped with two insults not long after. And he'd brought far more pain to my family than could ever be undone.

But beyond that, what would I do with a body of my own? I couldn't imagine it. I'd never let myself try before. Would I go back home and live a peaceful life as a hairdresser? No idea. I couldn't imagine settling down for a life of small talk about mundane things, much less a typical life with marriage and a house with a white-picket fence. It all seemed so...

"Boring. The word you're looking for is boring." Even though Nalem's hands were busy with the violin, he placed phantom impressions of them on my shoulders. *"No matter what could be changed with your body, your mind is marred with fantastic things that most mortals couldn't even begin to comprehend. You'd never fit in with them."*

"What you're saying is, I'm damned if I do, damned if I don't."

"You can't escape yourself or your past with a fresh face alone. One would think this obvious, but I suppose not everyone has the luxury of experience...or knows how to handle it, in the Ringmaster's case."

So, what was the right choice? Stick with Nalem, no matter what else he had in store for us, because it was familiar and I might be able to reign him in? Or cast it aside for a chance to be a normal person and probably fail? Either way, I doubted Dad would let me off the hook even if managed to snatch the skull from under the Ringmaster's nose. And if Nalem was dealt with, I wasn't sure if Dad would leave me be, or he'd watch me forever for traces of being "tainted" by his presence.

I dwelled on that for a long time, letting my senses drift with the music and the tide. By the time I came to, the sun was far closer to kissing the horizon.

I belatedly realized that when the sun next rose, it'd be my twentieth birthday.

Someone clapped behind me. I turned, expecting a random beachgoer, but there was Ginny. She called out to us, "Been a long time since I heard that tune, milord. Glad you got that viola back. Where did it end up?"

"Lady Delight had it," Nalem answered as he returned the instrument to its case. "I'm not sure if she plucked it from my body after that death, or if someone else did and sold it to her later, but it hardly matters now. I killed her, as is befitting a traitor."

Ginny nodded and hopped onto the rocks next to us. If the sharp parts hurt her callused feet, she didn't show it. "Sorry I didn't grab it first. Maybe we should put tags on all your goods. 'If this asshole lost his shit, return to Levi's Tomb so Ginny can hold onto it and laugh'. Or something of the sort."

I took control of my mouth to ask, "Then why don't you stay with him all the time, once you find his newest body?"

Ginny shook her head. "If we were together all the time, we'd see the same things, and neither of us would realize if the other had a bad idea. This way, if I find him digging himself into a pit with his plans, I'm prepared with a rope to pull him out."

She tugged on my sleeve until I looked her in the eye before saying, "You've got to realize, that's the problem with immortals. They don't get time to stop and reflect, like the rest of our souls do between reincarnations. All they know how to do is keep going, and while their ambition is grand, they don't always realize if they've been running in the wrong direction for a few hundred years. They need mortals like us to set them right now and again, show them a bridge was built in the years they spent trying to ford the river. You get me?"

"I...think I do?" It made sense, and not something Nalem would admit, which was why I'd asked Ginny. Having some perspective from another person familiar with Nalem but not trying to kill him was a nice change of pace. "That's why the Harvester keeps putting him in new bodies, and not just reviving the same one over and over. He can get a fresh view, right?"

Ginny didn't answer for a while. We stared out at the sea together. Would've been scenic if a seagull flying overhead hadn't nearly shat on us. I shifted away from where it nearly hit my shoe, and Ginny laughed.

"Never thought of it like that. Thought he was just as bad as...well, you might have it right. That's why I need you to help him, if things get too complicated. When he gets stuck, he's the sort to thrash when others try to free him. Change is hard, in a world without end."

Ah. So that's what she was getting at. "You think shit's gonna' hit the fan at the carnival."

"Gotta prepare for things like that, with two Fae involved, one pissed off lamia, and a potential poltergeist on the line. And even if things were half as easy, Nalem's got a way of complicating things. I'm sure you get that."

"I sure do. He's got complicated friends too, it seems." I smiled at her and didn't stop Nalem from drawing it too tight. "Say, how'd you know I was here? Stop by the hotel to chat with Jarrod and Farris first?"

"I don't even know what hotel you buggers are at. Though seeing how cheap your brother is, I've got a guess." Ginny shrugged. "As I said, I know Nalem well. He always finds his way back here sooner or later."

"Then how'd you know about the lamia? We didn't mention it at the bar, or to the Harvester." The viola case, which Nalem hadn't closed all the way, clicked open. "You knew there were multiple Fae involved before Jarrod mentioned Dad. And you knew that Bertha and the carnival were connected too."

Whatever Ginny swore under her breath was lost to the sound of crashing waves. "Should've figured you'd be more on guard after the shit Lady Delight pulled." She grabbed my sleeve. "All of this, I've done to help you out, my lord. Though I don't suppose you'll do me the luxury of coming quietly and trusting me, for old time's sake?"

Of course not. I tried to grab her wrist, but she yanked my sleeve and somehow twisted my arm and pinned it against my back without tearing the fabric. Nalem formed the backup bones into daggers and flung them at Ginny, but she wasn't fazed no matter how deep we dug the bones into her skin. Couldn't get any through her chest; she had chainmail under her shirt.

She pulled one of the daggers out of her arm and slashed across my back. Tore through my vest, shirt, and the corset piercings I used to keep my back shut in case I somehow lost my shirt around humans. I had no organs inside, just bones and Dad's curse. At least, that's what folks could see.

Ginny and I tumbled to the ground, me trying to warp her bones while she tried to hold me down, face against the stone. I was so preoccupied with trying to knock her off that I didn't realize who else had tagged along to kidnap me. Monica rushed in, and once Ginny had me down, she shoved her hand into my back. Sure, the thorns inside tore her up. But then she reached my chest and squeezed.

See, when folks ask how huldras (and empty hulderkind like me) live without organs, the usual answer is a shrug. But if one wants to get really technical, we do have an energy source, some combination of a brain and a heart that animates us. It floats throughout huldra bodies, generally somewhere in the chest, burning up anything that falls inside our bodies and turning it into pure energy through some pseudoscience I never quite understood. But if you want to kill a huldra, that's what you've got to hit or otherwise remove from the body, which is a bit difficult when it's intangible.

Turns out, a soul isn't the only intangible thing the Ringmaster can handle, and that power works even through Monica. I imagine having one's heart literally grabbed while it's beating in your chest feels a lot like Monica grabbing my ethereal power source.

I seized up. Brain halted. The same must've happened to Nalem; this was his body too.

I wonder what the other beachgoers thought, seeing two gals carry my body across the beach and into the car. I'm sure their minds glossed over my open back. Maybe that was enough to make them look away before I got tossed into the trunk of a car and driven to the woods.

"I don't give one flying fuck about your morals. We don't have *time* for morals. Either you fix them now, or we're all going to die."

No surprise Ginny's shrill declaration woke me up. I didn't need to open my eyes to know where we were; there was no mistaking the combined stench of paint fumes, spun sugar, buttery popcorn and spilled blood. I sensed Ginny standing between me and Monica, and a numbing static just behind her that had to be the Ringmaster. The skull wasn't anywhere nearby, and still had something living attached. So much for my plans. Figuring out that Ginny had been the traitor didn't help when we'd underestimated how well she could avoid Nalem's powers.

My chest ached and opening my eyes felt like too much effort. Mom never said anything about how much fucking up a huldra's core could hurt, since most people couldn't do it. But as Ginny said, there wasn't time. If I didn't move, I might as well kiss my body goodbye. I pushed up with a groan and opened my eyes.

The walls of this little tent were green and lined with mirrors, reminding me of the theater greenroom from back in school. But instead of makeup and scripts on the tables, there were operating tools and notes on body mods. Empty skins hung up from hangers in a macabre parody of costumes. I hoped none of those were for me.

"Perfect timing. We can ask him ourselves." The Ringmaster pushed aside the flaps to the tent and entered, so tall he had to stoop to avoid hitting his head on the ceiling. "You know exactly what kind of predicament you're in, don't you? Such smart lads. I do hope this means you'll both cooperate."

"So much for all of your guests visiting of their own free wills," Nalem muttered as he came to. He checked my memories for what happened before realizing I hadn't been awake much longer than him. *"The one time your bizarre anatomy turns out to be a bane instead of a boon..."*

The Ringmaster said, "You won't have to worry about such weaknesses in bodies crafted by yours truly. I do hope you enjoy them enough that you'll forgive me for this one day." His hands grabbed various tools, and his ringmaster outfit took on the light teal color of operating scrubs.

No surprise, my arms and legs were bound, but instead of with rope or handcuffs, it was with those long circus balloons clowns use to make animals and stuff. I said, "Changing our bodies if we asked is one thing. But you do realize doing this without our permission is...real fucking skeevy? And would be illegal, if y'know, body snatching was a normal thing."

"It's better than the alternative!" Ginny shouted. "I'm not going to let our world disappear because of your vanity. Just because you call yourself a god, doesn't mean you can damn us with your hubris."

Wait...what was this about the world? Sure, Dad was powerful and dangerous, but...

The Ringmaster narrowed his gaze at us. "Nalem, my friend...you didn't explain any of this to your vessel, did you?"

"I do not recall giving you permission to root around in my thoughts, or to call me friend, but here we are." Nalem sunk down deeper into his thoughts to avoid the Ringmaster.

Ginny shook her head. "The arrogance of it all..." She stomped up to us, staying just out of arm's reach. "Have you never wondered why the hell Nalem's immortal? Or why his old man protects him despite all he's done? Why the hell we worship him?" She didn't leave me time for a

sarcastic answer, gesturing outside at the technicolor
hellscape of Arcadia. "Years ago, before even I was born,
Arcadia sprung up and split our world in two.
Moonworld and Sunworld, 'case you were wondering.
And Arcadia's growing, trying to devour everything it
can. Know what's stopping it from eating our world and
turning it into a Faerie-ridden nightmare?"

Wait, was that... *"That's why you can't stand being in
Arcadia, isn't it? Because you're...repelling it?"*

"Like opposing poles on a goddamn magnet," Nalem
hissed. He kept the memories locked from me, but not
his rage. *"It's not a fact we advertise. I have enough targets on
my back already, without adding every Fae to that list.
Honestly, the Ringmaster should wish for my death as well, for
just that reason. He could spread his carnival everywhere if he
wished."*

"Which I do not." The Ringmaster had the gall to
sound hurt. "No matter what you keep thinking, I'm not
a mastermind or conqueror. I want to help people!
Humans and all those other beings I'm just now
learning exist! There's so much about the world I don't
know...I can't let it all go up in smoke." He smiled softly,
which might've reassured me if his hands weren't full of
scalpels and other sharp surgery tools. "Besides, I
already told you. I can't stand the idea of anyone else

dying around me, having gone through it myself. Even if your death wouldn't damn our whole world, Nalem...I'd still have a second chance for you here."

I shouted that we didn't need anyone's second chances, but the Ringmaster's free hands lunged toward me. My reactions were sluggish, but I managed to roll off what I'd been lying on—it turned out to be a table setup for a magician specializing in sawing folks in half. Nalem took control of my bones and popped the binding balloons with spurs on my wrists and ankles. Black ooze splattered everywhere, causing me to slip as I tried to stand. A knife narrowly missed my shoulder. Ginny had another one ready.

Nalem grabbed control of my mouth and called out, "Ginny, if your aim has gotten so poor, I'm afraid I'll have to retire you. But for your many years of service...I thank you." Venom dripped from those last two words. And Ginny began to scream.

"No time to watch, little one. We have to make our escape." I ran before the Ringmaster could shake off his surprise. Nalem directed me as he plotted out a course. His viola was trapped in the car they'd transported us in, but if we could grab the skull, we'd have an easy ride out. Hell, maybe we could make it out before any of my family arrived.

I'm no stranger to the sounds of bones breaking and reforming. I've heard plenty of muscles tearing and skin ripping. But it's different when the subject is alive. I didn't dare look back, but I felt those bones swell as Ginny's tiny boggan body took on the monstrous form of a boggart. Her voice broke as her vocal cords shifted. The Ringmaster panicked, seemingly torn between chasing me or helping this woman in such pain. I used every ounce of strength to take advantage of his indecision.

"What's happening to her? I know you said boggans can't stand being thanked..."

I felt Nalem also resisting the urge to look back. But if he felt any guilt over what he'd done, he hid it well. *"Without going into the full legend of it all...after boggans were taken advantage of for their kindness in days of yore, a spell was cast on their kind. If they end up unwillingly under the service of someone, they transform into powerful boggarts, so they either clear their debt faster or, well, destroy the source of it. And while the connotation has changed, thanking someone used to be dismissive of their efforts, implying it was only done out of obligation."*

"So she helped you out of friendship, and you basically claimed she did it 'cause it's her place to do so. Since everyone's lesser than you."

"That's the gist of it, yes."

We rounded a corner past some large tents and ran into a patrol of clowns. I didn't have any bones but my own on hand, but I couldn't risk anyone catching up. I grit my teeth to keep from screaming as three of my finger bones tore out of my skin and formed into daggers, piercing through clown heads. I ran over their deflated, flailing bodies as I tried to dry off my now ooze-covered bones with my shirt.

"And you thought taking advantage of a curse to turn one of your longtime best friends into a monster was...okay?!"

"She betrayed me! She knew the risks." Nalem dug his mental claws down my spine, as if the threat of more pain might make me run faster. *"How dare she assume what I want? What is right for me? And while I care not for the lives of mere townsfolk, she risked the afterlife of Sea Mother and the existence of the town I built...she is no better than these Fae! It is only befitting she serve as a distraction for the Ringmaster, so we may escape and live another day."*

So, she was the reason we were in this mess in the first place. Yet if she'd really believed she was helping Nalem out by getting him into his own body...shit, I didn't have time for moral dilemmas. If I survived 'til my birthday, I could go ahead and spend the next year of my life questioning right and wrong as much as I wanted.

Tents crashed behind me, followed by heavy thumps. Clowns silenced mid-honk. A quick check with my powers told me Ginny's transformation was done, and she was hunting down the certain someone who was to blame. My tired legs had almost given out but hearing those heavy footfalls behind me brought a second wind.

Nalem, you've got to learn to stop throwing your allies under the bus. Might be why they keep trying to ruin your life.

13 - JARROD

"**R**etz has been kidnapped. Monica was working with someone, didn't get a good look at who." Artemisia sighed, despite her lack of visible mouth. "I...wasn't able to stop them, but I think we both know where they went."

I want to make it clear how calm I remained. Despite everything that had gone wrong that day, I did not panic. I did not scream. Didn't even reach for my flask first thing. At this point, things going to absolute shit seemed an inevitability. Of course Retz had been kidnapped while trying to give me space. It was the punchline to a cosmic joke at my expense.

I undid the lock on our hotel door. "Come on in and tell me what happened."

"Wait one moment!" Farris shouted, almost too late as he scoured the hotel room for his pants. I counted backwards from ten. "Okay, it's safe!"

"As if I've never drawn a nude model in my life," Artemisia muttered as she entered. She wore a human face, realistic until one noticed she didn't blink or move her lips. The face closely resembled Monica's, and I noticed the stains around the lips where she'd had to paint over a smile.

I offered Artemisia a chair, then grabbed my notebook before sitting on the bed next to Farris. "Tell us what you saw. Starting with why you were there in the first place."

Artemisia explained, "I try to keep tabs on who Monica talks to. See if I can warn anyone away without revealing myself. It...hasn't worked many times, but I'd rather fail than say I hadn't tried at all."

"So how do you follow her? Do you...stalk her?" Farris asked. He hadn't bothered to find a shirt, so we had full view of the smoking hole in his chest where his heart had once been. Since Artemisia's eyes were painted and unmoving, I couldn't tell if she stared.

"I've got...let's call it a sixth sense for where she is." Instead of painting on herself, Artemisia fiddled with the fraying stitching on her denim jacket. "You might've noticed we're similar. I guess you could call us the opposite of Retz and Nalem. We're the same person. But when the Ringmaster shoved me into this body, not all of me made it through. Her body—my old body–is empty enough he can possess it when he wants to. Yet part of me's still there. Makes my skin crawl."

Any other day, I would've considered the implications, tried to narrow down if that meant her soul had broken and if such a thing might've also happened to Farris. I had more pressing matters right then. "So you followed Monica and found her with Retz. What did you see?"

"She and another woman were carrying Retz. He looked unconscious, and some of his clothing was ripped. They tossed him into the back of my old car, Monica's now, and sped off. Couldn't keep up with them on my bike. I've had someone watching the gate in the park that leads to the carnival, but when they phoned me to report, they were cut off mid-call."

"And did you notice any distinguishing features about the woman with Monica?" I had my suspicions, but I wanted to be certain.

Artemisia thought until green paint flowed from her fingertips, staining her jacket. "She was really short, and something on her head was this color. Like a really weird hat."

"Or a beehive hairstyle." I thought I'd noticed some discrepancies in some of Ginny's comments, but I'd foolishly believed Nalem had filled her in and paid it no mind. Gods damn it all, I should've...

No. I'd spent the past few hours keeping myself from the mire of dwelling on a past I couldn't change. All I could do was make up for it moving forward, starting with rescuing my brother.

"Farris, can you get us into the carnival?"

Farris crossed his arms. "Remember what happened the last time you rushed in there? I hate being the voice of reason babe, but we ain't ready. You and I can't tackle it alone."

"He's got a point," Artemisia said. "You've seen how strong the Ringmaster is. I know you were able to hold your own against the minotaurs, but...dying in Arcadia the first time is what made him this way. I can't imagine what might happen if he falls a second time."

"Faeries can be difficult to deal with, but they have their weaknesses." I glanced at Farris's chest. His skin still sported blistering burns where Bolton's iron rings had struck him. "Think the minotaurs might be willing to loan us a sword?"

Artemisia perked up at that. "Even if they wouldn't, they might want to break into the carnival with you. They agreed to leave us alone after you and your brother left, but they did ask a lot of questions about the carnival and its layout."

"Then what're we waiting for? Farris, grab some clothes. Artemisia, you're free to ride along if you want." I glanced down at my notebook and realized I'd torn up

the edges of the page instead of writing any actual
notes. I took another deep breath. Save that anger for
Arcadia, I told myself. I'd need plenty of it if I had to
face the Ringmaster, Alexander, and likely Ginny as
well.

We hurried out of the hotel room and into the car.
Artemisia hesitated, but ended up riding along. "If
nothing else, I can tell you what I know."

The start of her story was too familiar. Two humans
in the woods accidentally encounter a gate into Arcadia.
During their attempts to escape, a monster none of
them can fathom kills half the pair, but the one who
died rises again for revenge. And turns into...something
no longer human in body, however hard they cling to
their mortal face. Except Alexander and I were trained
to deal with the supernatural. Monica and Aiden had
been normal humans, childhood friends on the cusp of
becoming lovers, and they weren't equipped to even
comprehend Arcadia.

They'd wandered aimlessly for what felt like days,
Artemisia explained to us on the drive to the minotaur's
garage. Arcadia shifted around them like a
kaleidoscopic nightmare, assaulting their senses and
destroying any chance of ever finding home. But after a
long time, they found something familiar: the tune of a
circus calliope. They followed it to a small, worn-down

circus, almost right out of their childhood. It had a carousel, a Ferris Wheel, a few abandoned snack stalls where they could finally eat, and when they needed shelter...they entered the House of Mirrors.

It was the same circus Retz had accidentally fled to when we'd last been in Arcadia. Except when we'd entered, it had been abandoned. Aiden and Monica hadn't been so lucky. A Ringmaster–the original Ringmaster, as it turned out–chased them down those reflective halls. It caught Aiden and tore him apart. Except somehow, in the mercurial nightmare of Arcadia, Aiden's reflections reached out and put him back together again, and the arms from his reflections melded with his own body. He'd grabbed the glass shards of broken mirrors and stabbed the Fae to death, taking its costume as a prize.

And he'd looked upon the broken carnival around him and said, "Now this is a depressing relic of the place. A carnival's supposed to be fun, ain't it? Let's build something better."

He'd taken what he wanted from the circus, namely its big top, and went on his way. Monica stuck with him, of course. She had no choice; she couldn't navigate Arcadia on her own, and Aiden-now-Ringmaster had come to understand this world of his rebirth. He'd tried to help at first, she claimed. Spun her food and shelter from the candyfloss, tried to find a way out. But then he discovered he couldn't return to the mortal world. So instead, he found a way to keep Monica with him, as they'd been before.

"That's why he made this body," she said, gesturing to her canvas skin and fingers leaking paint. "I'd always loved art. He practiced other bodies first, made all those creepy clowns, thought they'd make me laugh...but then he made this. Said we'd match. I was so out of my mind, I agreed. I'd have given anything for the world to make sense again."

Except with that first body swap, something...broke. Artemisia hadn't been sure what it was, but hearing her explain it, I'm sure it was her soul. Not all of her memories or personality, not all of her *self*, made it in. Some of that stayed in the old body. The Ringmaster hadn't been able to put the pieces back together. But he discovered he could pilot Monica's human body, since so little of her soul remained. When Artemisia finally found the exit and returned to the mortal world, Monica followed under the Ringmaster's watchful gaze.

They hadn't been able to return to their normal lives. How could they? Artemisia wasn't human anymore, and she couldn't stand interacting with a stranger–once her almost-lover–in her old body. "And then Monica

encountered a human who was upset, and it turned out
they had an eating disorder related to their body image,
so of course Aiden figured that with his newfound
powers...I don't need to explain the rest to you, do I?"

No, and she didn't need to explain how the
Ringmaster and Alexander crossed paths either. The
Ringmaster must've still had ties to the old carnival and
sensed when someone else showed up. I imagined him
arriving just after we'd left, while Alexander was still
present. They got to talking. Alexander figured he could
use the Ringmaster's powers to fix his children. And if
the Ringmaster already had the leviathan skull...yeah, it
apparently went missing four months ago, and our
escapade in Arcadia had happened after that. So
whoever decided to lure Nalem in, which sounded like
possibly Ginny, had already roped the Ringmaster in for
her scheme. And once Alexander heard about the bait
for Nalem, no wonder he'd want to work with the
Ringmaster for a chance to murder his nemesis instead
of giving him a new body. But what did the Ringmaster
get out of it? Did Alexander simply offer information
and people to save? Or did the Ringmaster cooperate for
a simpler reason...fear?

I had a hypothesis that might get us all out alive
before Alexander arrived. "Artemisia, has the

Ringmaster ever turned away anyone with a ticket? Or ignored them, asked them to come back later…anything of the sort?"

She shook her head. "Far as everyone's said, he always drops everything the second someone flashes a ticket at his gate. Even if he's working with someone else, he'll just take the opportunity to help them all out. I've heard he'll occasionally summon Monica to him and use her as a second body."

"Good. And how certain are we that the minotaurs will back us up if we head into Arcadia?"

"I'd just about bet my life on it. Even if they were on the fence, we've got a couple ways to goad them into a fight."

Farris asked, "Got a plan, babe? And some way to work around the whole mind-reading thing?"

"I do, and I might not even have to hide my part in it. Doesn't matter if he can read my mind if he has no way of stopping it." I sped up the Merc and hurried on to the minotaur's garage.

Even though I'd volunteered myself as distraction and bait, I paused when I reached the Arcadian gate in the woods. My mind buzzed with all the ways this could backfire. Or if it instead went too well. Was this really right, forcing Retz and Nalem to remain in one body or stopping Nalem from being murdered at my father's hands? What if either of these Faerie's views, though extreme, were...

I dug my nails into my palms, crumpling the ticket in one hand until sharp pain returned me to my senses. Then I grabbed my flask for another quaff of liquid courage. I'd been raised to know right from wrong, even if those around me had forgotten. And I would not follow my father down the path of becoming a monster. As for Retz, I'd let him make his own decisions about his life and body, but I'd fight like hell to make sure they were truly his.

I ran off the path and into the gate before I could change my mind. Kept running so I didn't have to see my contorted face laughing at me from the carnival posters. My boots crunched across the cotton candy pathway as I reached the gates, the air rank with blood and buttered popcorn. The ticket thrummed faster than a hummingbird's heart on the verge of collapse.

This time when I approached the carnival, the calliope's song was punctuated by resounding booms and snaps. A tent on the horizon wavered before toppling to the ground. I hoped it meant Retz had escaped. I didn't see any vines or smell roses. Maybe we had time before Alexander appeared to steal the show.

The gate, resembling the opening to a carnival tent, was guarded by two clown guards, both wielding party poppers the way a cop does a pistol. One lolled its head at me.

"Hi-di-ho there, friend! What brings you to the biggest show off Earth today?" Much as they sounded like cartoon knockoffs, their poppers were aimed right at me. I resisted the urge to aim back.

I held up the golden ticket. "I've got an invite." They didn't lower their poppers. Could they sense I was plotting something? I faked a quiver in my hands. "Come on, you've got to let me in. I need help. *Please.*"

"Oh deary me!" The other clown stumbled over, holding up its head with one hand and accidentally dropping its popper as it grabbed my ticket and held it up to the light. "Yup and yep, this is one real deal of a ticket! We'll let the Ringmaster know you're here. But first!"

Without warning, the other clown threw its popper away over its shoulder. Both of them scurried forward, and I braced to run from their charge...only for them to hug me. They were about the height of children, save for their bulbous heads battering against my sides.

"You have been so brave, buddy!" One said in happy cartoon monotony.

"You've come a long way to get here, but everything's okay now!" The other agreed in the exact same voice. "Our pal the Ringmaster is gonna' get you all fixed up."

"Boy howdy, it'll be the best night of your life, once you're all reborn!"

I resisted the urge to shove them away.
"That's...great. I can't wait." And then, just to stall for time, "You weren't ever people, were you? Human or otherwise?"

The clowns tried to shake their heads, but this only sent them off-kilter. One toppled over, nearly pulling me with it, and flailed on the ground like an overturned bug. The other said, as if nothing had happened, "No sirree bob! We were made, not remade. We only exist to make people happy, the way good clowns are supposed to do!" Perhaps I was biased by seeing what happened when those bulbous heads popped, but I couldn't understand how anyone could find them enjoyable.

Still, my brother's safety was riding on this. I swallowed my pride and forced a smile. "Well, I feel better already with you two around. Say, do you know what'd make me happy?"

"Another hug!" cheered the one on the ground. I should note that the one who hadn't fallen over never let me go, just held on tighter.

"It's...something more fun than that," I said, easing the clown's grip on me. "There's a huge crowd heading to the carnival later. They're led by a man made of roots and roses. Maybe you've seen him before?" The clowns chattered that they had, and they still hadn't figured out how to make him laugh. "Great. Well, I'd appreciate it if you two could come let me know if you see him approaching. Can you do that?"

"We sure can! Wowee, having so many visitors today is great with a capital golly-gee!" The hugging clown finally released me and toddled over to help its fellow up. They both fell into the candyfloss, giggling as a wayward bug crawled onto one's head. I began to understand Retz's nascent coulrophobia. Damn it, why did the Ringmaster have to keep me waiting?

"Do you really have to ask that?" Asked the Fae who chose that exact moment to arrive. He appeared far more disheveled and frantic than our last encounter, top hat about to fall off his head, but he still wore that face-splitting grin. "After all, you purposefully marched in while I'm trying to get a handle on your brother and Ginny. Did you know about–yes, seems you did."

He stared deep into my eyes, scanning my thoughts for my plan. I had nothing to hide. Knowing his logic, he'd be bound to help me if I presented my ticket. With him and Monica split between Retz and I, he wouldn't have time to look for anyone else. Especially if I had no idea where or how they were entering the carnival. Would the minotaurs break down the gate? Farris warp everyone in through the shadows? Artemisia camouflage everyone with paint and walk in through the front gates undetected? Hell, they might have an even better plan than that.

I held up my ticket. "You've got two options. Take me to my brother now, or we both play along with this fucking charade until Alexander crashes down on both our heads. You thought the Fae who killed you was bad? Alexander's on a completely different level if you don't cooperate."

"And that terrifies you, doesn't it?" The Ringmaster asked back. He dared to sound sympathetic, even pitying. "You've never had to face your father, and you're afraid the little mercy he had as a human has all worn out. And much as you want to stand up to him now, you're afraid you might fold and give into his orders again, curse or no. Because it's easy. It's what you've done all these years without question."

Using myself as a distraction didn't seem so brilliant anymore.

The Ringmaster softly took my hand in two of his. "Walk with me. Maybe we can talk some sense into your brother and save him before Alexander arrives. If nothing else, trust that I want to save your brother as much as you do."

I let him lead me into the carnival and told myself it was part of playing the bait. "You're still waiting for him to offer his ticket, aren't you? I assume that's why you're not by his side right now."

The Ringmaster laughed, but it was a rueful sound that matched his bitter, tired smile. "I may not have the luxury of waiting. Which I hate, but we both know what'll happen if I'm not able to save him." He paused a long moment, staring down at me as we passed the gates. "Except you don't know. No one ever told you what's at stake."

"My brother's life is on the line. That's all the reason I need to save him, even if I didn't have this curse to protect Nalem too."

The Ringmaster let go of me, placing one hand on my back to slowly move me forward. That'd make it harder to break away if I chose to run. Smart. He didn't speak for a while, apparently debating whether he should tell me what else I didn't know. He must've decided against it when he said, "Sorry I'll have to delay the grand tour. Things are a bit hectic at the moment, as you know, and we've got a big show tonight. How about we hit the arcade and such afterwards, though? There's a shooting range game and everything. Could be a good opportunity to take your new body out for a spin."

The calliope played on overhead, punctuated by crashing buildings and honking clowns. But the carnival remained bright and cheery, right out of a painting that slowly leaked back into the candyfloss. Maybe if I took my glasses off, the world would be blurry enough for me to mistake it for the real thing. Instead, I turned toward the end of the carnival where Sea Mother's head rested. "You asked if I knew about Ginny. She the one who gave you the skull?"

"And the one who set this whole thing in motion, yes indeed. And for her devotion, the person she tried to save turned her into a monster instead."

"Like you?" If he was going to dig under my skin, no reason I couldn't do the same.

The Ringmaster watched the fall of distant tents. "Am I? I hoped helping others might change what I've become. But I suppose if one isn't human, there's only one other side of the coin. No matter how hard we try, we can't spin between heads and tails forever."

"You keep forcing folks to leave their humanity behind. I think that makes your position pretty clear." We were heading toward the cacophony, closer to the

skull and hopefully my brother. I wanted to grab my
guns, but I knew they wouldn't help me here.

"See, I'm sure I would've thought like you before all
this. Before I knew what else there was beyond being a
man." The Ringmaster flung his arms open, gesturing to
his carnival and everything beyond its borders. "There's
so much wonder to behold! Humanity rejects you if you
embrace the unknown, but let me tell you...being away
from all those unspoken rules of society, I've never been
happier. That's why people love the carnival! It's a
chance to cast aside one's restraint and simply live. And
with the bodies I make, all my guests find that freedom
too. They see how much more there is to the world!"

He stopped there and looked down at me. "I envy
you, you know. You grew up seeing the world for what it
is. So why do you fight so hard to pretend you aren't a
part of it?"

He knew full well why. Could pluck it right out of my
head and voice the damn words himself if he really
wanted to. That kind smile started to piss me off. I had
to keep a lid on it, for Retz's sake.

"And there it is. You think you're such a danger to
others. But you've only really felt alive those few times
you've given in." Those memories flipped through my
head. Losing my temper and going apeshit in battle.
Letting passion take me to the brink with Farris, the

only person I'd ever trusted myself with. Even fighting the minotaurs, when I'd been able to use my full strength, had been a relief in its own strange way.

The Ringmaster placed hands on the side of my face. "I know what to do with you. But again, we'll have to be quick. Your father tried to tell me how to build your body, you know. As if he could determine what you want! But I see it in your heart."

"Let me go." I pried hands off me; if he wanted me to use my monstrous strength, then he knew what he was in for.

"You're here to distract me while the others save your brother, right? And you already gave up your ticket. If you're really so dedicated, then save your brother by letting me save you." The Ringmaster kept that soft, borderline condescending smile plastered on his face. Even when I kept fighting his many hands, breaking fingers and wrists, that grin just widened, slowly baring teeth. "I'm sorry, but we don't provide refunds at this carnival. And I really hate to do this, but you leave me no choice. Hold still."

My scarf immediately went so tight around my throat, I gasped for air. My limbs fell limp. Stupid idiot I am, I hadn't even considered that he'd go for my curse.

But of course he'd know about it. And no matter how helpful he claimed to be, he valued control even more.

"Nasty curse you've got on you," The Ringmaster muttered as he scooped me up like a goddamn rag doll. "No wonder you're so wound up. But you've been living under these rules since before this touched your neck, now haven't you?"

I couldn't answer. My orders were clear: hold still, don't move. I wanted nothing more than to scream. But if I tried to fight, my curse would activate, and then I'd be stuck as a rosebush.

The Ringmaster prattled on as he marched through his carnival. "I didn't want to stick you in a catch-22 like this, but you've really left me no choice. Got a lot to do in such a short time. I bet if I have Monica bring your brother over, I can work on everyone at once...I've got enough hands for it, after all."

I'd throw hands at him the second I had the chance.

"I'm sure that'd be cathartic, but then you'd loathe your own penchant for violence, and it'd be a whole bitter feedback loop. Hurts to be bitter. That's why you've got to keep smiling, despite it all. You don't do that much, do you?"

Like I had reason to. I tried to be a realist. At least, I thought I did. Realizing how far Alexander had pulled the metaphorical wool over my eyes...maybe I wasn't the logical man I'd claimed to be.

"If you like logic so much, you'll appreciate this. Know why people like dogs so much? They always look like they're smiling. It's infectious and everyone around feels better. You should try it sometime. In fact..."

Hands reached into the candyfloss, squishing it down into black ooze and forming tools. Chains. Hooks. And what looked suspiciously close to a piercing gun. I remembered the tiny holes pierced into the corners of Monica's mouth.

"Allow me to help. After all, what kind of Ringmaster would I be if I let a guest leave without a smile on their face?"

14 - RETZ

All I had to do was make it to Sea Mother's head, and I could escape with my life.

That's what I kept telling myself, hard as it was to believe with Ginny barreling down the path behind me. I never looked back, but even if my powers hadn't told me how close she was, her heavy footfalls came so close I almost feared she'd step on me. I wove between carnival tents and bounded over every obstacle I could, but even my piss-poor parkour attempts couldn't put much distance between us. Every barrier I put up got crunched up seconds later, as it turns out a boggart is like a trash compacter with legs and a temper.

"Could you have thought of a distraction that wouldn't grind our bones into paste if she caught up?"

"Ginny would not be so crude, even in such a state!" Nalem hissed. I took this as meaning "I was feeling petty, and I still think I can walk all over anyone I want." I would've let him do the running to make him prove it, but knowing how and why Arcadia fought against him, we couldn't afford to take chances like that.

"Then save your daydreams of revenge for later and get moving!" Nalem pinged with our senses to gauge our surroundings. We'd almost made it to the skull. Ginny was hot on our heels. Monica wasn't, instead heading toward the big top, and the Ringmaster was on his way to the gate. Someone waited for him there. Was that...Jarrod?

No time to wonder what he might be planning, or where the others were. I couldn't wait around for a rescue.

I stumbled into a group of stalls filled with homemade goods and mouth-watering smells tinged with the tang of paint, more county fair than anything else I'd seen so far. I hopped over a pie stall, trying to ignore how the "fruit" squirmed under the crust. Even Ginny made a disgusted noise when she splattered them moments later. Sensing an opportunity, I grabbed a pie from the next one and threw it behind me.

I briefly saw the pure anger in her bloodshot eyes. It dwarfed anything I'd ever felt from Nalem, the huldra rage I'd rarely seen take over Mom or Jarrod, even Farris when he'd met his Faerie existence with a berserk rage. I hope Nalem saw too and realized what he'd done. He hadn't crossed a normal mortal or burned a bridge that had rotted through. If I'd had time, I would've waited for his guilt to pang through my chest, and I would've reveled in it.

But unlike him, I didn't value pettiness over survival. I chucked the pie into her face and struck at least half of it. Fake berries burst like the clown heads and black ooze dribbled down her face. I turned away. Maybe I should've said sorry. Doubt she would've believed me if I had.

I ran past baked goods, vegetables that were suspiciously organ-shaped and fingerling potatoes that looked a tad too literal. I half suspected these pieces were recycled from scraps of bodies that the Ringmaster didn't keep around. If that was the case, maybe fixing the aberrant was a lost cause after all. Welcome to the unfortunate fates club, everybody. I held my breath when running through a barbecue cook-off, and then came a petting zoo that looked like an artist who'd never seen a pig or a cow had been given a vague description and a bucket of cheap paints. With my earlier theory in mind, I didn't dare reach with my powers to see if these painted beasts were empty inside, or if they'd been built on repurposed bones.

Purposefully ignoring my senses is why I didn't notice the minotaurs until they tore through the blue-ribbon quilts and tackled the boggart behind me. How they'd kept quiet all that time, I had no idea, but when their movements broke the painted camouflage that was surely Artemisia's handiwork, they banded together with a rallying war cry.

Someone grabbed my hand, and I felt no bones. I almost pulled away before realizing it was Artemisia. "Follow me," she said, and led me out of the fair. Our escape was followed by a boggart's scream and the thuds of minotaur bodies hitting the ground, but no more footfalls.

"You came to save me?" I asked. "Not that I'm ungrateful, far from it, but–"

"I saw you get kidnapped and couldn't stop it. I figured helping your brother with this was the least I could do," Artemisia said calmly, as if we weren't running full tilt through a madman's carnival. We turned a sharp corner that put the fair and fight out of sight. She continued in a softer voice, "Having heard about the other Faerie on its way...I also wanted to try to talk Aiden out of this madness. See if he'll finally realize he's fallen too deep."

"Once a Fae falls to madness, there's no bringing them back," Nalem chided from the back of my mind. I didn't dare voice his words aloud. *"Those who stay close to humanity may be fine for a time. Farris, for all his faults, has handled his transformation better than any other I've met so*

far. But those who stay in Arcadia without contact from the outside, they detach themselves from humanity and its concerns. Once concepts like morals are lost, they're...difficult to relearn, at best."

"Might explain a couple things about you."

His smirk seared against my mind. *"Careful, little one. The Ringmaster might think you actually have enough of a spine to leave me."*

"Can you stop being an ass for two seconds while I try to save our lives?!"

I was sure he couldn't, but at least he kept any further thoughts to himself. We were close enough to Sea Mother's head that it rose over the tents. It had been propped up against one of those carnival strength tests. Chained to the front of the skull was a teenage girl's body, humanoid except for the hooves and cow hide. But in place of Bertha's head was another one of those damn clown heads, lolling around and rarely blinking. Guess it was enough to keep the rest of the body functioning and alive, so I couldn't control the skull from afar.

We reached Sea Mother's head. The sheer scale of it all, her antiquated majesty, was honestly awe-inspiring...and made Bertha's young and broken body stand out all the more in sickening contrast. I had to get them out and hope there was still some way to fix

Bertha. Sure, I knew what happened to her wasn't my fault and I didn't need to meddle. But wasn't that part of being a good person, like Jarrod always tried to do? Helping others because it's the right thing to do?

Maybe that's what I wanted out of life, regardless of what body I ended up with. To be a better person despite Nalem–hell, maybe even to spite him. Seemed as good a goal as any. But I had to survive first. I put a hand on the skull and reached out with my powers, preparing to move it out of this nightmare carnival.

But the skull wasn't the only thing I felt. On the other side of the carnival, Jarrod had gone limp. The Faerie-static of his curse was stronger than I'd ever felt it, tendrils binding him in place. Someone else I couldn't sense carried him toward the Big Top where Monica had gone, and I doubted it was Farris.

Nalem pulled the tendrils of our senses away, concentrating everything into the skull. It quivered and slowly floated off the ground. *We have to save ourselves. Leave Farris and the others to rescue him.*

I tried to pull away. The skin in my hand split as the bones shot out and melded to the skull. The skull was easily large enough to carry us, and Nalem planned on riding it out like a floating canoe. But I felt the strain it placed on him. Moving something that large in Arcadia took a lot of energy. I stopped resisting once my feet couldn't reach the ground.

"Are you okay up there?" Artemisia called. Her voice struck somewhere between worry and amazement. "Do you need me to cover your escape?"

"I can't leave yet," I called back. "I've got to grab my brother first." I took hold of as much of our powers as I could to get the skull up and over the tents faster, but I didn't plan on heading for the gate. I shifted the skull to point toward the big top.

Nalem tried to wrestle for control over our powers, freezing us in midair. *Imbecile! Use your damn eyes and look at the horizon. Our would-be executioner is almost here.* He forcibly turned my head. Past the gates, brambles surged toward us, uprooting the forest in their wake. They marched toward the carnival gates, making way for the group approaching. Some were human, some not, but all were decorated with the same intertwining green runes that Jarrod had on his limbs and neck. Leading them was a rambling mass of vines and roots covered in softly glowing white roses. It took me a minute to recognize my father, seeing as he no longer wore a human face.

Now I really had to get Jarrod out. Even if we managed to thwart Dad...seeing him this way would break my brother. I had no idea how he'd stayed together this long; sheer willpower, I guess.

"Why must you take my plans in the exact opposite direction as intended?" Nalem tugged the skull toward the path back to our world. *"Move or lose yourself completely, little one."*

"We both know you can't do that here and get this skull out on your own. You need me." I pulled the skull back toward the big top. I sensed Jarrod had been set down. Monica seemed to be reaching for something. Tools to carve out the few features on my brother's body they wanted to keep for his new one, I bet.

The two of us mentally wrestled in the air, Sea Mother's head moving in sharp jerks. Neither of us were strong enough to take full control and move the skull on our own; she was too big, too old, and we had to be careful not to break her. But just as Nalem didn't want any harm to come to his beloved leviathan, I didn't want any harm to come to my brother if I could help it. And unlike Sea Mother, Jarrod was still alive.

I dug deep into that well of stubbornness and good ol' hulderkind anger that I barely ever bothered with, and I pushed it out into my powers. The skull pitched down and shot toward the big top like the world's biggest arrow. We pierced right through the top, paint sludging over us as we tore through safety nets and tightropes on our way down. With our angle of descent, we would rip apart the walls and crash into the green room.

Then something struck the skull hard enough to career us off-course, splattering black ooze. Out of the corner of my eye, I caught a clown climbing into a cannon, in case the first one hadn't finished the job. We smashed through wooden bleachers on our way to the ground. The splinters that dug into my skin felt more plastic than wood. A generic laugh track sounded from clowns and remnant human bodies with plastic parts, likely the old bodies of aberrant, seated on the remaining seats.

The laughter ceased when the Ringmaster emerged from the back room, smile brittle and hands covered with disposable plastic doctor gloves. A few of those hands hefted a body bag. I didn't want to know who it belonged to.

"I've lost so many clowns to your little family. Do you know how sad that makes me? All they ever wanted to do was make you laugh."

I tried scrambling to my feet, but one of the bench beams had fallen across my back and my hands were covered in exploded clown goop. "I'm here to rescue my brother," I shouted. "You let him go, right now."

"I haven't changed his body yet," The Ringmaster said, as if offended by my accusations. "And he willingly offered himself as bait! Turns out it worked on both of us though, didn't it?" Those long arms and numerous fingers reached through the rubble and grabbed me before pushing away the beam. I tried to struggle. Bones pierced through my skin and stabbed him where he touched me. "Don't make me go for your...whatever you've got instead of a heart."

"Bold of you to assume I'm stupid enough to fall for that twice." I'd turn my body into a reverse iron maiden if that's what it took to survive. "Let me walk away with my brother and the skull, and we can all put this behind us. I'll even leave revenge to the aberrant and minotaurs if they want it."

"Wish I could," The Ringmaster said with a sigh, "But you saw how close Alexander is. If I let you leave now, he'll send his goons through the gate and after you. Curse 'em so they either catch up or turn into a literal man-made garden. You know there won't be any peace for either of you, much less survival, if I let you go."

He had a point, and that made me hesitate enough for him to open that bodybag and throw me in, even if I stabbed him like hell on the way in. The bag spurted ooze every time I stabbed it. Couldn't tell if the thick leather was real or fake, but whatever it was made of, I couldn't tear through it. The bag jostled as the Ringmaster moved, carrying us to who knew where. Somewhere he thought he could escape my father, I bet.

I wasn't alone in the bag. There was another body, plastic skin and no heartbeat. The hair almost felt real, like a high-quality wig, and an accidental misplaced hand informed me the body was feminine in design.

"Either the Ringmaster's figured something out about me I haven't considered, or this isn't meant for me."

I expected a sarcastic quip, but Nalem remained silent. He ran a hand through the body's hair and tried to remember someone else's. Memories of the Harvester brushing a young Nalem's hair, remarking how similar it was to his own, flickered through my mind. I remembered Jarrod's question about Nalem's original body after the possession.

"...This is yours, isn't it?"

"I fear it may be. Hard to tell, in the dark. What arrogance, to even attempt my true form; I should destroy the damn thing." But he didn't. He brushed his fingers along the face and down the throat, arms, fingertips. Racking his memory for anything familiar to what he'd missed since he'd last encountered this body. A bubbling mixture of rage and homesickness brewed in my chest. The mere existence of this body when he believed the real thing

was so close at hand infuriated him like nothing else, yet what if this really was as close as he'd ever get?

What did any of that mean? What was Nalem really fighting for?

Should we run together, or go our separate ways?

"We should be safe here," the Ringmaster announced. Light flooded the bag, and I was yanked out and slammed into a plastic seat. Belts snapped around my middle and my wrists. The other body was buckled into place next to me. In the full light, it looked so much like Nalem's sister Loresha, who I'd only ever seen in his memories. They must've been identical twins.

The Ringmaster said, "This'll be a little tricky to do in motion, but we should be safe until the ride is over. Hold on tight…Not that you have much else to do."

The world lurched, and I finally took in my surroundings. Back when I was a kid, a cheap collection of rides always rolled into town at the beginning of summer, and that included the spinning hammer ride. Nothing quite like being trapped in a tiny metal tube rocking back and forth, burning up in the summer heat with the stench of another kid's barf and the ever-present fear of getting stuck upside-down.

"You don't have any better rides to perform body-swapping surgeries in?" I yelped. "What kind of a moron are you?"

"The one about to fix your life! Try not to squirm, alright?" Those hands reached up for my head. I shut my eyes. Even though the idea of losing Nalem forever had its merits, I felt myself mentally reaching for him, as if thoughts of holding him back would keep him in place.

I felt him about to speak, and then...there's no easy way to describe an entire person disappearing from your head. The closest I can get is like a bubble popping, all the thoughts and feelings gone in a flash with nothing to replace them. It was too quiet. No one answered my thoughts except for me, and that allowed them to spiral without stopping. I never realized how quickly they could do that. And I had no idea how to make them stop.

"Oh dear. Retz? Retz my friend, I need you to focus on me, please." It took me a moment to notice the hands on my shoulders, the Ringmaster trying to smile calmly even as his other hands held onto Nalem's new body. "Retz, you're having a panic attack. I know this is a lot, but it isn't new. You've been alone in your own head before, even if you don't remember it. Can you take a deep breath for me?"

"I don't need to breathe," I said even though I did as he asked. It was harder than it should've been. My chest felt too tight. That was part of a panic attack too, right? Was that really the right word for having the person closest to you, for better or worse, ripped away in a matter of seconds? "I don't like this. Put him back."

"Retz–"

"I said put him back!" Now, I know there were plenty of benefits to having an ancient evil who'd ruined my life and others out of my head. But I couldn't remember life without him, and never imagined what it might be like. The Ringmaster had been right; hope had been the farthest thing from my mind, only way I could cope. I'd made keeping Nalem's worst influences at bay, piss poor as I was at doing so, my purpose. Imagine having that ripped away. Too much freedom all at once can be paralyzing.

Oh, I'm aware how unhealthy that all is. Just reporting the state I was in. Why I'd beg for the monster to go back to where I mistakenly thought he belonged.

The Ringmaster must've realized how strong my panic was. He loosened the strap on one of my wrists and moved my hand over to rest on Nalem's. Fingers twitched under my palm. Even if the skin was cold and unmoving, it brought a bit of comfort.

The hammer ride had kept spinning this entire time, flinging us back and forth and upside-down to make a bad experience even worse. So when it lurched to a sudden stop, I thought it was part of the ride. Freaking us out with a sharp break before spinning faster than ever, or some other cruel trick. Thorns piercing through the windows, attached to long vines wrapping around the carriage, changed my mind pretty quick.

The Ringmaster swore. His hands all got to work stretching and squishing orbs of black ooze into humanoid forms. Judging by the way he kept glancing out the window, we didn't have a lot of time left. "Rude of him to outright attack, don't you think? Or is this normal for Faeries? Do you think–"

Nalem cleared his throat and said in a feminine but still deep voice, "You have trapped his nemesis in a body he can easily smite while sparing his family, and the only thing in his way is this tiny metal cylinder. I think he's given up on being patient." Grey eyes blinked open. "Little one, while I appreciate how thoroughly I've ingrained myself into your entire existence, I need you to remain calm so we may both get out of here alive."

Easier said than done, but what choice did I have? I sharpened my wrist bones to break the restraints around my wrists, then tore the belt across my lap. Glad as I was to still have my powers with Nalem gone, they were slower without him, and making weapons out of myself hurt a lot more without him to share the pain with. I bit my lip and turned to free Nalem, whose new body didn't have any bones at all to control.

"I was about to release you, you know." The Ringmaster winced as a sharp tug pulled our carriage down. "If I carry you two to the top of this ride, can you summon that skull again and fly out on it?"

Nalem shook his head. "No, thanks to you. So long as the minotaur girl's body remains attached and theoretically alive, my powers are useless." He shot me a look since I'd refused to remove Bertha's body and hadn't fled when Nalem wanted. To my surprise, his gaze then softened. "I also could not move it alone, even if I wanted. You retained half my power. But I fear that for both of us to survive, we must briefly part ways."

"Because Alexander doesn't know about this body of yours," The Ringmaster said, reading and responding to his thoughts the way I no longer could. "If we cover your escape, pretend like you're still in Retz's head, he can't kill you. I'll just need to keep Retz alive."

"And find some way to return him to the mortal world immediately," Nalem concluded. The carriage jerked once more. "Retz, I know this sounds like a perfect time to betray you, but I well and truly require your trust if we are to reunite. For if we do not...you recall what will happen, I'm sure."

Right. I had already died once, and Nalem's presence was what brought me back. If he was gone... "I'll die again, won't I?" And if I died in Arcadia, I'd become a Fae, like Farris and the Ringmaster. And like my father.

Nalem nodded. "I do not wish to lose such a valuable vessel in such a crude manner. So...keep up the charade for now and know I will return."

We didn't have time to argue, as the vines were toppling the ride. The Ringmaster quickly crafted a cover to drape over Nalem, hiding him from sight until we'd departed. Then he threw open a hatch in the top of the carriage, pulling me out while scrambling along it like some humanoid spider. He paused before climbing down, and that smile of his fell into heartbreak. His world of joy and merriment was being covered up by my father-turned-monster's handiwork.

I'd seen Dad's realm once before, a forest of thorns and glowing roses. He'd brought the whole place with him, and those brambles invaded before he'd even reached the gates. They wrapped around every tent and sprouted, white petals flecked with rainbow splotches, and they spread along the gates and up, trying to blot out the sky. Roots dug deep into the cotton candy earth, and while they didn't uproot anything, they were poised to take this whole place apart and turn it from carnival to garden show.

The vines forced the front gates open, and in marched Alexander's cursed captives. I recognized plenty of them, since he'd "rescued" them from Lady Delight's gilded menagerie, but even those I hadn't seen before were familiar. They all wore the same cursed marks forcing them into obedience, with the same static staining their bones. And they all wore the same serious, downtrodden look I saw Jarrod wear so often.

Dad didn't. Dad didn't have a face anymore, and he didn't move like a human. I could only tell the roiling mass of thorns was him because when he stood, his upper half vaguely resembled a man, wooden ribcage and vines interwoven in a vague homage to muscles. Oh, and one branch on his head stuck out the way his nose did. In lieu of eyes, he had wilted roses, and I realized the rest of his body was covered in snapped twigs and chipped wood. Dad was falling apart.

"What kind of monster can tear beings like us into pieces?" The Ringmaster whispered. He must have realized godlike powers didn't mean he was immortal himself. I shrugged because I had no idea how to answer. Even if iron was a weakness, we'd never fought a Faerie before. I realized more and more I had no idea what Dad had been up to these past few years, especially since his untimely, unnatural demise.

The Ringmaster sighed, chest deflating like a plastic balloon. "Alright. Give yourself a moment, then chin up, my friend. The show must go on and all, right?" That damn smile carved itself into his face and his eyes lit up like a toy. I'm surprised there wasn't an on switch between all those arms. He put a hand on my back and pushed my posture straight. I didn't dare smile. What did I have to be happy about? I was back on death row again thanks to this idiot Ringmaster, my father, fucking everyone who'd brought me into this mess.

I should've been happy; it was my goddamn birthday tomorrow. The day I could finally say I'd made it two whole decades on this earth despite the odds.

"I'm so sorry about this," The Ringmaster said. "I truly thought I could save you both. Maybe I still can."

Dad waited at the gates. The Ringmaster marched us forward. He had the gall to sing "Happy Birthday" under his breath, and I wasn't sure if I should be touched or pissed.

15 - JARROD

It wasn't the first time this year I'd been strapped to an operating table against my will. Last time, I'd lost a toe. This time, I risked losing my whole body.

As Bertha had explained, the Ringmaster's operating supplies were set up in a room reminiscent of a theater green room. But mixed in with the carnival posters were sketches and notes about the new bodies for all the Ringmaster's "special guests". The wall I was forced to stare at, being unable to move thanks to my curse, had been plastered with bodies and faces that supposedly belonged to me. I hated all of them.

"Don't you worry," The Ringmaster said through Monica as she bustled around the room. "I've got your brother safe, and we're going to get him fixed up lickety-split. In the meantime, what eye color would you like? I could make them green like your brother's. Or maybe brown? I think you'd look great with brown eyes. Anything less gray and murky."

I couldn't speak, as moving my mouth violated the order to "hold still", but I growled to voice my opinion. Not that I could move my mouth much anyway. The Ringmaster's key to a forced smile were piercings, two for the corners of my lips and two pierced into my skull right behind my ears, with a chain connecting them to force my lips into a grin. My muscles hurt, my gums had gone dry, and the Ringmaster's pseudo-logic about smiles failed to make me any happier.

Monica held a pair of forceps to the light. "You're not exactly letting yourself be happy. You're still too hung up on what's going on right now, instead of the future. Your whole life is about to change! Your family can be together again without Nalem in the way. And you can finally be the man you always dreamed about! Instead of forcing your flesh into something it's not, we'll sculpt the perfect you. The way *you* want it, I might add."

I stared at the papers. Some looked like action figures rather than reflections. Others looked suspiciously close to family photos of Gallows I'd never met. Most of those had notes written by my father's hand. Keep the nose and eyes. Fix the jawline. Remove the tail. Erase this scar where Alexander had accidentally stabbed me during a job and never forgave himself. When I looked at those sketches, I saw no trace of my mother. I used to chide myself for the features

that came from her, but seeing them missing left a
hollow feeling in my chest.

Something out of view clattered. Monica clicked her
tongue. "Still getting used to those legs, my friend? I
suppose it's quite a change from slithering around
everywhere. But hey, we always get up when we fall,
now don't we? Let me help you." A resounding smack
followed this, and a hiss that didn't work quite so well
with a human mouth.

So Zalin ended up in a plastic body after all. I
wondered if she'd turned in her ticket, or if like with
Retz, the Ringmaster simply decided he was out of time.
Had she really wanted to be more like her human side—
like I'd thought I'd wanted? I had my doubts. For all his
claims of kindness, the Ringmaster seemed confident
he knew best when it came to making people happy,
regardless of anyone else's opinion.

And my opinion was that I'd made peace with myself.
Sure, I wouldn't say no to free top surgery if that was all
he'd offered, but I'd left the rest of my loathing behind. I
wasn't going to lose the body I'd fought so hard for
because someone else thought it wasn't enough.

How was I going to get out of this? If I disobeyed an
order, how long until my feet turned into roots and my
fingers into leaves? Or would the soft parts go first, eyes

into flowers like Alexander's? Maybe I'd have time. Maybe Farris would figure out how to break curses before Alexander and the Ringmaster got to me. But if all I had was one action, one shot, timing would be crucial.

Monica walked back into view, plastic skin seemingly unmarred from Zalin striking her. Her smile looked as wide as mine felt. "If we're going to get any work done, it's time I got started. Then if you want, you can get as much revenge as you'd like on me."

"As if doing so would get my body back once you've ripped me out," I thought at the Ringmaster. *"Don't touch me, and don't touch my brother."*

"Why are you two so adverse to help? I know you've suffered without hope for a long time, but please understand. I only want what's best for you." Monica's hand hovered over the selection of tools, but she didn't grab anything. "I will try to preserve as much of your body as I can. Then I'll move you to your new body, once it has some familiar parts. Most people find moving to a purely plastic body...disorienting." Still no movement. The smile drew tighter. "It may sting a little. Would you like to be unconscious for this?"

Out of my view, Zalin snapped "Stop asking him questions he can't answer. You can snag the answers from his brain, but if you're playing goody two-shoes about this, you're going about it the wrong way." Ironic for her of all people to lecture about a captive's rights. Except...she knew the curse I worked under. Maybe she'd been ordered to keep still and silent too.

"You've got a point," Monica said. "Jarrod, if I give you permission, can you speak again?"

My cursed scarf of leaves loosened ever so slightly. I drew in a deep breath. "Seems that way. And no, I don't want to be unconscious. Though I doubt that matters, seeing as I never asked for any of this."

"Neither did I." The smile slipped. Monica pulled her hand away from the tools. "Shit. Where am I...?"

"You're back at the carnival," I said. If the Ringmaster's hold on her was slipping, it might mean he was otherwise distracted. Hopefully by Retz making an escape. "Monica, do you remember this place? What happened to you here?"

"I don't want to." She slowly walked over to me and tried to help me sit up. I fell against her, limp. She flinched, seemingly torn between backing away and keeping me upright.

Zalin huffed in irritation and strode over, wobbling on plastic legs that clacked when she walked. She braced herself on the edge of the operating table. "Ringmaster told him he couldn't move. From what I've experienced, the only person who can undo an order is the one who gave it. But since you're so constantly possessed by him...want to tell this man to walk again?"

Monica seemed confused but had enough wits about her to recognize that there wasn't time to get the full story. "Will he hurt me?" Monica asked.

"I won't," I said. "You can order me to if you don't believe me. But if anything, I'd like to save you. Help you reunite with your other half."

Monica winced. "The Ringmaster?"

"No. The other half of your...soul, I think. Most of your memories got stuck in one of those fake bodies. Calls herself Artemisia, and she came here to help us. If you do too..." Maybe I could convince the Ringmaster to right his original mistake instead of trying to make up for it by "fixing" others. Or maybe the Harvester could help. There had to be some way to keep her from being broken forever.

Monica looked down at me, beads of black ooze bubbling at the corners of her eyes. "Okay. Please, take me to her."

Not quite a free pass, and Zalin swore under her breath like she knew it too, but it was enough. My curse loosened around my neck. My entire body filled with static fuzz as I moved off the table, that sensation of one's foot falling asleep but spread across my entire

being. I stumbled, but I caught myself on the wall. My
fingers dug into notes covered with my name but not
my face.

I asked, my voice low, "Before we go, mind if I do a
little redecorating?"

Zalin elbowed Monica in the side. "I'd let him have
some catharsis. Hey, those piercings..."

Right, first order of business. I should've taken the
time to remove them, but I didn't have the patience to
smile a second longer, and my huldra healing would
keep them from leaving lasting scars. I tore them out
and crunched the chains in my hands. The metal dug
into my skin, and blood flowed into my mouth as the
wounds knit shut. I spat red onto the papers. Then I tore
them to shreds, removing every last real and fake trace
of me. I looked at the operating table. Just past my head
was, well, a newer head for me. It was all sharp eyes and
harsh angles, though of course a smile was built in, and
the nasal cavity was bare for where my real nose
would've gone. I broke it. If nothing else, it felt
satisfyingly close to punching in an actual skull, even if
it bled black onto my knuckles.

I'm sure I would've found plenty more to break, but a
shrieking honk cut through the red haze filling my
thoughts. One of the gate clowns cheered, "Hey buddy

ol' pal! Your visitor is on his way and almost here! By golly, you sure are popular today. And look at that new smile too, wowee!"

I smiled back, teeth stained red. Even Zalin recoiled at the sight of that. "Thanks for the heads up. I feel...great. Say, can you find where people in this carnival are?"

"I can check with my fun-loving friends! Who're you looking for?"

I put up two fingers. "One is a woman who goes by Artemisia. Painted lady, made of canvas. The other is my brother, Retz Gallows."

"Sure thing! Lemme just call over the ol' honkercom." The clown waddled out, threw its head back far enough to almost knock it over, and emitted an ear-splitting honk. A cacophonous chorus answered back.

"I can't believe you're able to work with those...freaks. I don't think even Lady Delight would've let 'em into the menagerie." Zalin looked me over, her mouth twisted into more of a natural sneer than a smile. She stood unsteady on human legs, no traces of scales on her.

"Are you..." Okay wasn't the right word. And even if she'd been an enemy, she didn't deserve to lose part of her identity.

"I dunno. But I've done a lot of thinking while trapped here," Zalin muttered. "About how I ended up in

this mess. Why I slithered into it in the first place.
I...decided maybe I need a fresh start. And I...dammit,
I'm not spilling my guts to you. Look, you're up again.
Let's call this even, and you don't–wait, no, that's almost
an order." She hissed a breath through her teeth. "I don't
want your help anymore. You've already saved my life.
I'll handle the rest from here. Got it?"

I nodded. "Then you're free to go. I've got to help
Monica here, and then find my brother. But if you
follow the path outside..."

"And miss the chance to beat up the Ringmaster and
your old man? Hell no."

The clown toddled back into the green room.
"Alrighty boys, girls, and tilt-a-whirls! Artemisia is with
some pals, and they're a ways away but heading over
fast as they can. And your baby brother is taking a ride
on The Hammer with the Ringmaster himself! Though
it looks like the ride's stopping a little early, which is too
bad, don't you think?"

I ran to the clown and looked outside. The carnival
rides were being pulled down by brambles, including
the aforementioned Hammer. The Big Top also had
brambles surrounding it, though something else had
torn through the painted canvas up top; I'd heard

whatever it was nearly crash into the green room, and that's what had distracted the Ringmaster.

On one hand, I needed to rescue Retz before Alexander tried to fell Nalem. On the other hand, I'd promised Farris I wouldn't let my rage make me reckless. If Artemisia was with others, they were likely the minotaurs and Farris. Regrouping would be smart and let me reunite Monica and Artemisia. I asked the clown, "If it's not too much trouble, can you help lead us to Artemisia and our friends?"

"Boy golly, I'd love to help! Just call me your personal tour guide!"

Zalin, who'd been leaning on Monica to stand steady, pulled away. "Tours aren't really my speed. But I'm feeling nice, so I'm gonna' do you one last favor. Then we're settled for real." She gestured to the brambles and said, "Your old man's work is tough, but it can't stand up to my scales. I'll clear a path for you all to move. Just save me a slice of the ass-kicking once it starts."

Red and black scales broke apart the perfect plastic skin, legs melding into a tail. Maybe the Ringmaster hadn't known how to change a lamia's true form, or maybe he had enough sympathy not to take all of Zalin's monstrous side away, but I felt oddly relieved to see that part of her original body remained. She wasn't as large a lamia as her old mistress had been, but she was large enough to constrict a minotaur, and the fangs in both heads looked sharp enough to tear through any vines that got in her way.

Without another word, she barreled into the spreading brambles. She couldn't clear them all, but we had a path forward. I grabbed Monica's hand to keep her close. "Alright, let's get going. Think you can give me a warning if the Ringmaster's about to return?"

"I...don't get much warning myself, but I'll try." She held my hand tight. "I'm sorry about all this."

"You can't help becoming a pawn in someone else's schemes if you don't know better." Maybe if I told someone else that, I'd believe it too.

Movement was slow at first, the clown tripping over roots creeping through the candyfloss. I picked up the damn thing and set it on my shoulders, and it rested its bulbous, greasy head on mine in order to keep steady. It cheered directions as Monica and I ran through the maze of tents and whatever vines evaded Zalin's path of destruction. As the tents around us fell apart, I realized how many of them were empty. So much of this was an illusion, a facade meant to comfort when all it did was unsettle.

"I remember a place like this," Monica said, voice raised to be heard over all the crashing. "That's when everything changed, and I started seeing all the monsters. I thought I'd gone insane!"

I asked, "Do you remember what happened to the Ringmaster? What you did for him?"

"Sometimes. Hard to forget someone else being in your head, much as I wanted to." Her face pinched together in thought. "He said we were friends. That's why we kept...helping each other. He'd remind me of some things I'd forgotten if I didn't have my notes around. All he asked me in return was to talk to people. Don't remember most of those conversations though."

I didn't have the heart to tell her they'd all been offered tickets by the Ringmaster, had ended up here and were removed from their bodies like she'd mostly been. I think it might've broken her. Or maybe I was forcing myself in her shoes, imagining what wrongs I'd unknowingly committed in Alexander's name. I didn't know how I'd cope once this whole job was done. Good as a drinking binge sounded, for once I didn't think it'd help.

Before I could spiral too deep into my thoughts, the clown erupted with a shrill honk and yanked my hair backwards. I stumbled back, narrowly dodging a leathery red fist. Out of the wreckage came a towering figure, all muscle and wrath the way I'd feared

becoming in my huldra rages. I noticed vivid green hair
that had until recently been a beehive hairdo.

"You two, out of the way." I put the clown next to
Monica before placing myself between them and the
boggart. "Ginny! We're not your enemy. We've got the
same goal here."

"We do not!" She bellowed. "I want that bastard's
head."

I put up my hands in a vain attempt to placate
her. "This carnival is full of bastards. I need you to be
more specific."

She snarled, with more hatred than I'd ever heard,
"Nalem."

Of course the idiot had made one of his staunchest
allies want to kill him.

"Is he the reason you're a boggart?" I asked. She
snarled. "Listen, I...feel just as you do most of the time.
And I'm sure we can find time later for you to enact
some sort of revenge, but right now–"

"You don't know what I've done for him!" The
boggart bellowed. "The years I've toiled. Lives I've taken.
Schemes carried out on his behalf! Yet he throws me
aside and risks damning the world with his own
selfishness." She dug her fingers through the candyfloss
and earth underneath, unaffected by the thorns biting

into her skin. "Maybe he deserves to fail. For the world to burn because he forgot his place."

"I'm afraid I don't know what you mean," I admitted. Sure, I'd heard Nalem's speech right before Farris died, claiming he'd take over his father's place and return the world to an age where humans feared monsters again. But this sounded different.

Ginny lowered her head, slowly so as not to trigger my keyed-up reflexes, until we were face-to-face. "You're telling me you made a pact to protect him, and you don't know why he needs protecting?" Her breath was strong, reeking of blood and an entire bar's worth of booze. "The only reason freakshows like this haven't crept into our world is because his soul repels Arcadia itself. And the only way he'll get what he wants is to give that up and condemn us all."

So if Nalem died...if Alexander had his way, Arcadia would seep into our world? Then Alexander could go where he pleased. Order whoever he wanted around. Even if he hadn't already lost his morals, such power would corrupt anyone.

"Even more reason to get Nalem out of here, before my father shows up to murder him," I said, attempting to reason with Ginny. I didn't know if a boggart could be soothed back into boggan form, but even if she'd betrayed us, she'd thought she was doing the right thing. I had to try to do the same.

"Sure you don't want that, you fae-cursed boy? After all, you're the one who led your father here. My plan to save Nalem was perfect, until your old man showed up and saw an opportunity."

"I didn't know."

Ginny heaved a sigh and pulled back a fist. "Children like you never do."

It took both hands to catch the first fist, and then she threw another. I shoved her back, ducked low to avoid her punches, and closed in for a strike. She was faster than her size suggested, and nearly slammed a fist down on my back. I shut out the rest of the carnival, the encroaching thorns, any fears I had about what might happen. I kicked the back of one knee and tripped her up. Then I tackled her with all my strength and knocked her down. She grinned with bared teeth. I matched her and swung again.

I spent so much time dampening the temper of my huldra half that sometimes, I forgot humans got fed up facing hurt after hurt too. Wanting to fight back after being knocked down is natural. I'd been holding back to prove to everyone else I was in control, that I knew what I wanted out of life. But didn't shutting down and keeping quiet hurt just as bad? It did. And I wasn't going to take one more punch, one more threat to my world, with my eyes shut.

I was going to tear down this carnival and everyone in it, or die kicking and screaming. Starting with the fool who'd kicked off this whole debacle with the stolen leviathan head.

I won't give a blow-by-blow of the fight. Whole thing's a blur, as all good fights are once bloodlust dies down. I swung and dodged on instinct, having never trained to fight at close range. Always been too scared I'd be too effective, as if I could be worse than a gun. What mattered isn't what I knew, but that I never stayed down. We tussled on the ground. Swapped bruises the way I'd been too scared to do with my brother back at the bar. Ginny had centuries of experience. I was pissed off enough that it didn't matter. I pulled her back to her feet, or maybe she tossed me up and I nailed the landing, doesn't matter.

I never noticed much in my surroundings when in the throes of a huldra rage. I retained enough control to make sure I didn't hurt Monica in the crossfire. Still took me far longer than necessary to realize she was trying to get my attention. Her and the clown were pointing...down at the corner of a tent? I looked, risking a punch to the jaw, disappointed to find they weren't pointing out a tent stake to stab my foe with before reminding myself I didn't want to kill Ginny, not here at least.

Wait. They were pointing at the long, looming shadows. My drunken, battle-addled brain made the connection. I dodged Ginny's blows until my back was to the tent, and when she swung, I grabbed her fist and used her inertia to throw her over my shoulder. Took most of my strength to do it, but she crashed into the shadows as expected.

Then there was Farris, leaping from the tent to land on the shadow. The ground gave way, and the two figures sank into the dark. Farris winked and shouted, "Thanks babe!" before falling out of view.

My fingers twitched. My breathing refused to slow down. There was nothing in front of me to fight. But after keeping so much shit bottled up the past few days, I couldn't just shove it back in and proceed like everything was okay.

I punched the tent. Paint pooled over my knuckles, cold greasy sludge. That brought a bit of clarity back. I realized I'd been grinning like the aberrant and clowns the entire fight. I forced a grimace and turned to Monica.

She was rooted to the spot, pink fingernails digging into the squirming clown she clutched for dear life.

It almost hurt to unclench my hands. "I'm okay now," I lied.

"No, you're not," Monica said, but with a lilt that indicated that this was the Ringmaster speaking. "And I'm so, so sorry I helped push you to this."

"Are you really? Or are you finally realizing why it's safer for us monsters to stay in the dark?" To think, he'd been so excited. Looked at me like a curiosity, someone to pity. Not realizing that I could've crushed him at any point if I'd bothered to get out of my own damn way.

Monica, and the Ringmaster through her, took a ragged breath. Held their ground, though. Impressive. "You're not a monster. It's...normal to be upset, sometimes. No matter how hard you try to smile."

"Damn straight." I took a step forward. I didn't plan on hurting Monica, but I wanted the Ringmaster to feel my intent. How I'd snap every one of his arms if anything happened to my brother. Or just if I saw his stupid face. Maybe I'd return those chains and piercings, let him try them on for size.

Monica clutched the clown tighter; it emitted a strained honk. The Ringmaster said, "He's...unharmed, for the time being. But we're heading toward Alexander, no choice in the matter, and I have no idea how he's going to react. If you're going to stage a daring rescue and retreat, now's the time."

"I know how my father hunts," I growled. "I'm not going to be prey." After all, he'd lead me astray, hadn't he? We'd turned away from our real goal a long time ago. Why else would he curse me to follow any damn order? It hadn't been a mistake. It was all he'd ever wanted. He'd taken me under his wing so he could tame me. He wanted Nalem gone so maybe Retz could finally fake being a normal human like Mom did. And it's why he kept cursing others to follow his command or give parts of themselves up to defy him.

He was at the gate. And if I had to take the bastard down myself, wouldn't that be fitting? Didn't I deserve it, after all these years?

"Jarrod." Farris was right behind me. Smart to say my name first. "I know you're pissed. You've been through a lot. But right now—"

I snapped, "Don't tell me to calm down. I won't run from this."

"You don't have to." Slowly, Farris wrapped his arms around my shoulders and leaned in, resting his cheek against mine. His skin was so damn cold. "You're not alone, and not the only one he's hurt. So let's be smart for once in our lives, yeah? Team up with the others.

Maybe see if we can borrow that sick iron sword the
minotaurs have. But just because your dad ruined your
life, doesn't mean you have to give it up in order to get
back at him."

"Living is a far better revenge," The Ringmaster
chirped.

"Oh, fuck right the hell off." I grabbed a multitool
from my pocket and chucked it without thinking, didn't
even bother to open a blade first. It struck the clown and
bounced off its head. Monica backed away; must be her
in control again. I sighed. "I'm...I was aiming for the guy
controlling you."

"Sorry I wasn't able to warn you," she answered
quickly.

We had a moment of quiet. It wasn't long in the
grand scheme of things, but among the cacophony, it
seemed to stretch on forever. I counted time with the
heartbeats missing from Farris's chest. My fire fizzled
against his calm and undead cold.

"I don't know if I can fight him without my anger," I
finally whispered into Farris's arms. "I'm afraid I'll
freeze up. Bow my head to him like I've always done."

"You won't, 'cause you see the game he's playing now.
And because we're here to back you up." Farris squeezed
me tighter. "I love you, and even if everyone else leaves,
I'm here for you."

I almost said "I love you" back. But then someone started clapping.

"Even I find it touching, how you two keep each other from degrading into savage beasts. Clinging to your humanity when you're both anything but. Much as you'd refuse to believe me, we are alike in that way, you and I."

The deep, feminine voice itself was unfamiliar, but I knew only one immortal asshole who spoke like that. I turned and saw a face I'd only seen in Sea Mother's memories, but older. Deep brown skin, bountiful black curls, and eyes the color of a stormy sea. This, then, was Nalem's true form. Or the Ringmaster's facsimile of it, I suppose.

But when I looked at Farris, there wasn't just recognition in his eyes. There was an epiphany.

He asked with a tremble in his voice, "Sis...?" And in his hand, something began to glow.

16 - RETZ

Growing up, I didn't hate my father. I'm not sure if I could even say I hate him now, even with all that's happened. I'm almost sorry for what he went through before he lost himself and gave up on the rest of us. I hope that hadn't happened until after his death, that Nalem was right and it was becoming a Fae that poisoned his thoughts. That he never really hated us for not being human enough. That he hadn't given up on me before the night he pulled a gun on me.

Whatever he'd thought of me back then, he still tried. He did his best to teach me that twisting the bones of the schoolyard bullies was not an acceptable solution, and that I couldn't clean my room by hiding all the clutter inside my empty chest for a few hours. He even tried to reason with Nalem, back before we knew the full extent of what he was. I remember them once getting into a deep discussion about riddles that could confuse a Sphinx, and they almost seemed like they could be friends. Or at least not kill each other.

The Ringmaster and I were almost at the gates. Dad
loomed tall and watched us with the empty eyes in his
missing face. I tried to remember what those eyes
looked like, the ones that supposedly looked like mine.
Tried to trick myself into seeing kindness in them again.

I thought about when I was a kid. See, I ran away a
couple of times back then. Sometimes at Nalem's
behest, when he ignored being stuck in the body of a
child so he could work on his schemes. More often, I ran
out of guilt. I'd gotten kicked out of school again. I'd
fused Jarrod's teeth shut and locked him in a closet,
where he wasn't found until hours later with tears long
dried on his face. I'd forgotten that good and Nalem
could never be one and the same, and I'd given in
and *listened* to the damn voice inside my head. Dad
always found me before I got too far away.

One time when I was eight and sort of wanted to be
found, I'd walked along an abandoned road instead of
tromping through the woods. It had been dusk and
raining, late Autumn, and my flashlight had died. I'd
kept walking until a light blared behind me, followed by
the sound of a door slamming. Rain slicked back Dad's
hair, back when the early grays were creeping in at his
temples, and rivulets of red trailed down his left hand.
He'd lost his glasses, meaning he was practically

running blind. But run he did, until he'd reached my side.

"You're out late," he'd told me.

"You're wet and bleeding," I'd retorted. "School nurse says you'll get new-money-a from that."

"Pneumonia. I've dealt with worse." He'd crouched in front of me and hid his bleeding hand in one pocket. "What brings you out here? You hate the cold."

I did, which was why I'd worn two sweaters that day, but the rain still seeped through my clothes. "I was a bad monster again," I told him. I made a concentrated effort to stare at my shoes instead of Dad. "I broke someone's hands. I *forever* broke them. I fixed the bones, but they still wouldn't work!" At that point, I was too young to know much about the intricacies of muscles and nerves.

Dad sighed through his nose. "Did he make Nalem angry, or you?"

I'd shyly admitted, "Me. He kept hitting me during dodgeball. And then he took my sandwich! It was ham and cheese, too. My most favorite."

"But did you hurt him on purpose?" Dad asked, with a patience no other guy would have upon learning that his son crippled someone over sports and a stolen sandwich. When I shook my head, he continued, "We all get angry sometimes, Retz. And when that happens, we sometimes make mistakes we later regret. We have to learn not to let our anger get the best of us—and when we do, how to make things right."

Dad had been good about stuff like that. He later figured out a healing potion for the kid, which we brought to his hospital room with my attempt at a get-well card. And then he started teaching me about anatomy beyond the bones, so I wouldn't accidentally rupture anything on another kid. Maybe that was a test, in a way. Because once I'd learned, if I ever hurt anyone that bad again, he'd know if I'd done it on purpose.

Back then, by the time Dad finished consoling me, it had been so wet my feet squelched in my shoes, and the streetlights replaced the sun. Dad walked me toward his old Chevy Impala, the white paintjob splattered with red like he'd been. I later learned he'd been crushing kobolds before hearing I'd gone missing.

"Tell you what. After we find a way to heal your classmate, would you like to help me fix the Impala?" Dad gestured to one of the headlights, smashed by a particularly resilient kobold's head.

"Could I really help?" I'd asked, because Dad had never asked for my help with anything before. Fixing wasn't exactly my forte.

Dad said, "You're the only one who can help." Mom didn't like to work on cars, and Jarrod had a lot of homework to do.

I agreed, of course. Dad trusting me with something? Needing my help? That made me feel a lot less horrible about life. He'd held the passenger door open for me, and we drove home to dry off and let everyone know we were okay. Mom and Jarrod were glad to see us. They even hugged me. Dad, of course, didn't.

Because here's the thing; Dad never touched me. No hugs, no holding my hand to lead me back to the car. Not even a handshake. Even at my best, when I was as good as I could possibly be, Dad didn't trust me. He knew I could tear him apart in an instant, and with Nalem around, it didn't even have to be my choice. I was the one monster he couldn't shoot and be done with, because I was his son. And what kind of father pulls a gun on his son?

Dad finally did, years later, though he didn't shoot. That story's been told before. And I had to wonder, once I reached the gate, if he would've considered doing it again if those root-claws of his were able to pull a trigger.

"You didn't run," Dad said. No hi, how are you, how much are you fearing for your life right now, I'm fine thank you.

I answered, "Too busy trying to save others. Rescuing Jarrod from the curse you stuck in him. Getting that leviathan skull out so a poltergeist doesn't level the town. You know, playing the hero life. What've you been up to? Building an army, I see?" I kept my face firm, the way Jarrod always managed to. I refused to show Dad the fear he wanted from me.

"You could say I've also been busy with the business of saviors." His voice rumbled and rasped when he spoke, like he was speaking through the hollowed-out trunk of an old tree. "The question of the day, Retz, is if you deserve to be saved."

I tried not to think about the Dad who led me out of the woods, who handed me a wrench so we could work together, taught me about cars and veins and what it meant to make up for one's mistakes. The Ringmaster suppressed a shudder next to me, but I couldn't tell if it was in response to my thoughts or Dad's statement.

I put my hands up. If Nalem had a plan, I'd stall until he could pull it off. "I'll have you know, I haven't ended a single life recently. Unless those clowns were really alive. Or uhmm, I squished a spider that crawled out of the shower drain the other morning. Guess that's...maybe sorta' bad. And as I said, I've been helping people." Trying to, at least. Not that I'd gotten Bertha or any of the aberrant their bodies back, not that I actually got to Jarrod or fixed Sea Mother, or managed anything beyond running from the truth. But wasn't I trying to make up for all the wrong I did, like he taught me?

Dad made a sound somewhere between a sigh, a groan, and the rough breeze that stirs the empty branches that moment you realize you've gone just too far off the path in the woods. "That is good to hear. But I have seen how Nalem's corruption grows. His plans of domination have spread since he was last in Arcadia. And his influence is not only corrupting you, but your brother as well."

I wanted to argue otherwise, that Jarrod breaking out of his hero worship was no fault of ours, but I bit my tongue.

Dad continued, "Even if Nalem is removed from the equation, how can I be sure you will not follow in his stead? That you will be…"

"Normal? Dad, you know that's the one thing I'll never be. But I've made it almost twenty years this way, and considering the circumstances? I think I turned out okay." I tried to shut out the crashing and honking, the failing calliope playing on, from the carnival at my back. "You remember what tomorrow is, right?"

"Autumnal Equinox. Mabon. The start of the season of death and decay. And, coincidentally, your birthday."

To my surprise, Dad reached out and tapped a claw to my forehead. "Nineteen years longer than you would've had, if not for my failures. But we cannot dwell on the past. We must play the cards we're dealt. I want to know how you intend to play yours, once Nalem is gone."

The Ringmaster side-eyed me at this. He knew as well as I did that I had no idea. That Nalem *was* gone, and I'd begged for him to be put back in. I didn't know how to live without holding back a scheming, malicious evil at all times. And no matter how human I looked, I'd always been poor at acting like it.

"I mean, there's a world of possibilities, you know? I think I...maybe I'd travel. I've had fun doing that with Jarrod and Farris. I could see the world without stopping Nalem from running rampant through it. Find a place to settle down and cut hair. Finally adopt a cat. Stupidly mundane shit like that. But first, I'd go home to Mom. You could too, you know. Mom misses you. Even if you can't come into our world, maybe we could..."

Dad's claw lowered to my lips, shushing me. "I could not go back, even if it were physically possible. I have too much to do."

Time to tread carefully. Much as I'd love to call him out on his bullshit, doing so might earn me a ticket to the chopping block. "I thought your one goal was to stop

Nalem, and then you'd come home. That's what you and
Jarrod always said."

That made Dad falter. And dammit, I should've taken
advantage of that to run, either out of the carnival like a
damn coward or in to reunite with the others, help
Nalem get that skull out, something. But part of me
wanted to believe in Dad the way Jarrod always had.
That the real Dad, the one who'd brought his wayward
child home so many times instead of leaving me for
dead, was still somewhere under the roots of lost
purpose. Guess I get sentimental without Nalem to call
me a fool for it.

"I'd originally thought my condition a fate worse
than death," Dad finally said. Did I imagine it, or was
there a bit of that paternal softness back in his voice,
like when he'd explained things to me as a kid? "I
seemed no better than the monsters I used to fight. But
once I realized the power my words held...I could make
the wicked change their ways, with the right order. Hold
someone to a promise. Ensure someone carries on my
work once I became unable. If I could make the world
better with my newfound power, wouldn't it be
irresponsible to cast the opportunity aside?"

"That's it exactly!" The Ringmaster said, his sickening
grin back on his face. So that's why they got along,
thinking they were the only ones with the power to

reshape the world. But if you give that power to just one person, they only see their own rights and wrongs. They don't see how they ruin the lives of others in pursuit of their own noble goal.

I thought about what Ginny said about immortals like Nalem. How they'd stagnate in their own thoughts if left alone. The fact that Nalem was chasing after ghosts and bodies and curses all thousands of years old. With all that, she should've seen how putting Nalem in a body of his own was a terrible idea.

"Would getting rid of me really make the world that much of a better place? Even if Nalem was out of the picture?"

"That's the question, isn't it?" Dad asked. "Depends on many factors. Such as if you retain some of his power if he perished, how much of his plans you know and agree with...and how long you intend to keep up this charade. Nalem has already escaped from your head, hasn't he?"

I tried to mimic Nalem's posture, stretching myself out and leaning uncomfortably far back. "Do not turn your wishes into presumptions, you fool. I simply found your speeches too mundane. Uninspired, even." Hey, I thought I nailed it pretty well.

Dad shook his head. "You can mimic his mannerisms well enough, but not his arrogance. But you lying to me is no surprise. I'm sure it comes easier than breathing. But Ringmaster...I thought we were allies. Or did you simply wish to use my powers?"

The Ringmaster stepped back and waved several hands. "We're allies and more, my friend! But I stand by my word that I won't abide any more death in this place. If murder's the game you're here to play, you'll have to take it elsewhere."

"Fine then. I shall." And without warning, the root-claw Dad had tapped against my forehead pierced through one end of my skull and out the other. I screamed, because even if the blow didn't kill me the way it would normal folks, getting impaled still stings. Then Dad lifted me up. A body with no muscles or interior organs is super light, after all, and he was made of sturdy wood no matter how brittle he looked.

Dad continued, "If Nalem is truly gone, you'll soon die without his influence. Seeing as you've lived nineteen years past your initial death...perhaps it would be a blessing to let this one stick. I am certain your soul will fare better in the next life, one without monsters like Nalem or the rest of this family."

He turned his head toward the Ringmaster and the carnival falling apart behind him. "I will handle my son, as is my right as his father. When I return, it will be time for Nalem's reckoning. If you do not wish for him to die here, leave him at the gate. I will take him elsewhere."

Dad turned back toward the trail, lifting me high enough that I couldn't touch the ground. As he moved, a hand gripped my ankle.

"I'm bound to fix those that seek my help," The Ringmaster said, still smiling with grit teeth, "And this lad clearly needs it, whether or not he's given me a ticket. Yes, his head's messed up, but Nalem's not the only one to blame. Do you have any idea what you've done to these boys?"

Dad froze. I wondered how long it had been since someone outside his family had called him out. "If the death of one would drastically improve the world, would you still stand against it?"

"I would. No one learns anything from permanently dying. Especially not when their fate was forced upon them, and all they've done since is cope as best they can."

That raspy sigh tore through Dad's body again. "Arguing philosophy gets nowhere with you. Fine." The vines in his head pulled away, giving him the appearance of a distended mouth with thorns for teeth. His voice grew stronger and he ordered, "Tear this carnival down. Capture any within and bring them to me." A shudder rocked the air when he spoke, and though he wasn't necessarily louder, I got the feeling his whole cursed army heard it. Was Jarrod's scarf tightening around his neck too?

The smile slipped from the Ringmaster's face. His hands reached in every which direction, torn between standing his ground against Dad or protecting his carnival from cursed cronies trying to tear it down. I almost felt sorry for the guy. Even if his approach was warped, it seemed he really wanted to help people, even if it put himself at risk. And I needed to capitalize on that if I wanted to survive.

I reached into my pocket. Though Jarrod never handed me my ticket, I felt the gilded piece of paper in my pocket, just like in a twisted fairytale. Moving, or even thinking, hurt with a claw impaling my head, but I managed to pull the ticket out and hold it aloft. The Ringmaster stared at it a long moment. It was a risk I had to take; if I lived and didn't get out, he'd put me in whatever body he saw fit. But I'd live. And he'd fight like hell to protect one of his charges. Did that mean I was too much like Nalem after all, if I had to use others to save myself?

But to my surprise, the Ringmaster shook his head. "Friend, you've given me a lot to think about. And you've spent too long wound up in what others want. So this ride's on the house."

With that said, the Ringmaster tore me off the claws impaling me. Chipped me a bit on the way out, but I summoned the pieces and melded them into place; my skin would heal on its own, and I'd find some way to fix my haircut later. Though the Ringmaster pulled me away, vines wrapped around my arm. The two Faeries fought, a flurry of limbs and vines. The world spun and jerked as I was tossed around, a ragdoll in their power plays. Clowns ran in and aimed their poppers. Brambles crashed through to restrain them.

I waited for my opportunity to make a break for it. Literally; I planned to wait until only one person held me, preferably by an arm, then I'd snap whatever I needed to in order to free myself and reattach everything later. It'd hurt like hell, but compared to dying...

"How about you stop tearing yourself apart to solve your problems?!" The Ringmaster shouted, still snooping in my thoughts mid-combat. He tore me away from Dad's claws and held me aloft with all those arms, and I thought he'd hold me until either he found a way to carry me out himself, or his pride got us both killed. Imagine my surprise when he instead chucked me over the thorns. Before I hit the ground, a gaggle of clowns swarmed, their arms too short to catch me. They used their heads to cushion the fall.

"Get the skull and get out," the Ringmaster shouted. He held onto thorns to keep brambles from following me and held back Dad to stop him from lunging after his wayward son. "Just please, if you can, take Monica with you when you go."

"I'll do everything in my power." I ran soon as the clowns set me on my feet.

17 - JARROD

'd known since I met him that Farris was a shell of whoever he'd once been. A man whose past was a mystery that might one day swallow him whole. But somehow, the thought that he'd once had a different personality too, one shaped by those missing memories instead of a cocktail of madcap adventures and cheap motel TV fare, had never occurred to me.

When he mistook Nalem's plastic body for his sister, I saw someone else looking through my lover's eye. I'd always imagined Farris would've treated a reunion like a celebration, running up and scooping his lost family in a hug, grinning like a fool through tears. This stranger was solemn, relief and disbelief warring across his face. For a moment, I thought I saw a glowing white hilt in his grasp, and the hint of a short but sharp blade.

"It cannot be," he whispered. The inflection wasn't his. I'd never heard him speak with an accent either, not quite my mother's German but close. This was a man about to break, and I wanted to hold him, except I knew for this brief moment he wasn't mine.

Nalem shook his head. "Indeed, it is not. This is a charade forced upon me, and I will require the help of you bumbling fools to remove it. And to save Retz again, of course." He narrowed his gaze and took a step forward. "You...are familiar with this form?"

"I am. She's..." The stranger fell away and Farris grimaced, face scrunching up as if struck with a sudden headache. "Damn it! It's right there, but trying to remember is like shoving my head into a knife box. But I know you. I mean her." The light in his hand faded. "She's someone important to me. But it's more than that, and I can't remember why."

"How fascinating." Nalem didn't say anything more, then seemed to remember he was outside of Retz's head and had to control the body himself. "But if this musing isn't helping you summon Fatebreaker, it is a mystery that must wait. Hurry, follow me."

"Where're we going?" Monica asked, able to follow the conversation again. "Do you know a safe way out?"

"I had one, but Retz found it more important to try saving you." Nalem directed a glare at me. "He failed, obviously. Now he's the one in need of rescue before he dies, or I'm stuck in this body forever while Sea Mother tears apart the town I helped build. I know you enjoy

your petty vengeances where you can get them, but I
hope you understand how this hurts us both."

So, the crash in the Big Top that had distracted the
Ringmaster was my brother? For a strike that loud and
noticeable, he must've used something large. Such as
the leviathan skull. Somehow, I hadn't expected that
he'd get so close to rescuing me. That his will could
overpower Nalem's selfishness. Seems Retz and I had
underestimated each other–and the Ringmaster too. We
couldn't make such mistakes again with risks like these.
But first, I had to save him so we'd have such a future to
plan for.

"Lead the way," I told Nalem, "and let me take care of
any obstacles. But we also need to find Artemisia." I
pointed to my scarf. Nalem rolled his eyes but didn't
waste time arguing. Off we ran, helping each other
through the rubble as best we could.

While the Carnival of Bliss had been a kaleidoscope
of eye-searing rainbow, now roiling, verdant green
vines collapsed every tent they came in contact with.
White roses grew from the tallest, and some leaves
turned bright and shining red like poison oak. I hadn't
been fond of the carnival's attempts to force cheer, but
seeing it torn apart by my father's will filled me with
dread. I tried to focus on the rage instead.

Even with Zalin crashing through the carnival in her attempt to take out brambles, we were still inundated with thorns and debris. At one point I pulled Farris and Nalem both from a toppling tent. I looked back to check on Monica, but she made do while carrying the clown. It cheered, "Golly gee, I don't think we've ever had this much excitement before!"

"Why the hell are you bringing that along?" Farris shouted, almost tripping on a vine as he did so.

"It's cute and it helped us!" Monica answered, hoisting the clown so it could ride on her shoulders. If she thought it was cute, the carnival's design suddenly made far more sense. I just hoped she wouldn't ask me to save the clown's "life" too, considering how many others I'd popped.

"What're we heading for first, and how close are we?" I asked Nalem as we turned a corner in the maze of tents and brambles.

"Retz. He's trapped between the Fae and sustaining damage. Sturdy as he is, I doubt he can take much more before expiring. And I do not wish my most useful vessel in ages to turn Faerie on me. With the power he already has, and a crafty mind trained by yours truly, I cannot imagine the havoc he'd cause."

"Do you actually have a plan to save him?" If all else failed, the Harvester owed me a revival in exchange for protecting Nalem. I could use it...but that'd mean forsaking Farris once he finished whatever his quest was. I couldn't imagine losing either of them, not after all I'd done.

"If the Harvester can return me to his body, my essence should be enough to kickstart his body back to life. Again." Before I could argue, Nalem continued, "I've been in his head for as long as he can remember. When I was placed in this mockery of a body, he begged the Ringmaster to put me back. Your brother needs me in both body and mind."

Of all the times to get under my skin..."Retz would never ask for you back. Not after all you've done to him."

"And yet, until just this week, you did everything your father asked of you without question and bore his curse without blaming him."

Farris glanced between us and sighed. "You know what? All of you have some major issues with setting healthy boundaries for yourselves. And after this carnival, I don't want to hear any psychoanalyzing for a long-ass time."

I was about to chide him for the comment when I realized the world had gone silent and still. No more crashing, no honking clowns, no calliope playing its mindless tune. The sudden absence of sound unnerved me. The last time I'd experienced it had been when Alexander cursed Nalem to be unable to kill.

"Tear this carnival down. Capture any within and bring them to me."

My scarf tightened around my throat before the words even registered. Since when had Alexander's words had such range? I heard Nalem shout "Warp us out, *now*" at Farris, followed by hurried footfalls and a yelp cut off too fast. But they escaped before doing so would trigger my curse; an order this large took time to settle in. I took as deep a breath as I could and held it as those cursed leaves choked tight enough that I saw spots.

I was standing next to a small tent. My hands were already stained with blood and paint, so I struck at its beam and toppled it. My scarf loosened a bit. I reached into the wreckage and pulled out part of the wooden beam; better to use a blunt weapon than waste bullets.

I didn't have time to despair being alone. That meant there was no one nearby to hurt, no one I'd have to betray due to this curse. I clutched the beam until its plastic splinters dug into my skin. The pain brought clarity, the opposite of alcohol, and all I saw in that colorful wreckage was red. He wanted the carnival gone? So be it. I'd tear apart this carnival and all its mockeries—including the Faerie who'd claimed my late

father's name. It was time for me to admit Alexander
was truly dead, and nothing of him remained in that
impostor of roses and thorns.

I gave in to rage.

I do not know how long I kept swinging. Every blow
faded into background noise, an unsteady drumbeat
with percussive snaps and clatters in place of cymbals.
When my weapon snapped, I used my fists until I found
a new one. Everything I broke bought me another gasp
of air. I felt ready to burst all over. Why was this carnival
so big, and where...?

Drumming. And not the song of destruction I'd built
in my head, but actual drumming. Singing, lines
shouted as call and response. I knew those voices. And
one of them had an iron sword, bane to Faeries.
Alexander's orders never said anything about what to do
after delivering those I captured to him. That gave me a
plan, though the hard part would be convincing
everyone to go along with it.

I ran toward the chorus, trampling every tent in my
path. There were the minotaurs, locked in combat with
others of Alexander's cursed who were trying and failing
to capture the herd. Some of the minotaurs, like Isolde,
swung weapons and fists on the front lines. Others like
Bolton stayed back in a ring around those who were

injured, pounding a beat on their riot shields. They
flickered if I looked at them out of the corner of my eye,
but I wasn't in a state to question it.

They were stronger than the bulk of Alexander's
cursed collection, but he'd stolen a few more powerful
creatures from the gilded menagerie the rest of us had
destroyed. A blue-skinned oni swung a spiked stone on
a chain at the guardian minotaurs, attempting to strike
over their shields, while a beast I didn't recognize made
of swirling sand fought Isolde with seemingly no solid
body for her to strike. Other monsters hung on the
outskirts, waiting for their chance. Humans hung
behind them holding ropes and chains.

I reminded myself these beings were not necessarily
wicked, but victims of fate and Fae like me. Even if they
were evil, killing them in Arcadia would only create
more Fae. Do not kill, do not maim. But I sure as hell
could scare them off. I let my hulderkind instinct take
hold, let everything else fade away to the beat of the
minotaur's war song, and charged in.

Blood gathered on my skin and coat. Some of it mine.
Not much. I healed faster than others could harm me.
Struck harder than expected for someone so short. I
didn't pay attention to who or what I fought, as long as I
steered clear of the minotaurs. I didn't have to hold
myself back. We were all monsters here.

"What a brawl that was, cousin! I suspected you held out on us during our previous fight, and here's my proof."

I blinked. Hadn't the fight just started? I forced myself to turn slowly instead of swinging fists-first. Isolde stood over a sword's-length away from me. Pleased by the fight but watching me with a wary eye. I bore the same curse as the other attackers, after all, and everyone had heard Alexander's orders.

It took longer than I would've liked to remember my purpose and speak. "Yeah. That was...exhilarating." Part of me wanted to keep going, to duel the herd-caller on even ground this time. No, stay focused. Bigger threat first. "I've got to stop Alexander. Save Retz. I figured out a loophole for the curse. Need your help."

Isolde didn't comment on my failing grasp on language; she seemed familiar with huldra and our rages. "What would you have us do?"

I reached into my pockets and pulled out zip-ties. "You can break out of these easy. Curse never said anything about how well I have to capture folks, long as I get them to Alexander. And what happens after isn't my business either."

Isolde grinned. "Crafty. But are you certain he won't see through your ruse?"

"I...spent a long time working with him. He believes I'll see his so-called reason. That things will be like they were before." If I could keep up a façade of calm once I reached him, I might even be able to buy time for a surprise attack from the minotaurs.

Isolde looked down her snout at me. There was understanding in her eyes; she wouldn't dare offer pity. "I know how it can be, losing trust in your family. It's...how I understand why Bertha ran away." The herd-caller held out her hands, wrists pressed together. "We will aid you, cousin. Everyone gather round. We've a ruse to put on before we reach our final foe."

Each of the minotaurs came up to me and offered their wrists. I had lots of zip-ties, and a couple larger handcuffs from previous cases, but I eventually had to resort to rope. The rote actions cooled my head. I tried not to forget the anger, but let it pool in my chest, within reach the moment I needed it.

Bolton came last, and he offered me something appearing small in his giant hands: Nalem's viola case. "I found it inside Ginny's car. Figured Lord Nalem might need it. I mean, no dead people here, right?"

True. Which meant if Retz had to defend himself, all he had were the bones in his dying body. And he was all too willing to use himself as a weapon instead of waiting for others to save him.

I took the viola case and slung it over my shoulder. "I appreciate all your help, Bolton. Let's get moving."

The minotaurs lined up in front of me where I could keep an eye on them, and we marched toward the gate. I only broke away when I needed to smash tents in order to breathe. Much of the surrounding carnival had been flattened, thanks to Zalin and Alexander's followers. I saw a few of them through the rubble, but they stayed away. Did they note how much I looked like my father, and believe I was on his side? Or were they simply scared of how strong I must be if I'd "captured" a whole herd of minotaurs?

Brambles had taken over the entirety of the front gate. The bright colors of carnival posters barely broke through the gaps in the vines. The trail outside had been transformed into a battlefield, clowns impaled on thorns, leaves splattered with viscous black ooze. Alexander reclined atop a tower of roots, watching as the Ringmaster tried to tear away from the vines wrapping around his arms. He stopped when I approached, holding still except for the twitching of his many fingers.

Alexander no longer had a face. Barely a human form. He stayed still as a tree on his perch as he said with no mouth, "I knew you'd be back."

I tapped the side of my scarf, which went slack enough I no longer had to fight for air. "You didn't give me much choice in the matter."

"Sometimes, hard decisions must be made and ultimatums given in order to force a result. You should know that better than anyone." Alexander's voice had grown deep and gravely since his death, and it was little more than a low drone when he wasn't giving an order.

"Obedience or loss of bodily autonomy isn't really a choice." I bit my lip. I only had to keep my cool a little longer. "I did as you asked. Here's the minotaur herd. Shouldn't be many others inside, if any."

"Your brother is in there. Aren't you still your brother's keeper? Devoted to keeping him out of trouble?"

"Of course. We left on a mission to save him, and I've never forgotten it." I kept my face blank but was relieved to hear Retz escaped. I wouldn't want to risk his tenuous hold on life during this fight.

I thought I heard the wind blow through the silent forest outside the carnival. Turns out it was Alexander sighing. "I expected that, yet I'm still disappointed. Traveling with him has corrupted you too."

"Corrupted? No, having Retz back in my life *reminded* me what I've been fighting for all this time. Why I keep going instead of giving up and becoming a mindless plant. And dammit, I'm not going to listen to you argue why everything we've done has been worthless and we should pivot to building cursed armies or whatever the fuck you're planning to do with everyone you've stolen."

Behind me echoed a chorus of snapping zip-ties and handcuffs. Isolde said with a smirk, "And here I was worried we'd have to suffer a whole monologue from this fiend."

If Alexander still had a face, I'm sure he would've given me an exasperated look. "Have you forgotten? I can curse you all with subservience. If I tell you to be still, still you will be one way or another." I wasn't sure if this was a bluff or if he'd truly grown strong enough to curse multiple beings at once. I didn't want to find out.

Isolde brandished her iron sword. "Even more reason to cut out your tongue. Curses or no, I've grown tired of your prattling."

As she spoke, the other minotaurs lowered their heads. They charged before Alexander could speak an order, and either their hides were too thick for thorns to pierce or they simply ignored the pain. Isolde shouted a battle cry, words lost to volume, and the others bellowed their answer as they attacked. When Isolde struck the roots with her iron sword, they fizzled and burned the way Farris's chest had when struck by the iron rings.

That got Alexander to move. He forsook his body entirely, separating into a swarm of scattering vines, like long green and brown snakes. A few passed through minotaurs as if they were ghosts; Artemisia must be hiding nearby, adding illusory members to the herd.

Knowing I'd be easiest for him to order, as I already had his curse planted within me, I avoided striking him directly just yet. Instead, I grabbed my multitool from my coat and went to work freeing the Ringmaster, using the blades to cut through the vines as I attempted to avoid the thorns.

"I appreciate your help," The Ringmaster said. The smile had dropped from his face, and his clothes were stained with black ichor leaking from the scrapes he'd accrued. "But I thought you hated me? I know what you saw and destroyed. I'm starting to think I shouldn't blame you for it either."

I thought back to a couple months before, when I could've left Zalin to die and patched her up instead even though she'd captured me. How hard I was trying to save Retz and Nalem, despite all they'd put me through. And how if the Ringmaster could be redeemed before he lost all of his humanity to power like Alexander had, maybe there was hope I could keep Farris from that fate too.

Or hell, I could just be an idiot who put too much stock in second chances. "You can't fix any of the shit you've caused if I leave you tied up here."

The Ringmaster stared at the fighting. At what he might become, if he continued to claim he knew best while casting empathy aside. "Suppose I should start by saying sorry."

"It's a start. Though I think Monica needs to hear it first. And without you jumping into her head to do so."

I'm sure he would've agreed, but roots with rough bark wrapped around my ankle and pulled me away before he had the chance. I dug my blood-stained, paint-splattered fingers into the ground and held on for dear life. The Ringmaster held onto one of my wrists while his other hands finished freeing himself.

Alexander loomed over me, with the exasperated sigh of a parent. "I found the solution that solved every problem we had. Rid us of Nalem while saving Retz, if he's redeemable."

"If?!" I interrupted. Saving Retz had never been an "if" before. I looked past him to see why the minotaurs weren't attacking him. They were, but Alexander didn't need a solid body anymore. He could split himself how he wished. And it looked like his cavalry of followers had arrived, flanking the minotaurs.

Alexander continued unbothered, "We can put you in the body you've always wanted, while also removing your curse and the pact with the Harvester. This power allows us to help others in ways we never thought imaginable. It is a plan without flaw."

"Sure, if you stop factoring other people into your plans. But before you died, wasn't that the entire point? Why we listened to both the humans and monsters before deciding how to handle a case, instead of only doing as we're told?" Something I hadn't been able to do for a long time, thanks to my curse. So many lives that hadn't needed to end. "Did you forget the entire reason we left home in the first place? What we promised?"

"To stop Nalem," hissed the Fae that had once worn Alexander's face.

"To save Retz," I corrected, "and then we planned to head straight home. We never planned to save the world. All we wanted was to save our family."

Alexander rumbled, "Retz said much the same thing. But plans have changed." Roots dug into my leg, piercing the skin. The blueprints he'd made for my body had excluded the few scars I'd earned on his behalf; did he think this would be as easy to erase? "And if you refuse, there will be no place for you except for home, alone with your tail between your legs."

I'd never struck my father before. Especially not with the aforementioned tail, strong enough that it snapped the roots around my ankle so I could pull free. I think it shocked him, because he stood there like dead wood as I pulled out my shotgun and aimed it up at his head. Not like he had much of a face to ruin anymore.

The time for talk was done. He stabbed his claw-like roots down. The Ringmaster released my arm. I rolled out of the way and fired. I should've felt something when chunks of bark went flying, revealing the rot underneath. Alexander didn't strike with his claws again; more roots and vines burst from the ground to surround me. I fired at some, and the Ringmaster pulled me away from the remnants. His hands formed weapons from the ooze he bled, colorful blades and guns that resembled the cartoon poppers of his clowns. It was clear once he began his attack that the younger Fae was far less experienced with combat, but what he lacked in experience, he made up for with his sheer number of hands.

As we fought, the minotaurs bellowed a new song with renewed vigor in their voices and plant viscera scattered at their feet. Isolde cut down vines faster than they could grow. Bolton pulled more iron rings out of his jacket like faux throwing stars; not as effective as in the movies, but they still singed the Fae. The Ringmaster and I flowed together as a team, a perk to fighting alongside a mind-reader. Alexander slowly crumbled.

Except when the Ringmaster next stabbed a sword into the core of the roots, they surrounded his arm and pulled him in.

A sickening crunch echoed through the battlefield. The Ringmaster screamed and tried to pull away. The brief moment his arm was free, I saw nothing past the elbow but ooze. The roots...shuddered, like a throat swallowing. I stood there, frozen, trying to comprehend what I'd just seen.

Then fresh vines green as spring shot out and wrapped around the Ringmaster. Far stronger than their predecessors and with thorns longer than my hand, they pierced his flesh and pulled him close. The Ringmaster's hands frantically tried to pry the thorns out, his returned smile akin to rigor mortis. More and more of his arms came away in pieces, cut off at wrists and elbows.

I aimed my shotgun at the growing mass of vines and fired. "I don't know what you're doing, but let him go!" No response from Alexander. The Ringmaster cast a look of pleading terror at me, pinpricks of black in the corners of his eyes. I fired again. If this didn't work, I'd have to charge in myself and...

An arm came out of the roots, but it wasn't the Ringmaster's. The skin was lighter, closer to mine, covered in patches of bark, moss, and dark brown hair. Even with leaves sprouting from under the nails and thorns on knuckles, I recognized the scars on that hand. The old calluses from years of fighting. A tattooed ring on one finger.

The shotgun slipped from my fingers.

"Everyone back, and prepare to retreat!" Isolde bellowed. An arm wrapped around my shoulders to pull me away while the other picked up my fallen gun. I briefly glanced up at Bolton. He had the face of a bull standing before a slaughterhouse. I didn't struggle when he led me back to join the other minotaurs.

"Shouldn't we strike them while they're vulnerable?" One of the minotaurs asked in a hushed tone. "Or are we waiting for the one to finish the other off?"

Isolde said, "No one goes near them until they're done. Ginny said Fae are at most dangerous when devouring one another, and while I no longer trust her as a person, this isn't something to lie about."

"Devouring?" It took a moment to recognize my own voice. It sounded so small. More arms sprouted from the roots, far more than Alexander ever had, and the wet sound of snapping limbs and slurping hadn't stopped.

The Ringmaster's screams had. I could no longer tell where one body ended and the other began.

Isolde explained quietly, "It's why every inch of Arcadia isn't crawling with Faeries. The strong eventually realize they can sustain themselves by devouring others. Judging by how damaged the...your father looked, I wouldn't be surprised if another Fae tried to do the same to him. But if we get close to them in this state, they'll only kill us so we become more Fae to feed upon." She paused as we all realized we could no longer see the Ringmaster's head, and a bulb had sprouted out of the new growth. "I'm so sorry, cousin. May your nightmares be kind enough to ignore this."

I wanted to thank her. Or to figure out some way to stop this. I couldn't bring myself to move or look away.

A canvas-covered hand blocked my view of the Faeries. Paint bloomed from the lines on Artemisia's palm, depicting a cozy room with a warm fireplace that seemed to flicker. I stared deep into the false flames and resisted the urge to peek over her fingers.

"Thanks Artie," Bolton said, apparently also staring into the painting on her hand.

"Sure thing. And don't call me that again." She guided us away to follow the others, leaving the sounds of crunches and slurps behind.

18 - RETZ

A t first, I thought I'd been hit with wild hallucinations. Flowers burst out of the ground with petals of dripping rainbow paint. Roots grew out of popped clown heads, scuttling around like spiders. Trees formed with plastic mannequin arms for branches. A grotesque garden grew all around, and I realized that not even my brain was fucked up enough to imagine this.

Dad and the Ringmaster had been pretty firmly at odds when I'd started running. The combined aesthetic didn't match their particular brands of unsettling either. I wanted to ask Nalem what it might mean, but I was met with silence.

Confused yelps gave away the position of a group of Dad's minions hunting me down. They were behind a toppled popcorn machine, still churning out stale buttered treats. On instinct, I flung bones from one torn-up hand, forming them into daggers and slicing Achilles tendons. Agony struck me seconds later and almost threw off my focus. I didn't have Nalem to help shoulder the pain of my injuries, and my hulderkind healing factor had slowed way down as my life force sputtered out. I didn't bother to check if I'd immobilized my foes; I pulled my bones back and cradled my aching hand to my chest as I ran.

The path to the busted big top had been clear, thanks to everyone trampling the carnival. I'd even been able to see the far end where Zalin had been beset by Dad's minions. But with all these strange plastic plants cropping up, my path quickly turned into another labyrinth.

At least I could still sense the skull. I had no idea where Nalem and Farris were, and Monica's signal had disappeared. I should've been able to sense where Jarrod and the minotaurs were, but the range on my powers was getting...fuzzy. Wasn't helping me track my new stalkers either. Only the skull was big enough, ancient and alien compared to humans, for it to stand out. The loss of one of my main senses was admittedly freaking me out, but I suppose tracking bones is a less important than keeping me standing with what little energy my body had left.

"I am going to celebrate like hell if I get out of here alive," I muttered to myself as I ran. It helped me stick to one train of thought if I voiced it aloud, and with all the chaos going on, I doubted anyone could hear my ramblings. "I'll...shit, I've never even done much for my birthday. But we're gonna' change that! I'm going to do big things for me, not just 'cause Nalem's gotten me in trouble again."

I stumbled into an alley of mirrors where every reflection showed a different variation on my body. I ignored them and ran until a tree fell and blocked my path. Well, not so much fell as leaned over because it had sprouted bulbous clown heads too heavy for its trunk.

The heads chanted in warbling unison, "From porcelain and plants, from passers-by and ants, He made us. From creatures and trees, the wind and the bees, He made us! The river of life, the end of strife, this made us..." All the heads turned toward me in unison, as if my life wasn't enough of a b-rated horror flick already. "Golly gee, happy birthday and deathday! Both at once, what a lucky guy you are!"

"Fuck luck." I stopped myself from piercing the heads and hurting myself further. Could I double back and find another path? "Either tell me what's going on or shut the hell up."

"The greatest show has begun, and the grand tour starts here! The Rosemaster and his merry band will

bring joy and order to Arcadia, and then to Earth itself!
Won't that be wonderful? Every person will have a place,
and a smile for their face!"

I imagined the implications, none of them good for
my continued survival.

Before I could ask another question, glass shattered
and heads popped. I never thought I'd be so happy to see
the Mercury Marquis, so garish that being splattered in
ooze and rainbow paint couldn't make it any uglier. One
of the back doors popped open as Nalem shouted, "Get
in, little one!"

I stumbled over my own feet climbing into the back,
and the first thing I did was take a deep breath that
didn't reek of paint, sugar, and blood. After this, I'd
never complain about Jarrod's lack of showers for, like, a
month. He wasn't in the car, but Farris was at the wheel
with Nalem riding shotgun. And next to me was
Monica, clutching a clown that had somehow gone
unconscious instead of transforming like the rest.

"Glad to see you're still alive and kicking," Farris said.
The Merc backed up to splatter a few more of the tree's
freaky clown heads before rolling onward. "Alright Nal,
where from here?"

"Every time you use a nickname, the likelihood of me
murdering you again grows." Nalem pointed left, in the

direction of the skull we couldn't see. "This way. And do hurry."

"And here I thought it'd be nice to take a scenic drive through here. Maybe stop for a picnic."

Thank the gods, banter outside of my own thoughts. How I missed it. "Thanks for picking me up. So...any idea what's going on? And why isn't Jarrod with us?"

Farris said, "We had to ditch him the second your old man's order went out. Didn't want him to be forced to hurt us. I figured it'd be a good time to grab a getaway vehicle. Tried to drop Monica off too, but..."

"I've got to find the rest of me," Monica said, clutching the clown tight. "And...and see if I can get Aiden out too. Somehow."

"Your friend is no longer himself," Nalem chided, gesturing to the world outside. "Our surroundings can only mean that Alexander and the Ringmaster have fused into one Fae. That might have even been part of Alexander's plan all along...Either way, it's impossible to return those Fae to how they once were. Either we kill them, or they'll spread this garden through Arcadia, likely feeding on other Fae now that they've tasted power."

"Funny how you've never bothered to bring up Faeries cannibalizing each other before," Farris snapped. He cranked the wheel to avoid a painted flower as it burst from the earth. "Might've been nice to know before marching headfirst into this place!"

Nalem countered, "We didn't realize you had any power until recently, so they likely thought there was nothing to gain from devouring you. And while I'm not surprised at this turn of events from Alexander, the Ringmaster seemed far too naïve to pose a threat to you. But now? Be thankful your powers make you difficult to pin down."

Farris groaned and kept his attention on the road. Smoke leaked from his lips. I'd felt Ginny disappear earlier, so assuming he'd warped himself and the rest of the attack squad in, Ginny out, and then used his powers to escape Jarrod's curse...probably felt as drained as I did right now. Except I only had one foot in the grave he'd already fallen into.

The Big Top was already in tatters thanks to my impromptu entry by skull earlier. Now most of its painted canvas was scattered across the ground, with a broken beam propping up the rest like a gaping maw. In lieu of a tongue was Sea Mother's skull.

"Looks like a venus flytrap," Monica muttered.

I reached out with my powers; if Bertha's body had expired when everything else in the carnival went all Alice in Wonderland, we could control it from afar. Of course we weren't that lucky. Okay, I was glad there might still be a slim chance of restoring Bertha to her original body, but I wasn't keen on testing how lifelike this fake flytrap might be.

After a moment, Farris said, "I've got a stupid idea. Everybody out." We did so, Monica and I both stumbling. She didn't look injured; maybe the clown she carried was heavier than it looked. We watched as Farris eased the Merc toward Sea Mother's skull. Sure enough, the beam snapped and the big top collapsed once he drove onto the canvas, tattered edges resembling spiny teeth. They crunched down but couldn't actually pierce through that tank of a car. Farris whooped and punched the ceiling, though this only encouraged the faux-venus flytrap to chomp down harder.

Nalem grabbed my hand, and the two of us ran into the wreckage. The skull was still intact, but the fake head on Bertha's body had changed, now resembling her regular bovine face instead of a clown. At least the Ringmaster tried to fix something on his way out.

With our hands on the skull, we floated it out of the ruined big top. Much as I hate to admit it, joining my power with Nalem's was a relief, like something broken had been made whole again. He said to me as we freed the skull, "We're almost through, little one. You must stay strong a little longer. But this time we must do things my way. First, we must extricate this body from the skull." He turned back toward the others. "Farris, Monica, give me a hand?"

Farris eased the car back out of the clutches of the big top, its tattered "teeth" scraping the already crappy paint job. At Nalem's behest, Monica set the clown in the trunk of the car. She wasn't any steadier on her feet after letting it go. This world was a lot for a human, I reminded myself, even one missing most of her soul and usually body-snatched by a Fae. The two of them caught Bertha's body when Nalem released it from the skull. Though the plastic eyes didn't blink, the chest rose and fell. They put it in the back seat.

"For our safety, we will ride in the Marquis as we control the skull," Nalem explained. "This should help Retz conserve his strength. However, should we be attacked, the skull is large enough we can ride it out, as originally planned." I expected a withering insult that never came. Nalem, too worried for a jab at my expense? Never thought I'd see it.

We piled back into the Marquis, Farris and Monica up front to navigate while Nalem and I focused on keeping the skull aloft. I did all I could to stay conscious and steady despite how tired I was, since my only options for pillows were Nalem or Bertha's empty body.

I felt every bump in paths that weren't meant to be driven. Roots broke through the cotton candy, and the garden spread like ivy, consuming everything it touched and choking what refused to kneel.

"Man, I wish I had a giant machete to cut through these goddamn plants," Farris said. "Fatebreaker's a blade, right? And these sure as hell look cursed. Bet it'd slice through all this like butter."

Nalem scoffed. "Doing so would be an insult to the weapon, I'm sure."

I didn't laugh because I realized there were people trapped within those plants, which look like painted mockeries of the giant roses Dad had in his realm. I think most of them were folks whose curses triggered, flowers blooming from their mouths and torsos seemingly impaled on flower stalks until one realized the stalks had replaced their legs. I tried to sense Jarrod to make sure he hadn't suffered the same fate, but doing so made my hold on the skull waver. Whoever said ignorance is bliss must've been a bastard with even less empathy than Nalem.

...Hold on, were those people moving? Even with parts of their bodies turned into plants? Sure thing. Some crawled, with arms or roots. Others pulled themselves along the branches. One man, once human, aimed a hand that bloomed into a gun with its muzzle haloed by rose petals. He nearly blew his arm off with the kickback, but maybe that was worth it to break our back window, though I'm not sure if what pierced the glass was a bullet or a seed.

"Drive faster, before they surround us," Nalem ordered.

"Easier said than done." But the engine roared louder as Farris slammed on the gas and went off-road, smashing through a bush with popcorn "berries" and under a gate of twisted trees and limbs. Anything left standing in the Marquis's wake, Sea Mother's skull crashed into right after.

I let Nalem lead our motions, lending my strength just enough to keep the skull up and moving. "Think we'll make it?" I asked him.

"That will be entirely up to you," Nalem said. He maintained a calm tone, almost soft, the voice he used if he needed me to be cooperative. "I cannot tell how close to the edge you are, and there is nothing within my power to save you in this world." He paused, tearing his attention away from the battle outside to look at me. "Do you truly wish to live, even if I am returned to your head? Or would you rather die, alone in your mind as most other mortals are?"

"As if you'd give me a choice in the matter."

Nalem's mouth twisted, fighting against the smile ingrained in that fake face. "I would hate to lose my most useful vessel in ages. But considering the circumstances..." Nalem paused again. Normally, he would've let a thought slip so I might "accidentally" read his intentions, but now he had to voice them. Even a moment's hesitation felt like ages. "Whether or not I am as evil as some claim, I refuse to be categorized with one such as Alexander. And you are one of the few vessels of mine who never actually consented to my presence. That decision was made for you. So now, I put the choice in your hands."

I hadn't expected that offer. What was the right choice? Sure, Dad was of the opinion I needed to die with grace, even if he was the one who'd allowed Nalem to possess me in the first place....but this wasn't his decision, was it? It was mine. And damnit, exhausted as I was, I didn't want to give up. I wanted to live, and to figure out what I wanted to do with my life.

Surviving meant joining myself to an evil I knew all too well. A person who bent others to his will until they broke and were cast aside. Me included. I'd be a willing accomplice to his schemes, everything from petty maiming to displacing the Harvester and leading a monstrous revolt. And as much as I might delude myself, there was no way I could convince Nalem to turn away from that. One person couldn't convince a self-made god to cast aside thousands of years of plans.

"If I gave up now and died, everything my family and I suffered would've been for nothing." And maybe believing I could be saved from Nalem was a longshot, but I'd rather have that chance than none at all. I'd allow myself to hope. "Besides, if I let you go into some other rando's head, they wouldn't know how to deal with you. I'm doing favors for strangers now. Ain't that nice of me?"

It was the first time I saw Nalem truly smile, instead of just feeling it against my own face. Farris cast me a conflicted look in the rearview mirror, and I'm sure I would've done the same in his shoes. And Monica–

That wasn't Monica's face.

"I knew you'd prove my point. But don't you worry, son. I'm on my way." I couldn't think of the last time Dad had called me son, but the inflection wasn't quite his. More like the Ringmaster. The face looked more like Dad's, at least until I saw the second mouth opening in Monica's neck.

Monica reached over and grabbed hold of the wheel, cranking it as far right as it'd go. Farris pried her hands away with liberal use of his claws, but the damage was already done. The Marquis veered into brambles, which wrapped around the car and held it tight.

Nalem grabbed my hand, gesturing for me to be quiet so the Fae possessing Monica didn't notice while fighting with Farris. The back windshield of the car was damaged from bullets, so Nalem struck it with his elbow twice to shatter the glass; guess his new body was far stronger than mine. Still holding my hand, he led me onto the trunk as we floated the leviathan skull down. We could float right out if we climbed onto it before the vines had a chance to tie it down.

Except Nalem stumbled, nearly sliding off the trunk, as a blade dug into the base of his neck. I looked over my shoulder. Monica had wrenched open the glove compartment and grabbed the survival knife Jarrod kept stashed there. Farris pinned her before she could grab anything else. For some reason, one of his hands was glowing. Black sludge trickled down Nalem's back.

I swore my ass off while trying to hold Nalem upright. Was I supposed to remove the knife, or would that only make it bleed more? Everything I ever learned about the bloodier bits of humanity fled my brain, and even if it hadn't, I had no idea how different these Ringmaster-made bodies were. Likely not at all accurate, judging from the design of the clowns, but to what degree?

"C'mon Nalem, you've gotta' stay with me. We're in this together, right?" I lugged Nalem off the trunk, out of Monica's line of sight. I tried to float the skull but could only manage a couple inches off the ground.

The brambles wrapped over the skull and would've gotten us too if I hadn't pulled Nalem into the leviathan's maw and clamped it shut around us. I barely managed to fuse shut the eye sockets to keep vines from breaking in. They tried to pry open the mouth instead.

Nalem groaned next to me. "The Ringmaster clearly had no idea how nerves work when setting up this mockery of a vessel."

Spikes thudded against the skull. I felt the faintest fractures form in the bone.

I said "We gotta' cut ourselves out. Help me."

Nalem snarled in distaste at warping Sea Mother's bones but didn't argue. We covered the skull in small but sharp blades to cut through the vines. Then to actually slice through, we spun the skull like a long sawblade; the bramble bush had us so tight that even moving the skull that much would've tired me out on a normal day. As I was, I felt like my head was about to burst and my chest would collapse right after.

We couldn't see outside the skull, but it sounded like vines were still wrapping around us, so I didn't dare open the eye sockets to sneak a peek. We tried to float the skull again, but only succeeded in crushing plants when we hit the ground seconds later. I carefully slid the knife out of Nalem. The wound bubbled black, clotting the white dress the body had been stuck in.

Nalem hissed in a breath. "Better. Not great....however, we should only need to hold out a little longer. I sense the minotaurs closing in on our position. Jarrod is with them."

I tried to reach out, but I couldn't even sense Monica a few feet outside our spiky skull cocoon.

"Will we be able to get out of here, with you injured like that?"

Nalem opened his mouth to answer, but before he could say anything, we heard snipping outside, followed by stomps on the skull and loud sizzling. Like someone found fiery pruning shears to scare off the vines. I looked at Nalem. He shrugged. Then realization hit. He whispered, "Our White Prince may have finally remembered something useful."

Unsure of what to do–we couldn't move the skull if someone was standing on top of it–we waited in nervous anticipation. Nalem's hand was cold in mine, though I'm sure I didn't feel much warmer. I had no idea what to do with the knife in my hands. Soon, the noises outside stopped, and were replaced by knocking on top of the skull.

I opened the eye sockets of the skull and poked my head out. Around us, vines lay oozing and twitching, cleanly snipped and singed in pieces. Standing atop the skull was Farris, and he wielded a glowing white weapon of mass pruning: a pair of large scissors.

"Is that..." I wasn't quite sure how to finish.

Nalem poked his head out of the other socket. "Good to know my father's faith in you was not entirely misplaced."

Farris glanced at the weapon in his hand. "Is this really it? Seems kinda...I mean, it's a pair of fucking scissors." Don't get me wrong, they were gorgeous. They glistened like newly fallen snow, and not even the black ooze could stain them. The handles curled delicately yet protectively over Farris's fingers, like they were crafted just for his hands. But other than the blades being longer than anything they'd allow in school...

Nalem sighed in vague exasperation. "I admit, the last time I saw it, it was a more traditional sword, and a pair of daggers before that if memory serves me right. But I know not how the weapon works, other than its presence being able to break curses with a touch."

"Cut and stab things, break curses. Guess it can do that much."

We surveyed the battlefield to make sure nothing else was about to attack. The plants seemed to have gotten the hint–or their controller had, at least–and retreated. This section of the carnival's labyrinth was, for the moment, more of a field. And Monica was nowhere in sight. I should've realized if the Ringmaster could snoop in her body, this new Rosemaster could as well. Though how two Fae could become one in the first place...probably something I didn't want to imagine.

Nalem and I returned the skull to normal and crawled out of the leviathan's maw. Soon as we did, Farris had Nalem by the collar. "Tell me what you know about the gal whose face you're wearing. Because I only summoned this when I saw you get hurt, and I wasn't...I stopped being *me* until I saw you weren't dead."

"And you think this is the time for threats and revelations? Your sense of timing remains poor as ever." Nalem pried Farris's fingers and backed away, wincing from the wound in the back of his neck. "I have another sister, aside from the one who murdered you. Her name is Loresha. We were...I suppose you could call us twins."

"The eternal body to your eternal soul," I said absently, as Nalem had told me when I'd learned about Loresha.

Nalem shot me a glare. "Indeed. Her body cannot die, but her soul is in a constant state of reinvention. Usually by cobbling parts of the souls of others. I suspect your own fragmented soul may be because she...to be crude, ate part of it."

Confusion bloomed across Farris's face. "That can't be right. Why would I care for someone who's made me forget what I'm supposed to be?"

Because sometimes our sources of hurt and comfort are the same, I thought, but I didn't want to ruin his train of memory.

Farris continued, "I don't know shit about her, but I called her sis. I remember her smile and I feel...happy."

Nalem turned away. I saw how tight his fists clenched. "Perhaps you were an ally of hers. I cannot say. It has been...quite some time since I last saw my sister in the flesh. Since I last attended the Samhain reunion with my family, well before Retz was born."

Farris asked, "So...what you're saying is, now you regret getting me killed."

Nalem would never admit such a thing out loud. But the grimace that covered his face said yes just as clear.

19 - JARROD

When an ice-cold shock ran along my limbs and neck, I feared the worst. That the chimeric Fae had acquired some new power to affect my curse, or I'd failed a task and was about to become a mindless rosebush...or a twisted hybrid of flesh and flower like these other cursed littering the carnival. I looked at my hands to see if there were thorns erupting from my skin. They were shaking. Took me a minute to remember I hadn't drunk anything since arriving in the carnival, and that last encounter with Alexander and the Ringmaster was still replaying in the back of my mind.

But if they weren't behind this sensation, already come and gone, what was?

"I've not felt an aura like that before," Isolde said. The rest of the herd nodded and grumbled in agreement. She turned to me, seeming to notice my unease. "Strong enough for you to feel it, eh? Bolton mentioned you'd never learned to sense auras."

"I didn't realize they could feel so...visceral." I shoved my quaking hands into my pockets.

Bolton explained, "Only real powerful ones are, like Nalem's. Though I guess if you grew up with him around, you might be used to him? Whatever this was, it's near where he is. And everything else in the carnival's headed there too." Us included.

We picked up the pace, crashing through this twisted garden, a mockery of both the Carnival of Bliss and Alexander's realm, Artemisia weaving her illusions around us to keep us hidden from the plastic plant folk scrounging through these ruins. I didn't want to consider what else might go sideways at this rate. Something stronger than a Fae, and maybe even Nalem, if these auras were any indication?

I considered slipping a drink from my coat. Soothing as that sounded, I needed my head clear as I could manage for this. Needed to hold onto my anger, and maybe even the sorrow I tried to drown so often, in order to put this all to an end.

I felt Retz and Nalem's powers before I saw them. The viola slung over my shoulder vibrated, but it seemed my contact with it was enough to stop them floating it from my possession. I felt a brief brush against my bones, a jarring sensation I hadn't felt since childhood when Retz was learning his powers. He was usually far more subtle when reaching out. If Retz was weak enough to lose even that...

There, up ahead, was the leviathan skull. I burst into a run. Sudden panic filled me; was my brother still alive?

"Jarrod! You're okay!" Retz stumbled toward me, nearly tripping over his own feet. His skin was paler than the night he'd first died, covered in wounds that hadn't fully healed, including a gaping hole in his forehead. And he still had the gall to say, "Shit, you look terrible. Sorry I didn't get to you sooner."

"That's my line." I suppose I was covered in blood and paint, and I had gashes in my face from where I'd ripped out the piercings. I grabbed Retz and gave him a light one-armed squeeze. I feared he'd be too fragile for anything else. "Glad to see you're still standing. Are you okay? Aside from, well, I heard about Nalem. But the minotaurs and I, we sensed something strange..."

"Ah. Bet I know what that was." Retz turned and waved behind him. Nalem and Farris were bickering next to the Merc–when did our car get into Arcadia?– until Farris noticed. His face lit up when he saw me. Or maybe that was thanks to the glowing pair of scissors in his hands. He bounded over, and at his approach, that cold shiver traveled along my curse again.

"Babe, I did it! I summoned that super special weapon of mine, and even though it looks really boring, it did a number on all the goons that came at us!" Farris pointed excitedly at the scissors, which must've been Fatebreaker. "Now I can get that curse out of you!....Once I figure out how to do that without killing you, that is! I've only gotten to use it on plants and shit so far." And he could get his memories back from the Harvester too. I wondered how long that stranger I'd seen would linger behind his eyes once he did.

"That's great. I'm proud of you. And we're going to need it, I'm afraid." I grabbed his shirt collar and pulled him into a quick kiss. Cold. Better than nothing. The minotaurs were catching up, and so was Artemisia, but my scarf didn't unfurl. And I didn't see Monica. "Did you...drop Monica off in the mortal world when you disappeared earlier?"

The excitement dropped from both Farris and Retz's faces. They exchanged wary looks.

Nalem broke their silence. "The Rosemaster possessed Monica and attacked us." He strode up to me and handed me the survival knife I kept in the glove compartment. It was coated in black ooze, the same that stained the back of Nalem's neck and dress. "If Farris is able to remove your curse, I suggest you cut your losses and leave her. She will only prove a liability who could turn on us at any time."

I shook my head. "There's still a person in there, and she's lost and scared."

"What's this about my old self?" Artemisia asked as she joined us. For once, her fingers were almost dry, and I had to wonder if the paint was her body's equivalent of blood. The painted facsimile of her old face had smeared some time ago.

Nalem quickly explained what we'd missed. Getting the car, Retz, and the skull. Bertha's body, almost repaired, in the back seat. Isolde went to look when that was mentioned, lost for a moment as she pressed against the glass, staring at her daughter's abandoned body. Nalem went on to explain how Monica had been possessed, how the Fae had appeared. He didn't ask for details on what happened, but he gave me a knowing look, almost pitiable. He'd witnessed it before.

I asked when he was done, "Can Monica be rescued? I don't care about your opinion. I want to know if it's remotely possible."

Nalem grumbled, "I hypothesize that, should the two of them be reunited with the Harvester around, he may be able to fuse the soul back together. After all, that is technically how he will return Farris's memories.

However, if this fused Fae–we have heard their minions call them the Rosemaster–is able to insert their consciousness into a body without much soul to guard it, then at least part of them may try to escape into Monica's body upon death. After all, Monica's body is still flesh and blood."

I had to save Retz, or he'd die. Nalem too, or the world would be overtaken by Arcadia. But if we didn't save Monica as well, then this Rosemaster might live on by possessing her body once more, Alexander's twisted determination combined with the Ringmaster's savior complex. There had to be some way to save them all.

"How long does it take for a Faerie to...finish fusing, so to speak? To act on more than mindless hunger?"

"Depends on the Fae," Nalem answered, "and how tightly they cling to power and their own desires. Both the original Fae in this case were highly determined with clear goals in mind. I doubt they will dwell on their hungers long when there's work to be done."

"So we need to plan quick. Are you able to make the skull fly like you did earlier?"

"Not anymore," Retz said. "Nalem's hurt, and I'm...well. You know."

Nalem added, "I believe we could glide if we got somewhere high up, but floating is all we can manage at this point. Regardless of how we move, Retz is correct.

Both of us are...considerably more fragile in our separated state."

"I can hide them," Artemisia said. "Might be able to paint some copies of the skull to obscure their position. So as long as someone else is able to deal with the Fae and...the rest of me."

"And we can help clear the way of obstacles, and fight against this Rosemaster for another round," Isolde said. She spun her iron blade before resting it on her shoulder. "Our last battle was cut short. And if an empty body such as Artemisia's old body is at risk, then Bertha's is as well. I will not allow this monster to escape into our world."

Pieces of a plan fell into place. "Farris, how're you holding up? I know you've done a lot, with all the warping and..."

Farris grabbed my shoulder and squeezed tight. "I'm in my element here, babe. Kicking ass and saving the day. You need me to move folks around or cut up some curses, I'm here for you."

I had an idea coming together. But I wasn't sure if Artemisia would be enough to protect Retz and Nalem, and I couldn't separate the minotaurs since they worked best as a team. Farris would need to stick with them too, in order to remove any curses that might arise. But if I joined them, who would find Monica?

"So this is where you all ended up. Any of ya' know what happened to this carnival? Thought I'd flattened the joint, and then it grew back all...fucked up."

We all turned around at the newcomer's voice. There was Zalin, standing unsteady on plastic legs and liberally stained with black ooze and iridescent paint. I thought back to her giant true form, which she'd used to crush the carnival. It was...pretty big. And having had my leg broken by her old mistress, I knew how strong lamia were too.

"Zalin, we'll have plenty of time to explain later if we get out alive. Right now, I need to know: are you strong enough to lift up that leviathan skull?"

The lamia strode over to the skull, running a hand along the ridges. "Haven't had a chance to work out of late, what with being trapped here, but bet I could manage. Did a lot of my lady's heavy lifting back in the day. But see, I said we were even. What's to stop me from kicking the ass of those Faeries instead?"

Before I could plan a well-intentioned and logical speech, Nalem stepped in. "This task is of the utmost importance to me. As it happens, the town outside of this gate is under my domain, and I have an opening for a bartender at my tavern. You are in need of a safe place that will not shun you for your past, unless running for the rest of your life is your plan. Help us, and I will guarantee you room and board in exchange for handling my tavern, and I will ensure that the community of supernaturals treats you as any other, so long as you do the same." Nalem looked over his shoulder at the minotaurs. "Is that not correct, my friends?"

Isolde crossed her arms and snorted through her nose, but said despite her apparent reluctance, "We will welcome her if she is willing to reform."

Zalin didn't waste time considering the offer. "Sounds better than anything I had planned. Fine, what do you need me to do?"

All eyes turned to me. Felt good to plan again instead of running on instinct.

"We're going to split into teams. And so the Rosemaster doesn't read the entire plan out of our thoughts, I'll explain each team's plans only to them. I need everyone to group up as follows..."

The plan was not a complex one. Most of our remaining time was spent with preparations. The minotaurs had to patch up a few of their own, and they tended to Nalem's wound as well. Artemisia worked on camouflaging the skull with her paints, and Farris practiced with Fatebreaker, apparently trying to transform it from scissors to a more conventional weapon.

Which left me a moment with Retz. We walked over to the Merc; he had to lean against me to stay steady. Were we already too late?

"I heard you tried to save me instead of getting yourself out earlier," I said.

"Some good that did." Retz's half-hearted laugh sounded more like a dying gasp.

"I mean, it distracted the Ringmaster, and I was able to get through to Monica to escape, so...it did help. But this time, don't do anything stupid. I'll be fine, but you need to save yourself." I shrugged the viola off my shoulder and offered it to him. "This is yours. Well, Nalem's, but I know it's got some sort of power that helps you out. And gives you a weapon other than yourself and an oversized skull."

Retz took the viola and hung it loosely from his shoulder. "That'll be nice. This may sound stupid, but I forgot how much breaking your own bones can hurt."

I bit back an exasperated sigh. Only my brother could say such a thing so glibly. "I've got something else for you too. To make sure you make it out of here alive." I reached into my breast pocket. Out came a small hold-out pistol, custom ordered and polished to a shine. Most importantly, the hilt was inlaid with ivory, and so were slivers along the hammer and trigger. "I wouldn't call this a happy birthday, but...here. I got it for you."

"A gun?" Retz turned the pistol around in his hands. "Jarrod, it's beautiful and all from what I can tell, but...you've got to know as well as I do that this won't do shit against the creatures we're facing here."

"It won't," I agreed. "But it'll guarantee your survival, because you have to live long enough for me to show you how to use it." I closed his fingers around the ivory-inlaid hilt. "Now don't give me a reason to wish I'd said something mushy after the fact."

"Like what? That I'm smart, funny, and maybe kind somewhere deep down? That's what everyone says about dead people." Retz winked. He went to put the holdout pistol somewhere, realizing he didn't have a holster. "Er, is this thing safe to put in a pocket? Don't want to accidentally blow anything off..."

Before we could solve that dilemma, we heard a muffled thump and turned toward the Mercury Marquis. It didn't look like Bertha's body had moved. Another thump. Something was in the trunk.

"Shit, the clown! Monica insisted on carrying it, and we shoved in the trunk once it passed out." Retz exchanged a look with me. Was it possessed like

Monica, or was it just an exuberant clown with a
bulbous head and entirely too much cheer for the
circumstance?

"I've got a spare key in my coat. You pop the hood, I'll
pop its head if it's possessed."

We crept over to the car. I counted down on my
fingers, my other hand on my pistol hilt. Retz opened
the trunk and I braced to draw. Then my breath fled
from my body.

"Boys, don't shoot. I'm here to help, and I don't know
how much time I have until they notice me."

The clown was in the middle of morphing, much like
Monica when she was possessed and the Ringmaster's
face showed through. Except this clown's head shrunk
to match a human's and its limbs stretched out, shifting
to resemble Alexander. As the circus paint faded from
his face, he looked just as when I'd last seen him alive.
Same hints of gray at the temple, crooked nose from a
bar fight gone wrong, glasses that never sat evenly on
his face.

I aimed a pistol, right for the head. "Give me one
good reason to believe you."

The plastic Alexander put his hands up. One was
shifting from a short and pudgy clown limb to his lean-
muscle arms and long fingers. "I...the rest of me gained
the power to move souls between bodies at a range. Part

of me realized what I'd become was...wrong. So I took as
much of that as I could and sent it here, to the only
vessel I could find that was truly empty."

My gun wavered despite myself.

Retz asked, "So are you really...Dad?"

Acrylic eyebrows knit together in confusion. "Not
entirely. Part of me is. I have memories of you two,
when you were younger. And before. But there are other
memories. A childhood with Monica, clearly from the
Ringmaster. Other memories I'm not sure belonged to
either of us. When you...turn Fae, it becomes difficult to
tell where your self begins, and all the other voices end."

Voices? Farris had mentioned his thoughts "going
loud" when he became a Faerie, and unlike the
Rosemaster, I knew he hadn't devoured any other
Faeries. Some sort of madness peculiar to Arcadia or the
nature of being a Fae? I wanted to ask, but whether or
not this fake father spoke true, there wasn't time.

"How do you propose to help us?" I asked. I lowered
my pistol. I didn't entirely put it away but kept it close at
hand if needed. Yet if I imagined this head bursting like
all the other clowns, I felt ill. Not even my anger could
stand up to a familiar face.

"I already have. I've removed what humanity I could from the rest. No chance of...me, I suppose, using your sympathy against you."

I said, "Easier to us to fight, but if we fail, we leave a far harsher enemy behind."

"I raised you better than to fail. Though perhaps I was too harsh on that front." A wry smirk, more Ringmaster than anything Alexander ever wore, twisted his face. "Is it possible to make a sincere apology if I'm not entirely myself? Regardless, I can also tell you exactly where my Fae counterpart is. And where Monica has gone."

"And as our guide, you could easily lead us astray for an ambush! Freaking genius." Retz glanced over his shoulder and flashed a thumbs-up; the others must've noticed our distraction.

Though Retz had a point, so did Alexander, or however much of him this plastic person was. I had no idea where Monica might be. Artemisia might be able to vaguely sense her presence, but with the carnival in such disarray, we couldn't take chances. I tried to remind myself the Rosemaster would be craftier than either of the Fae that made it. Surely a trap like this would be too easy to set up...

Yet it was as I feared. The more this once-clown shifted, the more he looked like Alexander. Like his death and monstrous form had been a bad dream, and now it was time to wake up and get back to work. I didn't want to fight him. I wanted to let him take charge of our quest again, like all those years of traveling together.

I said, "This may be foolish of me, but I'm going to give you a chance." I put up a hand before Retz could interrupt. "But if I think there's even a chance that you're being possessed, we'll shoot. And no offense, but your aim was getting slow last time we fought together."

"Such cheek. Your boyfriend's rubbed off on you. But I would accept nothing less than those terms."

We stepped back so Alexander, clown-form shed to reveal a mimicry of his human self, could climb out of the trunk. Retz whispered to me, "You better know what you're doing. If I can't die here, neither can you."

"Duly noted." I turned to face the others. The minotaurs were patched up. So was Nalem, narrowed eyes darting between me and the trunk. I almost couldn't see the leviathan skull as Artemisia finished painting it, and Zalin impatiently tapped her foot nearby. Farris had those snow-white scissors in his hands, and he looked...worried. I flashed him a thumbs-up to claim I was okay. "Is everyone ready to go? Once we leave, it's either victory or death."

Everyone voiced their agreement, though their eyes were glued behind me. They wanted to ask. They doubted me.

But there wasn't time. Farris ran to the minotaurs, and Zalin shifted to snake form. Retz grabbed my hand and squeezed it one last time, his holdout pistol sticking out of the breast pocket of his shirt.

"Retz." Alexander looked down at his son, something almost close to regret in his eyes. "I'm...sorry I gave up on you. Don't make the mistake I did." He paused. "And when you head home, give Erika this. It's as close to the original as I could get."

He held out one hand. Retz offered his. I caught a glint of silver; Alexander's wedding band. Retz's face faltered, but he said nothing. Just nodded, dropped the ring into his breast pocket with the pistol, and ran over to join Nalem.

"I suspect you're more Ringmaster than Alexander," I told the doppelganger. "You're trying too hard to wrap up loose ends."

"I'm doing what I can to help you move on. I know my time's limited. Yours...shouldn't be."

Retz and Nalem climbed into Sea Mother's skull, which Zalin lifted up in her serpentine form; with Artemisia's paints, the skull and its cargo were hidden. She sped in one direction, while the minotaurs and

Farris charged in the other. That left Artemisia, though she paused upon seeing Alexander. "This is…"

"Complicated. We'll explain on the way." I pulled out my other pistol and offered it to Artemisia. "He's trying to help us. But if he does anything suspicious, shoot. He's plastic." Alexander nodded at this, at the paranoia he'd instilled in me from a young age. Thinking about it that way, I understood Retz's reluctance to leave Nalem more than I expected.

We climbed into the Mercury Marquis, me in the driver's seat and Alexander riding shotgun, just like when I was learning to drive. Except this time, we had Artemisia and a minotaur body in the back seat. Alexander glanced around the car. His nose wrinkled, almost human-like. Perhaps the most accurate thing I'd seen out of him yet. "What happened to the Impala?"

"Crashed it after you passed. But I also took out a troll with it, so I'd say that situation evened out in the end."

Alexander was quiet as I started the ignition. I'm sure the Ringmaster part of him wanted to voice all the apologies Alexander never got the chance to, but in a way, that'd make it harder to accept. Alexander had always stayed silent about his doubts, and I'd done the same. Those were hard walls to tear down after

building, and I couldn't let the flood they held back
sweep me away.

"You know the layout to this place?" I asked.

"Like it was a map of home. You'll want to
turn...hmm, cardinal directions don't work in this land.
The path on the left, that's where Monica went, and she
hasn't moved far."

"She was awful attached to that clown. Did you plan
this? Implant the desire to protect it in her brain?"

Alexander nodded slowly. "The Ringmaster did, yes.
The prospect of dying again terrified me–him, us,
whatever you'd say, and there was no telling what
Alexander planned."

He glanced at Artemisia in the rearview mirror. "If
it's any consolation, he saw reason before this
happened. He was going to reverse what he'd done. He
was scared their souls would break, like yours did, but
he was willing to try."

"Too little, too late," Artemisia said with a sigh. Her
fingers were dry again, her face nearly blank. "So, you're
the human parts that remain? Aiden tried to put on a
human form, early on. Couldn't get out of Arcadia
anyway."

"Nor can I. This is the land where we died, and after
what we've done, coming back wouldn't be right. We
already had more time than we should've, and

squandered every second of it. But dwelling on those mistakes won't redeem us." Alexander turned to me. I watched him out of the corner of my eye while I drove, trying to overwrite the Fae's face with this one. "Do you have a lighter?"

I nodded. "Didn't think you were poignant enough for a final smoke."

"I'm not. But there's a weakness you should know. Not for all Fae, but in this case...well. I don't suppose you've tried to set anything in this carnival alight?"

I hadn't. But sugar was fairly flammable. Plants too, especially with all the rot and dry bark that had covered Alexander's Fae form. "Hope Retz won't mind if I borrow some of his hair spray." And behind me, I heard Artemisia hum. I asked her, "Your paints...are they oil, or acrylic?"

"Oil. But it'll create toxic fumes, so make sure you cover your face." She put a hand to her chest. "Monica's near, isn't she?" Alexander nodded. "Yeah, I figured. The world's getting...clearer."

My scarf loosened around my throat. That mission was almost done. And if I got the two of them back to Earth, I might be able to convince the Harvester to put their soul back together. He'd likely show up to put Nalem back in Retz's body, after all. Question was, which body would remain? The human body that had been repeatedly possessed, or the one with power but no real face? Which one would make her happy? I didn't dare ask. She might not even know.

We drove the rest of the way in relative silence. I got Artemisia to root through Retz's bag of salon products for a can of hair spray, which I shoved into one of my many pockets. Another pocket housed a custom metal lighter Farris had gotten me as a present the first year we'd dated, among all the other supplies I always carried with me.

This had been Alexander's coat, the one this plastic tribute wore a copy of. I'd tried so hard to follow in his footsteps. And for what? I'd nearly lost myself for it. Part of me was glad to have my father back for a moment, but the other wanted to scream, to accuse him of warping me into his own image long before he'd gone Fae.

Words wouldn't change anything, I told myself. I tightened my hold on the steering wheel. The only thing that'd matter would be how I'd live my life after burning this damn carnival and its Fae to the ground.

Monica stood where the game stalls had been. Surrounded by a collection of plastic bodies with iridescent roses blooming from their bodies, she looked small and vulnerable. Some of those bodies had been people. Some had been meant for me or Retz.

Monica put her hands up. "Don't come any closer! I don't want to hurt you. Please." All around her, plastic heads turned.

Artemisia opened her door. "You don't have to be afraid anymore. I'm getting you out like I should've before, and we're going home together." Monica gasped. The plastic horde stepped toward us, forming a wall.

"We'll clear a path for you," I told Artemisia in a low voice. "Grab Monica and get out of here. We'll take care of the Fae."

"Appreciate the help, but I'm not leaving until everyone's out alive. I already turned my back on people trapped in here before."

"Fine. Get ready to run."

I rammed the Merc forward. Not right toward Monica, but veered off to plow through part of the crowd around her. As expected, they converged on the immediate threat. Plastic cracked and ooze burst along the car. I opened the door and rolled out, rising with a pistol in hand. I shot those nearest me. One almost got a strike in, one of those wearing my face. Alexander swept its feet out from under it with a swift kick, and I finished it off with a shot to the head.

I couldn't help but ask Alexander, "Did you really want me in a body like these?"

He reached for a gun at his hip that wasn't there. "When I learned you were transgender, I...blamed myself for not seeing it sooner. For not letting you grow up right. I thought this would make up for it."

"Can't fix everyone's problems for them." I handed him my pistol, and I grabbed the shotgun he'd given me years ago. "But we can pave the way for them to help themselves, right?"

"Right you are." And for the last time, father and son stood back-to-back against foes most humans couldn't comprehend in order to protect others. The way it should've always been.

20 - RETZ

At the beginning of last month I'd helped kill a lamia, five heads full of horrible, and ruined her dynasty. Now I was relying on her second-in-command to deliver me home, so I didn't die like her mistress had. Zalin should've wanted revenge. Maybe she did, but the promise of a safe haven and a fresh start outweighed her bloodthirst. How funny was that?

No, not funny at all. Ironic. Or maybe just sad. Words are hard when your brain's shutting down.

Nalem and I clung to the inside of Sea Mother's skull. Each of us had an eye socket to peer out of, watching the carnival fall apart around us. To keep us from falling out of the bottom of the skull, we'd pulled thin strips of bone over our wrists and ankles, shackling us into place. Good thing we did; Zalin slithered so fast, I probably would've lost my grip. I'm still impressed she didn't drop us, what with balancing the skull on her two heads. Nalem had offered to temporarily fuse it to one of her skulls, but no one else thought that was a good idea.

The edges of my vision blurred. I focused on the pain from my slow-healing wounds, letting their sharp prickling keep me awake. My chest felt like it got tighter, reminded me how the thorns inside me rested uncomfortably close to the underside of my skin. I stopped breathing. At this rate, I'd have to shut down every facsimile of humanity in order to stay alive. I forgot to breathe all the time, but not having the option to pretend, even in a place as inhuman as this, struck me in a strange way.

The carnival fence had fallen when Dad invaded, and the Rosemaster built it back up with, no surprise, more brambles. Carnival flyers hung from thorns, looking like wanted posters. We steered clear of the carnival entrance, since even if the Rosemaster had moved on from where Jarrod and the others had last seen him, the Fae likely had the exit guarded to keep folks from breaking out. Not a problem for us. If Zalin couldn't get over the brambles, we'd glide the skull down. We figured I'd have enough strength for that.

We had to keep quiet so we didn't give away our position. I wanted so bad to talk. Not because I needed to drown out my thoughts...but because those were leaving too. My head was going dark, shutting out the lights on the way out.

I shouldn't have been scared of dying, right? I'd done it once before. And long as I made it out of Arcadia before croaking, I wouldn't be a monster like my father, just quiet for a minute. Like falling asleep. Or had I just forgotten how bad it was? The Ringmaster had been so terrified of dying, he forbade it in his realm. I'm sure dying so many times hadn't done wonders for Nalem's mental health either. And there had to be a reason I kept wanting to run, though my limbs felt heavy and I had nowhere to go.

Feeling Zalin jolt as something cleaved her tail down to the bone didn't help matters.

My first instinct was to harden her bones and fix the damaged vertebrae, but a wave of dizziness struck when I did. Right, didn't have much power left. Felt too sluggish when I turned my head to see what had attacked. Zalin's tail bled, actual iron-smelling blood instead of black ooze, thanks to an axe sticking out of it. Nothing colorful or flower-themed about it. But no one was holding the axe–

Wait. There was a new, hulking set of bones climbing up Zalin's body. Knives pierced into scales and flesh to keep hold. And not much could get through a lamia's scales, so Zalin wasn't taking being stabbed too well.

"Ginny! Damn it, I thought those fools had already dealt with her–" Nalem was cut off as Zalin's heads thrashed, and we tried to keep ourselves and the skull steady. "We have to move! Now!"

"Oh no you don't, ratfink!" Ginny hurled herself from where she'd stabbed her daggers, and with all her strength, cleared the distance to reach one of Zalin's heads. Zalin couldn't shake her off. We tried to get the skull floating. Ginny grabbed the back of one skull, I couldn't even remember the proper term for it, and held us down. Rivulets of blood trickled down Zalin's back, red like Ginny's grin.

"Ginny you fool, are you blind to how the situation has changed?" Nalem shouted. He formed spikes in the skull to make Ginny let go. They pierced her skin, but she didn't budge.

"When it comes to you, nothing changes. That's the problem!" She pulled herself along the skull, closer to us. Her limbs were long enough she could keep from falling out through the jaw. Spikes and teeth didn't deter her. "You ignore the world around you, no matter how hard we shout. You refuse to change direction, even when disaster's dead ahead! You cast aside those who care about you so damn much, and for what?"

What would she do if she reached us? Choke the life out of us, then pummel the Fae to dust? Drag us back to the Rosemaster and let them warp us how they wished? If the skull couldn't stop her, and getting close enough to affect her bones was a death wish...

...I had a birthday present specifically gifted to keep me alive.

Since my hands were shackled and most of my remaining power was focused on keeping the skull from plummeting us to our doom, I could only move the pistol with aching slowness. I inched it out of my breast pocket and tried to remember everything I'd ever learned about guns. Not much; no one had ever expected I'd use one. Jarrod had even joked once that my arms were such twigs, the kickback of a normal gun might shatter my arm. I think he'd been joking. But I'd seen the weapons in action, and I'd felt at least some of the havoc bullets could wreak through a body.

Ginny chewed out Nalem, but her claims faded into a low buzz. Couldn't keep my attention on that much at once. Aiming the pistol was a challenge, and I tried to figure out what Jarrod meant by aiming down the sights, as this thing didn't exactly have a scope.

Zalin jerked, and we were shaken with her. The shackles on my wrist kept me in place, but it took longer than it should've for my vision to stop spinning.

Ginny, probably realizing this skull would fall soon with her in it, barreled toward us, using every nook and cranny in the skull as a handhold. Her gaze zeroed in on Nalem; she didn't even seem to notice me. I felt the twitch in her bones as she reached for Nalem.

A couple facts about guns. One, even the tiny pistols are loud. Felt like my ears blew out soon as I fired. Two, bullets ricochet a lot once they enter the body. They don't enter straight like in the movies. I wasn't aiming to kill Ginny, but even with her thick skin and bulked-out body, the bullet still pierced her palm and made a mess out of her arm. Bone fractured and shattered. And as she screamed, Nalem grabbed her hand and sent the bone fragments through her flesh.

Ginny lost her hold on the skull and fell through the jaw. Thought that'd be the end of her, but her uninjured hand grabbed bone at the last minute, pierced with teeth to keep it in place. She stared up at us with pure hate.

She spat, "I'll haunt you, you know. You think that leviathan of yours was a menace? I'll make your lives a living hell for your betrayal. Even the Harvester will shit himself at the thought of coming near me."

"Bold of you to assume I will grant you permission to die," Nalem said, sneering as if she hadn't come close enough to beat him into a pulp. "In fact, I believe you deserve a chance to repent for your actions. I can even make a room in your beloved tavern for your solitary confinement. Benevolent, am I not?"

Blood dripped from Ginny's arm to the ground far below. "That's not how you treat your devotees, asshole. Or a friend."

"Friend?" Nalem laughed. I knew that cruel sound too well. I almost preferred my thoughts spiraling out of control. "Ginny, who ever heard of a god having friends? What we have are tools to serve our needs, and only a fool befriends the means to their handiwork."

Ginny said nothing. She looked...sad. The red in her skin faded. Her body was shrinking back to boggan form.

Then she looked at me in pity. As if she knew my plan to join Nalem again.

She let go.

The skull lurched as if to follow her, and I realized I'd lost my focus. Shoved it back, only for the pistol to fall. I barely caught it, but I couldn't float it back up. It hung like a guillotine, pointed down at Ginny. She hit the ground, and though the cotton candy made the ground look like a cloud this far up, it still stained red.

"Is she...?"

"No. Even in her boggan form, she's far sturdier than she looks." Nalem floated the pistol back to my hand. "You did well."

I nodded. Then made the mistake of looking down again. The ground looked...a lot closer. Were we slipping?

"The bitch poisoned her daggers," one of Zalin's heads hissed.

"How can you be poisoned?" Nalem shouted.

"Just because I'm venomous doesn't mean I'm immune to all toxins! This isn't a video game!" She coughed and shuddered.

Nalem swore. "We need to head out. Now. Little one, are you ready?"

Honestly, no. I couldn't even lift the gun. But what choice did I have? Everyone else pushed themselves to keep going forward, despite the pain. I couldn't let them down. "Yeah. Okay."

With a thrust of power, Sea Mother's skull took to the sky. For a moment, it drifted nice and languid, perfectly cloud-like. But a skull's a heavy thing to keep up, our fading powers versus gravity. I tried to push as best as I could. Long as we could make it over the bramble gate...

"And where do you think you're going?" asked two voices, both eerily familiar and shifted out of character.

They sounded loud but far away. Maybe I could outrun them. Out-float? Out...

"Hold still," the Rosemaster continued, sounding closer with each word, "so we can end this. Then we can leave the easy work of killing behind and get to the hard work of building everything back up again. Though I might have to make a fake you for a time, in order to keep the rest of the family...cooperative."

Oh hell no. A hot red surge ran through me, clearing my vision and juicing up power I thought had run out. I didn't get angry often, sure as hell never understood what Jarrod meant when lamenting about the supposed short fuse huldras had. As my head cleared and thoughts realigned from survival to revenge...I started to get it. Except by that point, I didn't care. Not while the motherfucker who'd stolen my dad's voice was still standing.

"You won't kill me again without a fight. And you sure as hell won't fuck up Jarrod and Mom anymore."

21 - JARROD

In the middle of violence and bloodshed, a soul came back together.

I didn't hear what was said when Artemisia reached her other half, but they weren't words meant for me. She offered a hand. Monica reluctantly took it, tears the color of ink welling up in her eyes. She screamed and collapsed into her other half's arms. And when the Rosemaster's goons got close enough to threaten that fragile reunion, I shot out the minion's legs.

My scarf finally hung loose around my neck, the curse satiated for the time being; I'd brought Alexander his intruders, after all, even if what happened after surely wasn't what he'd planned. The air around us had gone from sweet to cloying, but I took a deep breath anyway. I'd gotten one damn thing right.

As the din of battle died down, I caught the mannequin who looked so much like Alexander staring at Monica and Artemisia with a distant sorrow in his eyes. Was it the Ringmaster in him, coming to terms with what he'd broken and been unable to repair? Or were all those jumbled bits of broken souls inside of him envious, aware he'd never be whole unless he gave in to either hatred or death?

I felt like I had to say something. "You'll be able to rest soon," was all I could come up with. "Then it'll stop hurting."

Alexander agreed with a curt nod. "I shouldn't have run from it. Humanity isn't a cheap bauble to bargain away, even for completing one's life work." He turned away from the ladies and I, so I couldn't see his face when he said, "I fear I understand Nalem now. This un-life must be what he's lived this entire time. And we handled it just as poorly."

Behind us, Monica sobbed into Artemisia's coat as she cried, "I remember! He broke me! Us! What have I been doing all this time?"

"You didn't know," Artemisia answered softly.

"That doesn't matter! I should've fought back anyway. I should've...!" Her words gave way to whimpers. It made the dam I'd built around my heart threaten to break.

But I didn't have time to cry. Even with wounded, cursed bodies around me, and fake mannequins that wore my face, I couldn't cry. Not until those responsible were put to rest. And with them, I'd put part of me to rest too.

Alexander stared off into the sky. I wondered if he was gathering his thoughts for another apology, full of words that blurred the line between Alexander's truths and what pretty lies the Ringmaster thought we "needed" to hear. Then I followed his gaze.

Even from so far away, Ginny stuck out, a red blot tearing her way up the shuddering lamia. Artemisia's camouflage on the skull smeared away under Ginny's hands, revealing Sea Mother's head like a glitch in the sky. What little I could see shuddered. Zalin's body writhed, and she had a hard time keeping her heads steady to support the skull she carried.

Retz was going to fall. Even if I hopped in the Merc and rammed through every obstacle in my way, I couldn't reach him in time. What worth did any of the past ten years hold if I lost my brother now?

The fight went fast. We saw Ginny fall. But then Monica whispered, "The Rosemaster's on their way to that skull." Zalin didn't look well, shuddering even as the skull slowly floated off her heads, then plummeted toward the ground. They'd be easy prey for a determined Fae.

How does one distract a monster who's lost all humanity, and whose sole reason for existing—in this

case, killing Nalem, and probably Retz too–is about to
literally fall in its lap?

Wait. That monster was Alexander, true. But it was
also the Ringmaster. All he'd ever wanted was to make
people perfect and happy. And I had his greatest failure
right in front of me.

"I've got a plan. Artemisia, can you help me grab a
few things from the car?" I turned to Alexander and
said, "And can you make sure Monica stays? She
shouldn't be alone right now." Both of them nodded;
they got the hint I couldn't have the Rosemaster listen in
through its vessels. Artemisia gently pried her other half
away with apologetic words before joining me.
Alexander went to Monica's side, and just as in life, he
seemed uncertain how to comfort a traumatized
innocent.

Artemisia and I met by the car. I handed her what
she'd need for my plan. She handed my pistol back. I
apologized to her for what I would do, because it had to
seem like a real threat. She said she trusted me. I almost
told her that was foolish, but I bit my tongue.

And I pulled a gun on her.

"I know both of you are still connected to the
Rosemaster," I said as I grabbed Artemisia's arm and
shoved the muzzle of my pistol against her temple. "Let

it know that since it wants to kill Retz and Nalem so badly, I'm taking two bodies of my own. Both halves of Monica, starting with this one."

Monica's mouth formed a perfect O of shock with black ink tears marring her pink lipstick. Alexander's eyes turned to ice as if he could read my bluff. Maybe those behind their eyes did. But then both faces split into tight smiles that tore the edges of their cheeks.

"Didn't we build you up better than that?" Alexander said in a singsong voice the living him never would've used. "Suppose we'll have to make time for remedial lessons after this is all done."

Monica cheered, "We can rebuild him. Better, faster, more human, and without so many rash thoughts in his head. Won't that be grand?"

"I gave you a ticket, didn't I? Yet you weren't able to change me and haven't stopped Nalem...so much for all the good you promised to accomplish." I slowly eased back the hammer of the pistol with my thumb. Artemisia's breath hitched, but she didn't budge. "You keep harping on about how dangerous Retz is under Nalem's influence, but I've learned from that necromancer *and* from you. You know Retz and Nalem aren't going anywhere fast. Their power's shot. But me? I'll tear you down, and I don't even need an iron sword to do it."

Eyes narrowed. Lips split and bled black. They said in unison, "All we have to do is tell you no."

"Bold of you to assume I care anymore."

"Don't shoot Artemisia." The words burrowed into my neck. The scarf tightened around my neck, and my fingers pulsed with pain, begging me not to fire.

I said, "Stop me if you can." And I released the hammer.

The ground quaked and rolled in waves as brambles tipped with hands instead of flowers broke through the earth. Monica collapsed to the ground, and Alexander barely caught her as their smiles broke. Artemisia flinched, but stayed standing. She'd seen me take out the bullet and toss it into my pocket; I knew better than to gamble with live rounds. I holstered the pistol, knowing it wouldn't work against the Rosemaster, but that was fine by me. I had plenty of lighters in my pocket, and all of the hairspray I could find in Retz's hairdressing supplies.

"Crafty," the Rosemaster crooned as they formed, "but you're a child playing a game far too complicated for his nascent brain." The Rosemaster looked much like the Ringmaster had, even if their arms were primarily made of brambles and their face had two mouths

stacked atop one another, a smiling one for the
Ringmaster and a deep frown for Alexander.

"I'm not a child anymore. Hell, I was an adult before
you died. Even if I followed your orders for far longer
than I should've, I'm not your puppet."

The Rosemaster simultaneously chuckled and
grimaced. "Claim that all you'd like, but it doesn't
change your curse. And that won't leave unless I deem
you worthy of a new body. But if you're such an adult
and don't want one..." Shrugs from the Rosemaster's
many shoulders rippled down their back. They spoke a
clear, definitive order: "You will not harm me. Now, how
will you stop me?"

With trust. Trusting that if I bought time, even with
my body, everyone else might make it out alive.
That Farris's Fatebreaker could cut through a curse even
after it had begun. That the minotaurs had their iron
and their anger in case all else failed.

I began to run.

The Rosemaster's many hands came after me,
stretching as the brambles grew like Spring on double-
time. They could've told me to hold still, but that'd be too
easy. They wanted me to squirm, to beat me down and
make me regret ever standing. I zig-zagged around the
broken game stalls as I tried to figure out where to
strike. I'd only have one shot before my curse kicked in.

Thankfully, I wasn't alone. And I'd handed Artemisia the key to the Merc. While the Rosemaster's attention was stuck on me, she jumped in the car and rammed it forward, crunching brambles and clipping the Rosemaster's side. She swerved before they could retaliate and drove on, leaving a trail of paint in her wake. The passenger door opened as she passed Monica and pulled her inside. Alexander wasn't with her, so where...

A bullet grazed my shoulder. He still had my other pistol. I turned and found him by a busted shooting gallery game, arms shaking. He must've been fighting the Rosemaster's control; he never would've missed otherwise. I wanted to put him out of his misery. But he was still part of the Rosemaster, even if only the humanity that managed to escape. Hurting him would trigger the curse.

I muttered an apology under my breath though it wouldn't be heard. Pointed to Alexander and shouted, "Artemisia! You know what to do." She flashed a thumb's up through the window before slamming on the gas. I didn't watch to see if she ran him down, or listen for if his body went crunch or splat.

No matter where I turned, the Rosemaster was already there. They could read my thoughts, after all.

When I climbed, they knocked down my support or grew brambles to force my escape. If I tried to get close, fallen bodies rose once more, moved by vines whether or not they were dead. The Rosemaster spun string out of candyfloss while they watched me, crafting cat cradles between their many fingers and thorns. For every decision I might make, they could craft a trap. Planning didn't matter when I couldn't out-think them.

I could give way to that anger I'd clung to. Let instinct and passion carry me through, the way Mom and all the other huldras did. But since I'd spent so long tamping it down, were those instincts dulled, those emotions washed out by will and alcohol alike?

"You know better than that," The Rosemaster taunted, both mouths taut behind their smiles. "You can't reach your anger because I raised you better than that. You're *human*, Jarrod. Not a monster."

The minotaurs were monsters, and they risked their entire herd to stop this Faerie and help one of their own. Ginny was a monster, and even if I didn't agree with her, all she'd done had been to save the person she cared about most. Farris became a monster and hadn't lost himself yet. My brother and I were born from a so-called monster who'd done nothing but love and care for us.

"I know what the hell I am," I said. And I let my thoughts go.

The world divided itself into isolated sensations. How my muscles moved, bones against joints, the push and pull of muscles. Vines snapping, a softer crunch than breaking bones. Viscous liquid on skin. Falling. A color of sky I couldn't quite place. Rising. Pulling away bonds. Blood and sugar and ooze all matting against my skin. Words washing over me.

Two smiles, teeth bared in fear. They grew wider, crept up to reach eyes and twitching fingers, each step I took.

"Damn right, you should be scared of me." I'm not sure if I thought that or voiced my threats. "That's why you tried to hide me so long, even from myself. But it's alright. I'm on my way."

My arms stung. So did my legs. Getting harder to breathe. A stray thought sparked; had I been cursed again? Or did I strike early without realizing it? The Rosemaster wasn't dead yet, but some of the thorns in my fingers seemed to come from the inside.

"There's nothing left for you after this," The Rosemaster said. "There won't be anything for your prince to recover once the curse takes hold. Unless you let me do my job and put you in a new body–"

I was close enough to see the rot Alexander couldn't escape, cracks in the plastic of the Rosemaster's perfect crafted skin. How wide his eyes had grown. And how the trail of paint Artemisia left behind had splattered onto the Rosemaster when she'd clipped them.

"I like this one. Thanks." My knuckles itched for blood. I pried my hands open and grabbed the lighter and hairspray instead. Crude but effective, just like me.

The pyre of the Rosemaster smelled of campfires, caramel, melting plastic and burning flesh all at once. Maybe some of that last element was mine. Even with the stench and screaming, my head refused to clear all the way. I tried to shake off the haze, but my body followed sluggishly. I couldn't move my fingers once the hairspray ran out. Couldn't move from the burning Faerie, so I had to stare at two familiar faces coming undone.

"I'm so sorry," one said. "This is what you get for defying me," hissed the other. And it didn't matter who said what. "You gave it all up," they both said.

"You pointed it out to me earlier, after all. I never planned on growing old." Except this time, I did. I trusted the others would find me and undo this curse. I'd have the rest of my life to figure out what I could do besides kill. There had to be something. Monsters could make as well as destroy.

I didn't want those faces to be my last conscious thought. I looked at the lighter in my hand. Farris had gotten it for me. Leaves sprouting from my fingers covered what was engraved in the metal: an open coffin and the words "Late to an Early Grave".

Let's hope I'd continue to be just that.

I stopped breathing.

And then, who knew how long later, came searing white pain in the back of my neck. I screamed, and air rushed into my lungs. My body hurt all over, like that brief moment of yanking out a splinter where it stings before the relief sets in, but spread across my skin. My limbs unfroze and collapsed. Hands caught me and pulled me close to a cold, empty chest so I didn't fall into the Rosemaster's corpse.

Farris gasped, "Holy shit, why did I stab there? Did I break your spinal column? Babe, say something, anything, I'm begging you."

My first attempt to speak resulted in coughing up rose petals. I then managed to gasp, "Give me a moment. Think I turned into a plant."

"You sure as hell did! Don't scare me like that again!"

I tested my limbs by reaching up a hand to pat Farris. Felt like pushing through a wall of mud, but at least I could move. The green runes of my curse fled as I looked at my skin, but left grooves in their wake as if my skin were bark. I've never been vain, but I did feel a pang of disappointment at the sight. But I'd stand by my body as I'd said. Besides, I had long-sleeved shirts.

I tried look around. After everything else that had happened, the pain from that almost knocked me out.

"How long does Fatebreaker need to stay in?"

"Shit, I...I don't know. Once you're flesh instead of flowers, I guess." Farris ran his fingers along my body. I winced as he found more wounds than I recalled receiving.

"Do you know what happened with Retz and Nalem? Are they okay?"

Somewhere behind me, Isolde spoke up. "We can no longer sense their auras. This can mean only one of two things. They escaped, or they perished. Either way, they did so together." She stabbed her iron sword into the earth moments later. Into the remnants of the Rosemaster, I bet, ensuring they stayed dead this time. I absently wondered what had won out in their final moments: Ringmaster, no, Aiden's fear of death, or Alexander accepting the inevitable had finally happened. Maybe both. Or neither. Maybe all that remained were hate and purpose. It didn't matter anymore, did it?

"Let's get everyone out of here," I said.

"Starting with you," Farris agreed. He kissed my forehead. "You've done a helluva lot today. Too much, I'd argue, but I'm biased. We'll handle the rest."

He slid the scissors out and held me. He seemed ready to heft me up and carry me out himself, but Bolton tapped him on the shoulder. The minotaur said, "Uh, you said that with all your warping, you might need help getting out of here. And it wouldn't be good if you both collapsed once we made it through the gate."

Farris groaned, but acquiesced. Bolton scooped me up into a fireman's lift, though I barely made the width of his shoulders. Then he scooped up Farris under his arm for good measure. Farris protested, but didn't struggle.

I had plenty I could've worried about. The past I'd just buried. The future and all the possibilities that might be waiting on the other side of that Arcadian gate. Instead of any of that, I closed my eyes to the carnival, which slowly fell apart without its master to sustain it. As if I were a plant again, I let myself just be.

I was free, and damn the cost of it all.

22 - NALEM

Hell hath no fury like a man fighting against the throes of death. Call me an expert, for I have been that man many times before. Yet seeing Retz consumed by wrath was not an experience I ever expected. Considering the way I'd reared him, he rarely held much fight of his own. He had to be stirred to action by others; even now, his fury was born of a desire to protect his family. As if they, instead of he, were the ones dying.

But while my empty vessel does not bite often, do not think his teeth dull. No, there's a fire in him, bright enough to entertain me and almost make me fear. Almost. I have outlasted many terrors, after all. This carnival and its twisted Fae were only the latest.

Sea Mother's skull crashed into the earth soon after taking flight, though we did successfully clear the bramble barrier. We'd freed ourselves from inside the skull; protective as it was, staying inside while earthbound would only lead to us being overwhelmed and trapped, as we had earlier before Farris had summoned Fatebreaker.

The Rosemaster taunted us with words while staying out of sight, making their minions do the dirty work. Their union was still fresh and thus chaotic, so their creations resembled mannequins with roots and thorns breaking out of the plastic. Given time, I am certain their designs would become equal parts deadly and elegant. They wouldn't if I had any say in the matter.

Nor would Retz. He was the one flinging Sea Mother's teeth through the encroaching horde, when minutes ago he could barely lift a gun. As I said, rage could work wonders. Of course, I feared it might also sap what little of his lifeforce remained. Thus, it fell on me to drag him away once we had a chance to flee. I refused to let his stubbornness and daddy issues doom us.

"Listen up, little one. You are doing an admirable job clearing their ranks, but as soon as this wave is extinguished, we must be away. You knock on death's door, in case that fact has fled your empty skull."

Retz had the gall to snarl. I normally would have chided him for this, but from outside his body, there was little I could do against a huldra's wrath. I instead offered a silent apology to Sea Mother's spirit before flinging a few of her teeth myself.

Where was my viola when I needed it? Right, Retz had it. As if he sounded better than a caterwauling drunkard when he played. I opened the case dangling from Retz's arm and slid the instrument out. With my powers so limited in this body without bone, I had to play it with my own two hands. It felt far too elegant against those clunky plastic fingers. Yet I found comfort in holding it again. As if Loresha were truly beside me, not distorted in this temporary reflection.

I would reunite with her soon, come Samhain. That was my primary reason for surviving, and furthermore keeping Retz alive as well. I needed a cooperative vessel in order to join my family for their sordid reunion. If I played my cards well, Retz could be my penultimate vessel before achieving my true form, an immortal body that would house an immortal soul.

But here in the present, I had to fight for survival. I pulled the bow along the strings and its energy thrummed through me. I couldn't quite reach the heights of power I possessed when working alongside a vessel, but I would make do. Sea Mother's skull trembled as it rose, barely clearing the grass and the scraps of candyfloss that had escaped the carnival, but that's all I needed. I launched into a shanty I hadn't heard since I'd last played it for her and charged her into the Rosemaster's forces.

I expected this to lure the Rosemaster out to face us in serious combat, but they dared not show their mangled face. Their taunts had also ceased. I reached out my senses, and it took far longer to hit the static energies of a Fae. In fact, I sensed Jarrod on the move, with Monica nearby. They'd somehow lured the Rosemaster to their position. I did not waste time questioning how.

After clearing out the remaining forces, I halted my song and grabbed Retz 'round the arm. "The Rosemaster's fled. We must take the opportunity to do the same."

Retz blinked the way that warriors do once the screams of war give way for the silence of solace and scavengers. "Where did they...?"

Telling him that Jarrod had lured the Fae away would only encourage him to give chase so he could keep his brother safe. I forsook honesty and said, "The minotaurs make a persistent distraction. Or perhaps Farris opened his mouth."

Retz let out a huff of breath I assume was intended to be a laugh. But he seemed steady on his feet for the time being, and when I strode toward the gate, he kept his arm linked with mine, keeping pace. We stayed off the path in an attempt to stay hidden, but I always kept it in view in order to find our way to the gate. I also flipped the skull onto its side and floated it along as a makeshift shield in case the Rosemaster was smart enough to station guards along the path. I had to keep playing the viola with my powers to keep everything moving, so if there were any guards, they'd be fools not to find us instantly.

I told myself the gate to the mortal realm could not be far away. As if such logic could stop Arcadia from spinning and lurching around me, its chaos battering against my soul. As if distance might keep Retz alive a little longer. I glanced over at him. He'd gone quiet and pale again.

"Little one, talk to me. I've grown so used to your incessant prattling, I am unable to focus without it." Moreover, I could gauge his condition if he spoke. And maybe, if need be, talk him back from the edge if despair set in. It often did once anger ran out.

"You too, huh? Thought I was just crazy. I mean. Maybe I am." Retz's lips twitched in lieu of a smile. "You've died before. Like, a lot. What's it like?"

Agonizing. I get the briefest glimpse of an afterlife, hazy imagined locales where souls purified themselves for their next lives, be it through joy or flames. They reached a respite from life and all its chaos. I only ever got to watch before diving back into heartbeats and heartache. Because the world needed me, disregarding if I needed it back.

"The pain leaves so swiftly, you'll scarcely recall it set in." At least he would only be dead for a moment, should we make it in time. But in order for me to rejoin his body, he would have to die first. The few times my soul with its infinite energies had been placed in a living body...well, let's say I usually needed another new body moments later, and spare the gory details.

Retz kept talking, mostly about his fears of death and his new resolution to live, nothing I hadn't heard a million times before. I paid only enough attention to mutter an answer as I kept us alive. Our progress remained slow. Retz grew quieter over time. Sea Mother's skull eventually scraped against the ground as we moved, even when I played my viola for power. But there, just ahead, were the fallen trees that formed the gate. A fern-covered ridge surrounded by redwoods flickered into view on the other side.

We were almost home.

Then gunfire. Pain exploding in the back of my skull. My vision going out. Of all the damnable things for the Ringmaster to get right, why was it how the occipital lobe worked?! My face struck the ground hard, even with the candyfloss giving it the illusion of softness.

"Damn it! I knew this was a trap. Or that you couldn't fight it. Either way, this is your fault!" Judging by Retz's shouts, I assumed my assailant was the mannequin copy of Alexander. I should have killed it the moment it climbed out of the trunk.

"I'm not here for you."

"I thought you were finally trying to make up for everything you fucked up! I don't care if you're being controlled by the Rosemaster or not; your way isn't going to solve anything. It never was, because you had no idea who the hell you were dealing with." Retz's voice shook as he spoke. Even if he hadn't worshipped the fool as a hero the way Jarrod had, a part of him still regarded Alexander with respect, shattered and broken as it was.

But Alexander was not the first self-righteous fool I had faced. I knew how his kind operated, even if I begged for it to turn out different every time I faced my own father.

See, mortals always believe themselves to be so important.

So bold, to assume their lives will have impact. They see change happen over the course of their lives and cry, "Look at me! I've made a difference!" But it crumbles the moment they turn their backs. Existence is like the tide;

good becomes bad, becomes good again. Empires rise, fall, rebuild themselves in memory, echo in inspiration to the point of wondering if they ever lost control.

I have seen all those fools fighting in the carnival, across six millennia of lives muddled by memory. I have faced those like Isolde in her Grecian home along the ocean, with Ginnys fencing beside me. I have stared down Farrises in a thousand fortresses and brought them low each time. Artemisia could give herself the face of a million different lost girls, and I would find each of them familiar.

And Alexander...Alexander was a type of man who'd cropped up everywhere from castle halls to trailer parks. There would always be those who thought they, and they alone, made righteous change in the world. Their conviction built into the very scaffolding of their existence, and once broken, they were a danger to all around them. Alexander could not allow his children a final gasp at happiness, despite the Ringmaster's best attempts. If they were not to his perfect standards, they deserved pain. So would the rest of the world, after enough logic. It was why he could justify damning it to kill me.

But I do not die easy.

I got back to my feet, vision clearing as the sugary ooze this body was built from melded back together, and picked up my fallen viola. I put myself between father and son and prepared to play.

"Retz, I will hold him off. Get through the gate, immediately." He shot me a look as if about to argue. "If you die here, then we'll have another Fae on our hand. Do you wish to turn out like this fool before us?"

Alexander's grip on his pistol–one of Jarrod's, by the looks of it–shook. Others would posit qualms of conscience or fighting against the Rosemaster's control. I took it for rage at being interrupted.

Retz fled. I ran toward Alexander even as I began my song, and the bones hidden inside the viola case flew to join me. Seeing me as the more immediate threat, Alexander fired. Sea Mother's skull almost blocked the shot in time when I brought it forward as a shield, but the bullet passed through my hair. I rammed the skull into Alexander before he could prioritize Retz as his next target.

Ah, to finally get away with pummeling this man into his grave without anyone raising a fuss. It almost made this whole debacle worth it. What a pity he lacked bones for me to warp. I'd long wondered if he could hold his arrogant scowl with cheekbones tearing out of his face.

"How kind of you to sacrifice yourself," Alexander growled. One arm hung limp as it oozed black, but it seemed that had taken the brunt of the skull's force. "After all this time, have you finally recognized your own wickedness?"

"I've been a bane to man and monster alike so long, your oldest myths feature my likeness whilst forgetting my name. Yet you believed yourself able to stop me."

Behind me, Sea Mother's skull yawned open. The bones I'd summoned sharpened into stakes. Alexander pointed the pistol at my head. His injured arm began to melt, and flecks of skin flitted away like ash. In the far distance, I sensed a shift as bone turned to plant. Jarrod had finally activated his curse. And nearer, another body drove rapidly toward the gate. Monica? Seems this party was coming to a close.

"Do you wish to know a secret? Something special you can carry to your grave?"

I pinned the stakes through his legs. I paused my song and leaned in, almost close enough to whisper in his ear but not quite. The rest of his body was melting, and I didn't want a single splash of it marring this body, even if it was false.

"I am the single force protecting the world you once loved. And to achieve my goals, I will also be the one to condemn it. Your son has personally helped me come closer than ever to my true form, and for bringing us together...I thank you."

Destroying a man's body is all good fun, but destroying his spirit seconds before death so he has no time to come to peace with the magnitude of his sins? Nothing quite compares. I couldn't help but take a moment to watch that plastic body melt away into ooze, seeping into the Arcadian dirt.

I heard the grumble of an engine behind me. There on the path were Artemisia and Monica, driving that eyesore of a vehicle Jarrod had acquired. I offered a languid wave and waited to see if Monica would attack. She watched me with her typical confused wariness.

"What're you doing here, and where's Retz?" Artemisia asked.

"I'm cleaning up the mistakes of others, as is typically my lot." I pointed down the path, where I could no longer sense Retz. "My other half has escaped to the mortal world once more. I will join him shortly. Is that why you two came here? Were you concerned?"

The two halves of one girl shared a look. Artemisia said, "We also came to wrap up some loose ends, but looks like you beat us to it. And...yeah, we were worried about Retz." She leaned out of the car window and drew a red X on her face with paint from her fingers. "He's a good kid. Only one who came looking for us without a grudge, and maybe the most selfless person here."

"He doesn't deserve a monster like you in his head," Monica blurted before covering her mouth, as if surprised by her own words. Artemisia stiffened, but she didn't take back the words; they seemed to be of one mind on this matter.

I shrugged and returned my bones to their case. I needed a moment to catch my metaphorical breath before bringing the skull home. I still had much to do before I could leave this town in peace to continue my plans.

"Retz may not deserve me, but in the same vein, I certainly do not deserve to be shunted between vessels for all of time. If what any of us deserved mattered, we would not be here."

I felt downright charitable, so I even grabbed Jarrod's pistol before sauntering to the car. "No sense in walking alone if our destination is the same. Would you mind unlocking the door? Crafting a skeleton key can take some time, you see."

Artemisia groaned, and Monica glared, but they complied. I sat in the back next to Bertha's body. I absently wondered, with the Ringmaster gone, if there was any way to reunite Bertha's true head and body. Not that the tribulations of mortals mattered to me any. This fiasco had only proven that even the most seemingly stalwart mortal will prove a flighty mess who thinks they can understand the depth of my experience. How bold to assume any of them know what's best for themselves, much less what's best for a god.

The car rolled slowly along the path, as if the ladies were scared that a trap waited for them at the gate. I floated Sea Mother behind us, her head bobbing as if drifting along the waves. I would need a new place to hide her. A place where she could find the peace promised by death. No one deserved an undeath of anger and pain such as mine, least of all her.

I mentioned off-hand, "The Harvester will be waiting for us on the other side. Have either of you encountered him before? A man covered in eyes, or a silver-skinned reaper of souls?" Both muttered that all they possessed of him were rumors. At least that reaction could be amusing, a rare occurrence when dealing with my father. "You know, he is perhaps the one being other than the Ringmaster who could reunite the broken pieces of your soul. But I have to wonder...which body will you choose to keep?"

They did not answer me, but in the rearview mirror, I caught Monica's furtive glances at her other self, while Artemisia's fingers absently leaked paint the color of blonde hair and pink nails. Either decision would cut them off from a world.

We passed the threshold, the damnable saturation and sugar giving way to dark skies overhead and the deep scent of redwoods around us. The path itself was not lit due to the trails closing after dark, but the car's headlights illuminated our surroundings. Close to the gate, lying in the ferns and propped up against a stump, was Retz. Seeing as he did not breathe, I could not watch his body for indication of life. Especially not with my father crouched beside him.

"Loresha?" He stopped when he saw my face. He knew, just as I did, that it was wrong. His face grew soft anyway at the memory of my sister. "Nalem. You made it." He gestured to Retz. "Would've been cruel to let him die alone like so many others, don't you think?"

"Not for me it isn't." How many death throes have drowned out my thoughts in past lives? I've witnessed the final thoughts of all my vessels, confessions and revolts, terror and peace. That is what truly numbed me to suffering; if I'd continued to hold their pain so close to my own, it would have long since mired me.

But Retz was young. He didn't remember his first death. And like me, he never asked for any of this. All he ever wanted was to live.

I walked over to him, knelt by his side, and held his hand. "Little one, you may rest now. I have returned. We made it." His fingers twitched, so faint I could scarcely sense it. I almost felt sorry, and I hated it.

I said, "Before you do this, I have a favor to ask of you. Ginny—"

"We will take care of her. Pity. She'd been a friend to you for so long." The Harvester sighed. "You really must stop burning through allies like this. One of these days, you'll be well and truly alone."

"As if you'd be so lucky to escape. We're stuck in this together, you and I." And I would never let him, or those he stood for, forget it.

It was hard to tell when Retz died again. He didn't have a heartbeat, and I could neither see nor sense that ephemeral life core that huldras possessed. But after a long moment, the Harvester removed his gloves and put a hand to Retz's forehead. "It's going to hurt, this time. He's sustained a lot of damage."

"Pain is nothing new. Get me out of this mockery; it won't do for me to look this way at Samhain."

The Harvester tilted his head, but whatever he considered asking, he was smart enough to choke it down. He reached for my eyes, and I felt my soul disconnect from the vessel with a pop. The body crumbled into a heap. Sorrow pure and cold choked me at the sight, even though I knew it wasn't her.

"The real one is safe," The Harvester whispered, "and you'll see her soon. Now, be good this time." He knelt next to Retz and pressed my soul into his body. Pain curled around me like those damnable brambles, and I set to work fixing as much of my vessel's body as I could before his life started back up. By my estimation, his death didn't even last a minute.

"Nalem?" was his first thought upon coming back to life for the second time in his existence.

"I'm here, little one."

23 - JARROD

I insisted on walking once we'd passed through the gate. My steps were slow and unsteady; I overheard a minotaur in the back of the herd compare me to a newborn calf. But, battered as I was in both body and soul...I survived. The day was saved. I hadn't lost my body, and everyone I cared about made it out alive. Yet for a moment, once I'd taken those trembling steps out of Arcadia only to be met by darkness and silence, none of it felt real.

Then the lights of the Mercury Marquis flicked on, and I heard Retz call my name. He got up from the hood of the car and tried to run over, but stumbled and crashed into me on the way, knocking us both over. It hurt more than I'd like to admit, but I found myself laughing at how ridiculous and unlikely our own survival had been, and Retz followed suit. I'm sure it seemed like the carnival had finally gotten to our heads, as we sat there battered and bloodied in the ferns. Farris and some of the minotaurs waited for us to finish before interrupting. The rest of the herd was leaving, carrying

Zalin, but there was no sight of Artemisia and Monica. Or the Harvester.

I finally regained enough of my senses to ask where they were. Retz blinked, reality settling in around the two of us as the laughter died away. "Oh. Right. Harvester figured you'd make it out fine, so he went off with Artemisia and Monica to put their souls back together in one body. Then I think they were going to wherever Bertha is, see if they could get her body sorted out."

Isolde said, "The Harvester is...helping us? I believed him to be a slayer of monsters."

Retz shrugged. "Maybe. But he's also a dad, and when we explained what happened to Bertha, I think it pulled on his heartstrings a little. Or maybe he's just bored."

"Then if we were to find the remaining aberrant bodies in the carnival and bring them back here, would he fix them too?" From fearing their existence to actively helping them recover...I wasn't the only one whose worldview had flipped these past few hours.

"Probably. Wouldn't hurt to ask, at least." Retz raised an arm and gestured past our clearing to where Sea Mother's skull rested. "Either way, he said he'd meet us at the beach when he was done. Didn't say which one, but Nalem seemed to get it. We'll have to pick up the rest of her bones on the way, but with how late it is, I think we can move them without too much trouble."

As if moving a giant leviathan skeleton from under a building in the town's main plaza and floating it over to the coast would be easy. Well, at least it was dark out. Easier for humans to forget what they'd seen and mistake it for something else.

I said, "So, Nalem..."

"Is back in my head, yeah. Only reason I'm alive right now. I...didn't last long outside of Arcadia. Surprise, surprise." Retz tilted his head, expression shifting. Nalem said, "He agreed to it. This partnership is now of his own volition. And we have plenty of work to do." His eyes flickered to Farris. "If you want to uncover the origins of your partner here, it may behoove you to cooperate."

I didn't answer, but really, what else was there to do? My curse was on its way out, and Alexander was destroyed. I had no direction. No clue where else to go, or what I could do with my life. So long as Retz and Nalem were kept alive, and Farris completed his goal so I could revive him, the world was open and full of possibility, and that was more paralyzing than anything else I'd faced.

Farris helped ease me back to my feet. "We can hash all that out later. For now, let's get outta' here. Don't wanna get jumped by a sasquatch. Or worse, a park ranger..."

Isolde nodded at Bolton, and he hurried to help Retz stand up. She said, "We should also depart. Those who are injured may return home to recuperate. The rest of us, we have bodies to find. We would be ashamed to leave others to the same fate as Bertha, or Artemisia after all her assistance."

The herd-caller turned to us before she left. "Cousins, you fought admirably, and we are grateful for your assistance in our quest. I do hope our paths cross again, further upon the Road." She glanced at the Mercury Marquis and its slapdash paint job but held her tongue regarding our "ride".

We were about to part ways when I realized that none of us were in any condition to drive the car. I didn't trust my body with fine motor skills, Retz had literally died a few minutes before we'd returned, and Farris was quickly crashing after returning from Arcadia.

Isolde seemed to notice this and said, "Bolton? As you have no ride of your own at the moment, please travel with the Gallows brothers. They may need help navigating to the beach." Even Bolton didn't need this hint spelled out for him. He waved goodbye as his clan strode off to wherever they'd parked their motorcycles, then led us to the Marquis.

We all piled in the back, me in the middle with Retz and Farris leaning against either shoulder. A wave of tiredness finally made it through the bulwark of determination I'd built up in Arcadia. Once Bolton eased the car back onto the trail and then to an actual service road, with Sea Mother's skull floating behind us, I let my eyes flicker shut.

I dozed fitfully, only opening my eyes again when we stopped at the plaza. Retz stumbled out with the viola in order to summon the rest of Sea Mother's bones from the ruins of Levi's Tomb. I kept fidgeting while we waited, as if stillness meant becoming a rose again.

Bolton cleared his throat. "Hey. Uhmm...wanted to say I'm real grateful for all your help. I mean, we didn't realize all this shit was going on in our own town, and...well, er, glad you came along. And sorry for trying to run you over when we met."

"It's the least we could do," came my automatic response. But really, we could've walked away so many times. And if we risked our lives this much again, we probably wouldn't be so lucky. If I wanted to live...I'd have to be more careful in the future. "Think you'll be okay? Don't think Ginny will come around for revenge or anything?"

Bolton snorted. "Do I look like an oracle to you? But even if something comes up, we'll be able to handle it. Especially if the aberrant are willing to work with us now, y'know? Guess they're more like us than humans now, after all." He shrugged his giant shoulders. "All I know is, it'll all work out. And cousin, you should take a break after this. Maybe a vacation. After all, I think Isolde wanted to compensate you for finding Bertha...but that can wait for tomorrow, right?"

I suppressed a yawn as Retz slogged back into the car and practically collapsed in the seat next to mine. I'd muster up excitement about getting paid tomorrow. Right then, comprehending a turn for the better was a far-off dream.

The drive to the beach was quiet. It was deep into the night, when even drunks like me had passed out, so there was no one outside to point out the giant leviathan skeleton floating behind us. We didn't turn the radio on either. A couple restless cows mooed as we drove past farms on our way to Nalem's specific beach of choice. We parked, rustled through the car and my coat for flashlights, and made our way onto the sand.

I'd never realized the Harvester glowed in the dark, a faint silver even in his human form. He stood alone, facing the ocean toward a lost home we couldn't see. He beamed when he saw us. "Congratulations on your continued survival, all of you!"

"No thanks to you," Farris muttered under his breath. We leaned against each other to stay standing. Bolton stayed at the car, watching with wide eyes and silent lips.

I raised my voice and asked, "Are our friends okay?"

The Harvester flashed a peace sign, though I think he meant a thumbs-up. "Okay as one can be, after such an ordeal. It has been some time since we have worked so extensively on multiple souls in a day. More to come too, as it seems your new friends have more bodies to ferry out of Arcadia. But no matter! You shall see the results for yourselves, come morning. For now, we must put Sea Mother back to rest. Nalem, if you would be so kind?"

Retz and Nalem seemed stronger with each step as they brought Sea Mother closer to the waves. Her ghost flickered into view around her bones, complete once more. She shrieked, followed by a warbling coo as the frills on her head vibrated. The Harvester embraced the tip of her snout with the kind of joy the Ringmaster couldn't manufacture. Nalem drew close, and the two of them spoke with their words drowned out by the waves.

An autumn breeze brushed through the grass at the top of the beach's dunes. Even with the lantern, the world was dark and nearly still. No garish colors or blooming flowers. No twisted faces that had once been familiar.

I sat down on dry sand, not caring if it got on my clothes since I was stained with paint and blood and stars knew what else. Farris eased himself down next to me. We sat with our shoulders pressed together, breathing in the cool night air. Watching as Nalem and the Harvester slowly walked into the surf, floating Sea Mother's bones out over the ocean. Her ghost followed, casting an ethereal light on the water below as she swam through the air. I thought of memories that weren't mine, "remembering" how joyful it was to swim and simply be.

I didn't realize I was crying until Farris gently removed my glasses and wiped my cheeks with his sleeve. I tried to blink my tears away. Farris nudged my shoulder. "Hey. You've put that off long enough. There's nothing to fight anymore, not right now, so...it's safe, okay?" He wrapped an arm around my shoulder. "I'll keep us safe."

That did it. I gave in and fucking sobbed, the kind where my tears felt boiling hot and snot dribbled down my face. I let go everything that had been stewing, not just during the carnival but so long I'd forgotten it was even there, and cried every last drop of it out. At least, that's what it felt like. No idea how long I sat there bawling, but by the time I saw Retz through a watery haze, most of my shirt was damp and my throat had gone hoarse. Through it all, Farris hadn't let me go. I'd have to thank him for that later. Thank him for a lot of things.

"Feel better?" Retz asked. He crouched and pulled out the folded handkerchief he always kept in his breast pocket, offering it to me. I nodded and made an absolute mess of the little red scrap of fabric. I muttered a garbled mess of an apology. Retz shrugged. "Least I could do. After all, you got me through to my birthday, right? I'm sure we passed midnight somewhere in all that." Retz slipped out the pistol and continued, "Thanks for this, by the way. Worked as intended."

"Good. I'm...glad." Finally, something coherent. "After all that, I hope you don't mind a...laid-back celebration this year."

"Are you kidding? If we did anything marginally exciting, I think my metaphorical heart would explode."

As if on cue, the Harvester strode up to us. While he had plenty of eyes blinking along his skin as usual, he rolled one around the palm of his hand. Every eye of his peered down to the three of us in the sand. "All of you have sacrificed so much. We wish we could do more to reward you for protecting not just our child, but the world itself. But we can at least offer this."

Farris stared at the eye in the Harvester's hand. His, of course. All he had to do was pop it back into his skull, and all the memories the Harvester had unlocked would return. And that stranger, whoever Farris had been before, would appear again. I felt like my heart rammed itself into my throat.

"You've got the worst timing, you know that?" Farris said. "We literally just left the carnival from hell. Need a bit of time before we chase any more mysteries, you know?"

"Of course." The Harvester waved his other hand, and a small drawstring bag covered in scales blinked into existence. He pulled it open and dropped the eyeball inside before handing it to Farris. "Whenever you are ready, White Prince, a fraction of your destiny awaits. And if you wish for me to see what we can scavenge from your other eye afterwards..."

"One thing at a time, buddy." Farris held the bag with the tips of his claws, as if afraid it would attack him. "So...is your ghost calmed down?"

"Now that she is whole again, yes. And for the time being, we shall keep her in the ocean where her spirit can be at peace. Perhaps one day, when there are not targets on our backs, we can build from her bones once more. Now, if you do not mind, we wish to commune with her awhile longer while she is awake." He turned away from us, heading back toward the water. But he turned to us once and called, "Rest up, and we'll see you again come Samhain!"

"That is coming up, isn't it?" Retz grumbled with a sigh, followed by a swear that might've been Nalem's. The date was just over a month away, the day after Halloween. Surely not a recipe for disaster. "Guess we can't ever catch a break."

"Such is life," I said. But at least we had that moment, and we had each other. Right then, that was enough for me.

ACKNOWLEDGMENTS

This book would not exist were it not for three important people. The first is my beta reader Charlotte, whose belief in the story and its characters helped me finish when I felt like giving up. The second is Bill Tracy, editor extraordinaire who whipped this book into shape with his concise observations. Third, cover artist M. Brackett, who brought the story to life with the most kickass cover I've ever seen.

I also never would've finished this book if not for the support of my family. Mom, Chris, Unka Don, as well as my darling wife Triss and all my new in-laws, thank you for your endless patience as I prattle on about my stories. In addition, thanks to all my friends and coworkers who supported me as I wrote this book, and a special thanks to Mindy for inadvertently fixing the plot by suggesting "needs more snakes."

Finally, to all my readers, fans, and fellow creators for all your support. I hope you enjoyed the book, and I can't wait to share more stories with you!

EXTRA FEATURES

Concept Art

JARROD
GALLOWS

**RETZ GALLOWS
AND NALEM**

FARRIS O'REILLY

GINNY,
"NALEM'S
TRUE FORM?",
AND THE
MINOTAURS

MONICA,
ARTEMISIA,
ZALIN, AND
THE RINGMASTER

ABOUT THE AUTHOR

Hailing from the mountains of Oregon and the lecture halls of Mills College, Dorian Graves is an artistic cryptid found in the Pacific Northwest. When not writing, drawing or working on tabletop RPGs, Dorian can be found adventuring in the woods with their wife and their mischievous cat.

Website: www.doriangraves.com

Email: pictureofdoriangraves@gmail.com

Twitter or Facebook: @DorianGravesFTW